Praise for Martín Solares and *The Black Minutes*

"Stunning. His characters simultaneously move toward resolution and the void, each success paradoxically dragging them down."
—*Nation*

"Solares's prose—alternately playful, poetic, and plainspoken—propels the pages." —*Booklist*

"Martín Solares uses the codes and formula of classic crime novels to create a universe where the reader is permanently on a fluctuating border between dream and reality, between fiction and the authentic violence of facts." —*Le Monde* (France)

"[Martín Solares's] debut novel is risky business . . . One of the most ambitious crime novels that Mexico has had to offer since the great works of Paco Ignacio Taibo II." —*Titel Magazin* (Germany)

"This first novel by Solares will satisfy—to an immense degree, believe me—those who enjoy impossible missions and quixotic adventures." —*El País* (Spain)

"Solares displays an impressive string of situations, and constructs an action-packed plot that never declines . . . A true novelist."
—*El Mundo* (Spain)

Also by Martín Solares
The Black Minutes

DON'T SEND FLOWERS

MARTÍN SOLARES

Translated by Heather Cleary

Black Cat
New York

Martín Solares is represented by Schavelzon Graham Agencia Literaria,
schavelzongraham.com.

Originally published in Spanish under the title *No manden flores* in 2015
by Literatura Random House, Barcelona and Ciudad de México.

Published simultaneously in Canada
Printed in the United States of America

First Grove Atlantic hardcover edition: August 2018

This book was set in 11.2-pt Perpetua by Alpha Design & Composition
of Pittsfield, NH.

Library of Congress Cataloging-in-Publication data is available for this title.

ISBN 978-0-8021-2815-7
eISBN 978-0-8021-4620-5

Black Cat
an imprint of Grove Atlantic
154 West 14th Street
New York, NY 10011

Distributed by Publishers Group West

groveatlantic.com

18 19 20 21   10 9 8 7 6 5 4 3 2 1

DON'T
SEND
FLOWERS

PART ONE

The Mysteries of La Eternidad

1

He told them there was someone who could find the girl: an ex-cop.

He told them that if this individual was still alive after the trouble he'd had with his own team, he'd be just the man for the job. He'd survived assignments like this one—where a death wish was more of an asset than deductive skills—several times already. He told them that if this man was still alive, which wasn't entirely unlikely, they might find him in one of the next states over, Veracruz or San Luis Potosí. Every so often an informant would claim to have seen him on the highway heading into La Eternidad. According to these reports, he said, the individual in question still drives a white car. He settles in at a certain restaurant down near the breakwater for a few hours, chats with the owners, sees to his business, and heads back the way he came. No one knows where he goes. Others say he's always in and out of town and might be mixed up in smuggling, but I don't think so, vouched consul Don Williams. He always kept on the right side of the law. You might even have hired him at some point, Mr. De León. In any event, if this guy does happen to still be alive, he'd be just the man for the job.

Mr. De León asked what the individual's name was and the consul replied,

"Carlos Treviño."

"Don't know him," the magnate snapped. He prided himself on knowing each of his employees, and Treviño had never been on his payroll. "I don't know him and the name doesn't ring a bell. I won't risk it. I can't take the chance he's working for them."

"Treviño would never work for a criminal," the gringo insisted. "Not knowingly, at least. Unlike most people in this city."

He was interrupted by a loud crack.

"What was that?" the consul asked, while Mr. De León's bodyguards craned their necks like two dogs sniffing out danger. "It sounded like it came from nearby," the consul insisted, but neither the woman nor the men at the table budged. The sound of gunshots—a single round or a hail of bullets—or a grenade blast in the distance as night fell had become a part of life around the port, no more unusual than the words *extortion* and *kidnapping*. Noticing the consul's anxiety, Valentín Bustamante, a.k.a. the Bus, the head of Mr. De León's security detail, stepped onto the terrace to have a look through the magnate's telescope. A fat man with a skinny mustache, he moved his six-foot-three frame with an agility unimaginable for someone his size, as if gravity didn't exist, and pointed the instrument at the next neighborhood over. Hunched over like that, his round face and childlike features accented by his ridiculous facial hair, he almost looked like someone who wouldn't hurt a fly. Which was true, as long as that fly was under three feet tall and posed no threat to Mr. De León. Meanwhile, Rodolfo Moreno Valle—second in command of the magnate's security detail and as serious as a heart attack with his bushy eyebrows, goatee, cowboy boots, and black leather jacket—walked over to cover his associate's position next to the door and stood there with his arms crossed.

For a few seconds, the rustling of the palm trees was the only sound. A northern wind was blowing in, one of those that haunt the Gulf and can hang around for ten or twelve hours, knocking down trees and old houses. The gale reached out to stir up a handful of paper napkins next to the coffeepot with the tips of its fingers; for a moment, the napkins seemed to come to life, as if they were trying to transmit a message. The meeting was being held in Mr. De León's mansion, one of the biggest in the luxe portside neighborhood next to a valley of slums on this side of the river. It was a three-story abode inspired by California's Spanish colonial revivals, with huge picture windows and terraces adorned with wrought iron and carved stone, in a gated community complete with a small golf course, swimming pool, and a natural spring. All this, of course, could be seen only if you made it past the walled perimeter accented by flowering vines and bodyguards. The windows looked out over the lagoon—without question the most beautiful stretch of La Eternidad's port—but no one was there to talk about beauty.

"Why play dumb?" Mr. De León's wife asked. She was a tall, prickly blonde used to getting her way: an overbearing woman who was still in shape at forty-five thanks in large part to her bad temper. "Go talk to the three bosses, offer them some cash, and put an end to this."

"That would put your daughter at enormous risk," the consul objected. "If they don't realize she's disappeared, that's one advantage we have. We need to find another way."

"Well, the two of you seem pretty relaxed," she snapped. "I can't even imagine what Cristina must be going through right now, kidnapped and terrorized by those animals."

The consul looked at his watch. It was true: thirty-six hours had passed since the girl disappeared, and every minute that went by made it seem less likely they'd find her alive.

A truck's brakes screeched on a nearby street. The consul looked Mr. De León squarely in the eye.

"We don't have time to waste. Instead of waiting for them to contact us, send a specialist in to find her. One who won't raise suspicions. The detective I'm recommending is fearless and discreet. He could run an investigation and come up with a strategy for getting her back. He knows the area and has a team, or at least he did a few months ago. He's brilliant, the type who can handle any situation. He could get himself out of a whale's belly if he needed to."

A shadow fell across Mr. De León's face.

"And why should I hire this guy, when I have an army of bodyguards at my disposal?" he said, gesturing toward the most threatening member of his security detail, the man with the goatee. "Moreno's an ace with this kind of mission; he was trained by the German military. Why would I hire someone I know nothing about?"

The consul, aware that the businessman was a two-hundred-pound bundle of nerves, replied as diplomatically as possible: "I'm afraid your bodyguards wouldn't be able to infiltrate their ranks without being detected, Rafael, especially not the ones you trust most. Whoever got close enough to kidnap your daughter must have been studying your security for months. As for La Eternidad's police and military, I wouldn't recommend calling them in on this. The police would sell their souls to the devil if he was the highest bidder, and the military depends on the politicians. And you know who they work for. This guy was the best detective the port had seen in years. He was the one who caught the Chainsaw Killer."

The businessman's wife eyed him suspiciously.

"The Chainsaw Killer? The one who murdered those girls?" They were talking about a maniac who kidnapped young women from different parts of the city and tortured them. "That doesn't mean a thing," she went on. "Everyone knows the guy they caught was just a scapegoat."

"Precisely," said the consul. "The man officially accused of the crimes is innocent, but the detective I've been telling you about caught the real killer and ended up in hot water with his colleagues because of it."

Mr. De León looked up when he heard this, intrigued. The case had been big news around the Gulf of Mexico because of the criminal's extraordinary cruelty, because of how hard it had been to find him, and, above all, because of the scandal that erupted when word got out they'd let the maniac walk while an innocent man rotted away in a jail cell.

"That was a long time ago," thundered the businessman. "If he's as good as you say, why hasn't anyone heard of him? Shouldn't he be famous by now?"

"A good detective doesn't get famous," said the consul.

"Will you vouch for him?" the magnate asked.

The consul cleared his throat.

"Listen, I'm not saying he's squeaky-clean. He's probably taken a bribe or two, like everyone at police headquarters. But in the Chainsaw Killer case, he was the only ranking officer who actually tried to catch the criminal, even if his enemies say he was only in it for the reward. You know how things are here. But as long as he was on the force, he always collaborated with the consulate and with me directly, to the extent permitted by Mexican law, of course. He kept it on the straight and narrow. That's why he only lasted four years on the job. Treviño's one of the few honest people I've met in the Gulf." Noticing the silence this last remark provoked across the table, he added, "An honest man who'd be worthy of a position in your family's company."

Mr. De León and his wife nodded, as if appeased, and the consul made a note in some corner of his brain to show more respect in the future.

The door to the terrace opened again and the fat man with the absurd mustache walked back into the room, wrapping up a conversation on his walkie-talkie with, "Affirmative." He installed himself next to Mr. De León and didn't say a word until the consul asked him, "What's going on out there?"

"There's activity in Colonia Pescadores. La Cuarenta's thugs. It's the weekend, they must be off their asses. I also hear the boy hasn't come to yet, but we're keeping an eye on him."

He was talking about Cristina's boyfriend, who was still in the hospital. Mr. De León turned crimson with rage.

"I told you to leave him alone!"

"It was my idea," interrupted the consul. "I didn't want to take any chances. We're watching him as a precaution."

It wasn't likely the boyfriend would ever speak again, but the consul desperately wanted to hear what he had to say since he was the only witness to what happened. Sitting there, a balding old man with a potbelly, dressed in a plaid shirt and construction boots, he didn't look like much. But he'd been the consul to the United States there in La Eternidad for more than ten years and was one of the people who knew the most about crime in the region. To his friends, he was Don Williams; to Chief Margarito and company, he was Our Consul, if they were on good terms, and That Asshole Don Williams, if they felt he'd stuck his nose in above his pay grade in La Eternidad. There was no doubt in Mr. De León's mind that if there was a security expert in La Eternidad, the gringo was it. The minute he heard they'd found Cristina's car and that her boyfriend, Alberto Perkins, was in critical condition, he chose Williams to lead the investigation and negotiations.

"If they're going to keep an eye on him, make sure they're discreet. Remember, his father's an associate of mine," Mr. De León said. "Damn it, Consul. Stop wasting time. It was Los Nuevos."

There was no evidence to support the magnate's theory, but the possibility worried the consul just the same. If it did turn out to be Los Nuevos, it was only a matter of time before they'd find the girl's body, probably with signs of torture. But no one was calling to demand a ransom, and there were no new leads to follow.

"Duckie, go talk to Margarito," begged Mrs. De León, calling Don Williams, a.k.a. Donald Duck, a.k.a. That Fucking Gringo, by a nickname only his closest friends used.

Since they couldn't keep the local police from getting involved in the case—they were the ones who'd found the car, after all—De León and Don Williams had met with Chief Margarito at the magnate's home the night before. It was a hostile encounter: they barely said a word to the port's chief of police. They listened to what he had to say—"We'll find the girl, don't worry, sir"—and sent him off. The consul thought he was a prime suspect. Given the chief's reputation, they couldn't rule out that he was involved in the kidnapping or that he might get involved: he was the kind who would rescue the girl just so he could hide her again and demand three times the ransom—which is why the only information they gave him was a recent photo of Cristina.

Unfortunately, it was pointless to turn to local politicians or the mayor for help: they were all the governor's lapdogs, even though Mr. De León had bankrolled more than one of their campaigns and had friends and relatives among them. There were two rumors circulating about the governor of Tamaulipas. The negative version was that the Gov permitted this wave of violence because he was the one who had founded Los Nuevos, the most terrifying criminal organization working in the Gulf, a huge operation that specialized in terrorizing the locals by torturing and dismembering its rivals. According to the positive version, though, the governor wasn't one of the criminals. He just turned a blind eye to their crimes in exchange for a generous monthly payout. When crime rose to truly outrageous levels in the state, a group of businessmen went to see the governor to complain about all the kidnappings, robberies, and extortion, and the cynical way Los Nuevos showed up each month to charge the Business Association an astronomical fee in exchange for so-called protection, just to let them work in peace. The whole time the businessmen were explaining the situation, even presenting photos of the men who were extorting them, the Gov never took his eyes off his BlackBerry; he typed away on it, all smiles, as if he were playing a game or sending jokes to someone. One of the businessmen eventually reached over to cover the screen with his hand and asked, "What are we supposed to do, Your Honor?" To which the governor replied, "Pay them, of course."

One of the businessmen who'd been at that meeting told the consul all this while drowning his sorrows in a bottle of whiskey. That's how things were around there. The gringo was no stranger to Chihuahua or Durango, Nuevo León or Coahuila, Baja California or Sonora, and he'd come to the conclusion that—though the competition was tight—for three years and counting, Los Nuevos had been the bloodiest, most ruthless criminal organization in the Gulf: a state within the state run by psychopaths who acted with total impunity.

The consul took a sip from his bottle of Evian, cleared his throat, and insisted, "We should get started on the investigation, on our own, before the trail goes cold. Instead of sending your people"—he tilted his chin at the Bus and Moreno—"I suggest hiring someone who can get past every security post in the neighborhoods held by the Cartel del Puerto, Los Nuevos, even La Cuarenta. And find out if one of those organizations is behind the kidnapping. If we can confirm that, we can plan a rescue mission or at least as close as we can get to one under the circumstances."

The previous night, as he made his way to Mr. De León's house, Williams could sense the tension hanging over the port: sentries from various criminal organizations walked around brazenly with walkie-talkies in hand, ready to report any suspicious activity to their bosses; pickup trucks drove down the street with armed men in the back, and the gringo counted at least three fake checkpoints set up along the main avenue to block access to the streets where the city's main capos lived.

The consul knew that Mr. De León had thirty guards assigned to his different businesses in La Eternidad; they worked in teams of two and were trained and ready for action. He also knew that the magnate paid Chief Margarito every month, just like all the other businessmen in the area did, just like he paid Generals Rovirosa and Ortigosa of the army and the marines, respectively. Still, the consul rejected the idea of going to any of the above for help. None of them wanted to kick the hornet's nest. Los Nuevos had a hundred highly trained men in La Eternidad alone, and more were arriving every day from the training grounds in the north of the state.

"We don't want to get the kidnappers' guard up," the gringo repeated. "Your best bet is to hire Treviño. People aren't exactly lining up to work in this city. The longer we sit here talking, though, the less chance we have of finding her."

Mr. De León clenched his jaw.

"Do whatever you have to do. Just get my daughter back."

"All right."

The gringo took a deep breath, stood, and went to the terrace to make a call. As the wind picked up, they watched him leaf through his agenda, take notes or jot down a number, then hang up and dial it; occasionally he'd cover one ear and shout in the general direction of the receiver. Every now and then, the wind would shake the treetops so violently he seemed in danger of falling from the second floor.

"Tell that idiot to come inside," said Mrs. De León.

Before they could go get him, though, the consul opened the glass door, sat down in front of them, and held up his phone.

"I found him. But he won't be easy to convince."

"These two will go get him," said the magnate, pointing to Moreno and the Bus.

"I should be the one to go," the consul suggested, but Mr. De León wouldn't hear of it.

"You're staying here. What happens if they call while you're out looking for this guy? Who's going to talk to the kidnappers?"

The gringo shrugged. "All right, but show him respect. And plenty of it. He can have quite a temper."

"Don't worry." Mr. De León laughed. "These guys are real diplomats."

Turning to them, he said, "Bring him here. Don't take no for an answer, understand?" And then he added, without looking at the consul, "If this guy lets us down, I'm holding Williams responsible."

"Where do we find him?" asked the Bus.

"He lives in Playa de las Ballenas"—the gringo drew a quick diagram on an index card—"in Veracruz, near Isla del Toro. Ask for a hotel called Las Ballenas. The man you're looking for runs the place."

"That's four hours away," said the Bus.

"Three and a half if you hurry," the consul corrected him.

Moreno and the Bus turned, puzzled, and headed down the monumental spiral staircase. When they stepped into the garden, three guys in black jackets walked over to them for instructions.

"We're headed out on an errand. We'll be back early tomorrow. Rafita's in charge," said Moreno as they got into one of the two black F-150 Lobos parked in front of the door.

"Carlos Treviño, a.k.a. the Detective." The Bus mopped the sweat from his brow.

"Fuck that fucker," grunted Moreno, turning the key in the ignition. "What bridge should I take? The Pánuco?"

"No, take the new one. We want to avoid the checkpoints."

As the Bus leaned back in his seat, Moreno hesitated for a split second, not sure he'd heard him correctly. The new bridge? Wasn't that where they'd killed Mr. De León's last driver, his immediate predecessor? But the Bus was clearly in a hurry. "Hit it, cabrón." So Moreno peeled out, leaving behind them a cloud of dust like a gateway to the terrible events that were about to unfold.

2

"Of course I won't go," Treviño said. "Of course not. You've got to be crazy."

The consul drummed nervously on the table with the tips of two fingers as he studied the new arrival. The detective looked tanner than before; he definitely wasn't as thin as when he'd been on the force, but he hadn't lost the legendary self-confidence that had landed him in so much trouble. He'd clearly gotten into it with the bodyguards along the way: the Bus glared at him with obvious hatred.

Treviño had been on the hotel's terrace when they arrived. It was early evening, and the taste of salt filled his mouth. He'd noticed them right away: most people who came to the beach had eyes only for the waves, but these two didn't seem to see the water at all.

He'd watched them park at the end of the road where the sand begins and walk up between the two rows of pines. Three black dogs sensed the threat and charged toward the curtain of vegetation. Their yelps, which grew increasingly frantic, were his second warning. Treviño realized he'd been found.

He watched them flag down one of the vendors who walked up and down the beach trying to sell coconut candies. The two men called out to the vendor, who froze in terror. He saw the taller of the two lean over him and watched him point to the hotel. The visitors examined the old wooden structure with none of the delight typical of tourists. It seemed like they could see him there sitting on the terrace under a throw blanket, but they stood motionless against the afternoon sun, calculating their approach. They didn't seem like military men or criminals—maybe hit men sent by the chief himself. Meanwhile, the dogs were going crazy: *There are two strangers here. Isn't someone going to do something?*

He saw the two men start moving and cursed under his breath. *I'll be damned*, he thought. He was grateful there was hardly anyone in the immense row of palm cabanas, at least: just four gringas playing volleyball in the distance and two old Canadians drinking fruity cocktails. He watched a big wave form and break on the shore with a deafening crash and realized this peaceful life was about to come to an end. So he stood and folded the blanket, which had a Bengal tiger printed on it, then headed into the hotel to get his gun.

The first things he saw as he entered the wooden building were the honey-colored eyes of his wife, who asked him if something was wrong. "Don't go out there," he ordered. "There are two men coming this way, and they look suspicious." He watched her face tighten with fear and headed down the hall. He passed four rooms meant for the guests, climbed a few steps, and opened a door marked with the number 5. The family's residence: a table, a bed, a crib, a sink full of baby bottles, a wooden wardrobe, and an array of plastic toys scattered across the floor. He looked out the window facing the road and saw them approaching. He had no time to waste.

He opened the door of the wardrobe and took out the shoebox he kept tucked in the corner. He'd promised his wife but never could part with his Taurus PT99—even though it weighed almost two pounds and even though he could be arrested for owning a nine-millimeter now that he was a civilian. The weapon held sixteen rounds and was both fast and intimidating. He'd never felt comfortable with a six-shooter. *Well,* he thought to himself, *it's not easy to walk away from your past.* Detective Carlos Treviño, who'd been living under an assumed name for two years, slipped the Taurus into his waistband, covered it with his shirt, and walked onto the terrace. There was no time to do anything else, because the men were already there.

He thought he saw the visitors exchange a glance to make sure they were on the same page as he took his place on the far side of one of the terrace's columns. The taller of the two, who was also the broader one—a man with a little round head and a Pedro Infante mustache—took a step toward the stairs but was discouraged by a wave of Treviño's hand: *That's as far as you go.* Far from seeming embarrassed by the incident, the man with the ridiculous mustache stopped in his tracks and asked for the manager of the hotel. He had to yell to make himself heard over the constant growling of the dogs, which were getting more riled by the minute, and the waves crashing against the shore. Treviño looked at the huge fellow without responding, until the mustachioed man repeated: "We're looking for Carlos Treviño." The man with the Taurus didn't blink an eye, so he added, "The one who used to be a cop."

Treviño studied him carefully and asked, "What do you want?"

The giant looked at him and said, "Mr. Rafael de León would like to speak with you."

It seemed like a joke: Rafael de León, one of the richest men on the Gulf? There was a rumor going around that he was the one who'd hired the guys that left Juan Gómez, the only journalist in the state capital who was even marginally respected, in a wheelchair.

"Mr. De León would like to contract your services," added the giant. "And will pay you well."

In the distance, the group of gringas erupted in laughter. The detective thought about it for a moment and shook his head.

"I'm not the man you're looking for."

The second visitor, more impatient than the first, thundered, "You were a cop, right? You worked for Chief Margarito?"

Treviño looked at him, more annoyed by the minute.

"You heard wrong. I don't do that kind of thing anymore."

That was when the two men's hands went to their waistbands.

"Well, we're sorry, but Mr. De León wants to see you."

This just got ugly, Treviño thought.

Less than four hours later they walked into a large fifth-story conference room with an impressive wall of glass that looked out over the buildings that made up the Grupo De León. Some of his employees were carrying poles; others were hauling sacks.

The meeting got off to a rough start. From the moment he laid eyes on the consul, who was supposed to be mediating the encounter, Treviño was primed to beat the shit out of him. *What's that fucking traitor up to now?* The last time they'd worked together, things had ended badly. To say the least. The mayor had offered a reward for catching the man who was butchering women in the city. After overcoming more trials than Ulysses and battling the corruption and apathy of his own colleagues, Treviño managed to identify and apprehend the perpetrator, a psychopath who also happened to be the son of an influential man. Without missing a beat, Chief Cavernosum let the killer go, found a fall guy, and then accused Treviño of running drugs and ordered him to be tortured. Margarito was even about to apply the Ley de Fugas—the anti–habeas corpus—to have Treviño shot while in custody. And the whole time, there was the gringo, comfortably tucked away in the consulate, not lifting a finger to help.

The detective rested a hand on his waistband and the consul saw that the bodyguards had not been able to convince him to leave his weapon at the door. That's why they were so edgy and why they stuck so close to him.

"Welcome," Mr. De León said, inviting him to take a seat. When it became clear that Treviño was not about to greet him in return, the magnate withdrew the hand he'd extended and let it fall to his side with all the grace he could muster. "Would you like a cup of coffee?"

Treviño shook his head and looked the man over. He'd heard a lot about Rafael de León, but he didn't expect him to be so young. The blond man behind the desk was almost six feet tall and probably pushing forty-five, though he seemed to have the energy of a twenty-year-old. They disliked one another from the start, but both tried to hide it. *He'll try to put one over on me*, thought De León. "This son of a bitch would sell his own mother," Treviño said to himself.

The statement wasn't unfounded. In the 1930s, the De León family had amassed one of the biggest fortunes in the state. The founding De Leóns were from Havana, but had been lured to La Eternidad by the Mexican oil rush. Their efforts paid off: within ten years these tireless entrepreneurs had opened nearly every automotive shop you could find along the Gulf of Mexico, and they boasted that they opened a new distribution center every year. Toward the end of the 1940s they got involved in the steel industry with the same success, and in the early eighties they founded a chain of pharmacies called El Tucán, managing to turn it into the biggest distributor of medical supplies in the northeast of the country thanks to a dozen important clients, including the teachers' and oil workers' unions and a succession of state governments. *But all that glory belongs to his grandfather and his father. Rafael de León is known for being a deadbeat.* There were enough stories of the magnate's immorality floating around to fill an encyclopedia, thought the detective. When his father died in 1980, the black sheep of the family was obliged to give up the international party scene and come back to take over the family businesses. To everyone's surprise, instead of destroying the empire his predecessors had built with his indulgent lifestyle, Rafael lifted the company and his partners out of the unstable position into which they'd fallen after his father's death. In less than three years, he got his family's businesses growing steadily again; after a disastrous start that had the shareholders calling for his head, the young executive achieved such impressive sales figures and opened so many stores that the investors could only sit back and smile.

Don Williams, consul to the United States in La Eternidad—and, by the look of things, security adviser to tycoons in a bind—glanced at Treviño's white guayabera shirt and cleared his throat.

"Mr. De León needs your help."

You've gotta give the gringo credit, thought Treviño. *First, because he's still hanging around here, where so many people hate him. Second, because he had the balls to come looking for me.*

"They kidnapped my daughter the night before last," said the magnate, picking up a small silver frame. "They took her as she was leaving Giza."

He was talking about the hot nightclub of the moment. It was built in the shape of a pyramid and all the kids went there to dance and get drunk.

"Talk to the law," said the detective.

"We don't want the police mixed up in this, and we don't want anything to do with Chief Margarito. What I want is for you to go find my daughter."

The magnate turned the frame around, revealing the image of a radiant blonde with green eyes who could have passed for a European actress. Though the pale, bottomless pools of her eyes and the glint of mischief behind them caught his attention first, Treviño's gaze quickly wandered to the waves of hair that framed the perfect oval of her face like a crown. Her nose was perfectly sculpted, and it was hard not to want to stare for a long while at the remarkable curves of her full, sensual lips. *This girl was born to eat the world alive.* Like anyone seeing Cristina for the first time, Treviño was floored.

"She's sixteen," said her father.

"About to be seventeen," her mother corrected him.

The detective examined the girl's face—her sparkling, defiant smile—and turned to Mrs. De León.

"Did the two of you have a fight recently?"

Mrs. Cecilia de León nodded, somewhat dismissively. "Like we do every weekend. Nothing important. It's not easy to be the mother of a teenage girl who's also an *only child.*" That last phrase, crackling with resentment, was aimed at her husband.

"Have you checked the homes of her friends and her boy-friend? If your daughter has the motivation and the resources, she might be hiding out with someone she trusts. They do that, at her age."

"She's not with any of them," the girl's mother shot back. "Her friends are responsible, serious girls, and their parents swear she's not hiding out with them. They wouldn't lie to me."

"Does she have a cell phone?"

"We call her every five minutes, but she doesn't answer."

"I know she liked to party," Mr. De León's voice grew more serious. "She's young and I taught her to do as she pleased, but this isn't a childish tantrum."

He spread a series of snapshots out on the desk. The first was of a pink luxury convertible with both doors open, abandoned in a parking lot; the next one showed a stain left on the pave-ment by a dark liquid. It didn't take much imagination to guess it was blood. The last one was a picture of a young man hooked up to a breathing machine in what appeared to be an expensive private clinic.

"Her boyfriend. They left him in a coma."

Judging by the number of tubes going into and out of his body, the boy was never getting out of that bed.

"They arrived at the club and left together. They found him, but my daughter . . ."

Mr. De León looked exhausted: his eyes were glossy and his jaw was slack. *This man's hitting a wall*, thought the detective. The adrenaline and the sleepless night had caught up with him.

Mrs. De León pointed to the photo of the boy in the hospital. "If that's how they left him, we don't even want to think about what they did to her."

Treviño thought for a moment before he added, "And I'm sure you did a thorough search of the local hospitals and the morgue."

The man nodded. "She's not anywhere, not in any local hospital, and we already sent her dentist to examine the corpses they haven't been able to identify. No one's called about a ransom, either. It's like the earth just swallowed her whole."

Treviño looked at a telephone that had been set up on a small base with speakers in the middle of the desk. Off to one side were a laptop and a sophisticated device with a map of the city waiting for the kidnappers to make contact. These tracking technologies were Don Williams's specialty, he recalled. That Fucking Gringo, right in front of him.

The detective sighed. It didn't look good for the girl. If her parents turned to the bureaucratic labyrinth of the law, his colleagues on the police force would take at least a week to produce any results. If the police in La Eternidad could be trusted, first they'd have to file a report with the prosecutor's office, which would then pass the case to the police, who would open a file on the case and, if they managed to identify the guilty parties or catch them in the act, would ask the prosecutor to initiate judicial proceedings against them. Then a judge would review the case and sign a warrant to arrest the accused. If they were to be brought in, they'd be given a sentence that would first pass through the prosecutor's office; then, once they were remanded, they'd have a hearing before the judge. It was a long and tortuous process that in other countries would take less time and yield better results. But we're talking about La Eternidad, Tamaulipas, where the law is sold to the highest bidder, and the police round out their salaries with payouts from the criminals.

"We need your help, Treviño. You know the port better than anyone, and you were a good cop," said the consul.

And because this was the exact phrase he'd used a few years earlier to convince him to do the right thing, Treviño struggled not to punch him in the face.

"You've got a shitty memory, for a pathological liar," he exploded. "Tell them to go talk to your friend, Margarito."

Everyone, including Mr. De León, could tell that the detective's answer had offended Don Williams. Sensing there was about to be trouble, Moreno and the Bus discreetly moved closer to Treviño, but the magnate stopped them with a wave of his hand and changed the subject.

"I want nothing to do with Chief Margarito. On the other hand, Don Williams insists that no one knows the chief's methods better than you, which makes you our first choice for finding our daughter. I've also heard that thanks to your time on the force, you know the people in the trade you'd need to talk to and how not to stir up trouble with them. That more than one of them owes you a favor. What I'd like to ask is that while we wait for their call you go out and see if either Los Nuevos or the Cartel del Puerto has my daughter."

Treviño shook his head.

"I don't have connections with either of those organizations."

"Not with La Cuarenta, either?" the girl's mother asked.

"Not with any of them," the detective insisted. "I dealt with them only as much as I had to and always kept it professional, back when I was a cop."

The gringo interrupted him.

"The investigation doesn't necessarily have to start there, though. It's too early to say for sure that Cristina was taken by someone in the trade."

"It was Los Nuevos," the magnate declared.

Streams of tears were running down his wife's cheeks. She cried silently, wiping her face with a handkerchief. Treviño looked suspiciously at De León.

"Why do you think it was them?"

The magnate fixed his gaze on the window before answering.

"Over the past year . . . or maybe two years . . . several people who identified themselves as belonging to those organizations have tried to extort money from me. Repeatedly." De León chose his words carefully. "My people felt compelled to respond to these aggressions. It's possible, though it would be the worst possible scenario, that they've taken my daughter as payback for the way we treated them."

His wife sobbed convulsively and he went to comfort her. In the meantime, the detective looked the Bus and Moreno over and realized that the giant with the ridiculous mustache and the guy with the goatee probably had no qualms about taking care of a few delinquents here and there. It couldn't be easy, meeting with and then neutralizing the criminals lining up to get the Grupo De León to pay dues.

"Who came here trying to get money out of you?" asked the detective.

"Pretty much everyone, it seems," the consul chimed in.

The magnate continued. "The fucking bums who terrorized my secretaries said they were Los Nuevos. There were others, too, who said they were with the Cartel del Puerto, Mr. Obregón's organization. They were more serious, respectful even, but they wanted their share just the same. There's also been plenty of derelicts who come by claiming to work for one of them: small-time criminals, gang members trying to run their own racket. Ever since things started getting really bad around here, any asshole can just grab a gun and come down, trying to collect dues."

"Any fatalities?" The ex-cop asked, eyeing the bodyguards.

"How should I put this . . ." Mr. De León replied. "I don't pay them to stand around with their arms crossed."

Treviño wondered how many of the execution-style killings carried out around the port over the past few months had been the handiwork of the two bodyguards standing in front of him and how much Mr. De León must have paid the police and the local press to keep the corpses off the front page of the papers.

"I'm sorry," Treviño said, resting his hands on his knees as though he were about to stand. "I hope you find your daughter safe and sound. I'd like to help you, but I'm not looking for any trouble."

"We haven't even discussed numbers. And it would only be until they called." Mr. De León insisted.

"You were given bad advice," the detective said, looking at Williams. "I don't do this kind of thing anymore. Investigating a crime always involves some risk, but investigating anyone in the trade is suicide."

"Wait. There must be some way."

"Why don't you send your people?"

"Because I need them here, keeping an eye on the company."

"Bring someone in from the capital." He shrugged. "Or get the gringo to help you hire a detective from the other side, someone from the FBI."

"They wouldn't last five minutes here," the magnate said.

"Do it for my daughter," Mrs. De León broke through the formalities and free of the magnate's arms. She took the detective's hands. "Think about her. My husband will reward you generously."

"I'm sorry"—Treviño looked up—"but I don't do this kind of thing anymore. I explained it very clearly to your people, but they insisted on bringing me."

"Treviño." Mrs. De León's pale eyes sparkled. "Please. Just until they call."

After gently removing himself from the woman's grip, Treviño felt obligated to explain. "Look," he said. "If I take this gig, I'll have to start over from zero in some other part of the country. I wouldn't be able to live around here ever again, and that's no good for me. I've finally got my life here set up, which wasn't easy, and I like it the way it is. Not to mention the fact that my wife would kill me. I promised her I'd never do that kind of thing again. You're a wife. I'm sure you understand."

"Look." Mr. De León wrote a figure on a piece of paper and showed it to the visitor. "With this much money, you and your family could start over anywhere you wanted. And start over right."

"If I make it out alive." A smile flashed across half of the detective's face.

"As a father I understand your position, and I ask that you understand mine. If anything happens to you, I'll take care of your family. They'll have everything they could possibly need."

Treviño looked the magnate in the eyes, less certain than before. He thought about it for a moment and said, "No, but thanks."

Seeing things take a turn for the worse, the gringo let out a heavy sigh, stood, and walked to the window, keeping Moreno between him and the detective.

"There's also your brother. We know he entered the United States illegally, running from Los Nuevos. Poor guy. He was a pretty good CPA, and now he's stuck parking cars in San Antonio, living off tips and whatever he can find in the trash. Just imagine: a man with his education and character, having a hard time putting food on the table. He's been having a rough go of it for months now, and he could be deported at any time. Just imagine what would happen if Los Nuevos got their hands on him. Your brother needs a green card and I can get him one. Otherwise"—the consul coughed twice—"he might end up back here, and that wouldn't be good."

Treviño clenched his fists and shot the gringo an eloquent look. Both Moreno and the Bus kept their eyes on the ex-cop, who weighed half as much as either of them but could still cause plenty of trouble, as he'd proved when they went to pick him up.

A cement truck passed under the window and the building shook for a few seconds. Right then, Mrs. De León caught sight of the figure her husband had marked on the slip of paper, rolled her eyes, and muttered, "Don't be so cheap. Offer him more. What you've written there is an insult."

"I'll triple the offer," said Mr. De León, also rolling his eyes. But the detective snorted and shook his head.

When the building stopped shaking, the detective turned to the magnate.

"Five days. If I don't find anything in that time, the deal is off. The only condition is that my brother gets his green card no matter what."

Mr. De León and his wife breathed a sigh of relief. Five days were better than nothing.

"Deal," said the gringo.

"You'll be paid in full when you find my daughter," said the magnate. "And there's a bonus in it for you if you bring her back alive. What do you need to get started?"

Treviño didn't even look at him. "Just a car. And some cash, to pay informants."

"The car you can have right now, just go out to the parking lot and take whichever one you want. And take one of these guys with you," he said, pointing to Moreno and the Bus.

"Take one of these guys?"

"It's not a good idea to head out alone. Getting around can be complicated here."

Treviño looked at the two gorillas standing across from him and shook his head.

"You have no idea how bad the city's gotten," the consul insisted. "And you'll be happy to have them around if you run into Margarito."

Treviño looked at the bodyguards and considered the offer. He didn't seem convinced.

"How much do you need to get started?" The detective didn't answer, so Mr. De León opened the top drawer of his desk, took out a stack of bills, stuck it into an envelope, and slid it across the table. "Here's two hundred thousand pesos."

The detective looked suspiciously at the magnate.

"Something important is still missing, you know."

"Whatever you need."

"My intervention here is illegal unless you sign a contract hiring me as a bodyguard. If the military stops me, or Margarito does, I'll need to account for this weapon I'm carrying."

De León shot him the smile he reserved for business deals that were working out in his favor. "The contract's been ready for a few hours. It just needs your signature."

He signaled to Moreno, who left the room. *Sweet mother,* thought the detective. *What have I gotten myself into?*

Just then, Treviño's cell phone rang. The detective glanced at the screen, excused himself, and stepped into a corner of the room to take the call. The consul caught every word of the conversation.

"Yes . . . I'm here in a meeting with Rafael de León . . . Yeah, the one from the pharmacies. I didn't go to him. He came looking for me . . . No, there's nothing to worry about. They're just offering me a job in his company. I'll be back soon . . . I'll call you in a little while and explain everything. No, don't think like that. I won't be here long. Nothing is going to happen. Okay. I'll call you soon. Bye, now."

The detective ran his hand across the back of his neck.

"My wife," he said and then addressed the consul directly for the first time that day. "I imagine you have surveillance on all the ways out of the city?"

"Absolutely," replied Williams. "Five people who know the girl are standing guard: one at the airport, one on the bridge to Veracruz. Another at the piers and two more along the highways heading out of the city toward the north and the west. There's no way someone could get out of here with her without their noticing."

"Unless she's unconscious in the trunk of a car," Treviño said, looking at her mother. "And they're probably not planning to take any of those routes. There are other ways to get in and out of the port."

"Such as?"

The detective shook his head. "In a motorboat, from some deserted stretch of beach. In a small aircraft taking off from a secret airstrip. In a cargo truck, hidden under piles of fruit or corn."

"Excuse me, but—" stammered the consul.

"No, excuse me," Treviño interrupted him. "You've brought me nothing but trouble as long as I've known you. Hear this: if my brother doesn't get his green card, it's going to be your ass."

"The contract is on its way," said the magnate, trying to calm him.

Standing at the window, Treviño crossed his arms and looked down at the workers carrying construction materials into and out of the factory until Moreno came back in and set the stapled documents in front of his employer. The detective sat facing the desk, picked up a pen, and read the contract.

"Let's be honest," he said as he signed the papers. "People have tried to extort money from you on numerous occasions over the past year, but now your daughter disappears and no one's asking for a ransom. The clock keeps ticking, and no one comes forward. To me, this comes down to one thing: Who are your enemies, Mr. De León? Is there someone who hates you more than anyone else?"

The businessman's jaw dropped, and it took him a moment to respond.

"I don't have any enemies," he said. "That I know of, at least."

The detective followed his gaze and realized he might be holding something back because of his wife's presence, so he flashed him that half smile of his and said, "Why don't you just think about it and start putting together a list."

"Where are you going to start?" asked the consul.

"At the scene of the crime."

"That might not be a good idea," the consul argued. "The police were still there just a few hours ago."

"It's where we have to start."

"In that case, I should take you in my car. I have diplomatic plates."

The detective scoffed. "Why don't you work on getting the video feeds from the cameras around the club? The city used to have twenty cameras on the traffic lights at all the major intersections. If you want to do something to help, get the last few hours of tape from the cameras on the Avenidas Costera, Gulf, and Héroes de la Independencia. Seeing as how you and Margarito are such good friends, it shouldn't be too hard for you."

"The chief and I aren't friends," retorted the consul.

"Call it whatever you like. Just get the videos. If you don't want to talk to Margarito, I'm sure you have plenty of other contacts on the force. One more thing"— he looked at Mrs. De León—"I'll need to talk to your daughter's best friend. Tell her I'm going to pay her a visit, or invite her here to save her the shock."

"I'm not sure she'll want to," Mrs. De León said. "And I doubt her parents would let her come here if they knew she'd be talking with a police officer. They're all terribly frightened."

"If I don't talk to her, the odds that I find your daughter drop by fifty percent."

"All right," said Mr. De León, looking at his wife. "We'll get her here. We just need to add one more thing to the document. What is your wife's name, so we can add her as a beneficiary?"

Treviño looked suspiciously at the two bodyguards and picked up a pen.

"Here, I'll write it down for you."

He saw the way they'd looked at his wife when they'd gone to get him at the beach. Against his urging, his wife had come out to see what was going on while he was dealing with the visitors. He realized she was there because the giant and his companion looked up and softened a little all of a sudden. Out of the corner of his eye, Treviño had seen her using one hand like a visor to get a clearer view of them. She'd looked incredible in her floral dress, playfully lifted by the wind. It hadn't escaped his attention how the giant with the mustache licked his lips at the sight of her.

"Are you two family?" he'd asked.

Treviño hadn't answered. The giant ran his eyes lustfully over the girl's slim waist and full breasts. A few steps away, the Canadians had sipped their pink cocktails and watched the drama unfold with the curiosity of tourists. Finally, the Bus spoke. "Come with us. You'll be back soon."

The detective understood there was no way out and held them back with a movement of his hand.

"Wait for me here."

Treviño walked slowly up the stairs and turned toward the house and his wife. She hadn't moved a millimeter until then, but she guessed what was about to happen and turned away, furious. He took her by the shoulders and she shook her head once, twice. The visitors watched her tell the detective off with angry words and desperate tears, until Treviño finally calmed her down and held her. Then he turned and cleared the stairs in a single jump, landing behind the bodyguards.

"Let's go."

The stocky one swung into action right away, but the man with the ridiculous mustache had been slower to leave the sand, focused as he was on the woman's curves.

Say good-bye to your man, gorgeous, he thought.

Then he'd turned and followed the others back to the road.

A few hours later, in the offices of Mr. De León, Moreno said, "Lucky bastard. He's going to walk away with a bundle . . . if he makes it out of this alive."

"Treviño strikes it rich," muttered the Bus as he watched him sign the contract.

3

"We have a copy of the police report." Mr. De León said before the detective left the office. "Would you like to see it?"

A smile flashed across half of Treviño's face. It was the only way he smiled now, after the beating his own colleagues had given him.

"Who wrote it?"

"A guy called Bracamontes," the gringo offered.

"Braca? Don't waste your time. It's not worth the paper it's printed on."

"Listen," the magnate interjected, annoyed. "It wasn't easy to get a copy of that report. Do you have any idea how much I had to pay for it?"

"And I'm guessing it was ready for you right away."

"More or less."

"Of course it was. Writing up lies is pretty fast work."

The magnate held firm. "There's no need to be so dismissive. Who told you there's nothing of value in that report?"

Treviño finished counting the money, signed a receipt, and slid it toward his interlocutor.

"If he wasn't too drunk or high, Braca would start out with a description of the scene: He'd say they found the car and that there were signs of a struggle, but he wouldn't go into detail or worry too much about the facts. He'd say the car was facing north when it was actually facing south, that there were no fingerprints without having dusted for any, and he'd name not a single witness, even though there must have been plenty of people around at that hour. In the second paragraph, he'd plant a false lead, probably mention the presence of mysterious individuals who never existed. If he's not too short on time, in the next few days he'll pick up some random citizen or a small-time crook and try to pin this thing on him. About the girl, he probably said that witnesses reported seeing a group of suspicious individuals of indeterminate age in a dark car without plates. An SUV, let's say."

Mr. De León leafed through the report and read: "A black SUV with no plates."

"He uses the same formula for every kidnapping." The detective stood to go. "It's the easiest way around the problem: invent the perp."

The magnate tossed the report onto the table. Treviño slipped a copy of the contract into his pants pocket and said, "I used to work in that unit." Then, since the two men were still staring at him, he added, "We're going to take a look at the evidence. Where's your daughter's car?"

The Bus took him to a garage that housed two Mercedes and a huge white crew cab pickup that had been armor plated, by the look of its tires. There was also a yellow Jaguar that looked new and, in the back, a pink convertible.

"That's the one," said the Bus.

The ex-cop walked up to the passenger side and shook his head at the dark spots on the door that once were drops of blood. "Animals," he said. Then he knelt on the pavement and inspected the door and the underside of the vehicle.

"How much does one of these things go for?"

The Bus did some math.

"Hundred and fifty thousand dollars."

Treviño's eyebrows went up.

"Two million pesos?"

"Something like that."

"But they didn't take it."

"They were after the girl."

"They're in no rush to demand ransom, either," said Treviño. "They haven't called here or contacted Mr. De León's office. Strange. How fucked is the crime scene?"

"They blocked it off, but not before everyone and their mother passed through. Starting with the parking valets, the police, the ambulance, the gawkers, and one of our people, who brought the car back here."

Treviño nodded. When he finished examining the door, he added, "It doesn't look like either my people or yours have made any attempt to lift fingerprints. I'd even go so far as to say someone wiped the door handle down. The paint's pristine on this side, but on the passenger side you see blood spatters and scratches. Now, why, if her father was being threatened by every asshole out there, was she allowed to leave the house without a guard?"

"She wasn't *allowed*," said the Bus, going red. "But, you know, she was headstrong. Sometimes she sneaked out."

"I bet Mr. De León is just delighted with you all," the detective said, cracking half a smile.

"It's none of your business. Could've happened to anyone."

"I see."

Treviño looked the Bus over. Furrowed brow, sweaty forehead. That ridiculous mustache.

"What are we driving?"

"We've got two Lobos out front," replied the Bus. "The boss said we could take one of those."

"That's not the kind of ride we need. Who does that beauty belong to?" Treviño pointed to a white four-door Maverick abandoned in a corner of the garage.

"That? That one's for the staff. The cook and the gardener use it for running errands."

"Good. It'll do just fine."

"What the fuck, man. Mr. De León said take whatever car you want. There are two brand-new Lobos sitting out there, and, what . . . You choose that piece of shit? It's older than fuck. If we run into trouble, those Mercedes over there have serious armor plating. They can handle assault rifles, Mausers, nine-millimeters, thirty-eight specials, and hollow-point bullets. What do you see in that old wreck?"

"Does it run?"

"Of course it runs."

"Does it break down?"

"No, they use it all the time. But it's more than thirty years old."

"That's our ride, then. It's the same model as the taxis around here, and I want to keep a low profile."

"Oh, for fuck's sake. Treviño wants to be discreet. We might as well kiss our asses good-bye."

They got into the white Maverick, which had seen better days, and headed toward the front gate. The bodyguards leaning against the two armored F-150 Lobos seemed surprised. As the Maverick passed, they laughed at the sight of the Bus being forced to drive that clunker.

As the guards opened the gate for them, the Bus asked the detective: "Listen. Between you and me, how likely do you think it is she'll be found?"

Treviño sized him up, not answering right away. When he was on La Eternidad's police force, at least ninety percent of kidnappings went unreported—to a large extent, because the kidnappers were said to be police officers themselves or criminals who could rely on the complicity of those same cops, who took a share of the ransom. A good deal for everyone involved, except the victims and their families.

There were the De Albas. They took the father and eldest son, and in three months extorted from the rest of the family everything they'd earned doing honest work from five in the morning until sundown for three generations.

And the Gonzagas: they kidnapped the son-in-law of a cattle farmer who was known and loved throughout the region and, after forcing the family to liquidate everything they had, they collected a huge ransom for him. But the kidnappers claimed they never received the money and cut off contact with the family. That was two years ago, and no one has heard anything about the poor soul since.

Back when he worked with Chief Margarito, it had infuriated Treviño that certain cases would be closed and archived without a hint of remorse. He'd figured out which of his colleagues would misplace files and even get paid for it, and it wasn't much of a stretch to conclude that his boss also got a cut from certain disappearances. As far as he knew, though, none of his colleagues on the force had ever killed any of the victims. That practice came later, with Los Nuevos.

On the other hand, the kidnapper might be a psychopath rather than a professional. Those sickos wait three days at the most before killing their victims, torturing them brutally in the meantime, and a long time had passed without any news of the girl. Treviño knew time was running out.

"No idea," the detective answered, eventually.

"One thing's for sure: it was definitely someone in the trade," the Bus asserted. "I'll bet you it was Los Nuevos. Are you going to go after them?" Since Treviño didn't respond, he continued: "Mr. and Mrs. De León didn't want to mention this, but they're afraid the kidnappers are going to stick her in some kind of prostitution ring . . ." The bodyguard was waiting for Treviño's response, but the detective didn't blink.

"Could be," Treviño said. "Even if the girl weren't so pretty, it would still be a possibility."

"Have you been on a case like this before? Other girls who got taken?" The Bus looked at the detective with tremendous curiosity.

Again, Treviño didn't respond right away. When he did, he didn't look up or at the driver, as if something very sad were happening around his knees.

"When I was a cop, I investigated kidnappings. Sure. But they always asked for the ransom right away. I did hear about cases like what you described, but those were mostly along the Pacific coast. Oaxaca. Guerrero. Michoacán. Jalisco. They'd take the girls and ship them off to Asia, where brunettes are a hot commodity. When I worked here in La Eternidad, we didn't get anything like that. If the kidnapper didn't call, you could assume the victim was dead, that an ex-boyfriend or some sicko wanted to have his way with her and things got out of hand. Or else the girl had simply run away from home. But usually, it wasn't that."

The detective's response deeply disappointed the Bus, who after a while asked, "Do you think she's alive?"

The ex-cop looked at him and said firmly, "I'd rather not speculate."

They drove through what appeared to be a ghost town. Most of the streets were completely deserted, even though it was only two in the afternoon. Traffic was timid and clumsy: two or three cars, maybe, that pulled over anytime a pickup came along. *These people are scared to death*, Treviño thought. There were dozens of buildings with FOR SALE or FOR RENT signs on them, armed guards outside abandoned-looking banks and businesses, a mall with shattered display windows, and homes with their windows boarded up. The building that housed the only newspaper still in operation was pockmarked with at least twenty holes that could only have come from high-caliber weapons. They passed a bar called England and saw its main entrance boarded up and its windows and neon sign destroyed, as if someone had shot up the place.

"What the fuck! That was my favorite bar. Has it been closed long?"

"More than two years now," growled the Bus.

"So there's nowhere good around here to get a drink?"

The driver shook his head. "As good as England? Nope. There are some dives down by the port, but someone in there's always packing. These days, folks drink at home."

"And what about you, Bus? You don't drink?"

The Bus tilted his chin and said, proudly, "Only red wine, and only on my day off."

"Ah, a real bon vivant. And dessert?"

"Sure, after dinner. Why?"

"Sweets and wine. An elegant boozehound," said the detective, half smiling, his eyes fixed straight ahead. The Bus shot him a look: *You smug son of a bitch.*

The first time the Maverick—a little banged up but ready for action—stopped at a light, an older woman with a sign on her chest came up to them. The photo on the sign showed a smiling young man, and the text read: THEY TOOK HIM ON MARCH 2. PLEASE HELP ME FIND HIM.

"Hello, sir." Before they could stop her, the woman shoved a flyer with the picture of a boy and a phone number into Treviño's hands. "I'm looking for my son. I'm not asking for money. They dragged him out of a bar one night. He was with his friends. If you see him, please call this number."

Treviño tried to give the woman some money, but she refused it.

"If you want to help me, help me with your eyes and ears. I'm his mother. I promised to always take care of him. I won't stop looking as long as I live."

As soon as the woman stepped back, the Bus hit the gas and drove along the main avenue. The flyer had text on the back: BAD MEN TOOK MY BOY. HE WANTED TO BE A POET. THIS IS THE LAST THING HE WROTE. Treviño was reading the poem when the Bus grabbed the flyer from him, crumpled it up, and tossed it out the window.

"Don't waste your time with that crap," he said. "There's a woman like that on every damn corner of La Eternidad."

4

The Bus kept his foot on the accelerator of the white '74 Maverick, which had neither air-conditioning nor the appropriate armor plating for their mission, until they saw the parking lot of the nightclub Giza. He down-shifted just as the engine started to sputter.

"Oh, for fuck's sake," said the driver, not managing to hide his nerves. "We're gonna die of heatstroke in this goddamn heap."

"All right," the ex-cop interrupted him. "Where did it happen?"

"Right over there," said the Bus, pointing to a parking space that had been cordoned off with police tape.

"Hold on." Treviño took out the papers the consul had passed him earlier: the list of objects found in the pockets of Cristina's boyfriend, Alberto Perkins, her classmate and the son of one of Mr. De Leon's associates. Nothing out of place for a rich boy his age: a white handkerchief embroidered with his initials, breath mints, driver's license, a wallet holding two thousand pesos in hundred-peso bills, his father's credit card, and a few business cards that despite his youth presented him as the financial adviser for several restaurants in La Eternidad.

"Don't tell me he's the son of the guy who owns El Vaquero Burgers."

"Mm-hm."

"They're not bad," said the detective. "We should swing by if we can."

"The gorditas in Colonia Guadalupe are better," said the Bus, irked. "What, you don't like gorditas?"

"They're good, but I prefer hamburgers. I'm up to here with corn," he said, lifting a hand to his chin.

"Well, you're not eating either today. Both spots are already closed."

The detective looked at his watch. "What time do things close around here?"

"For six months now, restaurants have been closing before dark."

"Why's that?"

"Since the shooting began, it's rare to see someone in the street after five or six. As far as restaurants go, people really only eat breakfast out."

"And how do they stay afloat, if most of their business came from dinner and the alcohol people only drink later in the day?"

The Bus was clearly starting to lose patience.

"Most of them only sell food to go. They fired a shit ton of waiters and hired delivery guys with motorbikes. Supposedly they don't deliver booze, because that would be illegal, but the delivery guy will bring you whatever you ask if you slip him some cash. It's been that way for a while now."

Treviño looked up and confirmed that the street was indeed empty and the windows of the businesses were shuttered or even boarded up, as if the northern wind that had slammed against the coast the previous night had taken with it all the neighborhood's residents.

"It's hard for me to imagine the good folk of La Eternidad hiding in their homes. When I lived here, people would be out barbecuing from Friday to Sunday. You could spend twelve hours at a party."

The Bus threw up his hands, annoyed: "Are you done reading yet?"

"Don't rush me, man, or I'll have to start again."

Toward the end of the page, Treviño noticed that the list mentioned a set of three keys, plus an envelope with three condoms approaching their expiration date and the little paper explaining how to use them. He couldn't help cracking half a smile.

"Oh, man. This kid. You said he's not awake yet. What kind of shape is he in?"

"They messed him up pretty good." The Bus looked at his watch. "He's still hooked up to a respirator. Listen, if you wanted to look through those papers, you could have stayed home. This heat is killing me."

"All right. Let's go," said Treviño, putting on his straw hat and sunglasses.

They walked over to where the girl's car had been, in front of a line of palm trees.

"Everything is just like I found it," said the Bus.

In addition to the blood on the pavement, Treviño made out some shards of glass. "Look at this," he said. Taking a tissue from a little plastic baggie, he leaned over to pick something up and showed it to the Bus: a white button. "Find out if the shirt the boy was wearing is missing one of these."

The driver held out his hand, but the detective slipped the evidence into one of the pockets on his guayabera. "I'll keep it right here," he said. He leaned over the pavement again, then knelt to take a closer look.

"You didn't find anything yesterday that belonged to the girl?"

"Like what?"

"An earring, her watch. Part of a necklace . . ."

"Nothing," the driver said, rolling up his sleeves. He already had an ample sweat stain on the front of his shirt.

The detective stood and walked over to the police tape. Less than two minutes had gone by and he was sweating too. But he examined the pavement with incredible care, as though he were cataloging every irregularity the fierce coastal sun had produced on its surface.

"According to the report . . ." he said, trailing off. "According to the report, the boyfriend has serious cranial contusions and scratches on his left arm, which he must have gotten when he fell. His shirt was covered in blood, and he had two broken fingers and a series of wounds on his forearms, the kind you get when trying to defend yourself from being hit with a blunt object. His blood alcohol level was low, not enough to consider him drunk. We don't know who attacked him, but . . . Finally! Over here, man. A tire track."

"Whoa, shit," said the Bus, and his face seemed to go a bit redder.

"It's blurry, but it'll do. Strange, you see that end over there? Looks like someone tried to clean the rubber off the asphalt. We've got a lead here. Can you take a photo of it?"

The Bus took out his cell phone and captured the evidence.

"Son of a bitch. When I came out here it was dark and I guess I . . . I just didn't see it."

"Hm. Take another one, make sure you get a clear view of the tread. We can't leave anything to chance. Look at that stretch, there," said Treviño, "how clear the tread is. They must've been burning rubber when they pulled out. You know any tire experts?"

"I can find someone," said the Bus. "I'll ask around at the repair shop."

"Good. Shame there's no cameras around here," said the detective, looking up at the club. "The place is oh so exclusive, but nobody gives a shit about the safety of the clientele."

"They sell drugs out here," the Bus replied. "The dealers park and people come out to buy off them. The dark is good for business."

After looking uncomfortably at the activity on the block, he added, "Listen. It's not a good idea to be out here so long."

"What's the hurry, my dear Bus? We don't want to screw this up, do we?"

"Come on, man. I wouldn't be surprised if your colleagues came back to check the scene of the crime, and I don't want any trouble with Chief Margarito. What are you even still looking for?"

The ex-cop scanned the block intently.

"We have to find the invisible witness. The one who isn't named in the police report. The one no one found because they were trying not to." The Bus looked puzzled, so he added, "The great tragedy in this country is that the clues are all right there, in plain sight, but no one wants to see them. Ha! There we go. Why don't you head to the shop and ask about that tire tread? Come back for me in half an hour. I'm going to have a chat with the invisible man."

"You're going to stay here alone?"

"Just me and my peace," the detective said, patting the Taurus he wore at his waist.

"Whatever, it's not my problem," answered the Bus.

The detective waited until the Maverick was out of sight, then he crossed the street and headed toward a taco shop in the middle of the block. An old man, probably in his seventies, was mopping the floor of the establishment.

"We're closed," said the old man.

"I didn't come here for tacos," the detective replied.

5

"Carlos Treviño. Well, I'll be damned," said the old man. "Sorry I didn't recognize you, but with that haircut and mustache, you don't look much like Doña Rosita's little grandson. How's your grandmother doing? Wonderful woman, give my regards to her and her husband. I haven't seen you around here since that time you came to break up that fight between those two boys. I can't tell you how grateful I was. It's good to see a real police officer around these parts again. Come in, come in. Hope you don't mind if I lock the door behind you. Security, you know. If you're here for a statement, all I ask is that you don't use my name in the report. Officially, I saw nothing, and I have no intention of filing a complaint. If you give me your word, I'll tell you what happened. I wasn't planning to come in today, but someone had to be here to meet our suppliers."

The ex-cop nodded and listened to the man's small talk until he reached a natural pause. Then he asked, "What time did it happen?"

The old man hesitated, then looked around him as if he was searching for an emergency exit before blurting out, "Nine thirty, God damn it."

"Are you sure? How do you know?"

The old man nodded. "For a while now, I've had the habit of checking the clock whenever I feel like something is off. I mark down the time and then try to find out if there's anything about it in the papers. I got into the habit because ever since this government's been in power, this governor I mean, it's been impossible to find any trace of violent crime in the newspaper or on the radio. The crimes happen. I'll be damned if I haven't seen more than one dead body out there on the street. But none of it gets reported. And the local news program you used to be able to listen to on the radio every night, well, they canceled it a while ago. Now the station airs zarzuelas, courtesy of the government. Imagine."

"Zarzuelas." The comment got half a smile out of Treviño. "The governor's old lady must have been a dancer."

The old man pointed to the cash register. "I was here, working. I had to cover the register myself because my manager was sick and the taquero can't make the food and work the register at the same time. It wouldn't be sanitary. I was standing at the counter, thinking about how the heat was unbearable and how a storm must be coming, a hurricane or El Norte, and that for the love of God, could we get some wind moving and do something about this weather. This whole week we haven't had so much as a breeze. Nine in the evening and you could still feel the afternoon heat: the headache, the taste of dust and gasoline in your mouth. Just when I thought it couldn't get any worse, those bastards show up and God damn them . . ." The old man paused to take a drag from his cigarette. "The city emptied out over the last five years. The wealthiest residents went first, business owners and their families, then most of my customers followed. Fewer and fewer people come by. Sometimes, like the night before last, I wonder why I stay open, whether I really think it's going to get better. But I can't open any earlier. Other restaurants can do delivery, but I'm stuck doing what I've been doing because my customers are night owls: most used to come when they got off work or when they left the club or a bar nearby. They're tired or drunk and think a few tacos are going to get them back on their feet. My shop is famous for its hot sauce: fastest way to an ulcer, my wife says. It's a good thing people think heartburn is some kind of magic cure-all: if you're hungover, tired, or hungry, you come get a taco at El Venado. If it wasn't for the red sauce I make every week—tomato, cilantro, green chiles, and a juicy, crisp onion finely diced—I'd be out of business. Success is in the sauce. Why do you think the burgers over at Perkins's El Vaquero are so famous?"

"They're not bad, actually. But they close around six."

"More like five," the old man corrected him.

"Shit," said the detective, checking his watch. "All right, tell me everything. What did you see?"

"To be clear, I'm only doing this because I know you, kid. If it was anyone else asking, I'd have nothing to say."

"What did you see?"

"Well, I was over there behind the counter, serving up sauce and doing the books, when I heard screams. A girl yells, 'Liar,' and a young man shouts back, 'Ask your father.' Then a loud screech. The first thing I see in the parking lot across the street is a red truck and a black one blocking in a convertible with a girl and a young man inside. The young man is having words with the guys driving the pickups . . . I remember when that kind of thing wouldn't amount to more than a shouting match between drunk drivers. A few insults tossed back and forth and that was it. Now, every idiot's got a gun on him. From where I am behind the counter, I see two guys get out of the red truck and another two from the black one. In no time, they've surrounded the convertible with the couple inside. One of the guys who got out of the red truck went over and started a fight with the girl: a young punk, but built. Not like one of them bodybuilders: the kind of muscle you get when you do a lot of heavy lifting, working at a ranch or a construction site. He was standing by the driver's side with his arms crossed, facing her. He said something to her, but I couldn't make it out. Then she opens the car door in a rage and goes right for him. She hits him two or three times but the kid just laughs. Beautiful blond girl, hair down to her waist. I have no idea what a rich girl like her could have to do with the guys in those trucks. They were dressed like gangbangers: caps on backward, baggy pants rolled up at the knee, flashy sneakers."

"Any tattoos?"

"I couldn't see. I did see their pants and sneakers, though. They were neon."

"And shirts? What kind of shirts did they have on?"

"The one who argued with the girl was the only one that got close enough to see. He wasn't wearing a shirt, exactly. It was one of those sports jerseys, red, the kind a basketball player would wear."

"Were they wearing chains, jewelry?"

"Listen, I don't come with a zoom lens."

A smile flashed across half of the detective's face. "Then what happened?"

"The boy in the passenger seat sees his girlfriend get out and goes after her, but the other two grab his arms from behind. He yells, 'Cristina! Get back in the car! Cristina!' I remember it clear as day. Then one of my customers says, 'Now they're *fucked*,' and I see the two guys wrestling with the kid take handguns out from under their shirts. Everybody freezes. Most of us, that is. My nephews were eating outside on the bench, so I took off my apron and told the folks out there, 'Get inside.' They took forever to react. They were right in the line of fire, but they had no idea what kind of danger they were in. I had to insist and even hit one of them to get them inside. I cleared three tables and then had to deal with a pair of brats who refused to come in. They preferred to stay outside with their beers in hand to see what was going on. When we were all inside, I heard one of them say, 'Yo! They're taking her!' And I turned and saw the tall one grab the girl by the arm and climb into the red truck."

The detective stopped him with a movement of his hand. "Hold on, hold on. Did she get in the truck of her own free will, or did they put her in the truck?"

"They put her in the truck, like in any kidnapping. The guy never let go of her arm."

"Did she put up a fight?"

The old man thought for a second. "Not really. She just said he was hurting her arm."

"Are you sure?"

"Why would I lie? The tall one opened and closed the door for her. As soon as she was inside, he got in on the driver's side and they pulled out through the main entrance. Then I heard shouts and turned to see the guys from the black truck pummeling the girl's boyfriend, but he was holding his own, so one of them gave him a few cracks with the butt of his gun. The kid froze for a second, suspended, and then his legs gave out. He grabbed on to the knees of the guy who was beating him, and the monster gave him two more, right at the base of the skull. It sounded like someone was splitting open a coconut. The kid fell backward, slowly, slowly. Then they climbed into the truck and peeled out. There were people on their way into the club, and several parking attendants saw the whole thing, but no one stepped in or called the cops. They just stood there, terrified, and didn't do anything until the two trucks had gone through the red light and turned onto the Avenida de las Palmas.

"My customers left without paying, like they always do when something like this happens: at least two thousand pesos, up in smoke. I didn't even cover my expenses for the day, because no one else came by after the incident. When the customers had gone and it was just me and my nephews, my taquero walked up, handed me his apron, and said, 'I quit. The guy in the red jersey, they call him El Tiburón. They say he's in the trade, and I don't wanna be here if he comes back.' I should have done the same, but who would accept our deliveries?"

Treviño was skeptical.

"El Tiburón. The Shark?"

"That's what he said."

"Does your former taquero know where to find him?"

"First we'd have to find my former taquero. I called his house this morning and was told he'd left town."

The detective looked over his scribbled notes.

"You're sure they didn't hit her?"

"No, just the boy. But that's not all. It started to get around that thugs were kidnapping people from the parking lot. I heard more than one person on their way out yell to those who were just getting there, 'Don't go in! They're taking people!' The club emptied out within a half hour and all my customers were scared away: no one wanted to be kidnapped, obviously. When everyone was out of the club and most of the kids were in their cars waiting to leave the parking area, a man walked up to the shop. He was tall, dressed all in black, and he was wearing a cowboy hat. I didn't see where he came from and only realized he was there when he was practically on top of me. The man in the black hat asked me, 'Were you standing here in this doorway a little while ago?' And I told him I was. 'And you saw the whole thing?' I didn't answer, and he laughed. 'The quiet type, eh?' Then he opened his jacket so I could see he was armed. He tapped the handle of his gun a couple of times to get my attention and asked me again: 'What did you see?' I thought about the tall, brawny kid in the red jersey they call El Tiburón and the animals who were with him, and I said, 'Nothing, sir. I'm an old man and didn't see a thing.' The man in the cowboy hat smiled and said, 'Congratulations. That's the right answer. If anyone else asks, nothing happened here. Agreed?' 'Whatever you say,' I replied. 'Nothing happened here,' he repeated, and he stepped back into the darkness. Right after that, I got dizzy and came over here, where we're talking right now, to sit down. I'm telling you this, Carlitos, in absolute confidence and only out of respect for your grandparents."

The old man smiled like a saint or someone who's had an epiphany, but a moment later his smile vanished and he shook his head, serious.

"I don't know why I'm smiling. Forgive me. We haven't come up with a facial expression to match the horrors we live every day. The kidnappings, the executions, the decapitations, the bullets flying all around, the quickie abductions. This is all new to us, the ones who want to leave but can't, the ones who've seen it up close, who are stubborn, who work here, who live here."

"Chief Margarito?"

"Speaking."

"Some guy by the name of Carlos Treviño's been asking about the girl."

"Treviño? Brown hair, around thirty, with a scar on the left side of his forehead?"

"That's the one. He's wearing a white guayabera and a straw hat."

"I've been wanting to bring that guy in. He has some unfinished business with the law. Where can I find him?"

"He's working for Mr. Rafael de León at the moment, but it doesn't seem like he plans to stay here long."

"Did Mr. De León bring him in, or did he just turn up to offer his services?"

"Mr. De León brought him in. Same difference, though."

"I'll take care of this. Just let me know when an opportunity presents itself."

"Yes, sir, Chief."

Police chief Margarito González, wearing three rings with gemstones on his right hand, looks at his underlings and says, "Carlos Treviño . . . Well, well, well. Who would've thought?"

6

Twenty minutes later, the Bus honked the white Maverick's horn to announce his presence. The detective crossed the street, then the nightclub's parking lot, and got in.

"What's up?"

"Turns out you were right: the Perkins kid's shirt was missing a white button."

Treviño didn't like what he'd heard. He studied the driver's face.

"And the other thing?"

The Bus looked at some notes he'd jotted down on a napkin.

"The marks on the asphalt are from the most expensive brand of tires on the market. Conquerors. They're imported and used mostly in the countryside on all-terrain vehicles. They're good on sand and dirt. They say the design is unmistakable, very rugged. Not just anyone's going to be using them here in the city. An expensive tire for a heavy-duty luxury truck."

"You sure they're not full of shit?"

The driver put away his notes. "That's what the expert told me. He works in one of Mr. De León's tire shops."

"A tire for drug runners, then. This is going from bad to worse." The detective looked at the Bus. "We need a contact at the precinct."

"You've gotta be fucking kidding me, Treviño!" the driver exploded. "You're *begging* them to come fuck with us."

While the Bus drove along the main avenue, Treviño called the consul. He picked up on the first ring.

"Any news, Treviño?"

"It was some guy they call El Tiburón. He may be working for one of the criminal organizations, and he's probably set up somewhere outside the city. We shouldn't rule out the possibility that he does manual labor, or did, before he started running with a gang. He's probably not any older than twenty or twenty-five."

The Bus stared at him, slack jawed. On the other end of the line, it took the gringo a minute to respond. "And your source can be trusted?"

"One hundred percent."

"Can they put us in contact with this person?"

"No, he's just a witness. I'll find another way. Still no call about the ransom?"

"Still nothing. What else do you know about this . . . Tiburón?"

"I'm working on it. I'll tell you everything in person."

"All right."

"I need you to do something for me while I'm on my way back."

"Name it."

"We have to tap the precinct's frequency."

"But Treviño . . . that's illegal."

"Well, it's what we need to do if you want to find the girl. We also need to get our hands on the receptionist's report."

"The what?"

"The receptionist's report. There are three girls who answer the phones at the precinct. Each one has an eight-hour shift, and they always sign a report detailing all the calls they took from officers or citizens before they leave. They take the complaints by phone and then pass them along to a sergeant, who puts the first available officer on the case. It's a form they fill out in shorthand."

"And why do we need that?"

"We need to know what violent crimes were reported over the past few days."

"Look, Treviño, I'd never do anything illegal, especially not if you call me from a cell phone to ask me to do it. But lots of people show up at my office with things I never asked for. Maybe I know someone who could help."

"Wouldn't surprise me. I'll be there soon, but I have to see someone first."

"Deal. We're thrilled to have you working with us on this."

"Go to hell. You said the same thing when I was looking for that chainsaw asshole." He hung up, knowing Williams had no comeback.

Seeing that Treviño was in a bad mood, the Bus took the opportunity to say, "That's one good-looking wife you've got, man."

The detective looked at him out of the corner of his eye but didn't answer. A minute, minute and a half, later, the Bus added, "She's not from around here, is she? I don't know why, but she reminds me of one of those immigrants from Colombia or Central America—illegal, yeah, but hot—who come here trying to make their way to the United States but then things go bad and they decide to stay."

Treviño turned slowly and stared at the Bus. The driver felt the detective's eyes boring into his right temple, but before he could complain, Treviño said, "You're not from around here, either, are you?"

"Sure am."

"No. You're not."

The Bus looked at him with something resembling disdain. The detective went on.

"No, you must be from Nuevo León or Coahuila. If you pressed me, I'd say Coahuila. But your last name isn't common around there."

"I'm from Piedras Negras."

"Aha," the detective continued. "And when did you get here?"

"Three years this February."

Treviño did the math. "I've been gone longer than you've been here. Did you know the girl well?"

The Bus looked suspiciously at the ex-cop.

"As well as anyone in the family."

"What's she like?"

"What do you mean?"

"How did she spend her days?"

Distracted by the road, the driver took a minute to respond.

"She loved exercising. When she lived here—she's been living in Switzerland for the past six months—she used to go to the gym every day. She took jazz and aerobics classes, plus French and Italian."

"Who took her?"

"I did. Her father had me keep an eye on her."

"Where did she take those jazz classes?"

"At her father's club."

"And she went to the nuns for language instruction. I bet you had to be careful when you parked around there, so as not to upset the ladies. And then the shit hit the fan and they sent her to Switzerland. They didn't happen to send her there to keep her away from a bad influence, by any chance?"

Curious, the Bus turned to look at the detective.

"What do you mean?"

"Does she do drugs? Does she know any dealers? Have any friends with ties to the narcos? Don't tell me she didn't have vices."

Before answering, the Bus took a sharp turn to the right. "Every now and then she'd sneak a glass of wine or a Baileys, a Midori, but always as dessert and always at home. I never saw her drink when she was out."

"Did they ever get any threats about her?"

"No."

Treviño reflected for a moment and smiled. "Lucky for the kidnappers, the boyfriend's in a coma. What can you tell me about him?"

"What do you want to know?"

"What was his relationship with the girl like? Aside from that nightclub, where people go to buy drugs, what other kinds of places did he take her to? Do you know if he took pills or did coke?"

The Bus mopped his brow with his handkerchief.

"He's from a good family, pretty low-key. He never raised his voice to us, not like some of the young lady's other friends, who were impossible. The kid spent all his time reading. He sent her handwritten letters. He was a poet."

The detective examined the photos that had been taken of the boy's personal effects and paused when he got to the short-sleeved Lacoste shirt.

"Did he wear a lot of pink?"

"He liked light colors. She brought that shirt back for him from Switzerland."

"Did you ever see him take liberties with her?"

The driver, uncomfortable, shook his head.

"Were they sleeping together?"

"No way."

The detective didn't say a word, so he added, "They didn't let her go out without her friends."

The detective nodded and went back to looking at the photo of the pink shirt.

"A poet in a country of machos. That's bravery for you. Was she a virgin?"

"Look, man. We all showed the young lady respect. That was our job. We aren't like the old drivers, that pair of deadbeats the girl called Uncle and who quit as soon as the shit hit the fan. We're here to take a bullet for her."

"Did you ever see her naked?"

The Bus stared at the detective, his jaw set, and didn't answer.

"You have a criminal record?"

"What's your problem, asshole?"

"You spent some time locked up. What did you do?"

The Bus didn't answer. They were driving along one of the city's main avenues.

"Drunk and disorderly? Robbery? Assault? Drug trafficking?"

The driver slammed on the brakes, turned, and grabbed Treviño by the guayabera. "Look, man. I'll say this once and only once. Don't even think about giving me shit."

Treviño gave a nod and added, "Bar fight."

The Bus's face turned beet red, like something was about to boil over inside him. Then he heard a click and realized that Treviño's Taurus PT99 had been pointed at his belly the whole time. Their eyes locked for a moment while the car's engine sputtered and popped. Then the driver let go of the detective and took a deep breath. Treviño slowly put the Taurus back under his shirt and smoothed the wrinkles in his guayabera.

"You're not the only guy in this fucking city who's been locked up over a fight. And if Mr. De León hired you, it's because you come recommended. Who put your name in for this job?"

The Bus took his time in responding.

"Representative Campillo."

"I know him," said Treviño. "He's the one who owns those tortilla factories. Good guy. Where'd they lock you up?"

The Bus didn't answer right away.

"Laredo. Just forty-eight hours."

Treviño nodded and the two were silent until they reached the next light, at which point the Bus said, "Why the fuck are you asking all these questions?"

"Because when a woman like Cristina is kidnapped, it's usually someone close to her, or at least someone who has at least one point of contact with her, and plenty of opportunities to make her disappear. There are two profiles: the psychopath who wants to satisfy his base urges and the businessman who's in it for money."

The Bus looked straight ahead and didn't respond. Then the detective asked,

"Do you find her attractive?"

They drove the rusted white Maverick down the Avenida de las Palmas toward a restaurant called the Grand Vizier. As they crossed the city center, they saw Chief Margarito's precinct office in the distance and Treviño said, "That's where it happened. It's a miracle they didn't kill me."

The Bus stole a glance at the scar Treviño had on his left parietal and discreetly stepped on the gas.

While they waited for a convoy of trailer trucks to let them cross the avenue, the detective phoned the consul.

"Did they call?"

"No, still nothing. I just wanted to remind you that the clock is ticking. If this is a kidnapping, the risk that they decide to get rid of her goes up every minute they have her."

"You don't have to remind me. Do you have what I asked for?"

"The transcription's ready, but there's some shorthand we can't make out. You'll have to come decipher it."

"And the videos?"

"We don't have tape from around the nightclub, since all the cameras in the neighborhood are pointed toward Avenida Hidalgo. We do have a video that shows the moment Cristina drives up to the club with her boyfriend at exactly eight fifteen, but that's all."

"Got it. Write this down: I want you to check to see if sometime after nine, maybe around nine thirty, any of the nearby cameras captured two new pickup trucks driving at full speed, maybe changing lanes or flashing their high beams at the other drivers or making any suspicious moves. One red and one black. See if you can make out their plates."

"This is good. We're making progress. We'll take a look right now," said the consul, and they hung up.

They finally made it across the avenue and Treviño signaled to the driver that he should turn left onto a tree-lined street.

"Here?" asked the Bus, and Treviño nodded.

A moment later, the Bus was parking the car grudgingly in front of a strip mall on its last legs.

"It's a bad idea to go in there," he advised. "That's where the cops hang out."

"Don't worry. It'll be a relaxed little chat. Intimate. Wait for me here. I don't want you scaring my contact."

Treviño got out of the car, slamming the door, and walked away.

The Bus chewed it over for a moment but ended up getting out of the car and running after Treviño. The detective stopped him cold.

"This is a private conversation, partner. Wait for me here," he said, indicating with an unequivocal gesture that the driver should beat it.

The detective wasn't messing around, so the Bus sat down on one of the two benches on either side of the entryway of the ice-cream shop next door. He calculated which one would best accommodate his enormous haunches, grabbed what was left of a newspaper from the seat, and collapsed into it.

In the distance, the Bus caught sight of a man with sideburns and a mustache. He was wearing a rumpled green military jacket and standing next to a newspaper kiosk reading, or pretending to read, a magazine. When he saw Treviño he gave a little nod, paid for the magazine, and entered the restaurant.

Treviño walked up to the entrance, and—after making sure none of his former colleagues were inside—headed toward the table where his contact was sitting.

7

OFFICER CORNELIO'S STATEMENT

Cornelio says he got a call from the suspect in the late afternoon. He claims he told him to go to the restaurant downtown where they used to eat all the time, years ago. He'd recognized his voice immediately when he heard it, but couldn't believe Treviño had the nerve to come back, like they hadn't been looking for him since he quit. He tried to discourage him, but Treviño insisted he needed to talk, that it was urgent. He says he thought twice about it, but agreed in the end: after all, it was the best excuse he had for taking another pill. He'd already had two. In the name of all that's holy, it's not like he went out looking for Treviño, much less asked him to meet. He just wanted to come down to earth, to be the one in charge of himself, instead of the pills, to take the reins of reality.

The last time they'd seen each other had been in the precinct parking lot. His colleagues had been giving Treviño, who was Chief Margarito's star agent at the time, a brutal beating. It was one against half a dozen or more, but Treviño didn't give up, and every so often he managed to give one of his attackers a head butt or a swift kick to the gut. Cornelio says that everyone, some more than others, was taking the chance to get back at Treviño. Most of them were jealous of him. Cornelio states that he was completely surprised by the attack. He'd just parked his car and didn't recognize his colleagues, which is why he drew his sidearm. And also why, when Treviño scrambled over to him, not only did he not shoot him, which he easily could have done, but instead he aimed at the other officers and asked them what the hell was going on. Which is why, Cornelio insists, in those ten seconds of stolen time, Treviño was able to stand up and get into his car, a white Maverick, and hightail it out of there. One of the cops threw a bottle of beer, which shattered on the back windshield, but didn't break the glass. "What's wrong with you cowards?" Cornelio had shouted. "It should be one-on-one." He knew he was in trouble when they yelled back: "Fucking stupid Cornelio. Why'd you stick your nose in? The boss ordered this. He's gonna be mad as hell." And he was: from then on, Cornelio's career went from bad to worse. Defending Treviño cost him his good standing and sent him into free fall, like a stone tossed into a gorge.

The waitress motioned to him that he should sit wherever he liked, there were plenty of empty tables. After all, who the hell would want to go out on a Saturday night in this town and risk getting riddled with bullets? Then she gestured that he should wait a second. She'd be right with him. He says he knew it was going to end badly when a cover of Walter Wanderley's "Beach Samba" started playing over the speakers: it was the kind of music Carlos Treviño liked. In this version, though, a talentless organist playing off-key destroyed whatever merit the song might originally have had. Cornelio says that he chose a table all the way in the back behind a column because he didn't want to take any risks, and that he scanned the faces of the other diners before sitting down. A few clueless tourists, low-level bureaucrats, at least two tables of retirees playing dominoes, a few women over sixty made up like hookers who were trying to get the attention of the much younger bureaucrats. Which is why he missed the exact moment Treviño slipped into the chair across from him.

"'Sup, buddy?"

He says he got nervous, like he'd forgotten about their meeting, and blurted out, "What the hell are you doing here?"

But right then the waitress appeared, set two mugs on the table, and poured them strong black coffee they hadn't ordered. For the past few years, ever since he defended Treviño to be exact, every time Cornelio sat down in a restaurant someone automatically served him a cup of black coffee, as if it was written across his forehead that they should bring something dark on the double, because a black hole just walked in the door. The waitress, a woman in her fifties making an obvious effort to seem nice, didn't wait for their reaction.

"Can I bring you a menu? Today we have carne a la tampiqueña, fish Wellington, and enchiladas." Then she ran through a long list of dishes they weren't going to order before finally reaching the end of her speech: "And for dessert, we have Tres Leches cake."

"No thank you, my friend," said Treviño.

Cornelio states that all of a sudden he heard himself saying something he shouldn't have. Like in one of those nightmares where you only do and say things that create problems for you: "The gentleman won't be staying long," he offered. "The police are looking for him."

Like a joke. He immediately regretted his words. He's felt for a while that the pills he'd been taking to relax weren't really helping him think, that they were making choices for him without having much life experience to back it up, those assholes, or much of a sense of humor. The result was that he was living his life like something that wasn't really happening or was happening to someone else or that didn't matter, like one of those horror films you watch on television after midnight, half asleep, not caring at all what happens to the characters because in the end you know they're all going to die. Or: like those video games where you're driving a race car against opponents who are faster than you, who box you in mercilessly and never give you a chance to break free, and every second that goes by, you go further out of control and you know you won't be able to stop, the kinds of races that rattle your nerves and always end with you driving straight off a cliff.

He says the waitress lifted her eyes slowly, slowly, and cast a sideways glance at Treviño, as if he was a wanted criminal and she was going to identify him. Even so, despite her fear, she managed to leave them a bowl of sugar, a little pitcher of milk, and two napkins each: napkins so minuscule they might as well not have been there at all. The poor woman took a step back from the table, and Cornelio added, "If they catch you, they're gonna to kill you."

Treviño smiled as though he were kidding. "You and your bad jokes, brother," he said.

The waitress left their table significantly paler and more frightened than when she arrived. Cornelio says he didn't care, because it was all happening to some guy who looked like him, some guy in his seat at the table that night. Which is why he went on to say, "Just don't say I didn't warn you. The chief has you in his sights, but you insisted, so here we are. I really don't know what you're thinking, Carlitos. No idea what's going through that head of yours."

He noticed that Treviño was leaning forward, as if he were studying the napkin dispenser. "Lower your voice, Cornelio," he said. "There's no need to draw attention to us." And it took the officer a few seconds to understand that the visitor was right, that he was an idiot, that he was yelling and didn't even realize it, and he fell into a shamed silence, staring at his little napkins until the detective asked him how he was doing, how things were at the precinct. Cornelio says he made a serious effort to answer the question like a normal person, instead of a pill head.

"You don't have anything on you to even me out, do you? Something to get my feet under me?" And Treviño shook his head as though he felt something worse than pity for him.

As Cornelio recalls, the high notes of the terribly flawed version of "Beach Samba" fell over them. He took off his dark glasses and rubbed his eyes to see if he could ground his body and stop flying around above reality. Treviño didn't ask him any more questions for a while. He was distracted by the scars around Cornelio's eyes. That was when Cornelio mustered the concentration to ask the visitor, "What can I do for you, Treviño?"

The detective leaned over the table again and said quietly, "Have you ever heard of a guy they call El Tiburón?"

"Javier García Osorio, a.k.a. El Tiburón. Why?" Cornelio was acting almost normal by now.

"He owes me some money," said the detective. And Cornelio says he couldn't help smiling.

"Ha! No way. Forget about calling that debt in."

"Why? What do you know about him?"

And he told him the kid was already in the trade, that he was young but dangerous.

"He's not from around here. He's from a ranch in the middle of the state. Like any other dumbass his age, he's good in a fight but useless at holding a job, a legit one, I mean."

And since Treviño didn't say anything, he added, "Story goes, he was playing with a gun one day and it went off. Killed his father. But then, some people think he wasn't playing, that they only said it was an accident because he was a minor and the family paid to get the charges dropped. You know, same old story. They say his own mother and sister went to live in the United

States because they didn't trust him and wanted to steer clear. Then the ranch went under, or he lost it in a bet, and he came to live here by the port. They tied him to two other bodies, but haven't been able to prove anything."

"What bodies?"

"A few months ago, a girl he was seeing disappeared right after she left his ranch. She was found beaten to death. They let him go. He could prove he was with friends when it happened, and he had ties to a major player in the trade."

"Where did you say this was, again?"

"At his family's ranch, in the northern part of the state. El Zacate . . . no, El Zacatal, it's called."

Cornelio recalls (or claims to recall) that Treviño repeated the name of the ranch, El Zacatal, and asked, "Why would you remember that?"

"I had to book him a while back," said Cornelio. "He was raising hell in a bar and hit two people. The kid goes out every weekend and gets shit faced, then beats the crap out of someone. And with that build, no one can really take him on. Once, he started raising hell in a Brazilian restaurant and the owners called it in, so I went and brought him down to the precinct. But he passed some money to the chief, who chewed me out in front of him and let him walk that same night."

He says Treviño gave a little grunt before going on with his questions.

"They say he's been seen with a gang. Maybe La Cuarenta?"

"No . . ." Cornelio remembers shaking his head more forcefully than necessary, to the point that a few retirees turned to look at him, but then he managed to restrain himself. "I don't picture him with the Four-Zero. And I know every asshole in that organization. If he's in the trade, he's working with someone else."

"Could he be with Los Nuevos or Las Tres Letras, the CDP?" Treviño asked, referring to the two other criminal organizations that had put down roots in the port city.

Cornelio says he answered, proud of himself for taking the reins not just of the conversation, but of reality itself.

"It could be either of them." And then the truth blazed in his mind, despite the pills, and he asked, "Tell me something, asshole: why does he owe you money, and how much are we talking about? Because if I help you find him, I expect a commission." A big smile spread across his face and he was about to burst out laughing but managed to hold it in. He didn't want to make another scene. Well, maybe he did let out a little snicker, but nothing too loud or demented, though it did catch the attention of all present, and also of the distraught waitress, who watched him with concern. And he noticed that Treviño was looking at him too, sadly, and that he was having a hard time regaining his composure, coming back to earth, fighting the effect of the pills, but that he was finally able to stop laughing and pick the conversation up where he left off.

"What's your angle, asshole? What are you up to? Whatever you plan on doing, count me out. Look at me. I can't take any more risks. If I help you, I'll be even more fucked down at the precinct than I already am."

"You serious?"

"Yeah, man. When you skipped town, they took it out on me. Yeah. That's how things are."

After a pause long enough for half the restaurant's customers to discreetly ask for the check, and for several of the old folks to leave cash on the table and slip out without looking back, Cornelio said, never taking his eyes off the overly primped old ladies who trembled as they paid for their food up at the register, "You have no idea, no idea, my dear Treviño, how bad the port has gotten. This isn't a city anymore. It's a fucking Western."

He saw that he needed to explain.

"All the top brass work for one of the major players, the heavyweights in the trade. They all carry two, three phones. One for the job, another to stay in touch with their sponsoring organization, and one more for talking to the competition, because you don't want them seeing you as the enemy. It's outrageous: all those phones on the table during meetings or hanging from the officers' belts."

Cornelio says he went on.

"You remember Roque? He's one of them now: driver, messenger, lookout, bodyguard. He even moves product for them in his spare time. A bit of everything. He's doing pretty well for himself, but it's just a matter of time before they lock him up or fire him: you can't get too close to those people or meet with them in broad daylight."

"And our team?" Treviño asked.

"What team? They've all been run out."

Cornelio says his memory gets blurry here, because right then a kind of black cloud settled over the table, but he thinks the conversation went something like this:

"Who's still there that I know? And turn around, stop scaring the waitress."

"There's a bunch, a bunch of the top brass, but none of them's trustworthy. There's Oscar Fayad. They took away his patrol vehicle and his badge, now he's El Quelite's stoolie. He got hooked, spends everything he makes on blow."

"And Ramiro?"

"The one who taught karate? He quit. About a week after they beat the crap out of you. One day he just didn't come in to work, and word got around that he was working as a bouncer at a brothel in Ciudad Miel, a place called Babydollz. I don't buy it, though. I heard he's with Los Nuevos."

"And my girlfriend?"

Cornelio smiled. "She's still there, doing her thing. Why does that broad love dead guys so much? Dead guys and washouts. The news is that she opened a store that sells plants, not far from the precinct. Gotta do something to make ends meet. Still miss her, huh? It's hard to get some women out of your head, am I right?"

"My interest in her is purely professional."

"Oh, sure. You and your professional interest."

"Lay off the lewd gestures, Cornelio. This is a family joint. What about the Three Stooges?"

The nickname referred to three officers—basically thugs themselves—who had killed numerous criminals in firefights over the past few months. Suspects had a strange habit of dying while in their custody. Cornelio's eyes lit up for the first time in their whole conversation.

"Ahaaa. So that's where all this was going. Pinche Carlos. You want to get even, is that it?"

"No, of course not. I don't want any trouble."

"Well, they haven't forgotten about you. They say Bracamontes still scours the beaches around here looking for you. He didn't appreciate the way you knocked out his front teeth."

"I knocked his teeth out?"

"You don't remember the head butt you gave him the day you skipped town?"

The song playing in the background had become intolerable. Cornelio leaned forward and said angrily, as if it were all Treviño's fault: "Get with it, Carlitos. Since you left things have gotten out of hand. The chief sort of used to try to hide his dealings with the trade before, but a little while ago he went ahead and invited a few heavyweights to meet *in the precinct*. As you can imagine, it's like a holiday when those bastards drop in. They show up with suitcases full of gifts for the guys on their payroll. The precinct fills up with whiskey, snow, porn, and chits for table dances at one of their joints. If the federales or marines are making the rounds, they distribute their goods in the parking lot of a mall or in a park, but they always pay their people."

"And the ones who don't sign up?"

"They ask you if you're in. And if you change the subject or fake dementia, they just shrug and walk away. Then headquarters suddenly starts giving you more dangerous assignments or just lamer ones, where you don't get the chance to make an extra dime on the side. Their bet is you'll quit: they want you with them body and soul, or they want you to walk of your own free will."

"What about you, Cornelio? Who are you with?"

"Nobody wants me. But I guess you could say I'm with the founders."

He was talking about the old guard, an organization known as Los Viejos or the Cartel del Puerto, the criminals who got the business up and running way back when. Cornelio and Treviño both knew that for thirty years the same organization had controlled the black market in alcohol, weapons, electronics, pharmaceuticals, and drugs. They also knew that, as the CDP found itself under threat in the late nineties from a growing number of rivals coming in from other states, the businessmen who ran it were forced to hire more bodyguards. First, they were armed agents who worked for the federales or the local police. But as the fighting over territory got more intense and began to demand twenty-four-seven security, they had to bribe elite soldiers from the army. Their agreement lasted maybe ten years, until the soldiers decided it was time to take over and founded Los Nuevos. Cornelio says that's what he'd been talking about and that he'd added, "Everyone wants to control this territory. They're throwing everything they have at it. And they've got eyes everywhere."

"When I left," Treviño interrupted him, "the heavyweights were using taxi drivers as spies. They'd report back on any suspicious activity by the coast guard or military in exchange for cash. Is that still going on?"

"No, no. That's over now. Used to be the taxi drivers took money from Los Viejos in exchange for watching their backs. Now they work for Los Nuevos for free, because they get killed if they don't."

They fell silent when they realized they didn't see the waitress or the restaurant manager anywhere anymore. No one else gets a policeman's sense of humor. Treviño looked at his watch and asked how to get to El Zacatal.

"Are you really going out there to call in a debt?" Cornelio asked with a crooked smile. "Or are you in the *transportation* business, too?" When Treviño didn't answer right away, he added, "Man, I never imagined you'd get mixed up in all this, with all this moving merchandise from one place to another. Fuck, Treviño. Everyone's fucked these days, but I never thought you'd get into the trade."

"I didn't, Cornelio," said Treviño, turning serious. "It's not my thing and never has been, whatever Margarito says, but you're free to think what you want. They owe me money, and I want to be sure I'm going to get it."

Treviño looked his former colleague over. Finally, he asked, "And you? How much do you owe the chief?"

"Why do you want to know?" retorted Cornelio.

Treviño passed him a small manila envelope.

"Right before I left, you were one of the guys who bought a gram off the boss's associates every month. I'm guessing you still do, or there's no way you could manage to stay at headquarters. Anyway, and I say this with all due respect, I just wanted to thank you. I hope this helps you get out from under that debt."

Cornelio opened a corner of the envelope with his fingertips and peeked at the bills. There were a lot of them, all new and orderly. He swallowed hard and looked at his former colleague.

"Thanks, Treviño."

"Thank you. You saved my life."

Cornelio ran his fingernail along the corner of the stack.

"Yeah, but your life isn't worth this much. Now I'm the one who owes you."

Treviño smiled.

"How can I find this ranch?"

The policeman looked at Treviño.

"Take my advice, Carlitos: Don't even think about it. Forget about getting that money from El Tiburón. It's not possible."

"Why not?"

"Well, for starters you've got the checkpoints, asshole. There are guards posted every couple of hundred feet, some by Los Viejos, others by Los Nuevos. No one drives alone at night or in the evening for that matter, because they just stop you and take your car if they feel like it. People prefer to travel by bus, and only before three in the afternoon. But they say that at some point not even the buses get through. They say Los Nuevos pull people out, rob them, and scream at the little old ladies. They say that every now and then Los Nuevos grab a bunch of dudes and no one ever hears from them again. That they use them for manual labor or as human shields, but that first they're taken for training on a huge plot of land, out there in the sierra. Don't even think about trying it."

And he says that Treviño checked his watch again and said, "I need a favor."

"Name it."

"I need you to go back to headquarters and check if any of these people has a criminal history, but be discreet." Then he

gave him three names, keeping his voice low: Valentín Bustamante, a.k.a. the Bus; Rodolfo Moreno Valle; and Rafael Garza
Elizondo, a.k.a. Rafita.

Cornelio says that since none of the names sounded familiar,
he wrote them down on a napkin. *This shitty little scrap's good for
something, after all.*

That's what he was doing when flashing lights out on the
street caught his attention. Cornelio raised his eyes and peered
into the patrol vehicle pulling up.

"You're fucked now, Carlitos. Get out of here. Now I have to
report that I saw you. I'll say you were holding me at gunpoint.
I'm sorry, buddy, but it's my ass or yours."

Treviño stood. "First, pay the check and leave a good tip, so
the waitress gets over the shock of all this. Don't go cheap on
me now, Cornelio."

Cornelio says it took him longer to find the woman in the
pink apron and ask her for the check than it took Treviño to get
out of there. That when he turned back around, his former colleague was already gone.

The man approaching the restaurant was one of the Three
Stooges: Bracamontes, the one they called El Braca, or the Snout.
The one with the gold teeth. And Cornelio López, a.k.a. The
Rolling Stone Headed Off a Cliff, a.k.a. The Car Driven by Pills,
says he suddenly understood how he was going to rejoin his
body and be himself again. There was only one path, and that
path was pain.

Bracamontes walked in seconds later, in his crisp uniform and
knee-high boots, with one hand resting on the holster that held
his sidearm. While the few remaining customers asked for the
check—it wasn't a good time to go out for dinner, not with so
many bad people around, spreading bad energy—Bracamontes

examined every corner of the place. He didn't find what he was looking for. He walked over and stood next to Cornelio.

"That was Treviño here just now?"

"Oh, hi," said Cornelio, thanking the gods for suggesting he hide the envelope with the money in his pants.

"Why'd you let him go?"

"He caught me by surprise. He's armed. He threatened me."

"Does the boss know?"

"I'm working on it," Cornelio said. "I'm working on it, but I keep getting a busy signal on his cell."

"Why don't you call him from the squad car?"

"I was just on my way to do that."

Bracamontes took out his own cell phone and passed it to Cornelio, who called their boss. Chief Margarito picked up right away, as if he'd been waiting for the call. In a sense, he'd been waiting for the call for years.

"Margarito here."

"There's news, Chief. Treviño is back in the port. I saw him in the Grand Vizier before he hightailed it."

"You're sure it was him?"

"Yes, sir. He even sat at my table."

Cornelio had to wait a long time before the chief spoke again. When enough darkness had gathered, Margarito said, "This is the second time you've let him go, Cornelio. I'm starting to get angry. Very angry. First, we get the call that one of our officers is high as a kite and screaming nonsense in a restaurant. Then I find out that you let this guy go. I'm going to have to send all available units out after him. One more thing, Cornelio."

"What is it, boss?" The officer's voice cracked.

"Come see me in my office, friend. I want you to tell me everything Carlitos asked you about, word for word. I'm sure that when you're here you'll be able to remember it all in detail.

Bracamontes will give you a lift. I'd hate for you to get lost on the way."

"What do you think?" Margarito asked the Three Stooges an hour later. He'd just poured four glasses of whiskey. "What message was Treviño sending us?"

"Whatever it was, he won't get to enjoy it long," said the Block.

"I'll find him," said El Gori.

"I'm going with you," Bracamontes insisted. "Obviously."

8

"A lot of activity on the street," the Bus observed and looked at Treviño. "Listen to those squad cars flying down the avenue."

"Must be the Three Stooges," the detective replied.

"The Three . . . Those guys that tore a suspect's arm off?"

"That's them. One walked into the restaurant just as I was leaving. Seeing as how they're all distracted, let's get something to eat. It's time for dinner."

"You're reckless, Treviño. No, what we're going to do is head straight home."

The first thing Treviño and the Bus saw when they stepped into Mr. De León's living room was the consul and a technician leaning over a pair of screens. When the consul saw Treviño, he blurted, "We have news!"

"Did they call?"

"Not yet. But we found the two pickup trucks."

After speaking with Treviño, the consul and his driver had started poring over tapes. Taking advantage of the gringo's contact at police headquarters and, above all, of Mr. De León's professional connections, they were able to get about a half dozen video recordings, mostly captured by private cameras mounted in front of the businesses near Club Giza. One of the videos showed two vehicles careening down the main avenue, not far from the nightclub, but it was impossible to make out their license plates. Not a single frame had captured them.

"We haven't been able to make out the plates at all in this video," said the technician. "The angle and the video quality aren't doing us any favors, and the camera itself is terrible, one of the oldest models out there: we both know headquarters only buys obsolete equipment. As this section goes on, the trucks change lanes and stay behind a bus the rest of the time. See here? We've watched this thing several times. They're too close together to see their bumpers, and then they drive under the camera and off the feed."

Treviño watched the kid riding in the back seat of the red pickup pass under the camera, his face turned back toward the truck bed.

"And the next one?"

"I was just working on it. We were able to get the feed from a camera at the next light, but the trucks don't show up in the video."

"Are you sure?"

"Completely. They're not there. Look."

The passenger van and a few cars from the previous tape were on this second one, but the trucks were nowhere to be seen.

"They went into Colonia Dorada," the consul said, clapping his hands. "They live there. We've got them!"

Treviño stood and walked over to a little table that held a plate of sandwiches and a pot with hot coffee. He studied the array as if it were a map of the city.

"If they turned off before reaching the next light, Colonia Dorada isn't the only place they could've gone. There's also Colonia Pescadores. There's a dirt road behind the wall surrounding Colonia Dorada that leads to the river. In trucks with that kind of clearance, they could get down there with no problem."

"Shit," said the consul.

Pescadores was La Cuarenta's base of operations. It wasn't going to be easy to run an investigation down there.

Treviño looked around the room. "Where's Mr. De León?"

"He went to bed. He was exhausted."

"Do you have the transcripts I asked for?" the detective asked, pouring himself a strong black coffee.

"Here they are."

"I hope you didn't buy them off Bracamontes."

"I know other people at headquarters, don't worry."

"Of course you do. How many cars does Mr. De León have out there?"

Williams looked over at the bodyguards, who did a quick calculation.

"Right now, two F-150 Lobos."

"I see. Well, there's also a black Grand Marquis parked at the entrance to the compound, and I think I see two of my former colleagues inside. When you get the chance, would you pay them a visit?"

"The black car?" The Bus reached for his walkie-talkie. "We'll get rid of them."

"Leave 'em, it's just El Carcamán, the old geezer, and El Chino. Laid-back types, not too sharp. But be aware that Margarito's got eyes on us. He wants to know who's coming and going around here."

"Do you think they saw you?"

"Not sure. But we have to proceed with absolute discretion. Can I steal a cigarette from you?" Treviño indicated to the consul that he should follow him to the terrace.

The gringo, confused, did just that. Treviño walked over to the farthest corner, lit the cigarette the consul offered him, and after exhaling a huge cloud of smoke said, "Now that you've looked into Cristina's bodyguards, did you check out their homes?"

The gringo nodded.

"Moreno's house? What about Rafita's, and Bustamante's?"

"We've been keeping an eye on them ever since this thing began. My driver went into each of their homes and didn't find anything unusual."

Treviño let out another cloud of smoke. "What can you tell me about Moreno?"

"He lives here. Mr. De León puts him up in one of the little houses on the way in. His things are all there."

"And Rafita?"

"He and the Bus both live in apartments downtown, near the market. There's no way they could have taken the girl there. There's hundreds of eyes around, and no one saw anything suspicious. And just so you know, everyone who works here, even the gardener and the kitchen staff, had to take a lie detector test. They all passed."

The consul's driver, Larry, stuck his head out to let them know they had a call, and Williams returned to the library. The detective took a few more drags on the cigarette, stepped into the house, sat at the table, grabbed a highlighter, and marked three or four phrases in the police transcript. Suddenly, he stopped and leaned over a page, as though he couldn't believe what he was reading.

"Do you have today's papers?"

"What are you looking for?"

"I'm guessing," said the detective, "that no one published anything about the three dead gang members that showed up in an empty lot in Colonia Pescadores. Am I right?"

The consul didn't answer, so he went on.

"What would we do without government censorship?" He leaned over the papers. Williams sat down next to him and looked at the transcript.

"Look, there were three bodies," said the detective, pointing at the document. "The operator sends patrol vehicles to investigate a firefight. Then later," he continued, pointing to another page, "Officer Bolívar Arzate, a.k.a. the Block, one of the Three Stooges, reports finding an abandoned vehicle riddled with bullet holes and three corpses: boys around twenty years old, dressed like gangbangers. Each had multiple bullet wounds in his chest and a kill shot to the head. This was two nights ago, the day the girl disappeared, just . . . let me see here . . . one hour after she left the club."

"Holy shit."

"We have to talk to the guards at Colonia Dorada, ask them if they remember two trucks driving through there on Saturday night. And we need to examine the scene," he said, pointing at the transcript.

They heard the unmistakable rattle of an automatic weapon somewhere in the distance. Just like the night before. The detective and the consul looked up as the Bus took out his handkerchief to dry his forehead.

"It's going on too long to be an execution or a confrontation," said Treviño. A minute later, the gunfire started up again.

"We heard something similar yesterday," said the consul. "At around the same time."

"It happens every so often," the Bus interjected. "It's La Cuarenta, marking their territory."

"Marking territory? Those guys are pissed," said the detective.

Mr. De León, who was just entering the room, noticed that the color had drained from the consul's face. He leaned over the transcript.

"What's going on, Treviño?" he asked.

"That's what we're going to find out," replied the detective, and he set his coffee down on the table.

An hour later, Treviño discreetly handed an envelope full of cash to the guards stationed at the entrance to Colonia Dorada and headed back to the pickup. In order to avoid his former colleagues, the detective had needed to abandon the white Maverick, predisposed as it was to stalling out and generally inappropriate for this kind of mission, and travel in one of Mr. De León's armored trucks. When he saw him, the Bus lowered the driver's side window.

"What's the word?"

"They didn't come this way. No residents match their description, and no one saw the trucks drive through. Looks like our next stop is Colonia Pescadores."

"I'm not about to go down there alone. Let's get Rafita and Moreno to back us up."

The detective thought about it for a moment and nodded. "We'll wait for them over by the gully that leads down to the neighborhood."

The Bus started the motor, grumbling the whole time, and Treviño climbed in.

After they had circled around a bit to shake the agents tailing them, a second truck carrying Rafita and Moreno pulled up next to them. Treviño explained the mission: they needed to get in and get out as quickly as possible; they should be efficient and respectful, but ready to throw their weight around if necessary. Right then, his phone rang, and the detective stepped away to hear better.

"Yes, I'm still in La Eternidad . . . No, no, I didn't get arrested. If I had, I couldn't have picked up my phone, right? Those guys who came for me weren't police. They were bodyguards. They work for Mr. De León. They came looking for me because Mr.

De León wanted to interview me for a job. That's why I'm still here . . . I'll be back soon . . . No, come on . . . Don't make me say it out loud . . . Okay, I love you too. Talk to you soon."

He hung up and turned to the Bus.

"All right, let's get going."

And they headed down the gully, toward the river.

It was a vacant lot about 250 feet long by 100 feet across, just barely marked off by a few stakes and some barbed wire. In spots, the bushes and weeds grew more than three feet high.

One armored pickup could go unnoticed in the city, but a caravan would always stick out in Pescadores and could mean only one of two things: rich people to rob or rivals in the trade who would need to be checked out.

"Step on it," said Treviño. He noticed the Bus was sweating, despite the air-conditioning.

They saw a few groups of three or four residents sitting in front of a shack, huddled around a little battery-powered television—the men drinking beer around a plastic table, and the women holding babies and herding other children. Invariably, they'd fall silent and turn to watch them pass. Treviño was surprised by the complete absence of old people: there wasn't a man or woman there over forty years old. Was that the life expectancy in the neighborhood? Then there was the constant barking of the dogs that escorted the vehicles through town. On two occasions, small groups of teenagers smoking marijuana around a garbage can bonfire or in the back seat of a charred car stripped of its tires stared at them suspiciously. Treviño watched them through the tinted windows and remembered growing up not far from there.

"Son of a fucking bitch." The Bus was a nervous wreck. "Just try and get us back here again."

"You're pretty jumpy for a guy who runs a security detail, man. What's the matter? Cat got your balls?"

"I've got them right here, thank you very much, and I'd like to keep it that way. Why take this risk?"

The Bus carried only the Colt .45 that Mr. De León gave to all his bodyguards (an ostentatious firearm with wood grips and shiny chrome plating, suited to a millionaire), but he knew Rafita and Moreno were packing, respectively, a sawed-off Colt twelve-gauge and a Steyr TMP compact submachine gun, a souvenir from his European coursework. For his part, Treviño had the Taurus tucked away in his pants and was holding only a flashlight.

"This is it."

They parked the two vehicles on the dirt road. The detective was the first to get out. A length of reflective tape blocked access to the lot. When the bodyguards caught up to him, Treviño lifted it and walked underneath, followed closely by Moreno and the Bus. Rafita stayed behind to keep watch.

"They don't waste time around here."

The windows of the dark-colored pickup were broken, and its left side had several bullet holes in it. The hood was up, and the motor and battery were gone. They'd also taken the tires, leaving the vehicle on four cinder blocks.

"Motherfuckers. I bet you a tow truck tried to get in here, and they wouldn't let it get close enough to haul this thing out." Treviño would have liked to compare the tracks they found outside the nightclub with the tires on this truck, but it was both impossible and unnecessary now. The crime scene investigators had already removed their plastic cones, but Moreno tripped over an evidence marker, number 66, that had been placed near the truck in line with the driver's side window.

"All right, detective, what do we have here?"

Treviño observed the flattened grass and ants around the marker.

"That's where the bodies fell."

He picked up a branch and fished a sneaker splattered with blood and covered in ants out from under the truck.

"If this is how they work a crime scene, I hate to imagine what the city must be like."

The detective stared intently for a moment at the sneaker and the evidence marker, then looked up and said, "This is where they were shot. They were standing here in front of the truck when they were hit by one, maybe two gunmen."

Moreno nodded and took three big steps backward. Treviño shone his flashlight at the grass near the bodyguard's feet, and the two of them combed through the underbrush until Moreno found casings that must have come from the assailant's gun. He picked up one of them: an elongated golden cylinder with a notch at one end. After studying it for a moment, Moreno tossed it to Treviño. "Seven sixty-two," he said.

"Hey-o. That's an AK-47."

Treviño slipped the bullet into his breast pocket, scratched his chin, and fell silent until the Bus approached him.

"Are we set?"

"Hold on a minute. There's something strange here."

"Strange? Come on, man. They did these guys, and that's that. What's strange?"

Treviño stood and scratched his chin again.

"Guys in the trade usually settle their scores with traitors and enemies with a bullet to the temple. Before, they used to bury the bodies on ranches way out there in the sierra where they'd never be found. But ever since they declared war on God and everyone else, they've been throwing the corpses in front of one of the competition's businesses with a sign explaining why the guy got killed. Sometimes, if they really want to go all out, they'll leave a flower or a fruit on the body to announce which organization just executed a rival or where they were from.

"Los Nuevos dismember their victims and like to leave the heads lying around. They drag the bodies to public places and, just to make sure their trophies don't go unnoticed, they tend to fire a few shots in the air when they leave them, to get the neighbors' attention. As a finishing touch, they leave calling cards with messages directed at their enemies or the authorities. La Cuarenta doesn't go in for calling cards, messages, or any other niceties. Ever since they got their hands on assault rifles, they're content to riddle their victims with bullets, whatever group they happen to be from. They don't do extra work.

"Here, though, there's no banners strung up, no flowers or fruit, no signs of a fight. They seemed to trust their killer or killers. They were caught off guard, facing their attackers and on their feet, judging by the height of the bullet holes in the side of the truck. That's what I meant when I said there was something strange about the scene. Smells like a double cross to me."

The Bus swallowed hard.

"We shouldn't stick around here too long."

"Goddamn it, Bus, you can't rush a crime scene investigation. How do you know we don't crack this case with a careful examination of the evidence here. It's tubs of lard like you that keep this country from making any real progress."

Treviño walked over to the truck and scrutinized its interior with manic intensity. They'd already taken the stereo and front seats; it seemed like they'd been planning to take the back seat, too, since it was no longer attached. On closer inspection, the passenger door was a little loose, too, as if someone had tried to take it off its hinges.

A sound in the bushes brought their guns out.

"Freeze!" shouted the detective. "Come out of there or I'll blow you to hell."

No one responded, so Rafita racked a round. When they heard the unmistakable sound of the weapon, two skinny, grease-flecked boys stepped forward with their hands up. They were barefoot and their shorts were in tatters.

"Don't shoot, boss."

The one in threadbare denim had three types of screwdrivers tucked into his waistband. Treviño aimed the light at their faces.

"All right, boys. What gang are you from?"

"None."

"Uh-huh. And that tattoo there, asshole?"

The young man raised his hand to his shoulder as if he needed to scratch it.

"If you weren't with La Cuarenta, you couldn't be here, so don't bullshit me. Hold on. Aren't you Doña Marta's son? The one who used to sell fish tortas with her?"

The boys let out a nervous laugh. They didn't know where to look. The thing is, this had been Carlos Treviño's beat back when was a police officer. There'd been a time when he got along with guys who passed the time lost in clouds of weed and mosquitos, when he made friends with a fisherman and even lent him money so he could get a little cart to sell his wares. But the fisherman died, and his wife had been running the business since then.

"Seems sandwiches aren't where the money's at these days. What was your name, again? Huicho?"

They answered with another nervous laugh.

"Lucho, sir."

"Your mother still alive?"

"Yes, sir."

"Well, don't break her heart, then. Tell me two things, and I'll keep this between us. Who's your chaka? Is it still El Carnitas?"

"No," the other boy scoffed. "They got rid of him, like, two years ago."

"Shot him in the eye," added his companion.

"El Toribio?"

The boy with the screwdrivers gave a nod.

"Toribio Villareal. He ran things around here for a bit, but didn't last long. Loved that Colombian."

"You don't say. So, who's your chaka, now?"

Both boys smiled, but neither answered the question.

Just then, Rafita walked over. "There are trucks coming this way. Let's get the hell out of here."

Treviño looked up and could see three or four pairs of headlights in the distance. Even so, he gestured to the bodyguard that he didn't want to be interrupted.

"One minute. What'll it be, boys?" The two of them just kept smiling, so he added, "I see they've taught you well. We've got two choices here, fellows. Either I arrest you for robbery or you answer three questions. Deal?"

"Fine, whatever," said the one with the tattoo.

"Some guys got killed here two nights ago."

"Two machine-gun blasts." The one with the screwdrivers nodded. "The whole neighborhood heard."

"The match was on," said the one with the tattoo. "It was during the second half."

Moreno did a quick calculation and said, "Ten thirty?"

"Something like that."

"Who was it? La Cuarenta?"

"No," the other one answered. "They weren't from the neighborhood. Came from outside, like you all."

"You see them?"

"No. No one did. Everyone was at home, watching soccer."

"And the dead guys? Did you know them? Were they from around here?"

The boys chose not to answer that one and just smiled cagily at the detective.

"Hey, Treviño. Those trucks are getting closer."

"Give me a second," he said and turned to the boys. "So? What's the word? Who did this?"

The one with the screwdrivers hesitated a moment.

"The night of the killings, folks saw a car drive through."

"A squad car?"

"No, not a squad car."

"A truck?"

"Yeah, a truck. They say it was red, one of the ones that sit real high, like they use in the trade. Or like yours. They saw it go that way, past the bar and the pool hall. They say it went up the gravel road to the motel. Then it took the highway headed out of the city. A lot of folks saw it."

They heard a *rat-a-tat-tat* in the distance. It was pretty clear that people around there didn't like having visitors. Treviño turned off his flashlight and said his good-byes to the kids.

"That'll do. Save me a couple of tortas."

Then he turned to Moreno. "I told you these trucks would draw attention. Step on it." The engines on the two trucks roared and they drove through a gap between the houses, heading up the gully as quickly as possible. It's not that they didn't want to stay and chat, but night was falling.

As they approached Avenida de las Palmas, the detective got a call from Williams. Rafita's vehicle was clearing a path for the

Ford Lobo carrying Moreno, Treviño, and the Bus. The consul sounded nervous.

"Any news?"

"Oh, nothing. We found the kidnappers' car."

"What?" The consul couldn't believe his ears. "Hold on. I'm taking you off speaker. All right, go on."

"We found one of the trucks, all shot up. A black four-door Grand Cherokee. Older model." The detective briefed him on what they'd learned.

"After taking Cristina from the nightclub, the kidnappers left the main avenue and headed down the gully toward the river and Colonia Pescadores. They stopped in an empty lot, where they were finished off with 762s, a caliber used in assault rifles. We don't know who the assailants were or who died or if Cristina was with them. And one other thing: they saw the red truck leaving Pescadores along the road that leads to the highway."

"Hm. That's no good. Did you check for fingerprints?"

"We didn't have the right equipment with us, but it wouldn't have mattered," said the detective. "By the time we got there, half the neighborhood had passed through to strip the truck. And besides, we had to hightail it out of there."

"Shots fired?"

"We were far away by then. But yeah, they shot at us."

The consul was silent for a moment.

"Do you think it was La Cuarenta? Do you think Cristina could still be in Pescadores?"

"It doesn't seem likely, but I wouldn't rule it out."

"But if they used assault rifles . . ."

"Everyone's got assault rifles: Los Viejos, Los Nuevos. You can buy one anywhere for under two hundred dollars, and that's nothing new. And I don't see La Cuarenta killing anyone that violently just a few blocks from their base. They'd be drawing unnecessary attention to themselves. Why not by the river or the highway? The way the city is right now, there are plenty of other options."

"So it was Los Nuevos?"

"Not sure. Right now, what we know is this: the evidence suggests that the attack was intense and only lasted a few seconds. The neighbors heard two bursts of gunfire. One to wound the targets, the other to finish them off. The boys were standing next to their vehicle when they were shot. Why would they get out of the car if they were in the middle of a kidnapping? Also, at least two of the boys were armed, but the truck had at least fifty bullet holes on one side, plus all the casings on the ground. If they'd sensed danger, they would have tried to defend themselves and might even have succeeded."

"We have to check the hospitals again."

"Go back and ask about anyone who came in with a bullet wound in the past forty-eight hours. And don't bring Mrs. De León with you. There's a good chance you'll find her daughter."

"Right," the consul agreed. "What are you going to do?"

"I'm headed to the morgue."

"What!" shouted the gringo.

The Bus was so angry he almost stopped the car.

"You arrogant son of a bitch."

The detective gestured to him to be quiet and went on. "Either the assailants killed everyone, including Cristina, or the kids fought and killed one another, in which case the girl could be injured. Or dead. Or worse."

"What the hell are you talking about?" shouted the consul. "What could be worse?"

"We're talking about luxury pickups with expensive tires and kids who wear flashy clothes and pieces tucked in their waistbands. Kids who carry assault rifles. If you do the math, everything points to guys in the trade. But first we have to con-firm that Cristina isn't with the dead kids found in Pescadores."

"All right, I get it," said the consul. "But listen. The morgue is awfully close to your former colleagues."

"I know where it is. A block from the precinct."

"Doesn't it seem like an unnecessary risk? There's something you should know: Margarito called the consulate ten minutes ago saying he needed to see me about someone I was working with. I think that someone might be you."

"It's pretty likely."

"What do you think he wants to talk about?"

"I'm sure he'll tell you a few lies about me and ask you to turn me in. You decide whether you want to believe him or not. Why don't you use the opportunity to ask him about the girl?"

The consul cleared his throat.

"I get the impression he doesn't have any real leads in the case and that he's coming to talk about something else. If I bring it up, he's just going to demand money in exchange for useless information."

"He's got a habit of doing that."

"Well, just be careful. We don't want them hauling you in before you find Cristina."

"Don't jinx me," said the detective, and hung up.

"Listen," said the Bus. "If you're gonna search the morgue, you should probably just stay there. As if you didn't have a mil-lion motherfuckers looking for you. If anything happens to you, we're the ones who have to answer to Mr. De León. We can't do anything for you if they take you in. I don't know about Moreno, but I don't want any trouble with Chief Margarito."

Treviño nodded. Everyone knew he had little chance of walk-ing out of the morgue a free man if anyone saw him there, just a few feet from headquarters.

"There's a park nearby. Drop me off there and wait for my call."

"Do you want me to go with you?" asked Moreno.

"There's no need. Just leave me there and park somewhere downtown. I'll let you know when I'm ready to be picked up. But be quiet. I'm calling an ambulance."

"An ambulance?" Moreno searched the detective's face.

"Pinche Treviño's finally cracked," said the Bus, under his breath.

9

"Here's another one for you," said the EMT.

"Is he in bad shape?"

"Terrible," he smiled. "A real mess. We picked him up over there, in the park. Well, see you tomorrow."

"Wait," said Dr. Elizondo, "I haven't signed anything."

"You don't have to sign for this one. He's a gift." The EMT smiled again and made his exit.

As soon as she was alone, Silvia Elizondo, known as Dr. Ugly among her many admirers, walked over to the gurney, her long, silky mane swishing behind her. When she was about two steps away, she heard a groan that was meant to be scary coming from under the sheet.

"Very funny," she said. "But I've heard this one a hundred times."

She pulled back the sheet that covered the new arrival. The sight of Treviño wiped the smile right off her face.

"What are you doing here? Don't you know Margarito's looking for you?"

"I need your help."

The doctor looked at her watch.

"A fine hour for a visit. This can't be on the up-and-up. Get down from there."

The head of the forensics unit locked the door and turned back around. Treviño hopped down from the gurney.

"Very pedestrian. You used to be more creative."

"Let's just say this is an emergency house call."

The doctor gathered her hair with a distracted movement of her hand and peered at her visitor. They studied one another motionlessly until the woman spoke.

"So, you're not dead?"

"Officially, I am."

"Well, you're in good shape for a corpse. Would you like some coffee?"

"I'd love some, but I don't have time. Will you let me see the latest arrivals?"

"Getting right down to business, as usual. Everything else can wait. What are you looking for? Men, women?"

"Men and women."

"Make yourself at home," she said, gesturing toward the metal drawers filled with bodies that covered the far wall.

"Thank you, Doctor."

The detective opened the first drawer and shook his head.

"Poor woman."

"Which one?"

"The one with the exit wound in her forehead. Stray bullet?"

"Exactly."

"Poor thing. But I'm looking for someone a bit younger."

"Look over there, then. Those are the last ones to come in. You still roughing it? I can't imagine you've gone back to the police force."

"No, of course not. Sometimes I do detective work, if the case is interesting. And I bought a hotel. A little one, on the beach in Veracruz. You should visit."

"Uh-huh."

"Hey, do you remember that white Maverick I used to have? The one we used to drive down along the river in?"

"The one you described as the mirror of your soul? I have nothing but bad memories of that thing. Why?"

"I've got another one just like it now."

"I hope it brings you better luck. Don't forget how that all turned out."

Treviño smiled.

"It's not a good idea for you to be out in public around here," she insisted. "Margarito's not the type to forgive and forget, and he's got it in for you. This afternoon he sent around a memo putting us all on alert. He says you're in the trade."

"In his dreams. Anyway, look who's talking. If anyone's in the trade . . ."

"I know. So, how's your wife?"

"She's great, very happy. And my daughter, she's two and already walking."

"You have a daughter?"

The young woman's face lit up and darkened in two quick flashes. Then she shook her head as though she'd just taken a sip of bad tequila. Treviño felt like a total idiot.

"I'm happy for you. All right, take a look at this, maybe it'll get you out of here faster," she said, opening a folder in her cell phone and handing him the device.

The screen displayed a series of faces: older men's and women's and every now and then a child's. Treviño pored over them until he saw one of a young man—and then another and then another, all with tattoos on their necks. They were all around twenty years old, and all of them looked as if they'd been cleaned up before their photos were taken. Two had a big red spot on their parietal lobes, and it was hard to make out the features of the third: he'd been forced to kneel and took the blast to the crown of his head.

"When did these last three arrive, the ones with the tattoos?"

"Two shifts ago, the night before last. They came in together, the Three Amigos." Missing a few locks that refused to leave her forehead, Dr. Ugly wove her hair into a loose braid. "They brought them in the night before last and I examined them yesterday morning. So many people come in looking for their family members, and since the precinct has a habit of losing information, I've gotten used to taking pictures of my cases. Other people document fancy meals or their vacations, but with me it's just work, work, work."

The detective listened to her carefully. When she'd finished speaking, he asked, "So there wasn't a girl with them?"

The doctor sighed.

"No, no girls. Just women between fifty and sixty."

"But no teenager, a blonde, green eyes, around sixteen years old?"

"No. You looking for a girlfriend or what?"

Treviño handed back her phone and surveyed the room.

"I see you've gotten more storage. Are things that bad?"

"The city isn't the place you used to know, Carlitos. The people are different."

"Tell me."

Treviño watched her settle into the only seat in the room, as lithe as a gymnast, and pull her knees up to her chest. A slender woman, angry with the world, who wore high-heeled cowboy boots and her hair down to her waist.

"A year ago, when I was still teaching at the elementary school, a representative from the ministry of education came to see us, supposedly for a course in classroom safety."

As long as he'd known her, Dr. Ugly had taught science at a private school in La Eternidad in the mornings before shutting herself up in the morgue in the afternoons. It was how she stayed psychologically and financially stable.

"He looked and acted like a bodyguard. If this guy has a fourth-grade diploma, it's because he bought it. I doubt whoever sent him made it through elementary school, either. We've been seeing strange things these past few months: military checkpoints at the entrance to the city, charred vehicles on the avenues, storefronts set on fire or all shot up, shell casings on the ground. We knew something was going on, but they hid the truth from us. Until the truth got so big that we were the ones who had to hide. One day the principal sent around a memo asking us all to stay late for an emergency training session. Long story short, she introduces this guy, and the rat explains how violence is terrible in the area, and it's going to get worse. I couldn't believe what he did next. It's inhuman.

"He told us if shots were fired in the school that we should make sure all the students drop immediately to the floor and keep their heads down." As she spoke her voice grew thin, like a sheet of ice about to break. "And if an armed assailant came looking for one of the children, we should point out who it was he wanted to take. I stood up and said, 'Who gave you the right to come here and ask us to do something like that? Who designed this "course"? Your boss in the government? The teachers' union? You have no right. How can you ask us to do something like that, when we're the ones responsible for these children?' I yelled at him, just like that. And you know what he said to me? 'That's just the way things are, ma'am.' By that time, we were all crying in pain and anger. Our ambitious snake of a principal wasn't even there, probably to avoid having to intervene on our behalf. All she cares about is getting ahead. Miss Charito, who always speaks her mind, the only teacher there with a degree, said, 'How can you ask us to do that? Whoever gave this order has no clue about the bond between a teacher and a student. What you're asking is wrong, we can't do it.' The bodyguard interrupted her and said that he wasn't asking. It was an order and whoever didn't like the idea was free to go. They gave him hell.

"Miss Charito asked us to quiet down and said, 'The president, the governor, or our union leader might be able to give that order, but can you imagine a teacher actually sending students to their death? We get up early every morning, take our kids to school, and then go teach other people's children. We do all we can to help them learn and treat them the way we hope someone else is treating our own kids at that moment. How could you think a human being would obey that order? Whoever complied, how could they go on being teachers?' When she finished, we all started yelling. He was angry but had to swallow it. He probably wasn't used to being treated like an idiot by a bunch of teachers, and we were really giving him hell, so, making a serious effort, he told us in a more or less conciliatory tone that even if the order didn't seem to make sense, when an armed crew enters a school looking for one child in particular, the child's classmates refuse to give him or her up. And that could be dangerous, because these guys could injure or kill several children before finding the one they're after, which is why they felt compelled to give this course to reduce the number of potential victims and why they were asking the teachers to do their part.

"Then one of the other teachers said, 'Don't you all have any other solutions, like finally ending the violence or setting up better security at our schools?' The guy said he was sorry but the class was over and that the guidelines he'd laid out were not advice but rather a direct order and we could either follow them or quit. We looked at one another and someone said,

'I'm sorry, sir, but we won't do it. We'll think of something, but what you're asking just isn't an option. We're here to give these kids an education, not be accessories to a crime. What you're asking is that we collude with the criminals and the morons who are supposed to be governing this country.' To which he responded, 'Your call.'

"Then he looked at our ambitious snake of a principal, who was standing in the doorway pretending to be distracted by the religious pendants on her necklace. And what do you think happened next? One month later, that bitch fired every one of us who'd complained. You know what else? Every time I turn on the television, I see the leaders of the teachers' union or our cretin of a principal, who has an important job with the ministry of education now. Just goes to show what a total asshole she is."

The young woman let her hair down and deftly redid her braid, as if she were trying to shake off what she'd just remembered. Treviño knew that if asked directly she'd never say why an incredible woman like her had dedicated her life to doing autopsies or why she was still here, in this city, doing them. You'd have to know her for months or even years before she'd bring up the subject herself, saying, "Three days. My father spent three days lying in the weeds before they went to pick him up. No one wanted to claim the body because everyone was afraid the killers would retaliate. I was the one who had to identify him."

The detective looked at the woman, aware of how deeply she was suffering, and felt like an idiot for not having anything to say but, "I'm so sorry."

"It doesn't matter. They fired me, remember? I don't work there anymore."

A moment later, Treviño asked, "Hey, did you ever have Cristina de León in one of your classes?"

"Rafael de León's daughter? Yeah, she was my student before they sent her to Switzerland. Very smart girl, very bold. She's got a bright future ahead of her."

"Did she have many boyfriends?"

The blood drained from the teacher's face.

"Why are you using the past tense? Did something happen to her?"

The detective cleared his throat. "They stole her car, and the family hired me to find it. They say it could have been one of her boyfriends. What do you think?"

"One of her boyfriends? That doesn't make any sense. She's only had one, for as long as I've known her: Mr. Perkins's son, a laid-back, handsome kid. He plays, or played, on the school volleyball team. A good reader, too: he went through *Little Women* and all of Louisa May Alcott's other novels the year they were in my class. That kid couldn't steal a thing, not that he needs to. He comes from a lot of money."

"What about other boys?"

"I mean, she's had plenty of suitors. But he's been her only boyfriend."

"Got it. And do you know a boy, around twenty, who goes by El Tiburón?"

"The one who was in the papers a few weeks ago for tearing it up in a bar?"

"That's the one."

"Haven't had the pleasure. But I wouldn't be surprised if he came here to retire. They say he sells pills."

Treviño thought of Cornelio.

"What else do you know about him?"

"That he's not from here, he's from a ranch near the state line I think. He just comes here for kicks. He has a bad reputation, but his parents are good people." The doctor went back to rebraiding her hair. "Maybe it's just the paranoia talking. What's going on here can be summed up in three rules." She counted them off on her fingers. "Keep your mouth shut. Suspect everyone. Cut off ties. No one reports violence to the police anymore. Why would they? You and I both know there's no point. People are convinced that if they report murders or other crimes, and we're not even talking about drug deals, on social media, then the bad guys are going to come for them like they did with the women tweeting from Nuevo Laredo. And if the bad guys don't get you, then it's the government accusing you of terrorism. The mayors and governors around here all sat down and agreed that anyone who spreads 'alarm' is a terrorist."

"Jesus."

"Right? And if they kidnap or blackmail or kill your best friend, your childhood neighbor, your favorite teacher, the doctor who saved your life, Mother Teresa, the pope, whoever, you have to cut off ties with them immediately. Because they were probably involved in organized crime, despite a total lack of any evidence against them, despite the fact they died for being in the wrong place at the wrong time. That's how people think these days. What's your take on it, Carlos? We've never been more paranoid, right?"

Dr. Ugly played with the end of her braid.

"We used to be the most peaceful little corner of the world. For as long as I can remember, everyone who visited would leave saying how lovely the people of La Eternidad were. We were known for making fair deals, always lending a hand, and being fun at parties. And for being tough: we can work like machines, even in the heat and rough weather. But for a while now, there's been nothing but slander: 'Don't go to the coast. They're thieves and murderers there.' As if we were all criminals."

Treviño sat across from the woman and watched her continue to play with her braid. When she twisted the elastic around the end of it for the umpteenth time, she said, "I'm not kicking you out or anything, but didn't you see all the squad cars out front? How are you going to get out of here?"

"Do you still park your car in the basement of the building?"

"Oh no you don't, asshole," said the doctor. "You're not dragging me into this."

"I'm just kidding. They're on their way." He said, scrolling through his text messages. "Actually, they're already here."

Three knocks sounded on the door, and Treviño walked over to it.

"Don't open it." The doctor tried to stop him.

"Don't worry. If I'm brought in on a gurney again, check twice before you take out my stuffing."

The woman looked at Treviño but didn't respond. Treviño opened the door for Don Williams and his driver.

"We don't have much time, Treviño."

"Allow me to introduce you. Doctor, do you know the consul to the United States?"

10

As he stepped outside, Treviño caught sight of the Bus in the passenger seat of the consul's car, nervously scanning the street. The five minutes that had passed since they pulled up to the building had clearly felt like an eternity to him.

There were a few squad cars parked nearby and two police officers eating tacos at a stand on the corner, but the detective, followed by the consul and his driver, walked briskly over and tapped on the Bus's window. Bustamante eventually reacted and opened the rear doors.

The detective climbed into the back seat and the gringo sat beside him. After closing the door behind them, the consul's driver walked around the vehicle, got settled in the driver's seat, and started the motor. The consul patted him on the back.

"Thanks, Larry. Now let's get the hell out of here."

The consul's driver pulled out and they drove along Avenida Héroes de la Constitución. He made sure to avoid drawing attention by staying under the speed limit and not making any abrupt moves, but they didn't make it as far as the next traffic light before a squad car homed in on them with its siren wailing and ordered them to pull over.

"Shit," said the Bus, sweating.

"There must be some mistake," said the driver. But the officers in the squad car were gesturing at them to get to the side of the road.

"Chief Margarito, rolling out the red carpet," said the detective. "Bet you anything."

After exchanging a glance with his employer, the consul's driver parked at the nearest intersection, as dictated by the rules of road safety. Ashamed, the driver tried to excuse himself to his boss.

"I don't know what happened. I was driving under the speed limit."

"Stay calm. This is a secure vehicle, so just raise the partition and ask what he wants," said the gringo, referring to the tinted divider that separated the driver from whoever was in the back seat. With the divider up, no one would be able to see him or Treviño. The driver complied immediately and was left alone up front with the Bus. Meanwhile, the consul opened a small panel in the back of his seat.

"Here, Treviño. Get in the trunk."

"No way."

"It's the only place they won't be able to see you."

"And the best place to shoot me if they open it up unexpectedly. I'll stay right here in consular territory, thank you very much."

The officer, who looked like a caveman and was probably somewhere between thirty and forty-five years old, took his time getting his enormous bulk out of the squad car and over to the consul's vehicle. When he arrived, the consul's driver immediately lowered his window.

"Evening," the officer greeted them. Then he peered inside the car like he was looking for someone, with his right hand on the butt of his gun, which seemed to be made of silver. The consul's driver eventually got annoyed and asked, "Is something wrong, officer? This vehicle is the property of the United States of America."

"Just a routine search, for your safety. Wait here," said the officer, and he walked back to his car, where they saw him talking into a two-way radio.

Next to the squad car there was a convenience store that sold things people bought before a long drive: junk food, nearly expired medicine, flawed or outdated maps, and La Eternidad's newspapers, which were about as credible as the advertisements they ran. Behind the store there was a taxi stand with just one car at it, and past that there was a gigantic boarded-up casino with signs out front that must have been there for centuries and that no one seemed inclined to remove. Inside the convenience store, a bored-looking girl painted her nails.

"I wonder who that guy's talking to," said Treviño.

"What do you mean?" asked the consul.

"The way things are around here, he could be calling one of the criminal organizations operating around the port."

"What are you talking about?" The consul turned toward him.

"A police officer makes a hundred dollars a month. Some of that goes to his supervisor in exchange for the right to be a cop, and some more to use the squad car. Officers cover all their own expenses: uniform, gas, vehicle maintenance. The thirty-eight that guy's wearing on his hip is worth between five hundred and a thousand dollars alone, and I guarantee you it wasn't a gift from the federal government."

Seeing the shock on the gringo's face, Treviño added, "I thought you were better informed, Mr. Consul."

In the sliver of shade provided by a dark plastic tarp, an old woman and a girl were selling bags of mangoes they'd piled on four wooden crates. The girl grabbed two bags and walked over to offer her bright yellow wares, which seemed to glow in the sunlight. A few bees buzzed woozily around her arms. The driver waved her off and she went back the way she came, the smile never leaving her face.

"These poor people," said the consul, looking at the women. "I tell you, that old woman can't be more than forty years old. People are born and die so quickly in this city."

"The mangoes down by the river are delicious," said Treviño, who'd had his eye on the movement outside the car. "They're one of the best things about this city."

The officer lowered the walkie-talkie and tossed it into his squad car, then headed back to the diplomatic vehicle, his black leather boots gleaming in the sun. Reaching the end of his catwalk, he said, "Follow me, please."

Before he could turn around again, the driver called to him.

"Can you tell us what this is about, officer?"

The officer stared him down.

"The United States consul is in this car, right? The chief needs to speak with him," he said and went back to his squad car. From the side of the road, the old woman and the girl watched every second of the action.

The consul groaned. "We're screwed, as they say. The last thing I wanted was to see Margarito. Treviño, this is your last chance to get in the trunk."

"No way."

The gringo told himself that with a little luck they wouldn't be able to see the detective through the tinted glass. Or, rather, with a whole lot of luck.

They followed the squad car along Avenida Cuauhtémoc. When they turned onto Héroes de la Independencia, they could see La Eternidad's police headquarters two blocks away. The Bus recoiled at the sight of the dark building. The squad car parked near the main entrance and the officer signaled that they should pull into the next spot over.

A sizable man around fifty years old wearing oversize dark glasses sat in a rocking chair under the building's portico, chatting with two police officers. The men, armed with rifles, looked up at them when they arrived. Nearby, an old man and a boy washed parked squad cars with a red rag and a bucket.

"The bastard really put on some weight," said Treviño.

The man in the rocking chair was the famous Chief Margarito, one of the most powerful individuals in the state. A top cop who got his start in a gang. After that, he was a lackey of one of the most ruthless politicians the country had ever seen. He finally joined the force with the backing of that politician and the man who founded the Cartel del Puerto, also known as Los Viejos. And it was through friends like those that he built his brilliant career in an institution dedicated to serving justice.

The driver looked at his employer out of the corner of his eye and then at Chief Margarito, wondering what was about to happen.

"All right," said the consul to Treviño and the Bus. "I guess there's no way around it. I'll go. You wait for me here. Come on, Larry," he said and opened the car door. Caught off guard, the driver took a moment to react.

When he saw the gringo, the man in the dark glasses stood and walked over to greet him. The consul pulled out a pack of cigarettes and lit one, perhaps to avoid shaking his hand.

"Mr. Consul, what an honor," said the chief. "Please, come in."

"This isn't a social call, Chief. As a representative of the United States in this city, I didn't need to come. I'm here as a gesture of respect for the local authorities."

Larry saw the man in the dark glasses smile ironically. How awful people could be: the gringo had turned rude on him. In the end, though, that was his lot: arresting thieves; catching the bad guys; helping good, innocent folk who got themselves into trouble. If life had taught him anything, it was that he couldn't expect anything in return—except money.

"When we caught the Chainsaw Killer, I thought we were going to be good friends, you and me. What happened?"

If the policeman wanted to move the conversation in a certain direction, the consul wasn't about to help him. "Tell me, Chief," he said. "Why am I here?"

The man in the dark glasses shook his head.

"I hear you've been advising Mr. De León on this business with the girl. I'm hurt you didn't reach out to us, your real friends, before talking to someone else. Weren't we a big help last time? The detective you hired is a criminal who has unfinished business with the law. You don't need to turn to that kind or get mixed up with smugglers and drug dealers. You know how those guys are. Why go looking for them?"

"I don't work with criminals."

When he heard this, La Eternidad's chief of police took off his sunglasses to clean them.

"I know you hired Carlos Treviño and that you've been in contact with him in the last few hours."

"As far as I know," said the consul, "the last ones to see him alive in this city were you and your team. They say you played a role in his exit."

The police chief concentrated on polishing his glasses.

"I don't know what you're talking about. Carlos picked up and left one day and never came back. Isn't that right?" He looked at his two bodyguards and the patrol officer. "He didn't even take his things. When we went through it to get rid of it all I found a stash of heroin, which he was clearly planning to sell. I'd never allow that kind of thing among the ranks, as you can imagine. Possession of that kind of substance is a crime, so I opened a preliminary investigation on him and then put out a warrant for his arrest. If you know where I might find this individual, I'd be grateful for the information. You'd be doing this city a lot of good. We can't have criminals like him walking the streets. It's why the city's gotten the way it is."

His bodyguards stared at the ceiling, two mindless mastiffs waiting to be sicced on someone.

The chief finished cleaning his glasses and said quietly: "I know the girl's parents are desperate so they sent this guy in, but he can't be trusted. It'd be bad news if word got out connecting him to you or if anyone heard our consul to the United States is going around recommending him to our leaders of industry."

The consul furrowed his brow.

"Who told you that?"

The chief smiled. "Don't be angry. Remember, I've got sources everywhere. It's my job. And I only mention this to save you headaches down the road."

The two bodyguards seemed to enjoy their employer's joke, but Williams didn't find it funny.

"Any news about the girl?"

"About what, now?"

"About Cristina de León."

"Ah, yes, of course. Yes. Soon forty-eight hours will have passed since she went missing and I'll open an investigation, according to the letter of the law."

The officers burst into laughter again. The consul, irritated, tossed his cigarette and said his good-byes.

"I rest easy knowing you're the one making sure justice is served in this city."

"We're still here, no matter who else comes and goes."

From where he stood, Larry Pérez thought he saw the consul's face darken with rage. But the consul had the presence of mind to retort, "The new mayor arrives in three days, right?"

"That's right."

"I hear they're bringing someone in to replace you, Margarito. I guess we won't have the pleasure of seeing you around here much longer."

"That's what they say, but we're still here, right? And anyway, the guy they're bringing in to replace me is my son." The chief smiled broadly, catching the light on his teeth. "On the other hand, do you know how many consuls I've outlasted?"

"Right. See you around."

"Farewell, my esteemed Consul."

As the gringo got into the car, his driver thought to look over his shoulder, and saw the chief mutter some malicious remark to his bodyguards, who found it quite funny. One of them even blew him a kiss, but Larry Pérez ignored the provocation and got into the car.

"Son of a bitch," said the Bus, sweating. "That was close."

11

As they approached Mr. De León's mansion, the detective noticed a sports car parked near the front steps: a Ferrari convertible. While the Bus and the consul walked down to that part of the garden, Treviño caught sight of Mrs. De León through the living room window. She was talking to two women who had their backs to him. Mr. De León came out to meet them before they made it to the door.

"Any news?" the businessman asked. Judging by the distressed look on his face, he expected to hear they'd found his daughter's body. Treviño deduced that the kidnappers still hadn't called, and he briefed Mr. De León on his progress.

"El Tiburón and Cristina weren't among the bodies brought in from Colonia Pescadores. Four men took your daughter from the nightclub, and three of them are dead. El Tiburón probably killed them himself, but we can't rule out that there was someone else involved: maybe a member of La Cuarenta, since they stopped over in Four-Zero territory. After that, it gets murky."

"What do you mean?"

"Those boys were killed with an assault rifle. Anyone around here could have a gun like that, from the army and local police to Los Nuevos or anyone else in the trade. But I don't think it was them. It doesn't add up."

"What doesn't add up?"

"Why would a twenty-something-year-old kid kill his bud-
dies? Did they try to take advantage of Cristina and he didn't
want them to? Did they want to rape her, and he wanted to keep
her for himself? I'd rather not speculate."

"Cristina . . ." whispered Mr. De León.

"On the other hand, your daughter isn't in the morgue, and
from what the consul's heard, she's not in any of the hospitals
around here, either. Not far from the scene of the crime, witnesses saw a red truck turn onto the highway headed out of
town, so there's a good chance that Cristina and El Tiburón got
away with the vehicle and their lives."

Mr. De León looked at Treviño through red, swollen eyes.
Finally, he spoke.

"Follow me. Ruth Collins is here with her daughter Barbara,
my daughter's best friend. They were at the club together that
night, so ask her anything you want, Treviño."

It would be hard to say which of the three women in the
living room looked most fetching. Mrs. De León was in a fitted
black cotton dress and had painted her lips an intense, glisten-
ing red, apparently to match the youth of her daughter's friend.
She wasn't wearing much jewelry, but she had styled her blond
hair to fall elegantly around her shoulders. When they saw him
walk in from their seats on the couch, her two guests immediately dismissed him as a mere domestic employee. Ruth Collins
was a forty-something who carried herself as if she worked out
every day. She had fiery red hair, blue eyes, and the same prickly
demeanor as Mrs. De León. Next to her was a teenager with
very pale skin, reddish-brown hair, small blue eyes, and lovely
full lips, just barely made up. She had the kinds of curves that
would look amazing even in jeans and a T-shirt. It didn't escape
Treviño's attention that both wore understated, dark clothes, as
though they were already mourning Cristina.

"This is Mr. Treviño, our detective."

The detective nodded in their direction and sat in the only empty chair.

"Afternoon," said the consul as he entered, causing a minor commotion.

"Uncle Bill!" As soon as she saw him, the teenager rushed over to give the consul a kiss on the cheek. The gringo's talent for making friends among the wealthiest families in the port never ceased to amaze the detective. The girl's mother, on the other hand, barely got up from her seat and pursed her lips as though she and the consul had a long history that involved a bed. As soon as the girl took her seat again, Mr. De León indicated with a nod that he could proceed, and the detective leaned toward her.

"Barbara, can you tell us anything about Cristina's disappearance?"

When the girl refused to look up, he insisted. "What is it?" he asked. But she wouldn't meet his eyes.

"We came because my dear friend said you wanted to speak with my daughter," the redhead interrupted him. "But we have nothing to say, other than that we're distraught over what happened to my goddaughter and that we're very sorry about all this. I can't believe the terrible things that are happening in this city."

Treviño noticed that the girl was biting her lip, hard. *She wants to say something,* thought the detective. *Her mother has her in a straitjacket, but she's a rebel.* He kept at her.

"What you tell us might save your friend's life."

"Treviño, please," said Mrs. De León, forcing a smile. "This is my best friend's daughter."

The detective was clearly annoyed and cut to the chase.

"Did Cristina have another boyfriend, aside from the poet?"

"No! What are you talking about?" the redhead interrupted. "Cristina could never, ever—"

The detective stopped her with half a smile and a full wave of his trembling hand. The woman fell silent when she saw the irritation written across his face. He leaned toward the girl and when he finally got her to look up, he locked his eyes on hers. The girl would have no choice but to answer.

"Who was he?"

"His name was Romain. A French guy she met in Switzerland."

"What!" shouted Mrs. De León.

"He's coming to visit her in two days. They message each other every five minutes."

Mrs. De León's jaw dropped so far it looked as if she'd dislocated it. Mrs. Collins let out a shriek and brought a hand to her mouth.

"And that's what Cristina and her boyfriend were fighting about?"

The girl nodded.

"Cristina wanted to end it, but Beto didn't."

"I can't believe my daughter . . ." Mrs. De León started to say, but the detective gestured that she should be quiet.

"What a mess," said Barbara's mother. "What will your godparents think?"

The girl turned scarlet and was about to stop talking, but the detective didn't let her.

"Did they have a fight in the club?"

She nodded.

"What else?"

The girl got her nerve back. "He told her he loved her, but she said she was with Romain now and he should leave her alone. He screamed some horrible things at her and she ran out of the club, but he went after her."

"Damn it, Cristina!" thundered Mrs. De León. "Beto was such a catch. How could she do this to him?"

"And you didn't see anything strange while you were inside the club? Any other boys watching her?"

"No," said the girl.

"Why didn't you follow her out?"

"I was dancing with my boyfriend," she replied. "And besides, Cristina and Beto fight all the time."

"All right, that's enough," the girl's mother said to the detective. "Time for us to go, sweetheart."

"One last question." Treviño looked at the girl. "What were they fighting about?"

Barbara's face twisted into an expression of sincere anguish as her mother stared at her agape, praying for her to keep her mouth shut. But sometimes there's no stopping a redhead.

"She told him she didn't want to be his girlfriend anymore, that she was going to have a French boyfriend, and he asked her how she could be so full of herself when everyone knew what her father did for a living."

"Barbara, shut your mouth," ordered the girl's mother.

The detective saw the color drain from Mrs. De León's face, observed her husband's volcanic anger.

"He told Cristina that her father did business with people in the trade. That she should know, if she didn't already. But she yelled at him, saying it was all lies. She got really upset, screamed she never wanted to see him again, and ran crying out of the club. A little while later, people started leaving without paying their tabs. We thought there was a fire, but when we got to the parking lot we saw Cristina's car with its doors open and Beto lying in the mud." *More like a pool of blood*, thought the detective, but he didn't interrupt her.

"Then a little while later, an ambulance came for him," she concluded.

Mr. De León was trembling with rage. The detective kept a close eye on his reactions.

"My dear friends, forgive her. The girl is clearly confused. We should go."

"Yes, perhaps you should," Mrs. De León agreed. "Thank you for stopping by." She was furious too.

"Please don't be angry. They're just a boy's lies. Around here, if someone does well the first thing they do is accuse him of laundering money."

Mrs. De León's eyes narrowed to slits, as though she were trying to hide them, but she forced a wide smile as she said her good-byes.

"I do hope you'll stop by some other day. Take care, now."

As soon as the women left, the detective looked at the magnate. The man's ears were aflame.

"Bitches," spat Mrs. De León. "The minute someone makes it in this place, people line up to sling mud at him. Isn't that right, Rafael?"

But the magnate didn't respond. His wife watched him sit down next to the bar cart, understood that he wasn't going to say a word, turned, and climbed the enormous spiral staircase, smoothing her black dress as she went.

After a prudent pause, the detective turned to the consul.

"It would have been better if you'd told me the truth from the start. I would have approached the investigation differently. I'll leave it at that." And Treviño stood to go.

"It's just slander, malicious lies spread by a bitter young man," the consul explained. "Isn't that right, Rafael?"

"Sit down," said the magnate in an unfamiliar voice. He poured himself a glass of whiskey. His face had darkened, as if he were having trouble breathing. He drank the whiskey in one swallow and snarled, "Everything I have, I built with my own two hands. When my father died, what I inherited was mostly debt. I started out with the deck stacked against me. If you look under the carpet, you'll find that three of every ten businesses in this city have dealings with the cartels in one way or another. No one wants to admit it, but in some cities, like this one, small businesses depend on the money these guys bring in. Malls, clothing stores, luxury car dealerships, residential developments, restaurants, sports clubs, language schools, liquor stores, fast-food chains, supermarkets, travel agencies . . . Even the airport does business with them. Throw a rock and you'll hit someone living off the cartels, sometimes without even knowing it. I have a relative, I'm not going to say who, who's always been a deadbeat. Whenever he runs out of money, he sets up a new business with a different set of partners, and that's how he makes his living. Going bankrupt and starting over, if you catch my drift."

He rubbed his eyes.

"We've always known who they were. You see them in church, at the beach. Their kids go to school with our kids. They come over for dinner, stay overnight or for a weekend. We sometimes go on vacation together."

"But not you, right?" asked the consul, conciliatory.

The magnate poured himself another whiskey and drank it down.

"When you run as many businesses as I do, you can't control everything. It's a lot of people we're talking about." He pointed a finger at Treviño. "I have nothing to be ashamed of or anything to explain to the law." The businessman looked down at the ice cubes floating in the amber liquid and went on. "You asked me if I had any enemies, Treviño. The truth is it could be anyone. This situation is forcing us to do things that would have been unthinkable back in my father's day. Four years ago, I noticed that the manager at a local bank I own was authorizing an unusual number of six-figure loans, mostly to people without collateral. I went to talk with him. He told me that every week or two one of his clients would come in, scared to death, asking for everything he had in savings plus the biggest loan he could get. And he would give him the money, because that's his job. The third time a guy came in, nervous and sweating, my manager took him back to his office and asked him what was going on. The man explained that Los Nuevos had threatened to kill him if he didn't give them the money that night. People still come in like that all the time. We give them the money, and they go into debt. No one can pay the loan back on time, so they end up losing their homes and their businesses. But what are we supposed to do? We're certainly not going to deny them the loan. Anyway, the bank doesn't take a loss. Insurance covers it, and then some.

"It's the same with car sales. I own dealerships for Mercedes, Ferraris, Toyotas, and Fords. Not a week goes by that my collection agents don't complain about some guy showing up, putting a down payment on the most expensive car on the lot, and then disappearing. We never hear from him again. But our insurance covers the loss. We're not willing to lose the sale.

"I could have made enemies helping people, too . . . One day one of my competitors showed up at my door, asking me to buy his company's nine branches right then and there. He needed the money to pay off the guys who'd taken his wife and children. He told me that over the past month he'd had to empty his bank accounts to pay the kidnappers several million pesos every week so they wouldn't kill his family. 'Can't you report them?' I asked. 'To whom?' he said. 'They show up to collect their payment every week in a squad car.' What could I do? I bought out the company he'd spent a lifetime building. At a small discount, of course,

because if I hadn't bought the locations someone else would
have, for even less.

"Two years ago, a man whose name I won't repeat came by
with a proposal to open a casino. He had good references. I'd met
him through a senator." He looked at the consul, who seemed
to want to escape his gaze. "It was an interesting offer and I got
involved. The numbers looked good, and it was going to be the
first casino in the area. We even signed a formal agreement, but
two months later they kidnapped and killed the man who was
going to be the casino's manager, then the accountant, and that
was when I figured out who this guy was. I called a meeting with
our lawyers and told him I'd changed my mind."

The detective waited out another prudent pause. When Mr.
De León had served himself a third drink, he asked, "What was
the man's name?"

"He's dead now. They killed him. Twenty years ago, anyone
could report them. Now they're everywhere. They want houses?
They just take them. Who's going to stop them? Guns? They buy
them off the Central Americans, or get them from their gringo
associates in exchange for drugs. If they're in a rush, they can
pick one up right here in town. Women? The Russian mafia
can deliver a hot blonde from any country that survived the iron
curtain. They've given money to the church, paved streets, built
hospitals, and formed alliances with the police. The government
used to lock one of them up every so often to appease the gringos, but that all ended when the politicians started getting cozy
with guys in the trade. And who's going to write that headline?

"These thugs even planted an editor in chief at one of La
Eternidad's major papers. He shows up right before they go to
press, sits down, and pores over the local and national news.
When he's done, he has the section editors take out any articles
that defame the criminal organization that bankrolls him. He

also makes them eliminate certain terms. To replace 'gang' with 'insurgent group,' to write 'business' instead of 'crimes against public health,' 'taken' instead of 'kidnapped,' 'marks' instead of 'wounds,' 'disappeared' instead of 'was murdered.' As if words were the private property of those bastards, too. Soon we won't even be able to say their names."

De León turned to look at Treviño with his bloodshot eyes.

"All I ask is that you honor the agreement we made this morning and find my daughter. I'll pay whatever you want, but please, get out there."

"Just tell me one thing," Treviño looked fed up and exhausted. "There's nothing else I need to know?"

"Treviño, Mr. De León just told you—"

"It's my life on the line. Do you or do you not have direct dealings with anyone in the trade?"

"I don't work for them or with them," the magnate responded without hesitation. "I don't know any of them personally."

Skeptical, the detective got to his feet. "I'll be back in five minutes," he said and went out to the garden.

As soon as Treviño was alone, he took out his cell phone and tried to call his wife. No luck. He got two messages in a row saying her phone was turned off or out of range, so he turned his attention to the scenery. There must have been forty palm trees bordering the path to the stairs: forty strikingly beautiful palm trees. Beautiful like his wife. There were also a few ominous vines clinging to the side walls that seemed determined to cover everything. The detective sighed and noticed a copse of pine trees across the garden that had probably been growing there since long before that part of the city was inhabitable, inhabited, and then uninhabitable again. He took a few moments to enjoy the view of the man-made forest around him: a gentle breeze stirred the branches on the trees, which from that angle looked like anemones caressing the air. Then Carlos Treviño took a deep breath and went back inside.

The consul and the businessman cut their conversation short when they saw him.

"Well?" asked Mr. De León.

"We have one lead left," Treviño said, turning to the consul. "Find the title for every ranch called El Zacatal. If El Tiburón survived the firefight, and if he has Cristina with him, he might have gone there to lie low." Meeting Mr. De León's gaze, he added, "It's all we've got."

After an hour and some help from his contacts, the gringo had managed to find three ranches in the Gulf region registered as El Zacatal. The first was in Veracruz and belonged to a well-known leader of the CTM, the Confederation of Mexican Workers, named Ranulfo Higuera. The second was in the middle of Tamaulipas. It was on the small side and belonged to a Dr. Luis Blanco. The third was less than seventy miles northeast of La Eternidad, near Ciudad Miel and far from any major roads. The title was held by a man named Óscar García Osorio.

"That's the one," said Treviño. "That was El Tiburón's father."

The consul located the ranch on the map.

"It's in one of the most dangerous parts of the state, right where two powerful organizations are fighting for control of the highway. It won't be easy to get in there."

"Who said anything about going in?"

"Please, Treviño," said Mrs. De León from the doorway. "Go get her."

"Cecilia," the consul erupted. "We don't even know that Cristina's there. We have to check out the lead. Right now, it's just a possibility."

"I'm begging you . . ."

"And besides, it wouldn't be a good idea to show up at that ranch without studying the area first," added the detective.

"Treviño's right," said the gringo. "Before sending anyone in there, we need to do some reconnaissance. Find out how to get to the ranch safely, how many guards there are, how many guys they've got inside, if there's an electric fence, surveillance cameras, alarms, and so on. And how to get in and out without running into a checkpoint."

"Exactly," said the detective.

"I could get us a satellite image of the area, and some useful information about the armed groups around the highways over there," added the gringo. It always surprised the detective how plugged in Williams could be, when he wanted to be.

At nine o'clock, after they'd been offered coffee and sandwiches—the first food Treviño had touched all day—the consul opened his computer and showed them what looked like a green cloud on the screen.

"There's a lot of activity during the day, but they're not planting anything. I bet no one out there's doing any farming."

"How many people are we talking about?" asked the detective.

"According to my sources, around two hundred."

"I'll be damned," said Treviño.

"Looks like there's a fence around the whole ranch," said the consul, pointing at the satellite image. It wasn't easy to see what he was talking about. "And then there are two more rings of fencing on the inside. It's all mountains over there. The nearest river is about thirty miles north, and from there you'd have to drive in on dirt roads. There's only half a dozen buildings inside, but they're big. They've got heavy security at the entrance, and freight trucks are always coming and going."

"Getting there probably won't be easy, either," said Treviño. "I imagine there's a fake checkpoint every fifteen minutes along those highways."

Williams looked at his notes. "There are fake checkpoints on every highway in the state, especially after dark. It's just the details that change, depending on where we're talking about. The weapons, for example. Los Viejos, mostly to the west of Ciudad Miel, have assault rifles, Spectre submachine guns, and a whole range of nine-millimeters and rocket launchers, the same ones the elite forces of the Mexican army use. You can pick those up at any gun shop in Arizona. On this side of the state, Los Nuevos have M16 rifles, hand grenades, Kalashnikovs. They get them from former guerrillas from Colombia and Central America. Former Kaibiles who've set up shop in the area training assassins. We're talking about guys who would eat a live dog without batting an eye."

Treviño latched on to the most important point.

"So, you have informants inside Los Nuevos."

The gringo turned beet red, realizing his indiscretion.

"Why didn't you say so before? You could have saved us some valuable time."

"I can't believe it," said Mr. De León.

"My informant's identity is classified," the consul said, defensively. "I couldn't endanger—"

"And have you asked this informant whether they took the girl? Or would you prefer that I risk my life so you don't have to inquire?"

The consul's embarrassment was written all over his face.

"I don't decide when we talk. He contacts me when he can. He's under constant surveillance."

"I'm sure."

"I can't tell you anything about this informant or any of the others. It would put their lives at risk."

"Treviño," said Mr. De León. "It's been two days, and no one's called. Go. Please. I can pay you more if that's the issue. But I'm begging you: go and negotiate on my behalf. Even if they've already killed her, we still want her back. Please," he insisted. "Go. Mr. Williams will go with you."

"I'm, uh, afraid I can't. I can't get the United States government involved in direct dealings with criminal elements."

"I expected no less of you," said the detective with half a smile.

"I'll double my offer" —Mr. De León sat down facing him— "and I'll go with you."

"Absolutely not," interrupted the consul. "It'll turn into a kidnapping right there on the spot. If they happen not to have your daughter, do you really think they'll let you walk out of there? Send a representative instead, someone who's not a family member or a close friend."

De León hadn't taken his eyes off the detective.

"You can handle the negotiation?"

Treviño stood and walked over to the window. The sky was gray, completely overcast. "What's happening with my brother's green card?"

"Things are moving along. He goes in to normalize his status in three days," said the consul, and he held up a legal document bearing the official seal of the United States. Treviño looked it over and studied the consul's face.

"All right," he said.

The clock was striking eleven by the time they finished reviewing the information they'd collected.

"Take my private plane to Ciudad Miel and rent a car there to get out to the ranch," said the businessman. The plan was that Treviño would go to where Los Nuevos had their training grounds, get in touch with El Tiburón, and offer him a ransom for Cristina. "Make him an offer he won't want to refuse."

"The airport's out of the question," advised the gringo. "They just tightened security a few hours ago. There's a squad car at the entrance, and three officers are stationed in the area. One of them is the Block, who knows Treviño. He'd never get past them."

The ex-cop took a long drag on his cigarette. Then he calmly studied the maps. "If I take the highway, it'll be three hours heading north and then another hour, hour and a half, along dirt roads. How old is this intel?"

"From early this month. It's the most recent we have."

Treviño shook his head and grumbled, "Give me a minute."

Then he made two phone calls that unsettled all present. First, he dialed the operator and asked for the number for Babydollz in Ciudad Miel. Treviño copied the information carefully and, after confirming the number out loud with the operator, hung up and dialed.

"Mr. Ramiro, please."

Ignoring the horrified expression on the consul's face, he launched in as soon as someone picked up.

"Ramiro, I was your karate student . . . It's me, cabrón. Treviño. Is this a secure line? Yeah, I know you can't talk. I'll be quick. I asked about you and they said you'd left the force . . . That's what I figured. Look, I need you to help me out with some intel on El Zacatel . . . Yeah, I know how things are. That's why I'm calling you and not someone else. It's for a job. Find out everything you can, but be careful. You want to make, I don't know, twenty thousand pesos?" Treviño glanced at the magnate, who gestured that the sum was fine. "Good. Deal. I'm counting on your discretion. I'll give you a call at this number when I'm nearby."

He hung up.

"A contact?"

"The only one I have around there," the detective explained. "I should get going. But first I need to see Cristina's room."

Mr. De León accompanied him to the foot of the spiral staircase and, once they reached the second floor, to a bedroom at the end of the hall. He opened the wooden door. As soon as he turned on the light, something moved on the bed. Treviño thought his eyes were playing tricks on him when he saw a woman with long blond hair emerge from among the pillows, but it wasn't Cristina. It was her mother. She was wearing white cotton pajamas. She rubbed her eyes.

"Ceci, go back to your room," the businessman said.

"I was dreaming that Cristina had been taken by crocodiles. One of them stood up on two legs and said that I was never going to see her again."

"You should take a pill."

"I've already taken two. Can I help you?" she said, turning to the detective.

"I want to take a look at Cristina's personal effects."

The woman sat up and closed her robe.

"She didn't keep a diary. My daughter never wrote so much as two words back-to-back, unless it was to sign a receipt. And all her recent photos are on the phone she took with her that night."

"Did she have a computer?"

"She left it at boarding school in Switzerland."

Cristina had only a few books, and all of them were from school. In contrast, her movies and music filled two small bookshelves. The closet, the door to which was ajar, was almost as long as the room.

Treviño took two steps forward and looked at the photos on the wall: Cristina and her friends at school, Cristina living it up in different countries, skiing through some snow-covered landscape, standing in front of the Eiffel Tower or Big Ben, dancing at different clubs, sunbathing on the beach in La Eternidad. The Perkins boy appeared in half the pictures. In others, Cristina was surrounded by handsome, well-dressed admirers she showed off like trophies, a mischievous smile on her face. She was young but already knew the effect her beauty had on men: in every photo, they looked as if they were standing in the presence of a queen. Treviño noticed the confidence of her pose: the long, inviting neck that looked like it belonged in an old painting.

Just then, something on the bed caught his eye: a little French flag, the kind you'd buy in a souvenir shop. Treviño cracked half a smile and walked out of the room.

When he returned to the library, which had been turned into intelligence headquarters, the consul immediately called him over.

"There's a few faces you should commit to memory if you're going in there."

The consul opened a different file on his computer and over the next few minutes went through pictures of around two dozen individuals with him. Most were between twenty and forty, most had a military buzz cut, and some had facial hair. At one point, Treviño stopped him and pointed to the photo of a man in a black hat with a shaved head and a thick mustache.

"Who's that?"

The consul explained that the man was known as El Coronel de los Muertos, the Colonel of the Dead, though no one could confirm he'd ever actually held the rank of colonel or that he'd been a member of the armed forces at all.

"He's a key player. A strategist in their inner circle."

"I had a run-in with this guy once, when I was still a cop. Asshole was raising hell on the beach in La Eternidad. He'd had too much to drink and disrespected two ladies, friends who were out with Officer Cornelio and me. We got into a scuffle, but he was pretty out of it, and I knocked him down. His guys were about to come after me, but he stopped them. 'Fair and square,' he said. When he stood up, though, he glared at me and said that next time it would be me on the ground."

"Are you sure?" asked the gringo. Treviño nodded.

"His voice is like gravel. I still remember it," said the detective, not mentioning that his first thought when he heard it was that it seemed like the voice of someone who held human life in low regard.

The consul shook his head.

"He's one of their main guys now. He runs the operation that collects protection money from the small business owners in La Eternidad. He makes the competition disappear or puts their bodies on display in the streets. You might not run into him, but get the hell out of there if you do."

"Good advice," said the detective, offering him half a smile. "I wouldn't have thought of that."

"Another thing: guys working for Los Viejos recently dug a new mass grave out by the Las Cabañas ranch, around Nueva Esperanza. They're taking their rivals out there to bury them. If Cristina's not at the ranch, it wouldn't be a bad idea to go out there." The gringo noticed that the detective was glaring at him and added, "This is the most complete information I have. Oh, also: a couple of miles toward the border as you leave Ciudad Miel, you'll see a checkpoint manned by Los Nuevos. They wear military uniforms and drive military vehicles, but they're not military. They stop all the buses that go by and haul off the young women and able-bodied men. People have reported it to the state of Tamaulipas, but no one's willing to look into it.

They say the travelers are just paranoid and are making things up. Try to steer clear."

"And the ranch itself? Were you able to find out anything useful? Any word from your contact?"

The consul took a sip of his coffee.

"There are usually around ten guards stationed at the main entrance facing Ciudad Miel. All well trained, former military."

When the consul finished his briefing, a silence fell over the room. Treviño served himself another cup of coffee and looked at the magnate.

"Remember, we signed a contract: you take care of my family if I don't make it back."

"Don't worry," Mr. De León replied, but Treviño didn't seem convinced.

"We don't have much time," said Williams. "You should head out as soon as possible. Maybe they'll let you through at the airport if we offer the police officers a bribe."

"We'll go by land," said the detective. "It's the best way. Margarito's looking for me here, but he can't do anything to me once we're out of the city. We'll take a car."

"Take one of the Lobos."

"I'd prefer the white car."

"The Maverick?" Mr. De León seemed surprised.

"Definitely," the detective insisted. "With all those checkpoints out there, we run the risk of losing the truck. Both Los Viejos and Los Nuevos love those things. No one will look twice at an old clunker, though. We'll take that one."

"It's a good little car," the magnate smiled. "It's never let me down. Take these two with you," he said, gesturing toward Moreno and the Bus.

"No way," said Williams. "Three armed men will draw a lot of attention out on those highways."

"The Bus can come," said the detective without missing a beat. "The courage he's shown throughout this investigation is exactly what I'll need."

The idea didn't seem to appeal to the bodyguard, who stood there slack jawed.

"Under the circumstances, especially with that surveillance team out there, we should create a diversion." The detective turned to the consul. "We'll need two other cars to leave right when we do."

"All right," said Mr. De León with a gesture toward Moreno, who stepped out to start the preparations. Treviño looked at the Bus.

"How soon can you be ready?"

"Give me an hour. I have to run home for some clothes."

The detective looked at him skeptically, but eventually nodded.

"Treviño," said the businessman, calling him over with a wave of his hand. "Come out to the terrace with me. I'd like to have a word with you."

The detective stood, stretched, and followed Mr. De León outside. Relieved, the gringo stood, as well.

Once they were outside Mr. De León said, quietly, "I'll give you another million if you bring her back alive. And if everything goes well, I'd like you to come work with me when this is over."

"Thank you, but I'm just fine where I am." Treviño thought about his wife.

"The invitation stands. Let me offer you a few words of advice about the negotiations."

Almost two hours later, the Bus opened the library door holding a little backpack that looked like a toy in his massive hand and a plastic bag of gorditas with extra sauce, by the look of what was slushing around in the bottom. The detective looked at his watch: three thirty in the morning. Mr. De León walked up to the Bus and said, "Don't leave Treviño's side, even for a minute, and do exactly as he says. He's in charge, and you're there to take care of him. I'm holding you responsible if anything happens to him."

"Yes, sir."

"And you, Treviño. Find my daughter. Report back as soon as you get to Ciudad Miel."

The detective nodded and turned toward the Maverick.

"Good luck," said the consul. "If anyone can get out there and back, it's you two."

"Asshole," said the detective, under his breath.

"Thanks a lot, pinche Treviño. Really appreciate the invitation." The Bus started the car and bit into his first gordita.

12

The '74 Maverick was warming up when one of the De León family's cooks ran toward them waving her arms. The gardener was with her.

"Mister," he said. "Please help us find our daughter. They say you're going to look for Cristina. Find my little girl, too."

The detective looked at the couple. The cook handed him a photo of a dark-skinned girl who looked around twelve years old. She was wearing a public school uniform.

"She was playing in the park with her friends. They came and took them all. Put them in a white truck. María Pérez López is her name. She was about to turn fifteen. Two months we've been looking for her."

"We can pay you with our car," the gardener added, pointing to a broken-down Nissan flatbed next to the servants' quarters.

Treviño looked compassionately at the girl's parents and slipped the photo into his breast pocket.

"I'll keep an eye out for her."

"Let's go," said the Bus, who couldn't stand those people.

Just as they were about to leave, the cook asked if she could grab a cassette of Juan Luis Guerra's greatest hits from the Maverick's glove compartment.

"Sorry. It's just, who knows if you'll be back," she said and hurried back to the kitchen.

"Goddammit!" the Bus exploded.

Moreno and Rafita, leaning on the two Lobos with tinted windows, watched them until the Maverick's engine turned over and the main gate opened.

When Treviño and the Bus reached the outskirts of La Eternidad, they stopped at a convenience store. A headline from the evening paper caught their attention: FIFTY CONSTRUCTION WORKERS DISAPPEARED NORTH OF LA ETERNIDAD: THEIR BELONGINGS WERE FOUND ON A TRAIN TO MATAMOROS. While the Bus picked up a few bottles of soda and a dozen or so bags of junk food, Treviño stepped out to smoke his first cigarette of the trip. Standing there, he noticed that the front yard of the house next door was being set up for a quinceañeara. Everything was there, even the cake. As he watched the preparations, Treviño thought back to a few months earlier, when an armed crew had killed seventeen kids at the same kind of gathering not far from La Eternidad. The killers got out of two huge trucks, took their time interrogating everyone there, then shot them all and left. Later it was revealed that they'd been released from federal prison by the warden for the express purpose of carrying out the crime.

He recalled how the hit men had opened fire on a group of kids (sure, maybe they were dealing drugs, but they were still a group of unarmed teenagers) and thought to himself, *God help us. It was a party just like this one. The guys must have driven up a street just like this one, fanned out across a garden just like this one, terrorized a group of people like the ones right here. People dancing, chatting, enjoying life. And how do you bring them to justice when there are no witnesses, the facts of the case are beyond reckoning, and they're backed by the prison's warden, to say nothing of the politicians. From one day to the next, right before our eyes, everything changed. The law doesn't decide who has the right to live anymore. It's them. It's the criminals who decide who lives and who dies.* "Holy shit," he said, tossing his cigarette. "What have I gotten myself into?"

13

Around fifteen minutes after clearing the city limits, travelers who take the highway north from La Eternidad see the landscape turn rocky. Tropical vegetation gives way to miles of yellow, sun-scorched brush. Just outside Ciudad Miel, the land turns to desert. Suddenly, the only things along the side of the road are huge, bright green cacti growing in forms so strange they're like something from another planet. This sight goes on for five or six miles, and there's nothing else like it. People used to stand in front of those neon green plants, their eyes wide with wonder and a smile frozen on their faces, hoping to catch those extraterrestrial beings in the middle of a conversation, maybe just as they reached an important conclusion about life on earth.

But that was then. Now, no one driving along that road notices the vegetation. What catches the eye instead are the wrecked cars riddled with bullet holes.

That's how things are, here.

That's how things are, now.

14

Treviño closed his eyes, and immediately heard a voice say, *Ditch the car. They've got to know where you are by now.* He ignored the advice, which slipped to the back of his mind where so much else was hidden. Every now and then some memory would venture forward, but when it reached the surface it would sense that the moment wasn't right and go back into hiding, like a frightened bird. He woke a few times in the back of the Maverick and stretched out his arms: the color of his skin stood out for a moment before the darkness took over, devouring him in inky blackness. *My arms, the night,* he thought and drifted off again.

He'd had trouble falling asleep ever since they kicked him off the force, as if he were trying to drive himself toward extinction. When he did manage to drift off, his dreams took him to terrible places, like the chief's torture room. For months, his insomnia was so bad he'd end up getting out of bed and putting on his boots. If he was staying at a motel, those were the best hours to slip out into the hall: there were only a few guests up and about at that time, and they were too tired or drunk to want to chat. It was strange: as dawn broke, the birds would invariably erupt into song just as he was remembering who and where he was, as if they sensed he'd entered the world and were announcing it. Birds, dreams, night.

Then came the heat and the mosquitos. *There you are, you bastards*, he thought. The burn of their bites brought him back to the world. The mosquitos always showed up right when he was in the middle of an idea, and he often lost his train of thought just as he was about to have an important revelation. He came to believe that in the strange balance of the universe the way mosquitos strike just as you're on the verge of an epiphany has kept far too many people from answering the big questions. Like what the hell they're doing with their lives, for example.

He'd tried to lead a peaceful life after being forced to leave La Eternidad, but his troubles with the law seemed to follow him wherever he went. He spent over a year doing odd jobs for whoever could pay him, as long as it didn't involve going back to La Eternidad: as the driver of a smuggler or a respectable engineer, finding stolen cars for their owners, tailing a businessman's cheating wife, working for companies whose activities ranged from questionably legal to downright criminal.

One time, when he was between jobs, he saw a big, fat crow staring at him angrily from the middle of the path as he headed down to the river to wash his clothes. It reminded him of Chief Margarito. Treviño made like he was going to kick it, but the bird barely moved: it spread its wings insolently and with one hop came to rest just two paces from the former policeman. *Son of a bitch*, he thought. *Have I really gone that soft?* He'd never seen such an audacious bird and took it for an emissary sent by his enemies, from the same realm as his demons and the nightmares that haunted him. Later, on his way back, he noticed his belongings spread out on the grass. He almost never carried his weapon when he wasn't working: he believed that anyone who carries a weapon ends up depending on it. One way or another, it destroys the character of its owner. Walking around his car, he

ran into a young man rummaging through the trunk. He had a
rifle strapped to his back.

"Hey, kid!"

The young man struggled to raise his rifle. Treviño could have
crossed the space between them and slugged him in the time it
took him to bring the gun up, but he told himself it wasn't worth
the trouble. *A real tough guy, this one,* he thought. *But harmless,
just like that crow.* He stopped in his tracks when the kid leveled
his weapon at him.

"This is private property," growled the boy.

Treviño looked around.

"I don't see any signs or fences."

"It's private property," the young man repeated.

Treviño turned his back on the young man as though he
didn't have a rifle pointed at him, gathered his things, put them
in the trunk, and sat in the driver's seat, whistling the first thing
that came to mind. And he left, feeling the fierce gaze of the kid
or the crow or whatever it was.

Sometimes his reputation preceded him. Once in Pueblo
Viejo he was hanging out at a roadside food stall when he noticed
a married couple staring at him from a nearby table. The man,
who wore a short-sleeved button-down shirt, a tie, and glasses,
rattled on and on to his kids without taking his eyes off Treviño.
After a while, the detective was able to make out a few snippets of
a different version of his life: the story of a cop who brought down
the man who'd murdered four young women with a chainsaw
and seemed impossible to catch. When he saw Treviño looking
at him, the husband raised his glass of orange-colored soda and
said, "To your health, officer."

Treviño watched condensation form on the glass the man
was holding. The whole scene made him uncomfortable, but
he gave the man a nod. Later he wondered how that version of

the story, far as it was from Margarito's official line, could have gotten out and who published the photo that allowed the man to recognize him. Maybe the truth just circulated among different channels here in Mexico. He felt strange, so he set his silverware on the table and stared out the window for a while. When he tried to pay his bill, he was told it had been taken care of by Dr. Solares, who'd just left.

Another time he went looking for work in Las Manitas, a little town where police headquarters was just a sentry box on the side of the highway. The precinct had two indios with guns as its only officers, a stake-body truck for a patrol vehicle, and a chief of police who got around in a wheelchair after driving through the front wall of his own station while under the influence. Treviño waited outside while the crippled chief talked on the phone. The officers stared at him, fascinated. One of them asked if it was him who'd caught the Chainsaw Killer. He had been asked that question so many times he'd learned to distinguish friendly from morbid curiosity and eventually nodded.

"What happened?"

Treviño summed up the entire affair in two sentences and glanced over at a brown horse walking along the highway. The officers reflected on what they'd just heard and told him it could have been worse.

"You came out of it alive and with one hell of a story."

Right then the chief came out to meet them.

"Looks like you'll be spending a few days in lockup, papá. Your boss issued a detention order for you. Cuff him," he ordered. The officers didn't move. He repeated the order and the men remained in their seats with their arms crossed.

"You're not going to arrest him? Sonofabitch, what lazy bastards you two are. The law won't mean a damn thing around here if you two keep this up."

One of the officers said something in his language.

"Don't talk shit about me in Nahuatl, or I *will* fire your sorry ass," the chief snapped.

Treviño stood. The chief was still arguing with his underlings as he turned the key in the ignition.

His nightmares got especially bad whenever one of his jobs brought him near the sierra outside La Eternidad. Once he even dreamed that his first wife, who died in a fire, was sitting on his bed. She had the fangs of a wolf and said to him, "I'm like this because of you." When he finally managed to wake up, he wondered if the torments that awaited him in the next life would begin with that image of her.

One night, a contact in the port warned him that the Three Stooges were on their way to the town where he was hiding out, so he got into the clunker he kicked around in back then—another old, beat-up Maverick—and drove until he was nearly out of gas. Just as he was losing hope of ever finding a place to sleep, he happened upon a modest hotel tucked between the highway and the beach. A rotted wooden sign announced it as the Hotel de las Ballenas.

When he saw the car pull up, an old man who'd been sitting out front stood and smiled at him.

"Come in, come in. If you like, you can leave your car in the garage."

Treviño gratefully pulled into the small wooden shed, away from prying eyes, and was pleased to see the old man close its doors as soon as he got out of the car.

"Do you have a room for the night?"

"Do I have a room? You're the only guest this weekend. If you like, the presidential suite awaits you on the second floor with a terrace facing the beach."

He was practically giving the room away, so Treviño accepted.

"This beach is different," said the hotel manager. "This is a special place. Whoever sleeps here is visited in his dreams."

Skeptical, the detective watched the rough surf and said he might fall asleep right then and there. The old man smiled and showed him to the suite. And so began a new phase of his life.

He liked the room right away. It was timeworn, but with its wood floors, paneled walls, and ocean views, it was the kind of place where anyone could imagine staying forever. A shelf beside the bed held a few books he'd heard of before: *Don Quixote, Tom Sawyer, The Black Arrow, The Odyssey, The Aeneid, The Iliad.* He picked up this last one and lay down, leaving his clothes on and keeping the Taurus in reach. A few minutes into the chapter where Odysseus and Diomedes agree to go spy on the Trojan camp, he noticed he was having trouble keeping his eyes open.

He sensed someone, dressed in black, open the door and stand there, staring at him. After jumping out of bed and realizing it was just a dream he said to himself, "If it's gonna happen, it's gonna happen." Then he flopped back down, this time free of worries. It must have been the chill of the night air or the soothing murmur of the waves, but he didn't feel himself drift off.

He dreamed he was looking out over a pond, its smooth surface disturbed by just a few ripples here and there, and he understood it was a reflection of his soul. He recognized his history in a few scattered objects: a guayabera like the one he used to wear in La Eternidad; a blurry photo of Daniela, the beautiful blonde who'd been his first wife; a pair of jeans; the Taurus; a leather jacket, a machete, and a pair of tall boots, like the kind he'd worn in the jungle. From there, he jumped to his sisters' bicycles, the steering wheel of his faithful Maverick, a straw hat, and the memory of his last true love. *It was all so unfair,* he thought. *I would have given my life to save her from that fire.* A booming voice enveloped him. *Would you really have given your life?* His heart felt like it was being wrung out and he sensed that every word, even the ones he didn't say, had real consequences in this world. That voice must belong to someone important, he thought, because his words reverberated like waves on the ocean. *Answer,* commanded the voice, and Treviño realized this was not a joke. "Yes," he said, possibly out loud. "I'd have given my life for her. I'd trade my fate for hers if I could. I didn't want her to die." As he said these last words, he realized he'd begun to cry.

Then came a silence that felt like a storm brewing, and the voice responded: *As you wish.* When he was finally able to make out the dream's landscape, he found himself in a dense forest thick with fog. Little by little, the form of a horse came into view a few paces ahead of him. The animal looked at him and turned to follow a narrow path that led deep into the forest. *Am I dead?* he wondered, and it seemed entirely possible. He'd lost so much in recent months that maybe he'd died as well. *Maybe they killed me in my sleep and I didn't even notice.* He asked, out loud: "Am I dead?" And the horse quickened its pace. "Wait!" he yelled, but the horse had no intention of losing him. If Treviño slowed down, the animal would wait for him, snorting and stamping the ground impatiently, as if to say, *Are you coming, or what?* The horse suddenly turned onto a wider path with fewer branches blocking the way and headed downhill. *Oh, good,* thought Treviño. *Everything will be easier from here.* Just then, the animal turned to him and said, in the voice of a human: "Think carefully before you go any farther: you get one last chance, then there's no turning back. Listen to the master." The horse fixed its eyes on a point in the distance behind the dreamer and said, "He's already here."

He was certain a shadow had installed itself in his suite. He might have opened his eyes for a moment but when he closed them again he discovered that in the dream there was only an immense tree. Treviño waited, but the master didn't appear. *How strange*, he thought. *Maybe he's not here, after all.* And out loud, facing the tree, he said: "This is all too strange. I'd better go." The tree said nothing. "Maybe I should go back to the port and ask the consul for help," he continued, but this time a voice interjected. *Do not trust the consul. Avoid flatterers. Crows feed on the eyes of the dead when the dead no longer need them, but flatterers devour the souls of the living.*

In the dream, Treviño was startled to realize that there was, in fact, someone there. *We rarely think about death*, the voice continued. *Almost never, really, during our lifetimes. From a young age, we do our best to avoid the subject, and suddenly it is too late.* It was then that Treviño realized there was someone sitting at the base of the tree. A man dressed in white and draped in shadows. "They call me the Greek," he said. "I have chosen you as my student. What a shame we have to die."

Treviño shuddered again in his bed, but the visitor went on. "You can shield yourself, but no man lives in a walled city when death comes. You will descend into hell," he continued. "And you will try to cross through. If you succeed, you will be given great responsibility. Every day when you leave your house, you will meet a friend, an unexpected ally, a liar, an enemy, and a traitor in disguise. If you manage to identify them, you will be allowed to return."

Treviño dreamed all this that night in the hotel on the beach. Five years later, as he slept in the back seat of the Maverick, he realized he was having the same dream again. The master said to him, "I entered the Trojan camp, where all sought my death, with no more than a sword and leather clothing instead of armor. We were the first to set foot in Ilion. We were showered with glory," he continued. "But the gods kept me from returning home. Prove that you are a warrior. And never forget: what is the point of being given life if you are going to fear death?" The master reached out and touched Treviño's forehead.

It was still night when he opened his eyes, but his spirits had lifted.

On that original visit to the Hotel de las Ballenas, as he observed the damage the ocean had done to the shoreline the night before and thought how peaceful the place was at that hour, he'd decided to ask the old man if he would sell him the hotel. The old man had looked at him quizzically. Before long, Treviño was the proud owner of a beachside hotel. He met his wife there. He had turned the page.

On Tuesday, November 8, 2014, Treviño awoke in the back seat of a white Maverick similar to the first car he'd owned and thought: *I've had this dream before. I've lived this life before.* The Bus looked back at him in the rearview mirror.

"You awake? About goddamn time. It's your turn to drive."

The detective sat up slowly. A few words and sensations had carried over from the dream: the pond, the horse, the master's visit.

15

Around two hours after they set out, they noticed it was hard to breathe and they couldn't see ten feet in front of them. It was as if someone had spread a dense layer of fog over the road.

"They're burning sugarcane," said the Bus from the passenger seat.

Not even the slightest breeze stirred the fields to either side, and sweat trickled into the copilot's eyes. It felt like the sun had landed right there on the ground.

"Fucking hell, Treviño." The Bus mopped the sweat from his face with the back of his arm. "You couldn't have picked a car with air-conditioning?"

Focused on keeping his hands on the wheel and his eyes on the road, the detective didn't answer. At times, the waves of smoke seemed intent on erasing all trace of the highway. They'd passed three or four ranches harvesting cane since leaving La Eternidad.

"Man! You detectives can be real dumbasses, you know that? Pull over at the first fucking gas station you see. If we don't get some coolant in this thing, it's going to overheat."

At a bend in the road they think they see three old indios with machetes, dressed in white muslin, watching them pass. Ever since the start of what many call the War, it's unusual to see young men working the fields in that part of the country.

"Hey, Treviño," said the Bus. "If you find the girl, Mr. De León's gonna roll out the red carpet for you. He'll probably invite you to come work with us. Or did he do that already?"

The detective didn't answer.

"Hey, Treviño. Don't act like you can't hear me. We've still got a long way to go. Just tell me one thing: you make good money, you private detectives? Can I ask how much you're getting for this job?" The bodyguard snorted. "Maybe I've been wrong all this time. Maybe I should consider a new line of work. Why don't you give me some lessons on this detecting business?"

Treviño couldn't help smiling.

"Look, my dear Bus. All I want is to keep my brother from getting kicked out of Gringoland. They're after him here in Tamaulipas."

"Shit, man. What did the little angel do?"

"He made some enemies." Treviño wasn't about to tell the bodyguard that his brother quit his gig with a company in Matamoros as soon as he figured out it was a narco front.

"And now he's scared? Doesn't sound like such a big deal."

The detective's brother never made trouble with his bosses, never reported them to the police. He just resigned, saying he wanted a change of scenery. But the fact that he was still alive was inconvenient for them.

As though he were just remembering the question, Treviño asked, "Hey, how long has Moreno been working for Mr. De León?"

"About two years. He arrived just after your humble servant here."

"Where did they find him?"

"He was a bodyguard for Manuel Sainz, who breeds cattle. Mr. De León offered him more money. He did a bunch of training in Germany."

"And Rafita?"

"He's been there ten years. He was Mr. De León's first bodyguard."

"Who were his references?"

"He worked for some of the boss's relatives. When he came to work with us, they sent him to train in Gringoland."

"And you? How did you arrive at such a distinguished post?"

The Bus answered him frankly.

"I worked my way up in one of Mr. De León's businesses. When he realized the situation in the city was getting worse, he sent me to take classes at the same military academy where Rafita went. And I just kept climbing the ladder. You know how it goes. Where there's talent . . ."

"And this was your first job?"

The Bus said nothing for a moment.

"No. Before, I was doing odd jobs here and there. I was even a soda delivery guy. I could carry three cases of soda with one arm. But the pay was bad, and it was boring, annoying work. Which is why I started on the security side of things."

"And when did your love affair with gorditas begin?"

"I don't like them plain. But add a little Tabasco, now that's a different story."

As they passed the billionth wave of smoke, the bodyguard said, "Hey, Treviño. They say El Tiburón's killed three or four people, but they haven't been able to catch him. Do you realize that if you get him it'll be the second time you've caught a serial killer? You're gonna be famous, pinche Treviño."

The detective kept his eyes on the road. After a while, the bodyguard spoke.

"Listen, if you don't make it . . . I just want you to know I'll make sure your wife is well taken care of. Brother to brother, no need to worry."

The detective shot him a look, but didn't respond.

*   *   *

After driving for a long time without seeing so much as a bent
sign or any other indication of where they were, they stopped at
a roadside orange stand somewhere in the vicinity of Ciudad de
Maíz. "Gotta take a leak," said the Bus, and he disappeared behind
the curtain of smoke. Treviño took the opportunity to stretch his
legs. The stand's attendant was a young man in swim trunks and
flip-flops dozing in the shade of a large beach umbrella.

Across the road, he could see something that looked like
it had been a food stand once, but was now just a collection of
rusted and scorched sheets of metal, scattered in the brush. As
he approached the fruit stand, Treviño caught a glimpse of an
old indigenous woman rocking nervously back and forth beside
the roots of a fallen tree. She made a move toward the detective
but stopped herself, as if she'd been kicked away by generations
of travelers.

"She's crazy," said the young orange vendor, without looking up. The detective walked over to him and pointed at a pile
of fruit. "Give me a kilo of those."

Before he knew what was happening, the old woman had
grabbed him by the arm. Her hand emerged so quickly from the
smoke that the detective almost jumped back.

When she saw his reaction, the old woman threw herself
on the ground, begging his pardon with her hands, and Treviño
understood that she'd also been scared to death. Trying to calm
her, he raised his hands and leaned forward, then offered her
an orange and rolled it toward her.

The old woman picked it up and flashed him a toothless
smile. Treviño took out a fifty-peso bill and set it on the side of
the road with a small rock on top to keep it from blowing away.

He gestured to her that it was for her, then turned without waiting to see the old woman's reaction.

The Bus rematerialized in the fog, zipping his fly.

"Why don't you just adopt the old bag? I mean, while you're at it."

The detective paid for the oranges and was getting in the car when he noticed the old woman beckoning him.

"Come, come here. Yes, you."

Treviño walked over to her slowly. When he was close enough, the old woman said, "That's where the spaceships are. Over there."

"The spaceships?" he asked, looking toward the horizon.

"Don't go that way. Better to go back," she said softly. Then she added, "That's where the spaceships are, over there. That's why no big trucks pass through anymore. Because the spaceships come flying over. People drive by here in their cars." The old woman pointed at the road, which disappeared into the fog. "And then later the same car comes back this way with a soldier driving. Better not to go there."

The old woman nodded in the direction of the sheets of metal across the road.

"There was a food stand once. Look. One day they took the owner, cut him up in pieces. Brought him back in four cans. Get out of here. Go back home."

Treviño saw in the smile the old woman offered him the same thing he'd seen in the face of the owner of the taco stand in La Eternidad. The terror. The smile that says, *You see what we have to live through. How could they leave us like this?*

"What's up?" The Bus had put the car in neutral and let it roll silently toward the tree.

"According to the lady," replied Treviño, standing, "we're not lost, after all. They're around here."

The Bus swallowed hard and looked straight ahead. The detective got into the car and held the bag of oranges out to him. The Bus took one and peeled it halfway, then took a bite. The juice ran down his cheeks.

"You have any sort of plan, even a half-assed one, for how the hell we're going to get out of there, pinche Treviño? Do you realize they're asking the impossible?"

"It's not impossible. There must be a way. And yes, I'm going. I gave my word. You can turn back if you want, I'll understand."

The Bus, a graduate of the school of hard knocks, spat orange seeds out the window, stepped on the gas, and muttered something that sounded like: *I fucking hate guys who think they're immortal.*

16

The second sign that things were about to get ugly waited for them a half hour outside Ciudad Miel: four cars riddled with bullets by the side of the road. The spectacle repeated itself every few miles, with a different number of vehicles. Most of them were pickup trucks, but there were a few regular cars and even the charred metal frames of what appeared to have been taxis.

They drove with the windows down, but the air coming in was scalding hot. Treviño's shirt was almost completely unbuttoned, and the Bus, who'd taken his blazer off as soon as they left the city, had recently loosened his tie.

"Aren't you hot? Why don't you roll up your sleeves?" asked the detective.

"I get sunburned."

"Man, look at you. I feel like my shirt's being ironed with me in it," said the detective, fanning himself with the fabric that covered his chest.

The Bus wiped his forehead, face, and neck with his handkerchief.

"Just one question. Just one. How do you plan to get in and out?"

Treviño flashed him half a smile.

"Don't worry, my dear Bus. I guarantee they'll let us in, and if you play your cards right, they'll let you out for good behavior.

You know the drill. You've been in the joint before." When the driver didn't respond, he added, "We'll leave our guns and money at the hotel. We're going there to negotiate and to make sure they listen. If they see me as a blank check and open the gates, we can breathe easy. If I were you, I'd relax."

"And why should I relax?"

"Because the most likely scenario is that they only let one person in, and that person will be me."

The Bus swerved to avoid a dead mule in the road and said, a little disdainfully, "Well, I don't know anyone who's made it out of one of those places alive. No one who's lived to tell the tale. I mean, if just *one* person could say what goes on inside those places, you could relax a little and think, 'Well, if that guy can do it, why can't I?' But there isn't anyone like that. No one!"

The detective shifted in his seat and covered his face with his hat. When he opened his eyes again, a faded twenty-foot-tall statue of a lion greeted them with its front paws in the air: WELCOME TO CIUDAD MIEL, HOME OF THE LIONS. It reminded him of the statues outside the bigger courthouses, and he noticed that the lion's eyes were so pale it looked like he was blind.

It didn't take long before they saw two big white pickups pass by, carrying men dressed in black who were pointing machine guns out the windows. For their part, since leaving La Eternidad they'd been careful to hide their weapons—a Smith and Wesson nine-millimeter for the Bus, and a Taurus PT99 for the detective—in different nooks and crannies of the car. The cover the consul had carefully planned for them had its risks, they thought, but with a little luck it would get them across the state and back.

"Goddammit," exploded the Bus. "What the hell are we doing here?"

It was four in the afternoon, but there wasn't a soul on the street. On the main drag they saw one house pocked with hundreds of bullet holes. And it wasn't the only one: they counted three more as they continued along the avenue.

They checked in at the first place they saw, the Hotel del Viajero. To the Bus's delight, there were no bullet holes in the facade.

"And that's a good thing?" asked Treviño. "If no one's shot it up, it means either they pay for protection or the place belongs to someone in the trade."

"You're a real ray of sunshine," said the Bus.

"I'll see you back at the front desk in twenty minutes."

"What's the rush?" groaned the Bus.

Treviño thought for a moment before answering. "I'm going to meet a guy who works for Los Nuevos."

"Shit," said the Bus. "Can you trust him?"

"He's one of them, man. What the fuck do you mean, can I trust him?"

The only reason Treviño dared reach out to him in the first place was that they'd known each other since they were kids.

"You know how this racket works: he runs with the organization, but he's only loyal to his bosses. He puts up with me because we go way back and because there's good money in it for him. Now stop asking stupid questions."

Treviño immediately regretted his outburst, but he had more than enough reason to be nervous. For almost a year, two cartels had been at war over Ciudad Miel. If you were to draw a T over the neighboring states of Tamaulipas and Nuevo León, the city sat right where the two lines crossed. Los Nuevos controlled everything to the left of the line, while Los Viejos controlled everything to the right of it, plus the federal highway that ran up from the south to eventually reach the US border. Ciudad Miel wasn't exactly on the border—the bridge was a few miles north, crossing the desert—but it was easy to see why the city was considered such a prize. Whoever controlled it controlled the flow of illegal goods into the United States for the entire region. The economic possibilities were infinite, which is why the two organizations had been facing off in the city for nine months straight. Whenever its spies announced its rival's presence, each organization would send convoys of fifteen or twenty trucks that would fan out and start shooting until there was nothing left to shoot at, for lack of a better way to describe this nuanced approach. The governor of Tamaulipas was always the first to respond, immediately issuing a statement: Nothing had happened. It was just another case of mass hysteria—because mass hysteria obviously could fire nine-millimeter bullets. The president's administration, still in the pocket of wealthy businessmen, was a bit slower than the governor to respond, but what it lacked in speed, it made up for in creativity. Eight days after a conflict like this, the administration would say that pacifying the region was the responsibility of the governor, not the president, who had more important things to do, or who simply didn't believe the outrageous accounts coming from the north. Which explains why five hundred thousand of Ciudad Miel's seven hundred thousand residents had decided to leave the city. The first to go, predictably, were the police: after a criminal organization attacked police headquarters, the survivors quit in droves—and because no one wanted to replace them, Ciudad Miel didn't have a single active police officer for more than six months. Since 2010, Treviño had seen more than one melancholy caravan on the road out of the city: entire families crammed into single cars filled to the brim with their belongings, looking for a safer place to call home. And to think that before the conflict began, the secretary of tourism had described Ciudad Miel as a magical town for its beautiful houses, churches, and fountains. People from around there would often say to Treviño: "Sure it's a magical town. It can make people disappear while they walk down the street."

Who would have thought, twelve years ago, that a bunch of killers and thieves would divide up the city's neighborhoods: *You do your kidnappings here. I'll run my extortion racket there.* Before anyone knew it, they'd taken the whole place. The superrich were the first to go, followed by the regular businessmen. Now that even the middle class has fled, who's left to extort? Who's going to buy their drugs? Even parasites know to show a little restraint so they don't end up killing their host.

Treviño and the Bus were given rooms on the top floor, looking out over the parking lot. The attendant said he'd be happy to move them if they preferred, since it was the off-season. In other words, the hotel was empty.

On the way to his room, Treviño noticed there was a bar in the lobby. Inside, he saw two women who looked like prostitutes chatting with a group of bureaucrats while the sound system spat out a melancholy ranchera.

As soon as he walked into the room, Treviño placed his small suitcase on the bed. It wasn't so much a suitcase as it was a cover: the thing was full of brochures for agricultural products. After making sure there was no movement in the parking lot, the detective stretched out on the mattress. A minute later, he was dreaming that two men had broken down the door with a huge ax and were coming for him. Waking, parched, he remembered where he was and looked over the objects on the bed: the suitcase, the hat, the Taurus. A few minutes later his alarm went off. It was time.

By a quarter past seven they were on their way to the city's red-light district, at the top of a hill on the other side of the main drag. Next to the Bus sat a bag full of gorditas he'd bought from a street vendor; he ate these as he drove, after drenching each one with hot sauce. He popped them like pills, a delighted look on his face. Catching the detective's expression, he explained, "They're really good around here."

There was actually very little going on: a few women in heavy makeup standing in doorways; a couple of cars full of students who'd ignored the warnings and gone there looking for a good time; half a dozen visibly drunk men dressed for the office, who, between fits of laughter, were haggling with a prostitute over the price of her services.

A few establishments were closed or even boarded up: Chicago, Manhattan, Gunz, Las Sirenas, and the Canoe. El Capitán and Babydollz, on the other hand, were open for business.

"This was a different place four years ago," said the detective. "Look, we can park over there."

"Aren't you going to meet with an informant?"

"What, are you scared?"

They parked in front of Babydollz. The neon sign above the place showed the outline of a curvaceous woman who swung her hips as she stroked her glimmering hair. A bouncer and an armed guard stood at the door. Luckily, they'd left their weapons at the hotel: they knew going around unarmed was dangerous in that town, but it was still better than the alternative. If they ran into either criminal organization, they'd have to prove they weren't working for the other side.

After they were searched, the guard knocked three times. A host wearing a cheap smoking jacket opened the door with a smile.

"Good evening, gentlemen. Are you joining us for dinner, or are you here to enjoy the show?"

"We're here for the show," said Treviño.

The host nodded and led them down a hallway paneled in blue velour. When he opened the door at the far end, they were dazzled by the vision of a dozen women dancing close together, in nothing but thongs.

"This way, gentlemen."

He brought them to a booth in the first row. A brunette with long legs and breast implants was strutting across the stage. It did not escape their attention that she was wearing a yellow spandex one-piece with black stripes up the sides and was carrying a samurai sword. The host had to clear his throat to get the Bus to take his eyes off the girl for a second and sit down in the booth. They hadn't even settled in when a waitress deposited two cold beers on their table. A moment later, two of the topless dancers turned up to wrap their arms around them and rub their oiled breasts in the men's faces.

"Hey, handsome. Like watcha see? I can show you a good time. Just say the word."

The women kissed the two men on the lips and disappeared again. Before the Bus could get up to call one of them back, the club's manager leaned over them to take their order.

"Welcome, gentlemen. What can I offer you? Would you like me to send some company over? Any particular size, type, or color?"

The Bus's eyes remained glued on the dancers.

"We came to see La Cat," said the detective. The manager seemed not to believe what he was hearing, so Treviño added, "La Caterpillar."

"Ah. Real men, I see." The manager turned to the waitress. "Sweetheart, bring over a bottle of the Tres Cruces serrano tequila. These gentlemen are hunting big game."

"Should I clear the complimentary beers?"

"Please. I wouldn't want to offend these gentlemen with such meager trifles. Bring these real men a real drink. I'll be back with you in a moment." And he left.

Almost as soon as he was gone, a one-legged man left his spot at the bar and walked over to stand in front of them, leaning on a wooden cane. Treviño almost didn't recognize him.

"Ramiro? What happened to you?"

The man looked at him disdainfully.

"Life happened. Who's this?"

"He's with me."

"That wasn't the fucking deal, Carlos. These conversations happen one-on-one. Let's just forget it."

"No, no. Wait." Treviño turned to the driver. "Bus: you have a mission to complete. You see that woman over there who looks like a tractor?" he said, nodding toward the back of the room.

Behind the topless dancers, the Bus saw the manager lean over and whisper something to a hulking mass that vaguely resembled a woman. She looked up at them.

Holy shit, thought the bodyguard. *Where did that come from?* La Cat, as she was known in artistic circles, was an enormous woman with the arms of a bodybuilder and a sour expression permanently stamped on her face. Aside from a pair of custom-made Greek sandals, she wore only a white silk robe and a rhinestone-studded hair comb in her black, shoulder-length locks.

"Her name is Constanza, but they call her Miss Ceiba or La Caterpillar. Her specialty is Greco-Roman wrestling. She's all yours," said the detective, patting the Bus on the back.

"Whoa, whoa, whoa. What the . . ."

"It's an order."

"But I have a girlfriend."

"We can't waste time on your scruples. Mr. De León told you to follow my orders, didn't he?"

"Yes, but—"

"If you don't go with her, we're going to draw attention. Go on, get to work. I'll see you at the hotel."

"Well, well, well. Look what the cat dragged in." La Caterpillar was already towering above them.

"We were just going," said the Bus. "We have an early morning tomorrow."

"Coupla queers, eh? How cute. All right, stop your crying and give each other a kiss."

"Madam," said Treviño. "We kneel before you."

"Don't be stupid. Nobody calls me out of my corner for nothing. You're here either because you want to have a good time or because you want to suffer. In the first case, you pay me. In the second case, I charge you. So. Whadda you tightwads want? What brings you here?"

"This young man would like to test his strength against you."

"I've squeezed diamonds out of worse trash. But I've got a short fuse today. Let's hope he knows how to treat a lady."

Under his breath, the detective said, "All right, Bustamante. Time to earn your keep. I'll see you when you're done."

Valentín Bustamante, a.k.a. the Bus, realized he had no choice. He stood up, ready to follow La Cat. Treviño grabbed him by the arm and said in a low voice, "If we get split up, wait for me at the hotel. Don't go anywhere. You hear me?"

"Right this way, sir," the manager urged. "We mustn't keep the *lady* waiting."

When he saw the Bus finally leave, the visitor leaned his cane against a column and sat down across from the detective. They waited until the Bus was completely out of sight, and then the detective asked, "What happened to your leg?"

The visitor flashed his incisors, reminding the detective of a cornered dog. Not trying to disguise his bitterness, the man explained that after successfully defending the area five times, he'd needed to push Los Viejos, the Three Letters, back to the highway and he hadn't been so lucky. The worst part was that a one-legged man wasn't out of place in the least around there.

Ciudad Miel was turning into a city of cripples. Looking at the sloppy patch job on the man's clothing and the cigarette burn on the front of his jacket, Treviño gathered that his bosses had tossed him aside. The informant followed Treviño's eyes and, embarrassed, covered the hole with his hand.

"Before we get started, tell me one thing: you're not with the DA or snitching to the marines or any of that, right?"

"Of course not, Ramiro. I'm here because of something else. They're paying me to find a missing person. You have my word."

The informant seemed to be rummaging through his oldest memories of Carlos Treviño. Luckily, the detective had never broken his word, at least not around him.

"Did you bring the money?"

The detective pulled an envelope from his jacket and passed it to him discreetly. The man counted the sum on his lap and slid the money into the inside pocket of his jacket.

"The ranch you're looking for was owned by the García Osorios. A good family, wealthy—one of the oldest in the city. The father died from a gunshot wound, and it was his own eldest son, a kid they call El Tiburón, who shot him. The family paid to get him out of the joint, but he kept making trouble, so they eventually distanced themselves from him. The widow and his other relatives sold everything except the ranch, which went to the kid, and moved to the United States. He's the only one of them left, that fucking parricide. He was always partying, so he ended up deep in debt to the dealers. One day he made the mistake of proposing an arrangement: he'd give them the ranch if they'd forgive his debt and pass him a little white once a month. He probably thought he was going to get rich selling the drugs they gave him, until they said no, that was for personal use only, and if they caught him trying to sell any, they'd waste him. What could the kid do? He does most of it, sells some to acquaintances at bars, just enough to get by. He never has a cent to his name and it seems like they stopped passing him cash. Or they pass him less than they used to, and whatever they do give him is gone in a hot minute. They say he's desperate. Los Nuevos have taken over his ranch and you can't even imagine what goes on there. The place is run by the boss of this whole area, El Coronel de los Muertos. El Tiburón is probably still living in one of the little shacks on the property, but he won't be there long. They're tired of him. Now, tell me, why are you so interested in the place?"

"I need to speak with the Colonel."

The informant recoiled and stared at the detective. Treviño knew something had gone wrong, because in a matter of seconds Ramiro had begun to look at him with absolute hatred. His upper lip peeled back, revealing his incisors again.

"He'll fuck you up if he finds out you're looking for him."

"He has no reason to. I'm just here to make him an offer."

That was when Treviño noticed that his childhood friend was pointing a gun at him under the table.

"Put it away, Ramiro. You don't need that. Put it away."

"Are you a rat?" the man asked.

"What?"

"Are you a rat for the marines?"

"What are you talking about?"

"You don't know?"

"Know what, man?"

"Seriously?"

"Fucking seriously. I have no idea what the fuck you're talking about."

"We know the marines have got something really big set up to take out the boss. We know they plan to use live bait to hook him. They're going to send him a messenger with an offer that's too good to refuse, and as soon as he shows his face they'll be there with a convoy of helicopters. So don't bullshit me: are you that messenger?"

"Man," said Treviño, holding up his hands. "Don't you know me at all? I don't have anything to do with the army or the police, much less the marines. Anyway, you and I both know that whoever takes that gig is a dead man."

Ramiro looked at him for a few seconds, then slid the gun back into his jacket.

"That's a nice piece. You don't have the Remington anymore?" Treviño asked, calmly.

"They took it," replied Ramiro, sizing Treviño up. "It just seems like quite a coincidence, doesn't it," he blurted out, "that we're waiting for a Trojan horse and you turn up, offering money. How much, exactly, are we talking about?"

"I'm not a fucking rat, Ramiro. Don't ask me again. And we're talking about three million dollars."

The informant considered the figure in silence.

"All right. What's the story?"

"Around ten o'clock Saturday night, El Tiburón and three guys from La Cuarenta grabbed a girl from a nightclub. They got her right as she was leaving, put her in a red pickup, and took the highway in this direction."

"Could be. Nothing surprises me when it comes to that maniac. Did you say he was running with guys from La Cuarenta?"

"Yeah. They were seen taking the girl."

"Not possible. The Colonel can't stand even the thought of La Cuarenta, and El Tiburón's not stupid. No one in the crew mixes with them."

"But you said he's on the skids and no one around here pays any attention to him. Maybe he did get involved with them."

"He'd be taking a big risk. Who's the chick?"

"Sixteen years old, blond hair, green eyes, five foot six, speaks a few languages. She's the daughter of Rafael de León. The three million is to get her back safe and sound."

"And what's in it for you?"

"They hired me to deliver the message."

"Interesting," said Ramiro. "But if I didn't know you, I'd already have turned you over to the boss. Like I said: his whole intelligence operation is waiting for some asshole to show up waving a bunch of money around, and they're ready to skin whoever it is alive. It's not a good time for this deal of yours."

"Goddamn it, Ramiro. I can't go back without trying. They don't pay me to sit around on my ass."

"Don't look at me, Carlitos. If I put you in front of the boss, it'll be bad for both of us."

Just then a band took the stage and salsa music began to pour from the speakers. That was the signal. Every waitress and cigarette girl in the place showered the patrons with confetti, while twenty or so topless dancers invited the regulars out for a spin around the floor. Two of the girls stopped in front of their table and held out a hand to Treviño with a smile and to Ramiro a bit more hesitantly.

"Can I have this dance, handsome?" said the one standing in front of Treviño.

Treviño said he'd love to, some other time, and the girls moved on. The dancers looked at Ramiro with obvious fear in their eyes, the way people look at a rabid dog. The informant finished his drink and the detective poured him another tequila.

After a while, he asked, "Is there any way you could tell me if the girl's inside?"

"Not sure. But, knowing El Tiburón, her body might already have been dumped out there somewhere. He likes to hit women. They don't let him in this place anymore. One time he took one of the dancers back to the ranch and spent the whole night beating on her. Later we found out she wasn't the first."

"Where does he live?"

The informant smiled. "He's always hanging around here, in the district, but he lives out at the ranch. I haven't seen him in a few days. You'd have to go out to El Zacatal, but, like I said, you won't get to see him."

"Are there security cameras at the entrance?"

The informant looked at him, annoyed.

"They're gonna kill your stubborn ass, cabrón."

The detective poured another round of tequila and didn't say a word. Their attention turned to the performance: a pale blonde walked up and down the stage, resting a foot on the shoulder of one of the men applauding her and inviting him to slip a bill into her thong. Then she'd give him a graceful little shove with her high heel and move on. The applause continued until the song ended.

Ramiro leaned on the table and said, "Do you remember what we talked about the last time I saw you?" Treviño did the math. They hadn't seen each other since 2006. "I told you things were going to get real bad for the country in 2010 and you didn't believe me. Was I right, or what?"

Treviño knew, because his informant had told him, that a while back Los Nuevos, bold from the success they were having against Los Viejos, started calling themselves the Rebels, like heroes of the Mexican War of Independence. They went around saying there was a war every hundred years—first in 1810, then in 1910—and that they were going to win the war of 2010. But the fact is that in Mexico the peace had already been broken for years. In 2005, during the presidency of Vicente Palafox, firefights were already a common occurrence in northern cities like Ciudad Juárez. Treviño had always thought that if Mexico was going to crumble, the first cracks would form in the south, with the Zapatistas in Chiapas or the EPR in Guerrero, and spread upward. But the two movements lost steam, and, who would have thought it, the chaos came from the north, right here on the border with the United States. This is where the wave of blood began to surge, and now we're floating in it and no one cares.

The violence got worse with the country's next president: the right-wing and much-maligned Felipe Calderilla, who forgot about the people who voted for him and dedicated his energy to creating a fantasy world where he could live surrounded by privilege with those closest to him. The worst part for those who voted for the right wing was that the other members of the party reacted like small-time speculators: they just sat back and let the instability escalate. Taking advantage of the fact that most of the conflict was taking place in states governed by their rivals in the opposing political party, they chose not to get involved and just let the people drown in blood. Deep down, they were hoping their political rivals wouldn't be able to resolve the situation and would lose votes as a result. As if they couldn't see they were all treading the same troubled waters.

"We're about to throw everything we've got at Los Viejos," said Ramiro. "We'll take whatever turf they still have. They have money and the guns they bought off the gringos, but they won't last forever. We're training hard for it. The government respects us and looks kindly on us. They'll let us do the dirty work and when we take care of Los Viejos, they'll do business with us. After all, the government made us what we are."

Treviño also knew, because Ramiro had told him over countless nights of hard drinking while they were on the force together, that Los Nuevos were formed with the support and complicity of the governor of Tamaulipas, who later installed his own successors and retained control of the state.

"They haven't arrested him. He's still right there. Everyone knows who he really is. Anyway. I've already said too much."

The last four governors of Tamaulipas were evading warrants from the DEA, and a few of them were wanted by Interpol. But they'd chipped in some of their state's funds during the last round of presidential campaigning and their party had come out on top, so they still enjoyed total impunity. To this day, no governor of Tamaulipas, Coahuila, or Veracruz has ever been arrested.

"I have to find the girl," Treviño insisted.

"Taking you to that ranch would be a death sentence. I suggest you drop it."

"Don't worry about me. Just tell me where it is."

"You're nuts, Carlitos. You know I can't do that. The only way into that place is to be brought in."

Treviño pulled a second envelope from his jacket and passed it under the table to his informant, who looked inside, counted the money, and didn't say a word. After a brief internal struggle, Ramiro dipped his finger in tequila and drew a fleeting map on the table.

"It's pretty much a desert out there. A few pines near the entrance, right off the dirt road, but after that you won't find a single tree for cover. Just a bunch of fucking cactus and shrubs. There's no grass anywhere and no way you're going to make it all the way to the first building on your belly. It's fucking far and they'll get you for sure. They've got dogs and patrol units. There's no way in."

Treviño's neck started to cramp. The ranch was divided up by three concentric fences guarded by men in trucks or on horseback. The first circle was where the vehicles were kept. It was a first line of defense. Most of the troops lived and trained in the second circle, and the third was reserved for the commanders. The hacienda at El Zacatal was now where Los Nuevos' kingpins would go to relax or hide out.

"El Tiburón lives in a small house, back in the woods. But they'll be kicking him out soon."

"There's got to be a way," said Treviño. His contact looked at him quizzically.

"Goddammit, Carlitos. People try to find ways out of that place, not into it. You know they're grabbing people off buses not far from here? Ten miles or so before you get to the border, right there on the highway, they stop the buses passing through and take everyone. I don't want to say what they do with the girls or how anyone who tries to stop them ends up. You'd have to be crazy to travel by bus at night. It's worst along the Paso de Liebre route. The only ones who still use the Gulf Line are the coyotes and a few folks desperate to cross the border."

The informant stood and leaned on his cane.

"It's late. Let's get going. Your friend back there with the mustache doesn't seem to want to come out."

"He can stay, for all I care. I'll take a taxi."

"Better to walk. Trust me. In case you haven't noticed, this city is a fucking snake pit. The streets are full of lookouts with walkie-talkies and cell phones ready to snitch to their local boss about any new face they see around."

"Why don't you drive me?"

"Because I don't have a car and I live around the corner."

Ramiro watched two women prowling around the front door in search of clients and added, "A piece of friendly advice: Go back to your beach. It's not too late. There's guys out there looking to tear someone just like you to pieces."

"Thanks for the suggestion," replied the detective.

Ramiro took one last look at the women and hobbled out of the bar. Treviño checked his phone, flipped up the collar of his jacket, and walked out.

17

"Taxi, mister?"

Treviño looked the driver over and turned him down. The temperature had dropped considerably, as it did in desert towns, but he would rather have shot himself than get into one of those cars. He lit a cigarette and walked around the block.

According to Ramiro, there was no way to get into the compound unnoticed. Treviño remembered the informant warning him that the main building was on the other side of three heavily guarded enclosures.

As he watched the smoke drift upward, Treviño saw the scarlet moon floating above his head. He suddenly felt he was in the presence of a ghost.

He turned and noticed that not only had it gotten colder, but a nocturnal wind was lifting the red-light district's garbage and thrashing it around in the air. It was hard to think of the wind as a single thing: it looked like an invisible pack of jackals tearing the alley to shreds. Isolated gusts rustled newspapers and plastic bags up and down the streets, whipping them around in a frenzy.

Maybe it was the moon or the vision of desert ghosts, but Treviño suddenly knew how to get into and out of the ranch. True, he'd be risking his life. But he learned back when he was a cop that if you want to solve a mystery, sometimes you have to take on challenges that are bigger than you are.

He asked himself several times if it wasn't the tequila thinking for him. If he set the plan in motion, there'd be no turning back. He had to get in, locate the girl, and get out like a bat out of hell. Just figure out if she's there or not, and if she is, let Mr. De León know they should start negotiations. *And if something goes wrong?* He fiddled with his cell phone. If he ever wanted to smooth things over with his wife, this was exactly the kind of trouble he needed to avoid. The moon slipped behind some clouds and he dialed Mr. De León's cell, waking the businessman up.

"Treviño? What is it?"

"I was just calling to see if the kidnappers made contact."

"No, no one's called." Mr. De León cleared his throat. "Would you like to talk to the consul? He's manning the phone in the living room."

"There's no need."

"Any news?"

Treviño took a deep breath. "We need to figure out if your daughter is with El Tiburón. If she is, we need to get the negotiations started. Otherwise she won't be alive for long. She's not the first woman this guy has taken. Trouble is, I've confirmed he's hiding out on the ranch held by Los Nuevos."

"Do whatever it takes. Please."

Treviño thought for a moment and added, "I figured out a way to sneak into the compound. I don't know how I'm going to get out just yet, but I'll deal with that once I'm inside. I need to confirm your daughter is there. If everything goes as planned, you won't be able to reach me for a few hours, so wait for my call."

"Is there anything we can do from here?"

"When you talk to the Bus, tell him to wait for me at the hotel. He needs to stay put and wait for me. Tell him the car should be ready and he should have guns on hand for whatever we might need to deal with."

"Where's the Bus? What's going on?"

"Don't worry about him, I gave him a special assignment. Another thing: if this thing goes wrong, my wife and daughter will depend on you."

"We made a deal, and I'll honor it. Go in there and find my girl. You have my word."

The wind stirred the garbage in the street. Treviño stared at the town's main drag in the distance and nodded.

"All right. I'll call you as soon as I can."

De León breathed a sigh of relief. "I'll make it worth your while."

The detective hung up and checked his watch. It was three in the morning. He did his best to close his jacket and walked toward the avenue; the bus terminal was just three blocks away. Travel and prostitution always go hand in hand. When he caught sight of the sign for the station, he checked his reflection in a store window to make sure he wasn't being followed.

The first thing he noticed when he stepped inside was that only the second-rate lines ran at that hour. He walked up to the Autobuses del Golfo counter and greeted the clerk.

"I'd like a ticket for the first bus to Paso de Liebre."

"You crossing the border?" the man behind the counter asked, giving Treviño's clothes a quick once-over.

"Yes, sir. Have to be there bright and early."

"There's one about to leave. You'll be there in forty minutes."

"That works."

The clerk took Treviño's money and handed back his change and a ticket. "Hurry up and get to gate five," he urged. "The bus is about to leave."

The detective walked through the back entrance and out to the parking lot. It wasn't hard to spot the only clunker with its engine running.

"Come on, get in." The driver hurried him along.

The first rows were filled by a group of teenagers dressed like basketball players who were passing around a bottle of alcohol poorly concealed by a brown paper bag. As he walked along the aisle he noticed a few of them looking at him with the professional interest of pickpockets. Several of them had tattooed arms. One pair of eyes, belonging to a sinewy, dark-skinned kid in shorts and a sleeveless T-shirt, bore into him like daggers. Behind that bunch: a woman nodding off with two little girls and a couple of old-timers. No one wanted to sit near seat thirteen, he realized, which meant he could have the row to himself. He took it and got comfortable.

"Paso de Liebre!" shouted the bus driver. The bus shook as he fired up the engine, and after slaloming past a few obstacles they were on the highway.

The bus swayed like a boat out at sea. Treviño rested his head on the window, crossed his legs, and decided he'd let himself close his eyes for five minutes. *Just five minutes*, he thought.

In his dream, a breeze caressed the fronds of a tall palm tree. He was on the beach with his wife, and it was that day they'd spent hours making love right after she'd moved into the hotel. The sun was strong but pleasant and it lit the ocean a blazing blue. The light disappeared as the bus rattled to a stop.

While the rest of the passengers panicked, Treviño checked his watch. It was five in the morning.

"What's going on?" moaned one of the old men. His accent suggested he was from Campeche. A moment later, he exclaimed, "Holy Mary!"

A group of men dressed in what looked like black military gear approached the bus. The leader of the pack had a gun tucked into the front of his pants.

"Don't be alarmed," the bus driver smiled. "They're just keeping the highway safe."

"Oh, God. Oh, dear God," the mother of the two girls intoned.

The driver opened the door to the bus and two of the soldiers stepped inside.

"Good evening, ladies and gentlemen," said a slim man with a broad smile. Treviño was immediately suspicious of him. "This is a checkpoint, for your own safety."

What he didn't say, though, was whether he was from the army or the marines, and the gun in his right hand was pointed straight up, contrary to military search protocols. Behind him, a man with a shaved head pointed an assault rifle at them. The man with the crocodile smile walked up the aisle and the detective noticed he was carrying a revolver—not exactly standard army issue.

Before reaching the rear of the bus, the man with the revolver turned, satisfied, and walked back to stand next to the driver.

"Close your curtains, ladies and gentlemen. We'll be passing a military base."

The driver started the bus and did his best to avoid a series of enormous potholes. The detective's traveling companions were concerned.

"What's he doing?" one of the old men said. "This isn't the way."

While his buzz wore off, Treviño tried to see through a slit in the curtains. The only thing he could make out in the five minutes or so they were on the road was a row of pine trees shrouded in the morning mist.

The next time the bus stopped he saw they were at an intersection: a dense forest and what looked to be an unwalled cemetery barely peeked through the fog. *It was a terrible idea to travel without Bustamante*, he thought.

"All the men get off here. The women stay on the bus," ordered the man with the revolver.

"Hey, what's going on?" yelled the woman.

"Just do as you're told, ma'am," he said, silencing her. "It's for your safety."

The detective got off the bus behind the group of boys, who, young and foolish as they were, kept cracking jokes. Six armed men immediately surrounded the group. One ordered them to line up with their identification in hand.

"Forward, march!" came an order from somewhere in the fog.

"Forward, march!" the smiling man repeated, and the line started moving.

After twenty paces, Treviño was able to make out a group of men sitting around a table under an improvised tent made of tree trunks and palm fronds. The travelers approached, handed over their papers, and lined up with their backs to the inspectors. More armed men (impossible to say how many) oversaw the operation.

When it was their turn, a soldier escorted them over to the table, where the smiling man who had boarded the bus, the one the others called Captain, was waiting. The man standing beside him was huge. Treviño was used to people in the north of the country being tall, but this guy broke every record. His black hair had been shorn into a buzz cut and one of his ears was grotesquely swollen.

When they got to the table, the captain asked for their papers. He didn't even bother examining the boys' passports.

"What's this?" he asked.

"A passe-port, sir," said one boy in shorts and a sleeveless T-shirt.

The officer shook his head.

"You're Mexican?"

"Yes, sir," said the boy, with a marked Central American accent.

"Where are you from?"

"From Chiapas."

"Then you can tell me where in the state Lake Pátzcuaro is."

The boy hesitated a moment before answering, "In the north."

While the soldiers behind him laughed, the officer replied, "North is right, boy. It's all the way up in Michoacán. Inside, all of you. Fucking cholo punks. Chiapas . . ." Turning to the other soldiers he said, "Time they came up with a better line."

As the officer compared Treviño's face with the picture on his fake identification, the detective discreetly scanned his surroundings. They were on some kind of ranch made up of what looked like a main house, a barn, and a small stable with a horse inside.

"Name?"

"Juan Rentería."

"Age?"

"Thirty-five."

"Occupation?"

"Salesman."

"What are you doing so far from Veracruz?"

The address on Treviño's papers indicated he was from there.

"I'm headed to the border for a business meeting."

"That's where you're going?"

"That's right."

"Let's see your wallet."

Treviño handed it over, along with the two hundred dollars in small bills and the fake visa that were inside. Like his identification, it had all been provided by the consul. The soldier hesitated.

"What did you say you do, again? What's your line of work?"

"Construction materials," replied Treviño.

"All right," said the man with the smile, tossing his wallet into the same sack that held the other travelers' belongings. The colossus made sure he wasn't carrying any weapons and gestured to him to get back in line.

When they'd finished interviewing all the men, they sent for the women and children and lined them up. The moment of truth had arrived.

The man with the crocodile smile called for their attention. "Good morning, fellow citizens."

"Good morning," echoed the fake Chiapans, expectantly.

"You're all headed north, and most of you don't have papers. Which means you're looking for work."

In a speech he seemed to have delivered many times before, the man explained that the coyotes working the border would charge them somewhere between two and three grand to get them across. That they'd leave them in the desert to die of hunger and exposure. That they'd probably get shot by either the rangers or one of those vigilante lunatics, and for what? To make a sorry fifty bucks a week working like dogs and being humiliated by gringos?

"We're offering you two thousand dollars per month, and you don't even have to cross the border. We're looking for a few brave men. A few real men."

"Listen," said one of the old men from Campeche. "We're just passing through. We're on our way to McAllen and were going to stop by Champotón on our way back.

The officer in the wide-brimmed hat ignored his comment.

"Last call. Anyone who wants in should get in the bus. Whoever doesn't, stay here."

The cholo and the fake Chiapans were the first to climb on board. Treviño slid in among them. The only ones to stay behind were the old men from Campeche and a couple of Canadians.

"All right, you'll stay with the women and children. Another bus will come pick you up."

"You promise?" asked the woman.

The man smiled. "Of course."

Treviño looked at the woman and her daughters with concern.

"Come on, keep your sorry ass moving," said one of the soldiers, pushing him forward.

Before he had time to regret his choice, he was sitting in the back of the bus as it drove along a narrow road into the compound. He was riding the wave now. Would he be able to get out?

When the bus couldn't go any farther, they were ordered off. The detective's feet sank into the sticky yellow dirt. Almost immediately, they heard a burst of machine-gun fire. He looked at the soldiers escorting them, but they didn't flinch. Terror was par for the course.

"Don't be a little bitch. Keep it moving."

They were ordered to climb a little hill. Slipping and stumbling, they reached a barbed-wire fence guarded by four armed men. Contrary to the gringo's intel, there were no cameras or alarm systems to be seen. There were even a few gaps in the perimeter.

He couldn't believe what he saw next. After that first fence, the plateau dipped into a depression the size of a football stadium. The space was divided into four camps of about fifty people each. He'd been hearing about this kind of thing for months, but had always thought the accounts were exaggerated. As the smell of gunpowder and burning rubber reached him, he realized how wrong he'd been. This wasn't just some little ranch. It was the size of a military base.

His heart leaped for a moment at the sight of what he thought was a row of electrical poles in the distance, which would have meant that the highway—and salvation—was within reach. But it was just a few cables strung between the trees for mountaineering practice. A voice inside him told him to give up hope. A man on horseback rode up to the other side of the fence, an assault rifle strapped to his back.

"Today, assholes!"

There was another fence when they got to the bottom of the slope; on the other side, fifty or so men dressed in tattered clothes, most of them shirtless, took turns shooting weapons of different calibers, first into a brick wall, then into a dummy or the dirt slope. Two pillars of dark smoke rose off to one side. One came from a tree; the other, from what seemed to be a pile of burning clothes. It took Treviño a minute to make out the charred human remains underneath.

A bald man in military attire stood in front of two dozen ragtag trainees, who hung on his every word. After aiming his assault rifle at a target and showing them how to shoot it, he handed the weapon to the guy closest to him: a leathery-skinned teenager with a strip of fabric tied around his forehead. The man in military attire pointed toward two dozen soda cans hanging in front of what remained of a house, and the teenager aimed, then fired four times. The man examined the results and passed the weapon to the next in line. As Treviño made his way down the hill, he felt his blood run cold: the bald man was the guy he'd had trouble with down at the beach. The Colonel, himself.

A skirmish suddenly broke out. In one of the other groups, the colossus with the cauliflower ear was kicking a man who was already flat on the ground. No one dared step in to separate them, and the giant didn't stop until the man was unconscious. Only then did he calm down.

The soldiers who'd piled them onto the bus walked them to the middle of the camp, where they met their instructor for the day: a man around fifty years old, whom the other men called the lieutenant. He'd been expecting them. A few yards farther in, yet another instructor was showing a different group of shirtless men how to make Molotov cocktails. Treviño was struck by the fact that they were using Coca-Cola bottles.

When it was his turn to shoot, Treviño made sure his aim was impeccable. He hit three bottles set at different spots on a tree trunk.

"All right, let's see that again," said the instructor.

Treviño repeated the feat, which wasn't really all that hard. It was a good rifle and just needed a little adjustment to the sight. The lieutenant asked if he'd had any military training.

"I used to be a cop," he confessed. Just as he and the consul had agreed beforehand, he went on to explain that he'd been on the force in Veracruz, where one of the gringo's contacts could vouch for him.

"Why'd you quit?"

"Wasn't enough for me."

"Who'd you report to?"

"Antonio Segura."

The instructor nodded and asked him to wait to the side until they'd finished this round. Treviño walked over to the row of pine trees, where the cholo was already sitting with the fake Chiapans. He breathed a sigh of relief.

They smoked in silence. Treviño looked the kid over from time to time. At around two in the afternoon, something like an alarm sounded over the loudspeakers and the newcomers had to line up. To Treviño's concern, the Colonel walked over to say a few words to them. He thought he saw the man recoil when he saw him, so he tried to make himself invisible in the crowd.

"You have three weeks to prove your worth, and that worth will be measured by your participation in real operations. You will be judged on the basis of your resourcefulness, teamwork, obedience, and loyalty. You will *not* question orders. An infraction will get you corporal punishment. Traitors will be executed on the spot. At the end, the best will be invited to join the organization; the rest will join the staff. Desertion is not an option: whoever sets foot in here is in here for good."

At three o'clock, they were taken to a barracks that must have been used for cattle at one point. A large, open space that held a row of at least thirty benches. On one of them, behind a column, a woman with Asian features and a body covered in tattoos was riding one of the fake Chiapans. She was naked except for a pair of knee-high cowboy boots. She caught sight of Treviño when he walked in and didn't take her eyes off him.

When the Chiapan finished, he put his hands on the woman's hips and said something to her that pissed her off. She slapped him jokingly, but hard enough to make it clear that she'd gone easy on him, and stood up. She took stock of her surroundings, then sauntered toward the newcomers, putting all her weight on one leg, then the other, as if they were industrial shock absorbers. It took Treviño a moment to understand that she was offering him her services. "Five bucks, sweetie." He declined.

They were given ham sandwiches and coffee. After the meal, Treviño walked over to the two soldiers on guard duty and offered them cigarettes. He introduced himself by his assumed name and told them he was at their service. He asked a few practical questions:

"Where do we sleep?"

"In one of the barns, they'll show you where later tonight."

"What time do we get up tomorrow morning?"

"We start at five every day."

A few minutes later he asked if it was true that they bused in prostitutes, like he'd heard. If it was true that some of the girls were foreigners, if there were any blondes, if they were hot. One of the guards told him to chill out, that he'd just gotten there and was already talking about taking a vacation, but he insisted:

he had his expectations too. He'd signed up because he'd heard that the guys who got in were treated right, and that there'd be plenty of honeys.

"It's pretty fucked at first," offered the shortest of the soldiers. "But don't worry, it gets worse."

The others, who were sharing a joint, ignored Treviño entirely.

"You'll be up to your ears in bitches, booze, pills, and weed, maybe even a little blow, but you've got a long way to go," said the runt. "You gotta earn it, cabrón. Now, I don't say this to get you all hot and bothered, but yeah, they bring us girls. Every month, month and a half."

"And there aren't any other girls around here?"

The runt went on teasing him for being impatient and asked him what was wrong with La Chinita. After beating way around the bush with talk about the cauliflower-eared giant's short temper and what he did to guys who disrespected him, the runt said that, yeah, there were a few other women around, but they were reserved for the bosses.

"Sometimes the bosses bring in broads from outside. Those ones stay for just a few days."

Treviño said he'd seen a blonde, maybe sixteen years old. She'd made an impression. They told him there were a few blondes hanging around, but he shouldn't get his hopes up. The only time they left the main house was to get some sun, and that was in a little attached enclosure. When they were done, they went right back inside. Mostly Asian chicks. They'd brought them in around six months before, but there weren't many left.

"There's blondes, too, though," said the other soldier, pointing at the main house. "I saw a few yesterday, from a distance. They were swimming in the enclosure with three or four buzz cuts standing guard. Real choice broads. They spent the whole time bouncing from the trampoline into the pool until they got tired and flopped into some colorful hammocks hung from the trees. They sunbathed out there and had drinks brought to them for a while. Three of them."

Treviño asked if they were Mexican or foreigners.

"More like Russians," the soldier replied. "A little long in the tooth, they'd had a lot of work done." He said they'd been speaking a sharp, explosive language that sounded more as though they were crushing gravel between their teeth than talking and that—judging by the way they shouted at one another—they didn't get along all that well. Mockery and contempt sound the same in any language. Treviño said he'd like to get a look at the women, anyway. He was just finishing up his cigarette when the colossus with the cauliflower ear walked up.

"Get to work, gentlemen."

They unloaded a shipment of bricks from the back of a truck and set them on a plot that had recently been cleared, at the back of which they could see barns and what was probably the main house. A third fence and another pair of guards stood between them. Just as Treviño was thinking there was no way to get over there, much less to explain himself if he got caught, the colossus got a call on his cell phone and asked if anyone there knew anything about plumbing.

Treviño raised his hand.

"Can you install a Jacuzzi?"

He nodded convincingly and was told to head straight up toward a two-story structure that was pretty run-down but still bore some resemblance to a house. He advanced cautiously until he reached the first guard, who leveled his rifle at him.

"They sent me to install a Jacuzzi," he explained.

"Who did?" The sentry looked at him suspiciously.

"The boss they call Tiny."

The sentry looked into the distance, nodded, then told him to head straight up there and keep it moving.

"Go around back and report to Sergeant Garlanza."

Treviño walked toward the house at a leisurely pace, as if he were admiring the landscape. He noticed four square windows on the second floor and two larger, rectangular ones on the ground floor. He estimated that if the structure was built like the estates of yesteryear, there were probably only four bedrooms, all upstairs. When he'd almost reached the front of the house, he paused. In one of the upstairs windows he could see an Asian girl of about twenty-five or thirty doing a line of coke. The plunging neckline on her dress revealed the beautiful woman's breasts as she bent forward. *So this is where the bosses hang out*, he thought.

"Go on, quit dragging ass," called the sentry, tossing a rock at him.

As he walked, the sentry whistled to another guard who was standing at the front door to the house. The second guard responded in kind, and when Treviño got close enough, he gave him a good kick in the back.

"Keep moving that slow and you'll catch a bullet. Around here, we follow orders."

"Yes, sir. Sorry, sir."

"This way."

He took Treviño around back, where a bunch of muscular dudes in swim trunks were chatting up three women wearing only thongs. It didn't take the detective long to notice that contrary to what the runt had said there was only one real woman among them, a tall brunette with shapely long legs and enormous implants. The other two were bottle-blond transvestites. *So this is how the "real men" spend their time, eh*, Treviño thought and looked away. A soldier was cooking meat on a grill nearby.

"The reinforcements are here, boss."

One of the more sour-faced members of the group stood and walked over to him without putting down his beer.

"You're a plumber?"

"I do construction, dabble in plumbing." Treviño saw an enormous eight-person Jacuzzi still in its original packaging and, next to it, a state-of-the-art water heater.

"How long will it take you to install?"

"About three hours, sir."

"You've got half that. And remember, it's your ass if you break this shit. What do you need?"

"Some bricks for the base. Cement. A set of wrenches. And help lifting the thing."

"The Jacuzzi is fine where it is. You move it, I bust your head. They'll bring you the rest of that shit now. Get cracking. This guy will give you a hand," he said, pointing to the soldier who had kicked him.

They were unpacking the water heater when Treviño heard new peals of laughter. Two blondes in their forties with spectacular fake tits had arrived. The man with the crocodile smile followed a few paces behind them, and all the way at the back there was the Colonel. Treviño hid behind the machine and tried to cover his face with his hat.

"Let's go get those bricks," he suggested. Just as he and the soldier were getting up, someone called out his real name.

"Carlos Treviño." The Colonel was right behind him. "What, you don't remember me? We met on the beach a while back."

The men held the detective's arms while the Colonel mercilessly pummeled his ribs and face. Eventually he got tired.

"Take him to the kitchen. I'll be there soon." The Colonel's knuckles were bleeding. The men lifted Treviño into the bed of a pickup truck. "Awww shiiiit," they said. "You're gonna get yours."

His body was floating on an immense wave of pain that made it hard for him to think. All he wanted was to get his hands on the cannonball lodged in his back, giving off flashes of black lightning.

They didn't take him to the kitchen. Instead, they drove a good twenty minutes across hilly terrain. He suddenly thought he smelled boiled chicken. Then one of his attackers grabbed him by the arm and rolled him onto the ground. Opening his eyes was as hard as lifting a truck.

The first thing he saw was three men heating a gigantic vat that stood around three feet tall. A long-haired guy in a shirt splattered with dark stains lifted a neon green bottle and emptied its contents into one of the containers near him, out of which a hand protruded. Treviño suddenly understood who they were, what they were doing, and that this would be how he'd meet his end too.

"Hey, here are a few more."

Only then did the detective notice the two bodies that had been thrown down beside him.

"How do you want them?"

"These two, same as the rest. But this other one"—he pointed at Treviño—"don't touch him. The Colonel will come pay his respects after dinner."

The guy with the long hair looked at him and nodded.

"Don't touch this one. We're waiting for the bald man," he said to one of his helpers, who stopped in his tracks, shovel in hand. The other one laughed and stared at the ex-cop, who looked the other way and discovered a dozen trees in bloom. The big, lush bougainvillea and canary-yellow golden chains were like beaming smiles amid the chaos. Flowers existing in a parallel dimension, blithely unaware of the terror.

The guy with the long hair poured himself a handful of pills and swallowed them with a swig from his can of Coke. Then he went over to Treviño, pushed him over to a nearby tree, and tied his hands and feet with nylon cords. When he was finished, he walked back and handed a machete to one of his helpers.

"This one goes in the gray drum, that one in the blue. But not right now. Right now it's time," he went on, raising his voice so the two men could hear him, "to get something to eat."

Treviño noticed a small piece of metal near him—probably the lid from a can of food. He covered it with his foot, praying no one else had seen it. The undertaker with the long hair looked at the detective, furrowed his brow, and planted himself right in front of him. For a moment, Treviño thought he was on to him.

"Who's going to watch him?" asked one of the helpers.

"The guardians of the mountain," said the man. "No one gets past them."

Flashing his jack-o-lantern smile, the undertaker leaned over the detective and tapped him several times on the forehead to get his attention.

"Be right back," he grunted.

And they left Treviño tied to a tree.

As soon as they were nearly out of sight, he grabbed the shard of metal and began rubbing it desperately against the ropes that bound his wrists and ankles. The moment they started to loosen, he wriggled out of them like an angry cat. It took a little while, but he'd cut himself free.

A bolt of pain shot through his back when he tried to stand, propping himself up on a shovel he'd found. He doubled over and had to take a deep breath before he was able to move his right leg forward, then his left.

He made sure there was no one in sight and, using the shovel for support, hobbled down the hill in the opposite direction from where the undertakers had gone. The good news was that there wasn't a soul for miles. The bad news was that there wasn't a rock, bush, or burrow to hide him anywhere, either. All it would take to catch him would be for someone to return to the execution site and look toward the horizon. Winded and trying to ignore the pain from his injuries, he made his way toward the crest of the nearest hill.

The evening sun painted the rocks a warm orange. He knew night would fall soon and the Colonel would be coming for him.

He reached the crest of the hill and saw that he was just ten feet from a large pond, probably stocked with fish.

Water was one of the things he needed most, so he carefully made his way down, knelt on the gravel, and drank like a dog until he couldn't breathe anymore.

He checked to make sure there was no one around and leaned over again to wash the dried blood off his face. He rinsed his mouth and spat several times onto the dry earth. Then he removed the torn, bloodstained rag that had once been his guaya-bera, leaving on his sleeveless undershirt. His tongue was in bad shape and he was pretty sure that if he wiggled one tooth too hard, it'd end up in his hand.

He suddenly felt a change in his surroundings, as if all the birds had fallen silent at once. His whole body tensed.

A shiver ran down Treviño's spine. He turned to see a straw hat appear at the water's edge and under it a diminutive man with an impeccable goatee.

The shock nearly killed him. *Jesus, Mary, and Joseph*, he thought. As the tiny man walked toward him, he wondered why he was so scared, and a voice inside him answered: *Because he's an evil spirit. A Chaneque.* He thought back to all the stories he'd heard as a child. If you were alone near a river or spring they warned, you might get a visit from one of these wicked creatures, who prey on the defenseless. If one of them asked you a question, you were supposed to lie or trick him if possible, because they'd ruin your life if they got the chance. You only had to say the name of a loved one out loud, and that person would fall deathly ill or have a fatal accident that exact moment. He told himself it was all ridiculous, but he couldn't stop himself from shaking as the visitor approached.

Unlike most dwarfs, the man had fine features, long fingers, and a harmonious build: a homunculus made to scale. The only shocking thing about him was his enormous eyes, tapered and yellow like a coyote's. Other than that, he was dressed in typical Huastecan attire: white shirt and pants and a red handkerchief tied around his neck. His legs were hidden by the grass, so Treviño couldn't tell whether he was wearing boots or huaraches.

The detective knew there was something dangerous about the visitor, but he couldn't say why he found him so terrifying. He was clearly unarmed and barely came up to the detective's waist. Still, when the little man walked up to him, Treviño's blood ran cold.

"Good evening," he said. "Because evening it is."

Treviño nodded, thinking he might faint, while the homunculus looked him up and down.

"You're not from around here. May I have some water?"

Treviño was about to answer that of course, he should drink all the water he liked, but then he saw the glint in his interlocutor's eyes. If he hadn't been nearly forty, callous, and deeply cynical, Treviño might have said that the visitor's teeth had gotten sharper from one second to the next. He felt a cold wind on the back of his neck and had to swallow hard before he could speak.

"Of course."

The little man smiled and knelt at the edge of the pond. He took three sips, using his hands as a bowl, then dipped his hat in and poured water over the crown of his head.

"Ah . . . sweet, sweet water . . ." He sighed, content. Then, without missing a beat, he turned to the former cop. "They don't give me water here. Not even water. Things were better, before. I'm famous over there, over there on that hill. Over there, some people even pray to me," he smiled.

Treviño mumbled that yes, things were better before and how terrible that they didn't let him drink the water here. The homunculus smiled and walked over to him. He seemed to enjoy Treviño's fear.

"No, you're not from around here," he said, locking eyes with the detective. "This isn't your place. You gave me a sip of water and so I have to help you, but only once. Only for a little while. Then I'll be watching you, and every time something bad happens to you, you'll know it came from me."

He took a deep breath, as if he were searching for something.

"The door you seek is down the hill, behind those trees. But take that shovel. You're going to need it," he added.

The little man leaned over, picked up some dirt, ground it in his left hand, and blew a bit in each of the four cardinal directions while muttering: "Brother Red, Brother Black, and all my brothers without names: clear a path so this Christian may leave unbitten. And now," he said, turning to Treviño, "get out of here before the door closes."

Treviño hesitated.

"Go on. It won't last forever," the tiny man insisted.

Aware that his life depended on that conversation, the detective extended his hand, palm up, and asked, "What can I offer you so you don't hurt me? I've already given you water."

Red in the face and trembling from the effort to control his temper, the little man spat: "Nothing you have is of any interest to me. If I want to hurt you, I will. Now, get out of here before I get angry!"

But Treviño didn't give up so easily.

"What can I give you so you don't hurt me?"

"Nothing!" the homunculus barked, purple with rage. "You can't give me anything. Everyone has his own luck. All you can do is pass yours to someone else." As soon as he'd said this, the tiny man clammed up, as if he'd gone too far, and waved his hands in the air. "Now get out of here, before the door shuts."

He thought he was going to fall, but Treviño made it down the hill with the shovel in his hand. When he saw a few cargo trucks parked near the fence there, he regained what little was left of his lucidity and wondered if he was walking into a trap. What if those men were waiting to kill him?

About a dozen men were shoveling gravel from a massive cargo truck into a smaller one.

"Hey!" a man with a walkie-talkie yelled in his direction.

As he got closer, he was met with loud whistles. The workers seemed to be giving him shit.

"Motherfucker!"

"Always there when we need you, right?"

Next to one of the trucks, a man lay on the ground in a dark puddle, surrounded by flies. No one seemed particularly worried about it.

"What happened? You fall?" the only guy with a gun asked him. Treviño remembered the bloodstains on his clothes and nodded.

"Dumbass," the man scolded.

"Everybody in," called the driver of the truck. "We're running late."

One after the other, the workers jumped into the back of the truck. Treviño limped after them, thinking there was no way he'd make it, but someone behind him pushed him onto the flatbed. He curled up in a ball in the far corner next to the other workers and looked up at the clouds and the spectacle of a perfect blue and an unforgettable red fighting for control of the sky. The truck drove down the hill and past a small copse of pines, passed through a wooden gate opened for them by the guards themselves, and then took the highway toward the city.

18

His luck seemed to hold for the next half hour. He lay down on his side with one arm covering his face and pretended to sleep in order to avoid talking with the other workers as the truck lurched toward the city. From what he could gather from the phrases they exchanged, they were all staying at the compound and had arrived more or less the same way he did. They were supposed to bring a new shipment back from Ciudad Miel, and more than one of them said they needed to hurry if they were going to get back in time to be allowed to eat dinner. When Treviño heard where they were going, he rolled himself into a ball. A few minutes after entering the city, the truck parked inside an enormous warehouse and the foreman told them all to get out. A visibly terrified man, who was either the owner or the manager there, stood trembling in front of the newcomers.

"Where's the stuff we ordered?" the foreman yelled. "From the list."

"We have everything ready, sir. It's just that the guys who do the loading ran out on me when they saw you coming."

"Cut the shit. Just tell me where the stuff is."

Taking advantage of the chaos as the foreman and the driver located the items they were sent to expropriate on different shelves around the warehouse and the other workers waited for instructions next to the truck, Treviño grabbed a yellow, grease-stained shirt with the warehouse's logo that someone had left on a shelf, put it on, and hobbled out. He made it to the corner as quickly as he could, then turned and walked toward a grocery store down the block. There was a public phone outside it that seemed to be working. He stopped to catch his breath. His face was so swollen he could barely see to his left. His ribs and his right knee hurt. He didn't have a penny on him after going through the checkpoint. He was just wondering how in the hell he was going to call the Bus to come pick him up when an old man pulled up in a rusted-out Lincoln.

He didn't like it, but it was either this old man's life or his own.

In the time it took the old man to engage the parking brake, Treviño slid into the passenger seat.

"Hey! What—"

"Don't move and don't raise your voice, if you want to get out of this alive."

"But—"

"Quiet. Start the car and drive toward the city limits."

"I don't have any money on me, just enough for—"

"Take me to the southern entrance to the city. Do you know where that is?"

"Yes, we're close. Please, don't hurt me." The old man started telling him about how many grandchildren he had and how he was supposed to be bringing them food.

"Nothing's going to happen to you, old man, but you've got to stop talking. Turn over there by that gas station." Treviño had just caught sight of the motel in the distance. He got out of the car and told the old man to keep driving straight and to keep his eyes on the road. He waited until the car was out of sight before crossing the avenue.

When he finally made it to the motel parking lot, he noticed that the lights upstairs were out. After checking that the Maverick was there he headed inside to the reception desk to ask for the key. He could still hear the music coming from the bar and above it the laughter of women: different girls with the same laugh, as if they were part of some endless river. Suddenly, he felt metal against the flesh near his right kidney.

"Don't move."

They pulled something like a ski mask without holes over his head, snapped a pair of handcuffs tight around his wrists, and patted him down for weapons. He guessed there were at least three people standing around him, all of them skilled at moving silently. He heard someone behind him say, "Let's go."

The guy with the gun on him must have been a professional, judging by how quickly and confidently he moved its barrel from Treviño's back to his left temple.

"Duck."

He was pushed into a large vehicle—maybe an old car or a luxury model like the consul's Mercedes—and then forced into the middle seat. Another man was waiting to his left.

"One move and you're dead."

He felt the car start up and back out. They weren't going to kill him—not there at least—so he let himself go with the flow.

From the passenger seat came the voice of an old man.

"Put your hands on the front seat and don't even think about moving. Why are you here, and who do you work for?"

"I'm a businessman. I'm in construction materials."

"Businessman, my ass. You work for Junior?"

"Don't know him."

"I'll ask you one more time. Do you work for Junior?"

"I don't know who you're talking about."

"Are you here alone?"

Treviño hesitated and it got him an elbow to the face.

"Answer me. Are you here alone?"

"Yes," he said, feeling a trickle on his face. One of his cuts had opened again.

"What's your name?"

Treviño gave the alias the consul had invented for him, without a second's hesitation.

"Juan Rentería."

"It's this one," said the man to his right.

"Get out of Ciudad Miel," said the old man. "If we see you or your car anywhere near here in an hour you won't live to talk about it." Then, to the others, he added, "Toss him."

They hit him with something metal, probably the butt of a gun, right at the base of the skull, and he saw a flash of lightning made of shadow. *Interesting,* he thought. *I didn't know there was a color darker than black.* And then he stopped thinking.

When Treviño opened his eyes, the young man from the reception desk was offering him a towel to stop the bleeding. He was on his back in his room.

"How are you, boss? Should I get a doctor?"

Treviño's head hurt more than it ever had, but he said no. As soon as he could sit up and get a handle on the dizziness, he saw the Bus staring at him intently, as if he'd given him up for dead.

"What happened, man? What happened?" the Bus asked when the young man went for more ice. The blow to Treviño's head distorted his image.

"Did you see them?" asked the detective. The Bus shook his head.

"I heard a racket down at reception, so I went to take a look and saw you lying on the pavement out front," the Bus grumbled.

"Let's go back. Stop fucking around. That was a warning. The big dogs know we're here."

The big dogs, thought Treviño. *How could I have been so stupid. Why didn't I think of that before?*

"Bus, give me your phone."

"What?"

"Give me your phone. I have to make a call."

The Bus handed it over and the detective dialed a number he already knew by heart. Mr. De León answered on the second ring.

"Treviño?"

"Yeah, it's me. Bus, would you give me a minute?"

The driver left the room, but he didn't like it.

"What happened?" shouted Mr. De León. "Where have you been? We haven't heard from you in a day!"

"I was in the Los Nuevos compound."

"What?"

"Your daughter isn't there, but I know how to find her."

"Where's Cristina?" his employer shouted.

"Am I on speaker?"

"Yes. I'm here with my wife and the consul."

"Turn it off." When this was done, he continued. "Your telephones are probably tapped, or else there's a leak among the people closest to you. I can't say any more."

"What are you talking about?"

"No one knew I was coming to Ciudad Miel, but they were waiting for me. A group of armed men jumped me a little while ago, and it's a miracle I got out alive. It was obviously a trap. They had the whole thing planned."

"Is she alive?"

"I can't say for sure, but I'll know in a few hours. Right now I need to see a doctor. If anything happens to me, don't forget about my widow."

He was about to hang up when he realized the businessman hadn't answered.

"Agreed?"

"Agreed," Mr. De León replied. He didn't sound very convinced. The Bus poked his head into the room.

"Take me to the hospital," said the detective.

They hit their first checkpoint not far from the hotel. Right where the road narrowed on the way to the private clinic, a group of rancheros stood in front of two parked pickups and a sports car with damage to the driver's side door.

"Fuck. Game over."

"Relax," said Treviño, but his heart was pounding like a jackhammer. Were they looking for him?

"Got your gun?" he asked, and the Bus responded by taking his piece out of its holster with his left hand and holding it close to the window.

Three guys were giving the car in front of them, a taxi without plates, a quick once-over. They waved at the driver and let him pass. In the meantime, something caught Treviño's eye.

"You see that black car?" he asked, pointing at the sports car. "I think it was parked next to the Maverick back at the hotel."

"Don't make me nervous, man."

A muscular guy with a military buzz cut signaled to them with his flashlight and they rolled up to the improvised checkpoint. One of the rancheros walked over to the passenger side while the guy with the flashlight aimed his rifle at Treviño.

"Where are you headed?"

"To the clinic. I just got mugged," said Treviño. The Bus, pursing his little mustache, kept his mouth shut.

"Not from around here?"

"We're from La Eternidad. I was attacked on the way into town. I need to see a doctor."

The man asked for their papers and the Bus handed over his passport, but Treviño claimed his wallet had been stolen in the attack. The fake soldier looked him over carefully, examining his grease-stained shirt, and said, "Stay where you are." He showed his colleague the Bus's passport and whispered something to him. Then the one with the flashlight said, "That'll be a donation of five hundred pesos. Each."

They paid up and the soldier handed back the Bus's passport and rapped two times on the hood of the car.

They parked in front of a sign that read EMERGENCY and the Bus got out to ring the bell. Two apprehensive nurses who had been stationed at reception came to the door, followed by a woman in a white lab coat with a stethoscope hanging from her neck. They didn't seem to be in any rush to let them in. The Bus helped Treviño to a bench.

"I was mugged and hit in the head," Treviño said. "I don't feel well."

"Where did it happen?"

"Near the city limits."

"I see." Treviño might have been imagining it, but the doctor and the two nurses seemed to go pale. "All right, then. Someone will . . . Someone will be right with you."

As the two men sat there, the doctor removed her lab coat and stethoscope with trembling hands, then threw open the front door and ran into the parking lot.

"What, did she forget something?" asked the Bus.

By way of an answer, the two nurses took off their smocks and threw them to the floor as they ran out after the doctor.

"Hey! Ladies! Hey!" a man in a nurse's uniform shouted.

From the front door, the Bus and Treviño watched them get into the doctor's car and close the doors as the car screeched out of the parking lot.

"The emergency's over here," said the Bus. "Where are they going?"

"Ah, well . . ." sighed the remaining nurse, then looked over at the detective. "You couldn't have waited until tomorrow?"

"He's injured and he needs to see a doctor," grunted the Bus.

The nurse took a deep breath and went to lock the front door. Then he dragged a chair over and wedged it under the knob so the door couldn't be opened from outside. The Bus never took his eyes off him.

"Yesterday a guy was brought into the hospital with a bullet wound, and an armed crew burst in to finish him off, right there in the operating room. Killed the surgeon and her whole team, too. That's why they ran."

The man's poor bedside manner didn't bother Treviño: after months of living in constant fear and anger, learning again and again to heed bad omens, of course these doctors were on edge. People from the north went from being the gentlest and kindest in the country to being the most nervous and cagey, the ones most afraid of conversation.

The nurse looked at the two men, knowing there was no point in asking whether they'd reported the incident to the police. There hadn't been any police for months.

"Do you have a credit card? We don't take cash here." Then, to the Bus, he said, "I can take care of your friend, but don't try anything."

"Don't worry, Doctor," said Treviño.

The nurse nodded and offered him a wheelchair. "This way," he said. "But he has to stay here. For security," he said, blocking the Bus's path. "I'm sure you understand."

"Wait here," repeated Treviño.

Not entirely convinced, the Bus watched as the nurse pushed the wheelchair down the hall and closed the door that separated the waiting room from the clinic itself. There wasn't another soul in sight.

Twenty minutes later, he saw two doctors head out to the parking lot for a cigarette. When they saw him they lowered their voices. He heard several buses drive past. Twice, the moon peeked out from behind the clouds and disappeared again.

When the doctors finished smoking, the Bus said to himself, "All right, that's it. It's hot as hell out here." And he sneaked in behind them.

"Can we help you?" asked one of the physicians.

"I'm looking for my colleague. He's being seen inside."

"I'm sorry, but you can't go in there," the physician replied, but the Bus was already halfway down the hall.

"Hey!" the man shouted.

Three doors led away from the reception area. The Bus stuck his head into the first room. It was empty.

"Hey, you can't—" The doctor tried to block his path, but the Bus easily pushed him aside.

"Don't try me, asshole."

In the second room, an elderly nurse was watching television. She nearly had a heart attack when the bodyguard burst in.

The third and final room was empty. The Bus swung around, furious, and saw the nurse who'd admitted Treviño filling out forms on the computer.

"Where is he?" he demanded.

The nurse looked at him, wide-eyed.

"He was right there, in that room. They took care of him and he said he was going to leave." When the nurse saw there was no one there, he lifted his palms apologetically. "I swear."

But the Bus didn't stick around to listen to his excuses, because someone was screaming out in the street. He drew his gun and ran down the hall until he found a door.

He had no choice but to take cover from the explosion. He waited a moment, then ran around the building to the front entrance.

Except for the nurses and doctors beginning to mill around, there were no suspicious persons or vehicles in the parking lot. The Bus holstered his gun when he realized that he, in fact, was the suspect. He watched silently as the flames grew higher.

"Enough!" the nurse yelled. "Can't you see we're sick and tired of all of you?"

The few vehicles passing by at that hour of the night slowed a bit for a better look at the fire blazing in the parking lot, then sped up again. Not a single squad car or fire truck ever appeared. In the middle of the blaze were the skeletal remains of the Maverick and something that had been sitting on the passenger side.

19

After walking for nearly an hour from the scene of the crime to his room on the second floor of the hotel, the Bus closed the door behind him and collapsed on the bed. He was disheveled and exhausted, with his tie undone, his blazer in his hand, and his clothing soaked in a sea of perspiration.

Fucking Treviño, you thought you were so smart. But sometimes things don't turn out how you'd expect. The doctors and nurses had fought the blaze tirelessly, afraid it might spread to the clinic. Not one had offered him a kind word, though. They were clearly convinced that he and Treviño were mixed up with the criminals somehow.

The fire department never did arrive, but when the medical staff finally managed to put out the blaze, he saw with his own eyes that there were no human remains in the Maverick. The car's interior—if you could say a car that's been blown up *has* an interior—and its chassis were burned to a crisp, but there was no corpse.

The Bus had stood frozen in the first row of the crowd, staring at the blaze. While the same nurse who'd reluctantly let them in finished spraying the remains of the car with yet another fire extinguisher, the bodyguard concluded that whoever did it had used grenades. He imagined several, though of course one would have been enough to destroy a car that old. A useless unarmored car with no air-conditioning. He didn't even want to think about how angry Mr. De León was going to be when he found out.

Typical, Treviño. You've got balls. I'll give you that, but you were way off this time. And look where it got me. He was good, sure, but not even all that good: it had been two days and they still hadn't found the girl. Besides, he should have seen this attack coming a mile away. *The problem,* he thought to himself, *is that this mess with the girl is on me now.* The thought annoyed him, especially because his first assignment was probably going to be to find the detective's body. It wasn't that his colleague's absence particularly upset him; he'd only just started to warm up to him. But he should have split a long time ago. *Fucking reckless Treviño, you should have gotten out while you still could.* After grumbling about the unpleasant work cut out for him, he wondered where the hell they might have taken the detective. *All I need is for them to send me into those two warring organizations, looking for him like I was the fucking detective.* For a long time—at least, for as long as he could keep his neurons focused—the Bus wondered what was happening to Treviño at that very moment. He imagined him lying by the side of the highway with a bullet in his back; in a safe house with his hands and feet tied, about to be asphyxiated with a plastic bag. He imagined a chainsaw slowly approaching his body. *Whatever, he was asking for it. Who does he think he is, anyway?*

Mr. De León hadn't picked up when he called right after the incident, so he called the consul to let him know what had happened. The gringo couldn't believe it.

"Stay right where you are. Wait for our instructions."

There was no way he was just going to stand around in the street, though, especially not since those guys could figure out Treviño wasn't alone and come back for him. He thought long and hard about his options and decided to go back to the hotel.

"Would you call me a cab?" he asked the nurse, who rolled his eyes.

"Do you really think a taxi is going to pick you up here, after what just happened?"

The Bus reflected on the implications of the question while the young man pressed the lever on the fire extinguisher one, two, three more times.

"You could walk. Or you could wait for the sun to come up and take the bus."

"What about the checkpoints?"

"I doubt they stuck around after the blast. They know the army or the marines will send a patrol. At daybreak, obviously, so they don't have to catch the guys who did it." Then, tucking the fire extinguisher under his arm, he said, "If you'll excuse me," and went back inside the clinic.

It took him over an hour and a half to walk back, hauling his 275-pound frame along the best-lit streets in town. Every now and then a pickup with tinted windows would slow down as it passed him, but no one got out to question him. Whenever this happened, the Bus was sure he was fucked: the mere fact that he carried his gun in a holster marked him to both criminal organizations. If anyone stopped to search him, he knew he'd have trouble getting out of there alive. So he kept walking, and when he finally saw the lights of the hotel, he told himself that at least that part of the ordeal was almost over.

The front desk attendant's jaw dropped when the Bus stepped into the lobby, sweaty and disheveled after his odyssey.

"What happened to you?"

The bodyguard didn't answer.

"My key."

The kid handed it over without taking his eyes off the driver.

The Bus kept going until he reached his room and threw himself on the bed, cursing the detective and his thing for old cars. Then he thought about how fond Mr. De León was of the Maverick, which he'd driven when he was young. As if he could read his thoughts, the magnate called five minutes later.

"What were you doing when they took Treviño? What the fuck were you thinking?"

"I was doing my job."

"Your job was to keep him safe, stupid. If we lose him, we lose my daughter too. Go find him. Now. Who took him?"

"Seems to have been Los Nuevos, sir."

"I don't know how you're going to do it, but you're going to get him back right now, you incompetent son of a bitch. And if we've lost him, *you're* going into that goddamn compound and *you're* going to get my daughter out. Do you hear me?"

He hung up while the Bus was still blathering apologies into the receiver. *Asshole*, thought the bodyguard.

This is your fault, Treviño, he went on. *You shouldn't have agreed to come with us.* Besides, who would leave such a beautiful woman alone on the beach? *With that smile, that smooth cinnamon skin, that silky hair . . . Who would leave her behind?* It was the detective's fault. That's how this all started. The things he'd had to do these past few days. That little assignment he'd been given with La Caterpillar. *How the fuck did I let myself get roped into that one? Why didn't I just tell him to go to hell?* He thought back to what had happened earlier at Babydollz. La Cat had swished her bulk down the hall and the Bus hadn't had any choice but to follow. The host walked in front of them, a room key in his hand. When she passed through the glow of a red light, she reminded him of a certain wrestler known for his bad temper. He could feel himself losing his nerve. "Listen, I'd rather just have a drink and talk," he'd said. "As friends.

Wouldn't you? Order a bottle of champagne, maybe?" But La Caterpillar had just stared at him.

It took him a minute to realize that his second cell phone, the personal one, was vibrating in his pocket. He had a text message:

> THERES NO FOOD LEFT AND WATERS SHUT OFF. WHEN R U
> COMING HOME?

He realized he hadn't touched base since the morning. His lady needed help. Of course she was anxious. He answered:

> RITE 2 THE BOSS AND SAY 2 BRING FOOD. BE THERE 2MORROW
> NITE.

Then he added:

> NEED SOME SPECIAL TIME WITH U . . . U HAVE NO IDEA WHAT
> HAPPENED HERE.

He looked at his watch. It was three thirty in the morning. Mr. De León was crazy if he thought he was going anywhere near that compound. How was he supposed to get past three security fences? His height and build meant he usually stuck out like a sore thumb. And he wasn't looking to get caught. He figured he'd probably get fired. *Fuck 'em*, he thought.

He didn't want there to be any doubt about what had happened, and since the police had abandoned Ciudad Miel months ago, he was going to need to get to the next town over—with all the risks that this implied—and file a report. But first, he needed to wait for the sun to come up; he was too tired, anyway, to take a single step. He didn't expect much to come of his visit to the precinct, besides getting a copy of the police report to show his boss. *With any luck*, he thought, *they'll tell me when they find Treviño's body, and that'll be that. I can't see why they'd keep him alive.*

Without taking off his clothes or his boots, the Bus pulled the blanket up over his eyes, then stuck his arm out and fumbled around until he managed to turn out the light.

The pain in his legs and groin nearly woke him up screaming. A line of fire ants was going to town on him. He seemed to recall leaving some gordita crumbs in the bed.

He tried to regain his composure after stripping down and shaking off the insects, but when he got back into bed he thought, *There really is something about this valley.* He wasn't able to fall asleep again. He lay there like that until dawn, when his work phone rang again. It was Mr. De León.

"Yes, boss?"

"Come back. We heard from the kidnappers." And he hung up.

The Bus did the math. *Four days it took them,* he thought. *Four fucking days. About goddamn time. They sure dragged it out.* He lay there a little while longer and thought, *What if they're not the real kidnappers? What if they're bullshitting?* News of the girl's kidnapping had probably gotten out by that point, and it wasn't impossible that a couple of smart-asses had decided to take advantage of the situation.

After his shower, the Bus put on the pants he'd worn the day before. He noticed a lump in the pocket and pulled out his notebook. During the drive, he'd convinced Treviño to discuss his experience as a detective, and he'd jotted down a few phrases he didn't want to forget when they got to the hotel. What had he said about the job? *There's not much to tell you. Don't trust anyone, and never leave home without your piece.*

When he went into Treviño's room to gather his personal effects, he found the contract the detective had signed with Mr. De León. The Bus was blown away by how much he stood to earn. *Fucking hell,* he thought. *I picked the wrong profession.*

He thought about Treviño for a long time, how all his hard work had come to nothing. *That stubborn son of a bitch. If he hadn't been so thorough, he'd still be alive. But hey,* he thought, smiling, *the bastard was asking for it. I'll have a burger or two in his memory when I get back.*

At exactly eight o'clock in the morning, the police in El Torito, six miles from Ciudad Miel, informed him that filing a report for kidnapping and destruction of property would cost him a thousand pesos.

"You don't want to examine the scene?" asked the Bus, surprised.

"What's the point?" said the officer who'd taken his statement. "We wouldn't be able to get prints off anything, anyway. Take your report and have a nice day."

As he left, one of the officers guarding the door remarked loudly, "Nice mustache. I'm gonna start trimming mine just like that."

Four hours later, after he got off the first bus headed toward the port, a taxi dropped him off in front of his employer's mansion. The guards at the gate could tell he'd been through the wringer and opened up for him.

"What happened to the car?"

"They burned it," answered the Bus, annoyed.

Mr. De León shook his head as soon as he saw the Bus coming up the stairs. With an expression of complete disdain, he read the photocopy of his driver's statement to the police, then crumpled it up and threw it to the floor.

"You let me down, Valentín."

His first instinct was to hurl insults at his boss, but he didn't have the energy. He was so tired and irritated that he asked for a personal day instead. He needed to go home and rest.

"You have twelve hours," said the magnate. "If you're not back first thing tomorrow morning, you'll be replaced."

"Yes, sir."

"Wait, wait. We should talk first." As if the exhaustion weren't enough, the consul wanted him to sit there and go over every detail again. When the gringo asked if he'd be willing to take a lie detector test, the Bus almost beat him to a pulp. But he agreed. He was there for an hour, and every few minutes he felt like he was about to keel over. Eventually, the gringo let him go.

"We should have sent Moreno," he said.

The Bus silently imagined dishing out another ass-whipping while he asked how the kidnappers had contacted the family. The consul signaled to Moreno, who showed him a sheet of yellow paper in a plastic bag. Close up, it was clear that the kidnappers had cut letters out of the newspaper to make the note's four lines of text.

* * * WE HAVE CRISTINA * * *
* * * SHE HAS A BIRTHMARK ON HER BACK * * *
* * * WE WANT THREE MILLION DOLLARS * * *
* * * GET THE MONEY READY AND WAIT FOR OUR INSTRUCTIONS * * *

They'd included a Polaroid of the girl with the note. In the picture, she was on her knees in a room with a concrete floor, trying to cover her face. There was no mistaking her for anyone else, though. No one else had her eyes or bone structure. Instead of the pink dress she was wearing the night she was taken from the club, they'd dressed her in white sneakers and a blue track suit that hung loosely from her frame.

"We found the note inside a plastic bag caught in a pine tree out back. We don't know how long it'd been hanging there," Moreno said. "Whoever left it didn't know the house well and didn't realize we wouldn't see it there, or else they knew it very well and knew it's the only place on the property where we don't have security cameras."

"So, there's nothing on the video feeds . . . nothing unusual?" asked the Bus, weakly.

"Nothing," Moreno responded, taking back the evidence. "Go get some rest. We'll see you tomorrow."

The Bus walked unsteadily down the stairs, dragged himself across the parking lot, and got into one of the Lobos.

On his way home, he stopped at the supermarket. He deserved to enjoy a feast with his lady, even if it meant maxing out his credit card. His life had been in real danger, after all. *I deserve it, sons of bitches.* He'd been sending her text messages since he got on the bus. She hadn't answered, but he figured she'd just run out of credit on her phone. *Who cares?* he thought. *I'm alive and we're going to celebrate.*

He grabbed a shopping cart and started grabbing food as if it was the last thing he was ever going to do. Three baguettes and a package of serrano ham, some sliced manchego, and two bottles of French wine went into the cart, followed by two rotisserie chickens, six cans of pickled chiles, two packages of corn tortillas, three jumbo bags of potato chips, and a big bottle, the biggest they had, of Tabasco. He started to head toward the cashiers but turned around and dropped two cakes and three pints of ice cream into his cart, along with a box of chocolate chip cookies, a bag of frozen strawberries, and a pack of Chocotorros. Then he threw in some Old Spice lotion and two boxes of condoms. *Too bad they don't sell gorditas*, he thought. *If I see a place that's open, I'm buying a pound. I've got lots to celebrate. I'm alive, and things are looking up.*

The Bus hadn't really had many long-term relationships. Or any, for that matter, aside from the ladies of the evening he visited regularly from the time he was a teenager. Women just weren't interested. Which is why he felt so lucky to have met

La Muda, despite the age difference (she was more than fifteen years his senior, but even in her forties she still had the body of a twenty-something). The only real problem was that he couldn't stand the wild gestures she used to make herself understood, since she couldn't speak, or the fact that she wasn't very pretty. The Bus, who wasn't exactly a model of loyalty, told himself he'd trade her in for a newer (more attractive) model the first chance he got. She would do for now, and they were going to celebrate.

It was a short drive, but he nearly dozed off more than once: the all-nighter and hours on the road had finally caught up with him. He parked in front of La Muda's house and got out, carrying the groceries. He had a small apartment downtown but spent the night at his girlfriend's place whenever he could: she had a three-bedroom home in a neighborhood full of public housing. It was the quietest place he'd ever spent the night, by far. It turned out that her house was so quiet because all the others on the street had been abandoned when their owners got tired of the constant clatter of gunfire. But La Muda, who had been a cop in La Eternidad for years, wasn't easily intimidated.

La Muda's going to love these treats, he thought. It was the first time he'd brought a bottle of French wine to her place, and he'd even bought one of those nice metal corkscrews, the biggest they had. He hated the little folding ones, which were made for smaller hands. *There's so much to celebrate. Things are looking up.*

When he opened the door, there was La Muda, sitting on the floor with her hands and feet tied and a completely gratuitous piece of tape over her mouth. He had no time to react.

Behind him, he heard a gruff voice he knew all too well.

"Hands up. Get on your knees."

The Bus immediately obeyed, dropping the groceries to the floor. The man who'd spoken deftly removed the driver's gun from its holster.

He turned his head as much as he could. There was Carlos Treviño, pointing the Taurus at him.

"Treviño . . ." he said, struggling to get to his feet.

"Don't move!"

The detective reached over to the table next to him and picked up a piece of yellow paper someone had gone to the trouble of gluing words cut out of the newspaper onto. The Bus went sheet white.

"As I'm sure you've guessed, I found the girl. I'm sorry, Valentín, but there's no good explanation for why she's in your house."

The Bus turned purple with rage.

"What are you talking about? This is my girlfriend's house, not mine."

La Muda let out a string of furious grunts.

"Don't play dumb. Cristina was here the whole time."

"I don't know what you're talking about. I don't have anything to do with this! I haven't been here in two weeks. Goddamn it, Renata, what did you get yourself mixed up in?"

When he grasped the direction the conversation was beginning to take and that Treviño wasn't kidding, the Bus took a deep breath and shifted his weight onto his right leg.

"What the hell is wrong with you, Treviño? What the fuck are you thinking?"

"Don't try it, Bus. Don't move. I'm telling you, don't move."

But the Bus did try it.

The bullet caught him in the right knee. The detective had known it was going to take more than one shot, even with a nine-millimeter, to stop Valentín Bustamante. In the end, three was the magic number. The Bus fell sideways, hitting his head on the wall, and then slid down onto his enormous haunches, a thin line of blood trickling down his forehead.

"That's enough, cabrón," growled the detective.

20

"When Moreno tried to take my weapon off me that day on the beach, I knew he was used to taking lives. It's written all over his face. He's ready to go at the drop of a hat, but he knows how to control himself.

"You're not that type, Bus, no matter how much you try to seem like you are, with the way you talk and dress and lift weights and pack heat like the others. Some people are born to kill, and others only do it when they absolutely have to. Moreno will shoot without thinking twice. You're a calculating, patient guy who waits for the right moment. The only thing you're any good at is lying.

"Since I arrived, you've done nothing but slow the investigation down: You said the tracks we saw at the club came from expensive tires, when actually they're cheap, the kind anyone could buy. I'd know that tread anywhere: they're the same tires I have, and I see the tracks they leave in the sand every day. You also said the young man had lost a button, but the button I showed you was from my own shirt. You didn't want me at the nightclub or the morgue because you didn't want me finding any evidence, and you didn't want me going into Colonia Pescadores because you didn't want me figuring out who the dead kids were. You didn't want me going to the compound, either, because you knew I'd figure out that the girl wasn't there.

"You've had her here all along, with La Muda keeping an eye on her. You obviously weren't planning to return her to her family, because she would have given you up. I don't know what you *were* planning to do, but those garden shears and the new shovel out back in the garden don't suggest anything good. You probably already used them to get rid of El Tiburón's body. In fact, I'd put good money on it. While I was waiting for you, I took a look at the garden. There's a patch of fresh earth out there and I bet we'd find him if we dug a few feet down.

"I have to hand it to you, though: you're not bad at planning. You waited until the girl sneaked out, and you followed her. You had the whole number laid out: you knew she'd go over to her boyfriend's house, since his parents weren't home, and that she'd take him with her to the club. You followed them at a distance and waited until they went inside. That's when you sent El Tiburón and the guys from La Cuarenta after them. You picked El Tiburón because you knew he needed the scratch, and then you found three guys from La Cuarenta to back him up as soon as you heard Cristina was coming to town for a few weeks. As soon as they grabbed her, you met up with them in Pescadores, took Cristina off their hands, and got rid of them. You killed them all, including El Tiburón, but you brought him back to bury him here. You wanted the evidence to point to him, to throw the rest of us off your track. You wanted us to think he was the one who'd orchestrated the whole thing so you could collect the ransom with total impunity. You'd promised the cartel boys a pile of money, but then you thought better of it and decided to knock them off instead. That's why La Cuarenta has been so pissed lately. Ever since you killed three of their own, a night hasn't gone by that they haven't been out there firing rounds into the air. They're reminding you of your debt. How do I know? You didn't want to roll up your sleeves on the drive to Ciudad Miel, and I'm willing to bet it's because you didn't want me to see the tattoo on your forearm you got when you were one of them.

"At first I didn't want you to come with me, but the second time you insisted it had been Los Nuevos, I thought it might be better to keep you close. I was hoping you'd contact your accomplice, but you managed to resist the urge. The problem is you made a few mistakes. Margarito's men had no reason to know I was hiding in the morgue or that I was riding in the consul's car. Except that you told them. You gave me up because the longer you waited to collect the ransom, the riskier things got. You needed to get me out of the way.

"Your last mistake was when I got jumped in Ciudad Miel. I knew it had to be you: I'd been careful to cover my tracks, so there was no way Los Nuevos or Los Viejos—the big dogs, as you called them—could have known I was there. If they *had* known, there's no way I would've gotten out of there alive. That's not how these guys operate, not in any of the three organizations. So it had to be you. You paid your acquaintances in Ciudad Miel to give me a scare, and you organized the whole thing from the hotel.

"I had to convince you I was dead so you'd lead me to the girl. That's why we're here. I still have to figure out who you're working for, but that won't take long. Now put these handcuffs on. Don't try anything, or I'll shoot to kill."

The Bus, who'd been applying pressure to his knee throughout the detective's monologue, gave the deepest sigh of his life and began to cry, his whole body shaking. They were the tears of a man who was so close to having it all. Three million dollars, gone in an instant. He was still bawling when he saw Treviño's silver-tipped boots approach. He threw himself at the detective.

The force of the impact sent Treviño flying into the wall next to the front door. At that moment, the detective realized he'd seriously underestimated the driver's strength. The first kick landed on his ribs before he could grab the Taurus. Then the Bus lifted him, arms and legs flailing, over his head and threw him at the glass dining room table. The glass shattered and Treviño landed on the groceries, breaking the two bottles of wine.

The detective struggled to maintain consciousness as the Bus lifted him by the shirt. He managed to land three useless punches to the driver's face. The bodyguard, on the other hand, held him against the wall with his left hand and drew his right slowly back.

The first punch broke the detective's nose. *I've got you now, asshole,* thought the Bus. The second punch left Treviño blinking like someone suddenly roused from a deep sleep. The third opened a gash above his eye. The Bus put both his hands around the detective's neck and slid him up the wall until they were eye to eye. The detective thrashed wildly with his feet, but the Bus leaned in with all his weight until Treviño couldn't move anymore. He wanted to say, *This is going to hurt, you son of a bitch.* But there was something scratching at the roof of his mouth. His tongue itched, too, and he couldn't move his jaw to form the words. He looked at the detective, who was about to pass out, and lifted a hand to his mouth.

That was when he realized it wasn't rage that had caught his tongue. It was the corkscrew, part of which was sticking out from under his chin. Terrified, he grabbed it and yanked it out. But he must have done something wrong, because blood started gushing onto the carpet.

La Muda let out a gut-wrenching groan when she saw the trouble her lover was in. She tried to stand, but her feet were too well tied.

Valentín Bustamante—bodyguard to Cristina de León González and native of Parras, Coahuila, a young man who'd been locked up only once for disturbing the peace, former member of La Cuarenta, current lover of Renata Hernández, a.k.a. La Muda—dropped what was left of Treviño, leaned his massive bulk against the wall, and stood like that until his legs gave out.

Treviño slowly got to his feet. He lifted a hand to his head and realized the blood pooling on the floor wasn't just the body-guard's. He must have hit something sharp, probably when he went through the glass tabletop. He noticed a few drops fall from his forehead, so he gingerly felt around the crown of his head and confirmed the blood was coming from there. *I don't have long*, he thought. When, much to La Muda's dismay, the Bus didn't react to the two sharp kicks Treviño gave him, he leaned over the bodyguard, carefully reached into his jacket pocket, and extracted his cell phone. He scanned through the list of contacts and dialed Mr. De León's house. As usual, the consul picked up on the first ring.

"Hello?"

"It's Treviño. I found Cristina. Send an ambulance to Twenty-Five Calle Doctores, in Colonia Huasteca. It's a matter of life and death."

"Is she alive? Treviño!"

"An ambulance," repeated the detective. "Hurry."

"We're on our way. Hang on, Treviño."

La Muda glared at him venomously, emitting a steady, angry groan. Her eyes said, loud and clear: *I hope you bleed to death, you goddamn son of a bitch.* Treviño hobbled toward the bedroom. Lying exactly where he'd seen her a while earlier, Cristina was starting to come to from the sedatives they'd given her. She still couldn't move, but she was blinking. When she saw him, she mustered a single word—*Help*—and broke down in tears.

Fifteen minutes had passed, help still hadn't arrived, and the detective felt like he was about to black out. *For fuck's sake, what the hell is that gringo doing?* he thought. He'd given him the exact address of the driver's hideout. But night was falling and there was no sign of the consul.

Finally, a truck screeched to a halt in front of the house. And then another. Thirty seconds later, someone kicked in the front door and there was La Tonina, a menacing character on the payroll of both the police force and at least one criminal organization. The last time Treviño and he had crossed paths, they were both still working for Chief Margarito. Cristina fainted when she saw him.

La Tonina shot a quick glance at the Bus's body slumped over near the door and smiled at the detective.

"My old friend Carlos Treviño. What a lovely surprise."

With the last of his strength, Treviño tried to lift the Taurus but La Tonina kicked the gun out of his hand. He'd always been faster, despite his imposing frame.

"Ay, mi amor. This is just how I'd dreamed of catching you. In flagrante with a kidnapped girl."

He enjoyed watching Treviño bleed out from above. He smiled again.

"There you go again," he went on, "messing with something bigger than you. This time, though, you're not going to get away. You wanted to take the girl home, but we had an intercept on the Bus's phone, asshole. We didn't leave anything to chance. That's how we knew you were here. And now you're gonna get it, you son of a bitch."

As Treviño's eyes fluttered shut, the image of his wife on the beach flashed though his mind. If he ever saw the consul again, he'd ask that asshole why the hell he ever thought he was the one to solve the mysteries of La Eternidad.

21

CONSUL DON WILLIAMS'S TESTIMONY

According to his final report on security in the Gulf of Mexico filed before he tendered his resignation in November 2014, as requested, the United States consul to La Eternidad went to an abandoned house in Colonia Huasteca, on the outskirts of the city. He was helping a couple who had recently gained United States citizenship find their daughter, also a US citizen. The consul states that he went with his consulate-assigned driver and two pickup trucks carrying the magnate's security team, and that when they got to the house, they found the front door open and chaos inside: as soon as they entered, they saw bloodstains on the floor and bits of food scattered all around, as if there had been a fight. A bit farther in, they found clear indications that at least two women had been living in different rooms of the house, based on the clothes they recovered. And that was all they found. There wasn't a living soul in the place. The consul states that he was surprised not to find Treviño or the US citizen there and told the others to park the trucks at a good distance. Following his orders, they reentered the residence without touching anything and left the doors open, as they'd found them. He says he knew none of it would do any good.

The consul's report states that he left the magnate's bodyguards at the scene and told his driver to take him home. They passed the university, which had been practically deserted for months, then the gas station and the empty lot beside it; and then, as they neared what once was the fairground, the consul told his driver to stop the car. He got out and walked over to what was left of the rides. Next to the carousel and the bumper cars, a couple with three little girls were boarding the old, run-down Ferris wheel. They were the only customers, but the attendant agreed to start up the wheel. The consul spent a long time standing there, watching that Ferris wheel go around and around. Watching the girls. They were the only people in La Eternidad he'd seen smile for a long time. His cell phone had been ringing the whole time. The consul glanced at the screen, but he didn't answer.

PART TWO

Chief Margarito and
the Conversation in the Dark

1

It wasn't the sea hurling its waves at the shore that woke him or the piercing yellow light of the streetlamp that supposedly kept the block safe at night; the party across the bay was winding down and a heavy silence hung over the beach. What woke him was a feeling of dread. He got to his feet and walked over to the window.

The rain had stopped; tomorrow the fog would roll in. It unsettled him to be able to see the stars so clearly. Sagittarius loomed above him, and a scarlet moon peeked through the dark. For a moment, he thought the sun had risen on the wrong side, but then he realized that the red sphere in front of him was a blood moon. He felt the hair on the back of his neck stand on end.

He remembered the last time he'd seen one like that. How long had it been? Ten, twelve years? It's an image you don't forget. The officer who'd taught him everything he knew had just died, and it was a troubling omen. He thought about the mess down at headquarters, where he was the one in charge now. About the man who'd sworn to kill him. He felt a strange disquiet take hold of him. *That's the moon,* he thought. *I'm the chief, I'm sixty years old, and they're going to kill me.*

When the moon vanished behind a cloud, he turned his attention to the stars, but Ursa Major and the North Star, which had soothed insomniacs for centuries, were nowhere to be seen. Instead, there was only Sagittarius, the archer, pointing insistently at La Eternidad.

But, then again, there's no such thing as a policeman who can read the stars.

2

Like every cop in La Eternidad, Margarito had learned fast how to tell a real threat on his life from all the fake ones. True, at one point he'd needed to hire a driver and a security detail, and he never left home without the nonregulation weapons he'd bought himself—like all the other guys on the force, since the city never had money for that kind of thing—but that was it. He'd never armor-plated his truck, and he never wore a bulletproof vest. When he was appointed chief of police, twenty-nine years and nine months ago, officers wore their street clothes and had to provide their own weapons, which meant that every investigator on active duty looked like a beggar. That's why it was so lucky he got the job. No one liked his style, but it was him, a known torturer and a cruel, corrupt son of a bitch who'd walked out on his own mother as she lay dying, who managed to bring the force up to speed with uniforms, weapons, office furniture, and even a few vehicles. The only squad car they'd had before was an old Jeep Wrangler bought for a song after World War II. It was a sight to be seen—the chief had felt like John Wayne the first time he drove it—but it broke down every ten miles. Luckily, the port wasn't very big. Anyway, there had never been a need for a car chase before: robberies were usually committed by cattle thieves who went straight back to their ranches. If you were lucky, you'd get there before they'd eaten their haul. There was the occasional burglar who waited in the dark for the right moment to strike, the hustler looking to swipe anything that could be pawned, and the drunk-or-crazy prostitute making a scene in the street. Instead of spending a night in lockup, those usually got sent back to their pimps, who'd straighten them out and make sure they toed the line. Most common were the shoplifters who distracted the clerks and stole without hurting anyone and pickpockets who came to town during Carnival and winter break. That's how things were when he started. Smugglers and drug dealers? He certainly didn't invite them or welcome them in, as the newspapers were so quick to say. They arrived with the explosion of activity in the port, had their boom in the seventies, and consolidated their power in the eighties. But they'd always been there and always would be. He'd known dozens of these guys, always cut from the same cloth. Every case started and ended in a working-class neighborhood like Los Coquitos, where you always caught the culprit. His guilt could be real or invented, current or retroactive. It didn't really matter. It was all there on the pages of *El Imparcial de la Sierra*, which had tracked his career on four pages of crime reporting every day for almost thirty years. The bank robbers, stoners, bad trips, and that psycho who went around cutting people up with a chainsaw—those all came later: in the last six, maybe seven years. There were no kidnappings, no shoot-outs, none of the problems they had now. Thirty years ago, who could have imagined how much La Eternidad was going to change?

He'd wanted to be a cop as long as he could remember, and his dream came true. What Chief Margarito hadn't anticipated was that after all those years, being a police officer in the port would feel like rowing solo into the eye of a hurricane. And sometimes the hurricane even called you on the phone to give you a direct order or to say, *I'm coming for you*—which is what happened the night before.

The day that was supposed to be his last on the job was one of those when you couldn't tell the sea from the sky, when you knew a storm was coming because you heard the sound of the thunder pushing through the fog and it felt like bombs going off somewhere far away. It was stifling, unbearable, like being inside a pressure cooker: the minute you stepped out of the shower, you were already covered in sweat. After a brutal week when not a single cloud bothered to pass over La Eternidad, when the port's residents and those few, clueless tourists still drawn in by the malecón decided to huddle in the shade from noon till six at night, the deluge felt like a miracle. It was a furious, thousand-armed giant that knocked down three palm trees and didn't rest until it had flooded every working-class neighborhood, fishing settlement, and slum. But under the normal summer sun, the city would be a sauna until nightfall. *What a difference,* he thought. The day he took the job had been clear and sunny with a gentle breeze blowing in off the water. Now, the heat and the fog multiplied his misgivings.

As he finished his usual breakfast (a cup of coffee and a Coca-Cola), he mulled over who could have called to threaten him the night before. *When I get my hands on that motherfucker* . . . Hardly anyone had the number of the cell phone he reserved for his most trusted colleagues, his contacts in the trade, a few snitches, and a certain high-ranking military officer. His ex-wife and son were in the respectable phone he used for his professional conversations, even if she only ever dialed his number to yell at him, and his son wouldn't take a call from him in a million years.

As he lit his second cigarette of the day, he noticed that his hands were shaking. He hadn't been able to take his mind off the threat or his imminent retirement long enough to fall asleep. What were the guy's exact words? *Your days are numbered, Chief. I've got bullets here with your name on them.*

He'd been heading out of the office after delegating a few loose ends and saying good-bye to the team who had been at his side for so long. El Flaco was the only one who'd volunteered to keep him company on the way to the beach, more as a friendly gesture than out of any real need.

He got the call on the highway, right in the middle of the storm. His pickup was full of his belongings, and he'd been slow to react because he was at the wheel. El Flaco's run-down truck was a few yards behind him. Margarito's phone rang about six times before he noticed the words UNKNOWN CALLER on the screen and picked up—against every instinct he'd developed in three decades of working for the worst kinds of men.

"Hello?"

"You're going to die."

Understandably, he didn't respond right away. Death threats weren't a common thing, not even for him. He could count on the fingers of one hand the times someone had dared to threaten him directly. One time, Don Agustín's bodyguard tried it when they picked him up for selling amphetamines without permission from the local wholesalers. Margarito had told the other officers to let him go and knocked the man's teeth out with two or three right hooks and a few well-placed kicks. Then he'd grabbed him by the collar and snarled, "Say it again, sweetheart, and I'll bury you alive right here on the beach." Word must have gotten around, because it never happened again. The guys he worked with didn't beat around the bush. If they didn't like something, they told you straight out or acted accordingly, but they didn't telegraph things beforehand. It was true that since marijuana took off in the seventies, the precinct had been getting more prank calls, especially on the weekends, when the dumber brats had a little too much to smoke or drink. But this was Margarito's private number, the one he saved for dangerous contacts, and very few people had it. So he slowed down.

"Who is this?" he asked.

"Your days are numbered, Chief. I've got bullets here with your name on them."

It sounded as if the mouthpiece was being dragged through sand or gravel and then the call cut out.

He pulled over near some palm trees. There wasn't another soul anywhere on that stretch of highway.

His initial train of thought was shattered when El Flaco tapped his keys a few times on the passenger's side window. It took Margarito a second to register that the man standing there was his bodyguard and to lower it for him.

"Die on you?"

"What?"

"Your car, boss. Did it die on you?"

El Flaco was completely soaked from the storm, despite the plastic bag he'd torn open and was using as a hood.

"No, I have to return a call. Give me a minute."

When Flaco Ibarra didn't move, he added, "Go back to your car."

Fucking Flaco, there's no point in kissing ass now.

The voice had sounded familiar, but he didn't think it was one of his contacts in either of the organizations engaged in a war of atrocities over the port. He racked his brain but couldn't think of anything he might have done to anger them. Nothing much had changed in the past few months: the same two groups were still armed to the teeth and determined to massacre each other. La Cuarenta still held uncontested control over Colonia Pescadores. The only difference was the body count. But he'd been instructed to limit his involvement to clearing away the remains.

Did I screw up somewhere? His only arrests in the past few days had been of three gangbangers who'd insisted on selling drugs on the pier, outside their designated territory, but the voice on the phone didn't seem to come from a gang. *No, they wouldn't go that far,* he thought. *And whoever it was sounded too well educated to be from the Four-Zero.* The face of the young man who'd taken over the leadership of Los Viejos flashed before his eyes, followed by that of the Colonel, who'd recently moved to La Eternidad. *Could I have pissed one of them off? You never know with those guys. They can't be trusted, not with all the shit they snort.* It'd be just like the Colonel to want to get rid of someone like him, an associate who knew too much. Still, he wasn't the type to telegraph his intentions, and Margarito was confident he'd be useful to the warring factions even after leaving his post. He wasn't surprised when his godson had insinuated there'd be room for him in the ranks. It was what the young man's father, Obregón—Margarito's dear friend and the organization's founder—would have wanted, may he rest in peace. *In any case,* he concluded, *I can't just leave this threat hanging there. I need to find out who called me. The minute I'm off the force they're going to be lining up to settle accounts.* The new administration had made it very clear he shouldn't expect any help from them. We all have skeletons in our closets, but Margarito's closet was especially big. He'd made a lot of enemies over the course of his career, and now they all wanted to get even. But how else was he supposed to have done his job? A cop who doesn't strike first is a lousy cop.

Just the thought of what awaited him was exhausting. He was sixty years old, about to go into forced retirement, and had one of the worst reputations of any police chief in the country. Not even hell itself would give him a second chance—which is why he needed so desperately to speak with his replacement.

As if the prospect of being killed or hauled into court weren't enough, there was also a rumor going around that he was the one who'd kidnapped Mr. De León's daughter the week before and that he was the one who'd demanded the ransom. *Well, isn't that just the goddamn cherry on top.* As his former mentor, Elijah, used to say, rumors like that could ruin a gentleman's reputation.

It might not be such a bad idea to get out of town for a while. With a little luck, he could talk his son into letting him stay at his apartment in Canada until things settled down. If memory served, Canada didn't require an entry visa—and it didn't have an extradition treaty with Mexico.

Now that his career was coming to an end, he asked himself what he was going to do with his life. He didn't have many options left. He pictured himself investing his depleted savings in honest but short-lived businesses; he'd never been much good at those things. He pictured himself down and out, driving his old partners around or working as a bodyguard to the rich and infamous. He pictured himself getting arrested and not lasting long in jail, ending his days beaten to a pulp and carved up by the guys he'd sent through the system. He pictured his immediate future, and he didn't like what he saw. Which is why he was so grateful for the ace he still had up his sleeve: it was a risky move, but it might just save his hide. First, though, he had to win his successor over.

He set his coffee on the table in front of the window and looked at the two cardboard boxes sealed with packing tape next to the bookshelf. Those files had been his insurance policy for years, especially certain documents signed by or implicating politicians who were still in office. As the chief took them out of his car the night before, he'd thought to himself that those kinds of precautions were going to be useless before long. Knowing his enemies in the mayor's office, he wouldn't be surprised if he were detained within hours of being removed from his post. *I wouldn't be surprised, either, if the kidnapped girl suddenly turned up and they tried to lay the blame on me.* The proceedings scheduled for the next few hours at city hall were just the start of the public execution they'd planned for him.

Fresh beads of sweat began to gather on his forehead and he realized he'd strayed too far from the air conditioner. He was going to need to jump from one artificially cool bubble to the next all day if he didn't want his clothes to end up soaked through.

He walked over to the console table by the front door and looked at the objects he typically attached to his belt: key ring, dark glasses, two cell phones, gun, lucky knife. He put on his favorite straw hat and, just before he walked out the front door, looked down at the loafers his ex-wife had given him years ago. For some inexplicable reason, he still had them. The simple elegance of the loafers, more appropriate for a dentist or an accountant, clashed with his button-down shirt and jeans. He'd gone barefoot until he started primary school, which he was forced to attend in flip-flops; he got his first pair of boots when he was twelve and had never worn anything else since. The loafers seemed hypocritical, almost fraudulent. *Then again, my whole life is a fraud*, he thought, and he decided it was time to break them in.

He couldn't remember ever having walked through a denser fog: it was hard to see to the end of the block. Just as he was about to open the door to his truck he heard a strange noise coming from the palm trees behind him. Faster than a lightning bolt cuts through the sky and disappears, he'd thought: *It's them. They've come for me and they're going to kill me, right here.* But it was just the horrible screech of an owl: it had emerged from the vegetation, beat the air with its wings, and vanished into the fog. *An owl*, he thought. He'd crossed paths with them before, way back when he and his mother lived out on a ranch in the middle of the sierra, but they never used to frighten him. *You scared the shit out of me, fucker.* The tiny bit of his brain that had managed to survive the sleepless nights, poor diet, and stress of his thirty years as police chief produced the only remotely profound thought it would have that morning, and Margarito understood why people freeze in terror when they hear those birds screech in the dark, as if they'd spent thousands of years as mice. He got into the truck and thought: *It was just an owl. My nerves are shot, it was just an owl, let's get the hell out of here.*

A few moments later his extended cab Cheyenne pickup, purchased with funds from one of the criminal organizations operating in the port, pulled out of the garage and headed straight into the storm.

Among the few possessions he'd managed to hold on to after being extorted by Los Nuevos were his two residences: an apartment in an old building downtown and a house on the beach, which he considered the jewel in his crown despite the fact it was only half finished and he spent barely any time there. Luckily, the title wasn't in his name. He'd never forget the day Los Nuevos arrived. *Bunch of fucking assholes*, he thought. *I bust my ass my whole life and they drop in and take it all away.* He'd gone to check out two decapitated bodies that had been left on the outskirts of the city. It didn't make any sense; executions just weren't done that way. The fingerprint database back at the office was such a joke it would take forever to identify them. The chief was examining the crime scene when one of his investigators shouted, "Heads up, Chief! Incoming!" He looked up to see a caravan of five white pickups speeding through the neighborhood. As the trucks got closer, it dawned on him that this wasn't a visit from the governor. When the first few guys got out of the trucks and nonchalantly leveled their assault rifles at him like they owned him, he studied their clothes and weapons closely. This was before the rash of firefights began, so even with their guns pointed at him, he had no idea what danger he was in. His first thought was that the army had finally come to arrest him for corruption. *There's been a shake-up in the state police,* he thought. *One of my enemies made it to a position of power without my knowing it.* Looking more closely at the new arrivals, though, he quickly realized that no officer in the Mexican military would let his men go around with those handlebar mustaches, sideburns, and goatees.

"What do you want?"

"Get in, Chief Margarito González," someone shouted from inside one of the trucks. "We're going for a spin."

He was so surprised he didn't even put up a fight when they took his gun.

The truck they hoisted him into seemed like a recent acquisition—by one means or another. The leather smelled as if the vehicle had just rolled off the assembly line, and inside two rows of seats faced each other with a minibar between them. From one of the seats, a man in a suit with a shaved head, a thick mustache, and a black cowboy hat on his lap addressed him.

"Welcome, Chief. Do you know who I am?"

Margarito gestured toward the street.

"The guy who left me those bodies?"

"That's right. I'm the new boss around here," the man replied. "We should talk."

"I'm listening."

"It's very simple, Chief. You do business with Mr. Obregón's son. But that stops now. You're either with us or you're against us. With the job you have, you've got to choose. We've tolerated your presence until now, because you didn't make trouble. You were always the type to live and let live, and as long as we didn't draw too much attention to ourselves we never had any problems with you. But not anymore. We're coming for all of it. We're in charge now."

Margarito took a good look at him but didn't recognize his face. He spoke and moved like a military man, but he wore expensive clothes from up at the border. A soldier couldn't afford that luxury.

"Mr. Obregón and his son are on their way out. They'll either make a deal or they'll die. In the meantime, we're calling in the debts some of these local entrepreneurs have racked up. You know who I mean. If they think they get to keep the money they made off us, money they were just holding for us because the army took out our boss a couple of weeks ago—well, they won't think that for long. And just so there's no question about who's in charge here, we're going to start with you."

"What are you talking about?" asked Margarito.

"We know you're close with Mr. Obregón. They pay you five thousand dollars a month for your cooperation."

It was true. When his friend decided to dedicate himself full-time to the trade, he'd invited Margarito over and said, "If I'm greasing the palms of the federales and every customs agent between here and the border, how could I not pay you a little, after everything you've done for me?"

The man who'd been speaking, known as the Colonel, slid a blue plastic cooler toward him with his foot.

"Open it."

One of the guys sitting next to Margarito jabbed him in the ribs with the barrel of his gun, so he leaned over the cooler.

Inside were the heads of two men he knew: Antonio Gallego and Roque Linares, who dealt drugs for Mr. Obregón in La Eternidad's nightclubs.

"They didn't want to work with us."

The Colonel shut the cooler with the tip of his boot.

"Five thousand a month over fifteen years comes to nine hundred grand. Figuring that you probably spent half of it and that you built a house in the middle of the city, we're asking for four hundred thousand and the house. That's for letting you, your wife, and your son live. If you say no, the three of you will end up in a cooler like this one. Your wife teaches history at the university from nine to five. Poor thing, she stays so late the parking lot's practically empty when she leaves. Your son goes to the same university; he takes classes in the evening and then goes for a run between eight and nine in La Huasteca. The boy's in great shape; not bad for a civilian.

"Don't take it personally. We're doing this to send a message to everyone carrying a debt with our organization: if we start with the chief of police, the others will know they've got nowhere to hide. You should be grateful you're not already in one of these coolers.

"Oh, and another thing," added the Colonel. "Starting today, you're going to be seeing a lot of these," he said, kicking the cooler. "Open whatever investigations you need to, but don't waste your time trying to solve any cases. You know who did it. In six months, it'll be your godson and everyone close to him, if they don't kneel to us. If you want to stay alive, you'll report to me from now on." He tossed him a cell phone. "I know you, Margarito. I know you'll accept our proposal."

The only thing the Colonel had been wrong about was that much more than six months had gone by, but his godson was still alive and there was no end in sight to the turf battle announced that day. Los Nuevos ruined everything when they showed up. Not only did they take his house and all his savings, but the day after that meeting he'd been forced to give up fencing stolen cars.

Taking all the necessary precautions, he went to talk with Obregón about the encounter and was told to accept the Colonel's terms.

"Those bastards used to watch the border for us. Now they want to break off and start their own organization. The most important thing is to stall them while we get our counterattack together. Give them the money and I'll pay you back."

Later that week, though, his friend had a stroke. He didn't bounce back from it, and his organization never did, either.

That's why we're in this mess, concluded Margarito.

As he always did when he stayed out at the beach, he avoided the potholes that were more like ditches, skirted the tall screen of pines that divided the shore from the rest of the world, and merged onto the interstate. The fog lifted in patches, offering him exquisite views, as if everything were stepping out from behind a vast curtain.

It took him longer to cross the row of pines than it did to spot Flaco Ibarra, who was tailing him at a discreet distance in his run-down pickup. The night before, he'd asked Ibarra to keep an eye on the barely passable road, but the guy was hardly a marine. *As a bodyguard, he's not worth shit. He couldn't hide from a blind man in a dust storm.* Chief Margarito hit the hazard lights and pulled over. El Flaco, who'd been going about three miles per hour, pulled over near a billboard and stared at it like he'd never seen anything so amazing in his life. *Why is he stopping? What's he thinking?* The chief honked the horn and El Flaco slowly pulled forward. When he was right alongside him, Margarito stuck his head out the window.

"You get worse by the day."

"We've got you, boss. There won't be any surprises. Hey, did you turn off your radio?"

He was talking about the shortwave they used on the force. The chief nodded. He preferred to communicate by cell phone, since a new technician had just started in the mayor's office, and he was certain the radio was the first thing they'd tap.

"I did."

Rather than complain about this, Ibarra simply asked, "Are we still going to the airport?"

Margarito furrowed his brow.

"Hell yes, we are. And the rest of my boxes?"

His escort nodded.

"We already cleared them out of your office. We also fixed that button on the air conditioner and tidied the whole place up, so the new boss finds everything perfectly in order."

Just the mention of the chief's successor hit a nerve. It's never pleasant to walk away from a place you've worked at for thirty years, and much less so when the guy filling your shoes wants to throw you into jail.

"See you at the airport." He had to hand it to El Flaco: he was definitely the most loyal of his security detail. In recognition, he gave him a little nod.

"Make sure everyone's in position."

"Right away, sir. Should I get a head start?"

"Of course not."

If they're going to shoot me they can take this asshole out, too, for not knowing how to do his damn job.

He closed the window and blasted the air-conditioning. If the people threatening his life wanted to catch him off guard, they'd have to wait until he was in the city. That's why he'd gone to the beach house: so he could head straight to the airport along the highways and main roads, avoiding La Eternidad's traffic. He wasn't about to make any rookie mistakes. It would be too cruel a twist of fate if the man who'd weaseled his way into Margarito's job had to figure out, right out of the gate, who'd killed his predecessor. *It wouldn't surprise me if he just left the case open.*

The fog was lighter as he passed the refinery, allowing him a clear view of its three flare stacks and the twenty-story spherical holding tanks around which the lives of the oil workers in La Eternidad revolved. As far as he knew, they hadn't found any pre-Columbian pyramids around there because the people who lived near the Gulf five hundred years earlier used shells, rinds, plants, and other perishable items to build their dwellings. To Margarito's mind, however, the refinery's immense black spheres were modern-day pyramids that had shaped the people's destiny over the last century. Now a new industry had taken over La Eternidad. He never would've thought it would be bringing him a little extra cash on the side.

The fog lifted again, providing a moment of spectacular visibility. There were no other cars around, no one waiting to shoot him: just him and the open road and the dunes. Still, there was no reason to tempt fate. He stepped on the gas, trying to escape the fog and his fear. He spent the next few minutes well above the speed limit imposed by a rusty sign. When he looked in the rearview mirror, he saw the little yellow fleck of El Flaco, following at a prudent distance in his compact pickup.

He left the wasteland of potholes and scattered palm trees behind and looked back at the flames from the flare stacks, still partially hidden by the last ribbons of fog that finally let up as he reached the municipal dump. He turned off the air conditioner to keep the smell out of the car and hit the gas. *Why not, it's a special occasion.* In less than a minute, he'd hit seventy-five miles per hour and was enjoying the relatively good condition of the highway. The chief had always had a thing for speed. Seeing that red light loom in the distance at the city limits was his first reality check: he realized that he'd need to start going a bit lighter on the accelerator when he turned in his plates. Come to think of it, this was really his last chance, since they wanted the transfer of power to take place that morning. Which is why, even though he saw the orange Caribe and the stake-body truck slowly approaching the intersection, meekly respecting the rules of the road, Margarito ran the red light, forcing the other drivers to slam on the brakes. They hadn't yet recovered from the shock when Flaco Ibarra sped past in his trunk, tapping his horn twice as he crossed in front of them. The man driving the Caribe, one Dr. Solares, saw them and said, "A strange chase: two old-timers trying to outrun death." His son, who was in the car, made note of the comment.

Margarito took the beltway to avoid the military checkpoint on the way into the city. Not only were he and the general in charge of the area not on the best of terms, he also wanted to be able to see any possible threat coming from a mile away. Before long, he was where the avenue leading to the airport began, at the end of the malecón. Ever since the violence started, there were three kinds of roadblocks you might run into: First, there were the ones the military set up at the entry points to the city in order to confiscate weapons twenty-four hours a day. Only an idiot would go that way: the soldiers were famous for seizing everything down to your nail clippers. Second, there were the barricades his department had to raise around the perimeter of a crime scene, at least until they found a good enough reason to drop the case. And third, there were guard stations you'd see here and there, which had been set up by the criminals themselves in neighborhoods recently acquired by their organizations and anywhere a local capo lived. He'd often see guards on his godson's payroll posted at strategic intersections in fake military uniforms. The most confident—or the most cynical—ones didn't bother wearing a disguise at all.

As he turned off the beltway, the sky was a dark mountain falling across the earth.

Right before he reached the airport, Margarito saw two trucks pulled up across the road. They were patrol vehicles—at least they looked like the new patrol vehicles—but he didn't want to take any chances. He slowed down and set his gun on the seat between his legs after releasing the safety in a fluid movement he'd learned over the years. He looked in the rearview mirror and was surprised not to see El Flaco behind him. *Goddammit*, he thought. *Some bodyguard I've got.* He'd had a bad dream the night before: None of his men had gone to the airport like he'd asked them to, and he was forced to get out of his car in the middle of a downpour. In the dream, he'd noticed as soon as he stepped out of his vehicle that the water was up to his knees. He took a few steps, and it had risen to his waist—heavy like silt, like sand, like cement in a mixer. He woke just as he realized the water was an impossibly deep red. Maybe it was age or his experience, but at this point he didn't need anyone to interpret his visions for him, not even La Santa. "There's your warning right there," he said to himself. "Plain as day."

He honked the horn once without coming to a complete stop. If the guys waiting up ahead were hit men, it would be the perfect place to shoot him: they'd left just a small path down the avenue, between the trucks. *All one of them needs to do is move a little and I'm boxed in.* But then La Tonina, recognizing Margarito's truck, jumped out from one of the vehicles and waved. Margarito pulled up alongside him.

"Where's the Suburban?"

"It's in the lot already, boss. I came out here to coordinate. Everything's in order. There are just two security detail vehicles: one of them with the guards sent to pick up the notary, Carrizo, and there's some dude from the mayor's office in the other, his personal escort. The mayor's in a van, and he's got a girl with him."

A bad start for the mayor, Margarito thought, *if he only sent two civilians to pick up his guest of honor.*

"Find El Flaco for me." After their many years of working together, he didn't need to specify that he wanted an escort from the airport to headquarters, one vehicle in front and one behind.

"Yes, sir. One more thing: Dr. Antonelli just went inside."

Goddammit, of all the days for her to turn up. There was only one person in La Eternidad who could insult him, scream at him, and make a scene without his being able to do anything about it. That person was Dr. Antonelli. She was one of the most respected professors at the university and, as far as the chief knew, the only historian who studied La Eternidad. He was certain one day he'd wake up to the news that she'd published a lengthy tell-all about him. All she'd need to do was write down what she heard while they were together. Which reminded him: "How are we for reporters?"

"A TV station showed up, and a photographer. Their credentials checked out so I let them in."

"Move the barricade closer and give me some backup. I don't want the press in there, no disturbances."

"Yes, sir."

He needed to talk with his successor about how it was all going to go down, and the twenty-minute drive from the airport to headquarters was his last chance before the guy took office and started making trouble for him. Everything had to run smoothly.

He drove past his men, who followed him in their trucks, and immediately recognized Dr. Antonelli's old Ramcharger in the parking lot. *Goddammit.* Dealing with her wasn't going to be easy. And he was going to have to deal with her, of course: there was only one waiting area.

From his car, he watched the plane land. El Flaco was nowhere to be found, but he did have to acknowledge that the whole thing was going like clockwork. A government van dispersed the drivers who insisted on idling near the entrance and the chief parked behind the mayor. The typical short, potbellied driver, who was about to become an official budget line, opened the side door of the vehicle and a pair of long legs emerged, followed by a designer miniskirt, a girlish waistline, and a pair of small but exquisite breasts—a tall woman with curly red hair, carrying a thick folder. The chief watched her with more disdain than desire. *And what are you planning to stop the bullets with, sweetie?* He got out of his truck as soon as he saw La Tonina jump out of his vehicle, rifle in hand. He was a good officer, La Tonina. Out of the corner of his eye he confirmed that El Dorado, the golden boy, was behind him, and finally, there was El Flaco, trying to catch his breath as he approached.

"Where have you been, asshole?"

The answer sent a shock through him.

"I thought I saw suspicious activity."

"What was it?"

"A blue vehicle with two cholos inside, headed this way. They turned around two blocks back, though. I'm telling you, we've got this place secured. Oh and, hey, your wife's in there."

The chief glanced at the airline service counter, where Dr. Antonelli was checking that the flight from Mexico City was on time. She wore a dress and heels, with a shawl draped over her shoulders. Her makeup suited the occasion. Without saying a word to his subordinate, the chief made his way across the parking lot.

They stood across from the domestic arrivals waiting area, making the civilians around them nervous—and with good reason. When you see someone with the Chief Margarito's build coming at you, with that look on his face, you know you have nowhere to turn. Not even to the law. On his way through the door, he'd determined there was nothing suspicious about the group beyond the general commotion of those waiting for friends and relatives. The young woman in the miniskirt, who'd probably been out of college for only about fifteen minutes, was chatting with two photographers and a television crew. Like everyone who worked for the new mayor, she brimmed with excitement and good intentions. As she distributed copies of his replacement's résumé, the girl extolled the man's virtues: two years on the local police force; a grant to study modern investigative and combat techniques abroad; a four-year residency in Quebec, where he'd worked in the private sector; absolute respect for the law and for human rights.

The girl gave her speech at a volume that was hard to ignore.

"The officer arriving today is a man of integrity ready to transform the city. The mayor himself went to meet with him in Canada, where he was living in exile, and convinced him to come back and join his team. Will you be at the induction ceremony? It will be at city hall at ten o'clock sharp."

One of the journalists cleared his throat and gestured, with a discreet movement of his mustache, in Margarito's direction. When it became clear the girl wasn't getting the message, he ended up greeting the officer.

"Morning, Chief."

"Juan de Dios, good to see you. Let me borrow the young lady a second."

The girl blanched but allowed herself to be pulled aside.

"There's been a change of plans. I'm going to be escorting our guest of honor."

The girl opened her round, strawberry-colored mouth.

"But they sent me to get him! I have to explain his itinerary."

"You'll explain it later, sweetheart. Juan de Dios," he called to the reporter. "Come over here."

The journalist walked over, white as a sheet and looking like he might faint, despite the fact he used the byline Fearless Juan. Over the past fifteen years he'd written hundreds of incendiary articles about Margarito in newspapers of increasing irrelevance, criticizing the chief's every move. Recently, instead of celebrating the opposition party's victory in the mayoral race, he'd been applauding the shake-up at police headquarters. He'd been the chief's staunchest critic throughout his career, and there was no way he was going to miss the arrival of his replacement.

"I enjoy those little jokes you write," Margarito hissed.

Over the past few days, Fearless Juan had, in his capacity as an informal adviser to the new mayor, suggested to the politician that it might not be a bad idea, after the transition at headquarters, to look into the current chief's ties to the organizations wreaking havoc on the region. With this on his mind, the reporter looked like he was about to burst into tears. *Fucking Margarito,* he thought. *Always with an angle. The devil really is on his side.* The chief, however, just patted him on the shoulder and said, "Will you take a picture of me with the man of the hour? A good one, cabrón—good enough for your column." And he pushed him toward the crowd.

"Sir . . ." the girl insisted.

Just then he saw the first passengers to get off the plane filing in to collect their luggage. With a "We'll talk later," he left her standing there, stunned, in the middle of the crowd.

"Chief," someone behind him called.

He turned to see a morbidly obese man in shorts and a T-shirt big enough to serve as a camping tent. The man was wearing a cap with the logo of a private security company on it, and the smile he was aiming at Margarito looked sincere. But the chief didn't recognize him until the other added, "It's me, González. Panda González, remember?"

His eyes and hair were exactly as the chief remembered them, but the man's face and what used to be his body looked as if they were wrapped in a layer, almost a tire, of fat. Margarito struggled to hide his surprise.

At that point, his bodyguards relaxed and the man was able to give the chief a hug, or the closest thing to a hug his girth would allow. You could tell from a mile away he had a very high opinion of his former boss.

"I saw you from back there and wanted to come over to congratulate you. They tell me you're retiring."

Of course he had to bring that up.

"I'm being fired," the chief corrected him. "And they took away my pension."

"Oh, man. I'm sorry."

"Don't sweat it," Margarito said and shrugged his shoulders.

"Anyway, I just wanted to say hello."

Ten years ago, Panda had been one of his most trusted officers: he was always ready to mix it up and never lost a fight. He was the shortest of Margarito's men, but his stocky five-foot-four-inch frame commanded plenty of respect. Panda González, El Flaco, El Dorado, and La Tonina were his right-hand men, but Panda couldn't handle the pressure. He quit a few weeks after he was forced to discharge his weapon during a bank robbery, accidentally killing a woman and her husband. The papers published the couple's story in a multipart series: a model husband and wife who ran a charity and donated generously to the local hospital, which was always in danger of closing. They were in the wrong place at the worst possible time, and the arrogance and incompetence of the local police did the rest. *He was a good* cop, thought the chief. *One of my most seasoned, and a good man. Come to think of it, that's why he left.*

"What are you up to these days, my dear Panda?"

His former associate held out a card that read:

Lightning Bolt Surveillance

Security personnel * Bodyguards * Cameras * Alarms

We're with you 24/7

Then he gave an address at the outskirts of the city.

"You're working for Mr. Chuy?"

"Hey, yeah. That's right. We're with you, whatever you need."

"And how's it going?"

The Panda cleared his throat.

"Good, you know. Relaxed. I'm on residential security detail. You know the Garza Blanca condominiums? The ones you can see from the highway? I work there, at the gate."

Margarito knew the place and could picture the inconsequential guard station at the entrance to the luxury condominium. Sizing up visitors through a little window, asking for identification, lifting that needle of a barricade a hundred times a day for every car that came or went. He pictured a small, smelly bathroom; a cheap blanket; nights spent on a cot, catching a few winks here and there—always at the beck and call of the residents and their stuck-up kids, afraid some burglar might take advantage if he nodded off—that zombie state where you can't think clearly, which steals one day after another until the end. He pictured a little television switched on around the clock until it breaks.

Under different circumstances, he would have said, *Stop by the office, I'm sure we've got something for you.* But this was his last day on the job, and soon he wasn't going to be in a position to help anyone, not even himself.

"I'll come visit you there."

"I'd like that, Chief. But I don't want to distract you. Here they come."

It was true: people were starting to make their way through the frosted glass doors: Carrizo and his bodyguard, followed by a rancher who burst out of the building like a charging bull after seeing the policemen gathered inside; a young man whose sweatshirt bore the name of a prestigious foreign university and who hugged his parents and sisters in turn; a slender woman in her forties with pearly skin, blood-red lips, and hair the color of a raven's wing. She wore an expensive suit, and no one had come to pick her up. Then came two clean-shaven businessmen who smelled like lotion: a young woman greeted one of them with a peck on the cheek, and the other, probably her husband, with a passionate kiss. Behind them, people in the crowd waited to pluck their luggage from the conveyor belt.

He recognized him right away, even though the young man had his back to him. Certain bonds of blood and hatred simply can't be broken. They say people in this line of work always know when an enemy is near. As if he could sense Margarito's presence, the newcomer looked up and scanned the crowd. *He knows he's going to need all the help he can get,* thought the chief. *Given the state of things here.* Just then, the man saw him and shook his head disapprovingly. *It won't be easy to get him to listen,* he went on. *But I have to try.*

The newcomer grabbed a medium-size bag and headed for the exit. He stood out from the crowd, not only because he was tall, but also because he was obviously in excellent physical condition.

"Now," he said to El Flaco and waved the journalist over. "Hey, Juan, over here."

La Tonina, El Flaco, and El Dorado stepped in to cut the new arrival off from everyone but Juan de Dios. The head of public relations for the mayor's office and the rest of the journalists clamored to get closer, but who could get around those three? With one smack, La Tonina dropped the only guy who refused to back off.

Thrown by the fact that no one from the mayor's office had come to meet him at the airport and above all at seeing Margarito waiting there for him, the young man who was going to be inducted as the new chief of police later that morning stopped dead in his tracks and quietly greeted the current police chief of La Eternidad.

"Hello, Dad."

A few paces behind them, Juan de Dios Cuevas, better known as Fearless Juan, thought, *Only in this line of work . . .*

Sensing that destiny was about to step in and ruin everything, he took the last photo in which the two men would appear together.

Conversation in the dark

"Did you hear?"

"About the new guy?"

"Yeah. He starts today. Margarito's finally retiring."

"About time. He's been at that job forever, and lately he's been totally useless. Nothing like how he was twenty years ago. He was a pain in the ass, but reasonable. You could work with him."

"They say there's going to be some big changes."

"Like what?"

"Looks like they're rolling out the red carpet for the new guy: weapons, cars, intelligence advisers, trained agents. They say the mayor is getting funds from Washington and that the money is about to start pouring in. He promised to put an end to the shootings."

"And I promise you, that's not going to happen. It's always the same thing. Talk is cheap."

"Who knows? We've already had a few surprises this year."

"What's he going to do? Get out there and walk the beat? His patrol cars are heaps of junk and he may have guns, but without ammo, they're just decoration. A kid could beat most of his men in a race, and I've seen slingshots more dangerous than his rifles."

"We'll see."

"I don't know. If he really wanted to change things, do you think they would've let him get this far?"

"Sometimes they get there, but they're not allowed to stay. Remember what happened in La Nopalera? How long did that new police chief last?"

"An hour and a quarter."

"He got an hour and a quarter to show for it and five pounds of lead. We'll see."

"Yeah, we'll see. Place your bets."

3

"Ricardo. Welcome," Chief Margarito stepped forward and patted his young replacement on the back. It's not every day you get to see your child appointed to such a prestigious job, even if that job is rightfully yours. "I'll take you to your meeting."

His son nodded but didn't say a word or make any attempt to hide his disdain. Luckily for him, he looked more like his mother. You could say he got her bone structure, the color of her eyes, her eyebrows, her athletic build and height, her thirst for knowledge, and her drive, whereas all he got from Margarito was the Y chromosome. There was even a rumor going around that the chief wasn't his real father. How could someone who had tortured and killed so many people, maybe the worst cop on the Gulf, have such a kind and upstanding son? There's that law about kids wanting to grow up to be the opposite of their parents, but Ricardo always focused on pleasing his mother: good behavior, good grades, mastery of English and Italian, graduating with honors, a nice honest job abroad. They knew the young man was ashamed of his father, that he wanted to sever all ties with him, which is why they chose him as the chief's replacement. To add insult to injury. But instead of taking offense, Margarito saw the choice as an ideal solution. He preferred they name his son to the post rather than anyone else—that son of a bitch Bracamontes, for example—because at least his son might think twice before sending him to jail.

He'd been calculating every move since the newly elected mayor had sent his personal assistant to pay him a visit, a month before he even took office.

"We want a seamless transition. I want us to see eye to eye on this: what do I have to do to get you to retire?"

But there was no way they were going to see eye to eye. They wanted him to leave and offered him nothing in return. That wasn't going to work. No one would've taken that deal. They spent four weeks negotiating his exit, and Margarito had insisted the only way he'd step down gracefully was if they announced his flesh and blood as his successor.

Now, there was his son, staring deep into his soul, trying to figure out just how many of the terrible rumors that had spread all over the country were true or if maybe there was some good in there, somewhere. For his part, Margarito wondered what had happened to the sweet, affectionate boy with a permanent smile on his face. It was as if the resentment fermenting inside him had turned him into a different person. The chief was just about to ask if he'd kept up with his karate in Canada when Dr. Antonelli burst through the wall of police officers.

"Ricardo!"

The young man hugged his mother as if they spoke often or had even seen one another recently and accepted a kiss on the cheek. Margarito didn't like the situation one bit: the last time he saw his ex-wife had been more than a year ago, and the encounter hadn't ended well. Watching her embrace their son, he was surprised at what good shape she was in, how muscular her arms and legs were. He could picture the evening salads, the intense regimen of diet and exercise. The mortification of the flesh in the pursuit of lasting health. He, on the other hand, kept needing to buy bigger clothes. If he ever actually made it into an operating room, the doctor would find a heart wrapped in layers of cholesterol.

"Hello, Márgaro."

The chief was uneasy. If he let himself get distracted by his wife, he'd lose the chance to speak with his son in private. But he said, "I'm taking him to his meeting. Come with us."

His ex-wife jumped back as if he'd tried to touch her. "Absolutely not," she replied. Then she added, "I'm sure you gentlemen have important matters to discuss. I'll see you at city hall, Ricardo, and then at home for dinner, as we planned."

Margarito was surprised by her relative friendliness: after their breakup twenty years earlier—or to be more exact, after she'd asked him to move out—Antonelli had harbored a complete and absolute hatred of the chief. She didn't take his calls, she refused to see him when he tried to speak with her in person, and she hired a fancy lawyer who managed to win her the house he was still paying off. At first, she bombarded him with phone calls and yelled at him for hours on end. To get her feelings out, she said. For his part, he refused to sign the divorce papers until eight years had gone by and it wasn't even legally necessary anymore. She'd almost killed him back when he'd invited their son to join the police force and didn't speak to him again until Ricardo quit. So he couldn't figure out her change in attitude. *Did she turn Buddhist, or what?*

The chief watched her hug their son.

"I'm so proud of you. Be careful out there," she said and gave him another kiss. Then she turned and left without saying good-bye to Margarito.

"Well, well, well. Look at little Ricardo . . ." El Flaco was the first to shake his hand, which made things easier.

A smile flitted across the son's lips when he saw his father's men. He'd always had a good relationship with them, except for El Dorado, whose height and bushy mustache frightened him as a child.

"Pinche Flaco, I almost didn't recognize you."

"How are you, Richie?"

The young man didn't answer. Behind him, La Tonina and El Dorado held their rifles and smiled. They remembered watching him play down at the station when he was just a brat; it was going to be strange to take orders from him now. Margarito stepped in to break up the tender moment. *A bunch of sentimental crap—like we have time for this.* He walked over to his son and pointed to the exit.

"We have to talk."

Not seeming to care whether the reporters heard him, his son replied, "You and I shouldn't be talking at all." The chief's face darkened as Ricardo went on. "I'll tell you right now. I'm not sure I can do anything for you. The mayor hired me to bring peace to the area and told me to make an example of my own family, if necessary."

Margarito tried to stay calm, just like he'd practiced.

"Listen, Ricardo. In any business, whenever there's a changing of the guard, the old boss offers words of advice to the new boss, who listens, if only out of curiosity and so he can avoid surprises. I only need a few minutes of your time. These are sensitive matters. After that, you can do what you want."

"I imagine the mayor's office sent a car and someone to pick me up."

"They didn't. You're the new police chief: you can't go around without a security detail."

The young man hesitated for a moment, then sighed and nodded. They crossed the airport lobby behind La Tonina and El Dorado and stepped into the morning heat, which was like walking into a lit oven. They got into the Suburban, which had seen better days but still got the job done. The two bodyguards sat up front, their boss and his son in the back. Looking out the window, the chief checked to make sure one of the new patrol vehicles was clearing a path for them and saw El Flaco climbing into his old bucket of bolts.

The last time he'd spoken with his son on the phone was six months earlier. When the young man moved to Canada, Margarito had started calling him once a month, much to the discomfort of his son and the daughter-in-law, who had always hated him. The chief had gone to impossible lengths, not all of them legal, to get his number. Annoyed at first, Ricardo chose to let his father do the talking. "Listen, son. There's a great job opportunity here in the capital. I heard it straight from the governor. Why don't you come back?" Or: "They say it's fucking cold up there where you are. Is it really thirty below? Aren't you freezing your balls off?" The calls usually came during the week from police headquarters or else in the evening, in which case the chief would sometimes hang up when he realized that he'd had a bit more to drink than he thought, his jokes were falling flat, and the alcohol was making his voice sound awful. They were all caught up on each other's news, so there was no need to waste time on niceties.

"What was it you wanted to talk about?" the new arrival asked.

His son had been using that formal tone with him for years, so the chief cut right to the chase. He'd been planning this conversation for over a week.

"I want to ask you to look past our problems. The situation here is delicate. There are people you should meet, introductions I should make. I'll need at least a week to bring you up to speed on who's who."

"I prefer to start from scratch. And let's get one thing straight: if I find proof that you're involved in any of this, be advised that I will proceed according to the letter of the law."

"You be advised: the law is just an excuse to throw people in the can, especially in this part of the world."

"I disagree."

"That's how it's always been, whether we like it or not." Margarito felt his patience thinning and tried to regain control. "Look. Dealing with these people hasn't been easy. Have I gotten close to criminals? Fucking A. It's my job. You put up with some of them, sit down with others: it's the only way to keep the peace in this city. And if someone snaps a picture of me with some capo, I'm there because I'm doing my job. Maybe I was the one who suggested the photo op. Though I'm not surprised the new blood in the opposition party wants to use it against me," he said, referring to a picture of him at one of Obregón's weekly banquets, which Fearless Juan had published in a newspaper in Monterrey.

"Look. You and I haven't seen each other since you moved to Canada, but keep this in mind: somebody has to do this job. No one else could. So they called me. The problem is now these assholes are lining up to screw me."

"Like who?"

"Your boss, for one. He talks about developing drug rehab programs, but whenever he throws a party he brings in mountains of blow. He talks about ending violence against women, but he has girls wandering around those same parties who were probably trafficked from Europe. What more could you expect from the douche bag who calls himself an environmentalist and publicly advocates for the death penalty? Anyway"—he took his time with this—"some people say he's on the way out. That he's only the mayor because they parked him here. By now he should be in congress or doing something on a national level, but it seems he rubbed someone the wrong way and the only job he could get was back here, where he started out."

Rather than answer, his son stared intently out the window. As the highway brought them closer to the city, all kinds of businesses started to appear and the young man greedily took them in: a taco stand and a pharmacy, a nightclub called Brisas and the Seven Seas motel, a restaurant called the White Whale, repair shops, car washes. Then there was the Sagrado Refugio de los Pescadores and the Carmelite convent.

They said nothing as the convoy entered the city. After making sure there were no suspicious vehicles at the off-ramp or behind the trees, the first truck honked its horn and turned onto the main avenue. Margarito's son turned to him.

"What else did you want to say to me?"

"That it's worse than ever here. A new organization is throwing everything it has at the older generation."

Murder wasn't a crime of passion anymore: it was a matter of business that claimed dozens of lives with every attack. It was that way in most border towns. Once or twice a month, the bosses behind the biggest operations looked over their returns and said, *No, no, this is no good.* Then they decided they'd make more money if they did away with the competition. They'd kill ten or twenty at a time, but their competitors would hire replacements the same week. The last mayor's strategy had been to tread water for his entire final year in office. He just stood there, arms crossed, with no intention of doing anything. He and Margarito had seen the violence coming long before it began, but they never thought the conflict would escalate the way it did. The working-class neighborhoods emptied out and people started arriving from who knows where to fill them back up, but they didn't last long there either.

"These guys know La Eternidad is going to be as important as Acapulco and Vallarta, and they want to get in on the ground floor."

When the first group of fifteen was massacred on the outskirts of the city, the mayor went to Mexico City to explain the situation and ask for federal support. He was carrying a thick file

Margarito had prepared. He returned the same night. Margarito went to meet him and found him more taciturn than usual.

"They didn't even hear us out," he'd said. "They threw your report in the trash. They gave us one suggestion: pass every mass killing to the federales, because the crimes involved don't fall under local jurisdiction. Translation: if you don't find drugs on the bodies, plant some, and leave it for the attorney general."

Over the next twelve months, the criminals grew increasingly cruel in their attacks, trying to outdo one another. Instead of driving out their competition, though, they created a spiral of hatred and revenge. And all the weapons coming into the port! Ten years ago, you had to order the standard-issue police sidearm from the state capital. Now you could buy one at your local supermarket if you were desperate enough to pay ten times what you would if you just drove to the gringo side of the border.

"I know," said Ricardo. "I got the report. Your name is all over it. If you had any idea of the things you're accused of . . . They even have statements from people close to you. If I were you, I'd be looking for a good lawyer."

The chief bristled at this last remark. Could there be a traitor on his team? It took him years to find a few efficient, loyal men who couldn't be bought. He could be proud of Macaria, the lawyer in charge of his paperwork; of Herminio, La Tonina, El Dorado, and of course, though to a lesser extent, El Flaco. Oh, and then there was Roberta Pedraza, a.k.a. La Gordis, fresh out of the police academy, a good officer with good attitude. They'd hit it off right away. So he leaned forward and said, "At the moment, there are two documents circulating that mention my name. There's the *Report on Criminal Activity in the Gulf of Mexico* prepared by the US consul to La Eternidad, and the study that hack from the Commission on Human Rights put together. No one cares about the second one, so it's got to be the first. Right?"

Noticing the surprise on his son's face, the chief added, "The consul has no idea where his bread is buttered. Diplomacy's great and all that shit, but we're the ones who have to bail him out when his plans go ass up. Day before yesterday he stuck his foot way in it, and they asked for his resignation."

"Maybe so, but the part about you is this thick," retorted his son. "They even have statements from the DEA."

There that Don Williams goes again, thought Margarito. *Sticking his nose where it doesn't belong.* His son looked him in the eye.

"Find yourself a good lawyer. It's the only advice I can offer you."

Margarito shifted in his seat.

"Look, Ricardo. All I want is for you to ask yourself if maybe, just maybe, they're using you to get to me before throwing you out on your ass too when it's over. No matter how well you do your job, you might find yourself in the same position I'm in after a few years. It comes with the territory."

"No, I don't think so. Two things make us different: torture, and the company you keep," he said. "There's no excuse for that."

From the driver's seat, El Dorado looked at his boss in the rearview mirror to gauge his reaction. The chief shook his head.

"Three years ago, while you were in Canada, we caught a guy who'd cut up six women with a chainsaw. When we brought him in, he was beaming with pride over what he'd done. He was a rich kid from a good family; he'd killed all those girls out at his parents' beach house. There were reports of two other women who'd gone missing, and he told us he had them, that they were bleeding to death in some hideout. He wouldn't tell us where. We searched the whole port and the surrounding areas and came up empty. You know how we got the clue that led us to them? I locked myself in with him for the night. And we saved the girls, even though one of them lost a leg. Gangrene had set in by the time we got there."

"There are other ways to interrogate someone."

"Sure there are, but tell that to those girls. And that goes for all the other cases, too. As for the other thing, the questionable company I supposedly keep: any asshole who gets hung up on that doesn't have a clue what this job is."

His son stared out the window for a moment before responding.

"You talk about the end justifying the means and all the good you're trying to do, but the Chainsaw Killer was an exception, not the rule. What *is* an everyday thing, though, is the money you take from them and your abuse of suspects in your custody. What do you think you're known for in the national papers? I know. I've seen the clippings."

Now I see who turned you against me, thought the chief. His wife, who'd always saved every newspaper article that mentioned him. He stifled the urge to go off on her. Ever since Ricardo turned fifteen, his parents had been at war for influence over their only son. His mother, the eminent Dr. Antonelli—an Italian who decided to move to Mexico, the first woman with an advanced degree in the port, and the dean of its budding university—bought him books, CDs, foreign and art house films; encouraged him to study Italian and other languages; took him on trips to the capital and abroad; sent him to finish high school in the United States so he could perfect his English. In short, she always wanted him to have horizons broader than his father's. On the other end of the spectrum, his dad: the man who'd sponsored and facilitated his first night of drinking, his first party with mariachis, and even his first experience with a prostitute—or would have, if Ricardo had let him. He'd treated him and his friends to endless banquets at trendy restaurants. The chief had thought he might be able to get closer to his son once he moved abroad, far from his mother, but that wasn't the case. The wounds the boy had suffered as a child never did quite heal.

The chief had tried to put his best foot forward when they worked together and always sent Ricardo on interesting errands, but his son wasn't blind; it didn't take him long to notice how shady the people were who came to visit his father or how his meetings were always at strange hours and places, like a massive unfinished hotel, a ranch on the outskirts of the city, or yachts that never spent more than a couple of hours docked offshore. He was also quick to realize that his father had a safe house off the highway where he took the more difficult detainees, the ones it was better to interrogate in private. Once, after he hadn't seen him in the office for two days in a row, Ricardo had gone looking for him in the cantina and found him there in a foul mood, with bandages on his knuckles, drinking tequila with El Flaco and El Dorado. The Commission on Human Rights had recently filed a complaint against his father for inflicting permanent damage on a suspect in his custody. Ricardo had asked if beating detainees was a regular thing for him, and Margarito replied, "Look. Sometimes we bring people in who just aren't going to talk. Who have so much confidence in their connections and their resources that they figure instead of charging them, we'll end up letting them walk and apologize to them, to boot. When you're dealing with the real lowlifes you can't just put them back on the street. You have to break their confidence. And the only way to break these guys is to go after them little by little, like cracking an egg without crushing it. You have to be patient and let it sink in that no one knows where they are and no one is coming to help them until they confess what they did and sign a statement. That's how police do it across the country, how we've always done it. There are even classes on how to do it."

His son's face darkened and he'd walked out of the cantina. He never set foot in headquarters again, not even to tender his resignation.

The theory of the egg wasn't the only thing that had put distance between Ricardo and his father. There were also the rumors accusing him of protecting Los Nuevos, all those mysterious meetings, and the fact that he so obviously lived above his police officer's salary: a house in the city and one on the beach, trips to the border, a new car and a younger lover every year, jewelry, watches. For as long as Ricardo could remember, especially in middle and high school, his classmates had either beaten him up or avoided him entirely. His mother got him a scholarship to study in Montreal. He hadn't spoken to Margarito much since then, and when he returned to La Eternidad, it had been two years since the last time he'd seen him.

"We can go case by case. But I need you to hear me out, and you should meet the players you'll be dealing with. These guys mean business."

"You mean your friend's competition? I know a thing or two about the individuals in question. They defected from the Mexican military."

Margarito nodded.

"They're military, yeah, but not just Mexican: we've picked up guys from the Guatemalan armed forces too, and even a few Kaibiles. Then there's the little gang that went to the United States and came back as La Cuarenta. Keeping them from shooting each other or killing anyone else is a tough job."

"Not that you've been all that good at it."

He opened the local newspaper, which had been on the seat next to La Tonina. The headline read: TWENTY MASSACRED. Below the words was a photo of a pile of corpses in a vacant lot on the outskirts of the city. The killers had set fire to the bodies and left them out in the open, making it clear they had no intention of burying them. Though local residents had been tipped off to their presence by the unusual number of buzzards circling, it had taken them two days to find the bodies or maybe to gather the courage to report what they'd found. Somehow twenty people were murdered out in the open, and there were no witnesses or forensic clues. According to the article, all had been shot execution-style. A professional job, the kind Margarito knew all too well: it took only a crew of three, maybe four, highly trained individuals to round up that many unarmed civilians, bring them out to the lot, and execute them. He'd told these guys over and over: "Rob them, run them off, but don't kill them. That's no good for any of us." But they didn't listen. Ever since war broke out between the two organizations, at least ten people would disappear every two weeks or so, which was how long it would take either group to kidnap the men who divided up their competition's product for sale on the street. At first, the victims would just vanish, buried out on some ranch. These last two months, though, they'd been turning up whole or in pieces at key locations around the city. The twenty they killed this time broke all the records. At the press conference, Margarito said only that the investigations were ongoing, per his agreement with the cartels.

"It's very convenient, washing your hands of all this by bouncing it up to the federales."

"I can't give you all the details on the fly like this, but it's a temporary situation. It'll be over soon."

"When they finish killing each other off, you mean?"

"When they reach an agreement. Did you hear about what's going on in La Nopalera? Do you know how long the new chief of police lasted? An hour and a quarter. An hour and a quarter," Margarito repeated.

The conversation ground to a halt just as they pulled up to a red light.

"What are you going to say at the press conference?" Margarito asked. "Think carefully, because there are going to be reporters there from *Proceso* and *La Jornada*, and they're going to ask you some tough questions."

"Such as?"

"Such as what are you going to do about all the mass killings we've seen this year." The chief gestured toward the newspaper that rested on the seat between them. "How will you respond to that?"

"That solving those crimes is a top priority, even if they did occur on the outskirts of the city. In fact, I plan to handle those cases myself."

"Are you fucking crazy? That's a fight you can't win. Let those assholes kill each other off and stay the hell out of it," Margarito bellowed as his son watched him with something like pity. "Think about La Nopalera. An hour fifteen."

As they waited for the light to turn green, Ricardo said, "I heard they kidnapped Mr. De León's daughter. And that you were behind it."

Margarito shrugged.

"Day before yesterday I brought a suspect in, a guy from Veracruz. I've got him in custody and we're preparing his statement. Looks like he's about to confess."

His son looked at him, trying to gauge if his father, who was an excellent liar, was telling the truth.

"They say you're asking for three million dollars," Ricardo added.

Margarito smiled at his son.

"If someone wanted to give me that much cash, I certainly wouldn't stop him. Now that I'm retired and all."

"And what do you have to say about the Three Stooges?"

Bracamontes, El Gori, and the Block were always popping up in *El Imparcial de la Sierra*, and Fearless Juan had written about them in *Proceso*.

"The mayor forced those guys on me. I have to put up with them."

Ricardo shot him a disgusted look.

"How can you stand to have those psychopaths on your team?"

As they reached one of the city's shopping centers, the light caught beautifully on the mist rising off the street, but the chief didn't seem to notice.

"You like what you see here?" he asked, pointing at the car dealerships and restaurants that so fascinated his son. "You might be surprised to learn how many of these places, even the ones run by folks you know, have ties to the trade in one way or another. You can't get around it these days."

His son said nothing.

"Have you heard anything about Treviño?" Ricardo asked eventually. Margarito shrugged and looked out the window.

"Not a word."

Technically, it was true. But he'd hear something soon enough.

That was all he said. If there was one thing he knew, it was that his son was going to try to get Treviño back on the force. The chief wasn't surprised they'd gotten on well when they'd worked together, but he couldn't stand Treviño.

Margarito looked at his son and saw the hatred in his eyes. After a few moments of silence, he added, quietly, "Do me a favor. Keep El Flaco, El Dorado, and La Tonina around. They've known you your whole life. If anyone can keep you safe, it's my men."

"The boss wants me to bring in a new team, fresh from the academy. A team that isn't crooked."

"Then make sure they get early retirement. Don't leave them hanging."

"I'll see what I can do."

Margarito watched his son stare out the window at a few grubby children washing cars nearby. This man was nothing like the son he'd raised, that generous, understanding person who never had a harsh word for anyone. Something had killed his compassion. *If only he knew*, thought the chief, *the metric ton of shit that's waiting for him. Come see me in three or four years and tell me this job is easy.*

"Yeah, see what you can do," he said, still following his son's gaze.

It wasn't even ten in the morning yet, but the malecón was already full of trios, soloists, nomads, masseurs, tai chi instructors announcing their services on sandwich boards, hairdressers braiding cornrows on the sand—droves of tourists, beggars, and vendors walking up and down the beach selling rosaries and other religious paraphernalia, blankets, rugs, crafts, beach attire, sandals, embroidered blouses, grilled shrimp on a skewer, silver jewelry.

Two guys walked past dressed like thugs. Police instinct cut through Margarito's reverie and he sensed the heavy, dark energy criminals give off.

"Pass me the radio," he ordered La Tonina. "See those guys over there at nine o'clock?" he asked El Flaco as soon as he had the microphone in his hand. "Go see what they're up to."

"Yes, boss."

"But don't go yourself. Send a squad car."

"I'll get out here," said Ricardo. They'd reached the parking lot of city hall. Margarito knew there was something important he still had to tell him, but the Suburban had pulled up to the front gate. Before his security detail got out of the vehicle, the soon-to-be chief of police looked at him and said, "See you, Pop. These were tough times you had to deal with."

The minute his son stepped onto the pavement, picked up his suitcase, and headed for the stairs, Margarito grabbed his walkie-talkie and ordered his men to keep an eye on him.

"Flaco, go with him. Don't let him out of your sight."

"Are you coming too, boss?"

"I'll be there in fifteen minutes."

He turned to La Tonina and El Dorado.

"You go keep an eye on him too. And leave the keys."

When they stepped out of the vehicle, Margarito got into the driver's seat and ran every light until he got to El Santo Refugio de los Pescadores.

For a long time already, nothing calmed him like visiting that church and its adjoining convent. He parked the Suburban next to an immense ceiba tree and hurried inside. The novices, who had just finished their morning chores and were getting breakfast ready for the senior citizens they cared for there, saw him come in.

"Will you be staying for breakfast, Chief?"

"No thank you, my dears. I'm in a rush. I'll just be seeing to something."

He crossed the atrium, where the three nuns in charge were seating the convent's fifty or so residents in chairs around the garden.

"Coming to pray at this early hour, Chief?"

"If you only knew what time I woke up this morning," Margarito replied, without slowing down. "Very busy these days."

"Goodness! And you're going to the chapel?"

"I promised my mother."

"May God bless you."

The nuns smiled and watched him head toward the chapel. The chief walked in—there was no one inside but a cripple in a wheelchair—and out again through the back door. He reached the four-foot wall at the edge of the property and, after making sure that no one was watching, hopped into the empty lot on the other side.

No one had cleared the weeds from the lot, or from his soul for that matter, in at least twenty years. The underbrush was up to his knees, but he advanced confidently along the path he himself had worn over the past few days. When he reached the run-down structure, on the outside barely more than a few stacks of cinder blocks and exposed metal support rods, he gave the metal door three rhythmic knocks. A forty-year-old woman peeked out and, when she was sure it was Margarito, slid her gun into her waistband. The main room was empty except for a cot, a patchwork quilt, and a small television set resting on a chair.

"How are we this morning?" Margarito asked, glancing at the two heavy black metal doors on the far wall.

La Muda, who still wasn't over losing the Bus, nodded several times to indicate that the girl had slept well and everything was under control. He had to admit it. La Muda was an asset: there she was, doing her job, even after they killed her boyfriend.

"She slept?" the policeman asked, a bit surprised.

The woman signaled to him to hold on and showed him a glass vial that contained a powerful sedative, indicating she'd given a dose to the girl, who immediately dropped like a ton of bricks.

"Go easy, that stuff can do some real damage," said the chief, and the woman shook her head furiously as if to say, *I'd never do something like that, not in a million years.*

Margarito crossed to the far wall and looked through a peep-hole in one of the metal doors at the gorgeous sixteen-year-old blonde lying half naked on a mattress on the floor. The cherry on top. If he hadn't asked La Tonina to tap Mr. De León's phones, Treviño would have made off with her, and good-bye retirement plan. With what he was about to get for her, he could finally think about taking a break. But you really had to see the girl. It was true what everyone said. She really was the most beautiful thing in La Eternidad, which is saying a lot in a place known for long-legged women with tiny waists, fine features, and blue eyes. To keep her from running, they'd taken her clothes and left her in just a pair of white underpants and a pink cotton T-shirt. The chief admired, as usual, the long blond hair cascading cheerfully across the mattress. He pounded on the door until the girl stirred.

Once he was satisfied she was alive, he turned back to La Muda, who threw her hands up to ask what they were going to do with her.

"It's almost over. Don't worry. This will all be behind us tonight. Yes, tonight. Hold on."

He hurried to the other door and looked through the peep-hole to make sure Treviño was still here, hanging by his wrists from a chain attached to the ceiling. Margarito told himself he could afford to be a little late to the event and opened the door. He walked over to the man and gave him a quick succession of right hooks to the ribs. Treviño writhed in pain.

"I know it hurts, but relax. You're not going to die. At least, not in the next two weeks. I've been looking for you a long time, and I plan to enjoy this little reunion. I'm in no rush. In case you hadn't heard, I'm about to retire."

The chief took off his shirt, hung it on a nail, and turned to give his prisoner another round of right hooks. He paused only to mop the sweat from his face.

"Those were for the Bus. He was one of my favorite associates. If you had any idea how long it took us to plan this kidnapping . . . I trusted him completely. It wasn't easy getting him a job
with De León. You made it harder for me to collect when you took
him out, but things are running smoothly again. When Daddy
didn't hear from you, he gave you up for dead and agreed to pay
not just three, but four million dollars for his little girl. A pretty
penny, no? I consider it a donation. To my savings account. But if
that runs out, it's no skin off my back; my son Ricardo is about to
take over at police headquarters. So you see, it's all in the family."

Blood had started to pool at the prisoner's feet.

"I didn't like that one of my most trusted men left me swing-
ing in the breeze five years ago, right when we were about to
make some real money with our contacts in the trade, but that
was your call. What I can't stand is that you won't stay gone,
given everything you know about yours truly."

Margarito banged on the door. Within a minute La Muda
stuck her head in and he told her to bring him a length of hose.
She gestured to ask him if he wanted water.

"No, not water, just the hose. For the gentleman," he said
and made a whipping motion with his arm.

La Muda nodded and closed the door. The chief walked over to
the dangling mass and spun it around so they were nose to nose.

"I told you I was going to break every bone in your body, and
here we are. You see? I'm a man of my word."

The door opened and La Muda handed him the length of
hose. She also pointed to her watch: it was almost nine.

Margarito squinted at the prisoner.

"Aren't you lucky. But don't think I'm done with you. I'll be
back soon to finish my workout. Exercise does a body good."

He thought about how, in just a few hours, he was going to
be filthy rich and Treviño was going to be behind bars or dead,

after taking the fall for kidnapping the girl. Working for the law
in La Eternidad had always been a lucrative gig, but he had a lot
of overhead—the ex-wife, the son at school in Canada, and Los
Nuevos. Those bastards just loved collecting dues. But Mr. De León
was going to be generous or he'd never see his daughter again.
God damn, he hated that guy. Margarito was going to make sure
he got what was coming to him. He had to deliver the girl safe
and sound if he wanted his ransom. But *sound* is a relative term.

He needed to hurry. He mopped the sweat from his forehead
and put his shirt back on.

"Enjoy your last moments on earth. Hope you like the smell
of piss."

La Muda closed the door behind him and the chief hurried
back to the living room and put on one of the two hoods they
kept on top of the television. Then the woman, who was already
wearing the other one, stepped out of the room for a moment
and came back dragging the girl by the hair.

"No, please no. No more."

"You're prettier when you're quiet," Margarito growled. "Now
let's say hello to Daddy."

The pressure of La Muda's gun against her skin kept their
guest from bursting into tears. Her knees buckled. She didn't
have the strength to run.

The chief took the cell phone the woman handed to him and
dialed the only number stored in its memory, holding a distortion
device to his throat. A man picked up after two rings.

"Hello?"

"How are we this morning, Your Excellence?"

"I want to talk to her. Put her on the phone!"

"Not so fast. Do you have what I asked for?"

"It's been here for two days. How is my daughter? I demand
to talk to her!"

"You're not in a position to demand so much as a scrambled egg, Your Excellence. Shut up and listen." He turned up the volume on the phone and brought it close to the girl's face.

"Say something."

The girl broke down in tears.

"Daddy? It's me . . . I can't . . . Please come get me . . . Please."

"Sweetheart!"

"A sweet fucking pain in the ass is more like it," interrupted the chief. "She won't eat, so she doesn't' have to piss. You'd better hurry. She's not looking too good."

"Honey, are you there? What was your first pet's name?"

"Oh, for the love of . . ."

"Bugs Bunny," said the girl, between hiccups.

"And where did you used to think Santa Claus lived?"

The hiccups kept her from responding for a moment.

"At Grandpa's."

The policeman pulled the phone back.

"You'll receive instructions at noon today. Do as you're told or you're all fucked." He hung up.

La Muda dragged the girl back to her windowless room, locked her inside, and approached the chief. They took off their hoods.

"Good, right?"

She nodded without much conviction. She'd heard a few calls of that kind and this wasn't the most inspired, but it was fine.

"Stay focused. Don't open the door for anyone but La Tonina."

La Muda nodded again. *I get it. I get it. There's no need to yell.*

The police chief closed the door carefully behind him and retraced his steps. After checking that there was no one nosing around on the other side, he hopped the wall and walked back through the chapel, passing the man in the wheelchair and exiting the way he'd come.

The mother superior was waiting for him as he reached the main entrance.

"May God bless you, Chief."

"And you as well, Reverend Mother."

As the Suburban drove off, the mother superior looked at the smiling, blue-eyed nun at her side.

"The world could use more men like him."

4

Margarito arrived at city hall just as the ceremony was about to begin. The new mayor and his team saw him enter the legislative chamber through the side door, but acted as though he didn't exist. Unsurprisingly, every aspect of the event was designed to keep everyone at least ten feet from the new mayor, so he wouldn't have to shake anyone's hand.

He wasn't yet forty, but the port's highest-ranking councilman was already a household name nationally. The chief had contributed to his fame—though not as the mayor would have liked—with that business about the foreign girl who took a ten-story fall from one of his parties. More recently, after announcing his candidacy he'd visited every major tourist beach in the country—Isla Mujeres, Cancún, Puerto Vallarta, Huatulco, Ixtapa, Los Cabos—and then moved on to Miami, Cartagena, Rio de Janeiro, and even Mar del Plata. He claimed that those places had inspired him to turn La Eternidad into a first-world waterfront and that he was going to transform the town into a tourist destination of their caliber. At least, that was his campaign promise.

He seemed younger than he had the last time Margarito had seen him, like he'd gotten rid of a few wrinkles. And then there was that blond hair—as silky as a woman's and teased so high it eclipsed even his bad reputation—and his lips, which plumply suggested a plastic surgeon's intervention. When he saw Margarito, the mayor pursed those lips and thrust out his chin, shaking the locks that framed his face. The chief said nothing, but he was not a fan of the man's coif.

A moment before the ceremony began, he noticed El Flaco gesturing to him from the hallway.

"What's up?"

"We got them, sir. They say they're from Chiapas, but their accents are Central American." The chief had almost forgotten about the suspicious characters he'd seen near city hall. El Flaco had done a good job. "Their arms are covered in tattoos. Could be a couple of the Maras they're looking for in Tampico. I sent them to headquarters for a chat."

"Were they clean?"

"They didn't have weapons or drugs on them. One other thing . . ." El Flaco gestured toward the parking lot with his chin. "Your son's security detail wants us to turn over the patrol vehicles. I told them they can have them once we've gone back to the office and signed what needs to be signed. That until then, they can walk. Right, boss?"

The chief looked at his son. "Give them your vehicle and tell El Dorado to take my son in the Suburban. You and I will follow in the other squad car with La Tonina. Everyone else should go back to the office after the event."

"Yes, sir," El Flaco replied and left.

Just then Margarito's cell phone rang with a call he needed to take: it was the federal agent investigating the threat on his life. The night before, fully aware of the risk, the chief had decided he'd need the help of Adrián Melgoza, a young technician from Los Coquitos he'd personally sent through the police academy and who was now working for the federales in the Department of Intelligence. Extortion and kidnapping had become such a huge problem in the past few years that the government had been forced to train a new generation of police officers in computer science and cybernetics so they could identify and trace suspicious calls from the country's capital. The chief had called Adrián on his private line and asked him to trace the threat, without his superiors' finding out. The kid had promised to look into it the next day, as soon as he got to the office. So the chief slipped out onto the terrace with all the discretion he could muster.

The best thing about city hall was the little terrace on the second floor, overlooking the water. It was a shame he'd spent so much time inside that building over the years and so little time out there. But he hadn't come to admire the view.

"I'm sorry," the agent said. "I did the best I could, but I hit a wall."

The young man apologetically explained that the caller had used a distortion device, which made it impossible to know exactly where the signal had come from. The only thing he could say for certain was that the call had been made somewhere in the vicinity of La Eternidad.

"Could the call have come from the federal prison?"

The chief knew, because he himself had allowed it, that there was no shortage of prisoners in La Eternidad's penal system who extorted money over the phone and who used devices to distort the signal so their victims couldn't trace the call. They called random numbers or homes suggested by a contact on the outside in the middle of the night, claiming to have kidnapped a close relative of the person on the other end of the line. If the victims got scared enough, they'd take out a bunch of cash from an ATM and leave the supposed ransom in a remote location. It was one of the most common forms of quickie kidnapping: the fake kind. The chief knew all the culprits. He'd trained them himself and taken a share of their profits. He had to make money somehow, now that he wasn't allowed to sell stolen cars. But the specialist put an end to his concerns.

"Not plausible. It's too far outside the area." When Margarito didn't respond, he added, "Would you like us to put a tap on your phone, Chief? That would let us see where the call is coming from, if they contact you again."

Margarito didn't even have to think about that one. He couldn't afford to have them record any of the other conversations he had on his personal phone. And that thing was going to be getting some serious use over the next few hours.

"No, thanks. I'd rather not. But I appreciate your help."

He was about to pull a cigarette from his pack when he noticed that someone had followed him outside.

A gringo with thinning hair approached, offering a light. It took Margarito a minute to place him: it was Consul Don Williams, one of the most annoying men he'd ever met. He looked gaunt.

"My dear Consul, how are you doing?"

"Margarito. I didn't think you remembered me. I've been waving at you."

The chief told himself it was time to get a good pair of glasses; he hadn't seen the man at all.

"Tell me, Consul, what can I do for you?"

"I was just wondering if you've found anything in connection to Cristina de León's kidnapping."

A seagull flew by.

"Ah, my dear Consul. I can only divulge that information to the girl's parents. And, as I understand it, you're no longer advising them."

Williams shot him a fiery look.

"It was interesting, don't you think, how your patrol vehicles blocked the exit of Mr. De León's residential community. Cost us valuable time."

"I already told you, we were pursuing a fugitive. It was a matter of public safety."

"Say whatever you like, but when we were finally able to respond to the call for help, all we found was one of Rafael de León's bodyguards, dead in an empty house. And the lead detective on the case, missing. As if the guilty party wanted to cover his tracks."

"Don't get too wrapped up in this, Consul. I know more than one guy who spent his last days mulling over these cases. Let it go. Enjoy your retirement."

The gringo exploded at him.

"You'll see soon enough what it's like to fall from power. Everyone's going to be coming for you. Run while you still can, Margarito."

The policeman smiled broadly.

"I appreciate the advice. Hey, do you remember the package of product that went missing when they seized that American plane? They say a package like that could buy a house on the beach. In California, say . . ."

He heard a round of applause and looked inside to see that the mayor had started without him. *You son of a bitch,* he thought. *What an asshole you turned out to be.*

"If you'll excuse me, I should head back inside. See you around, Williams."

He turned back one last time before opening the door.

"Malibu. That's the beach I was thinking of."

They'd had so many run-ins over the past few years they hardly bothered him anymore. He'd lost track of the consul for a while, and now he was back. Some gringos could get attached to a jail cell after working there for a day.

Margarito took the first empty seat he saw in the audience. He scanned the other attendees and was surprised to see his ex-wife in the front row, next to the deadbeat who followed her everywhere, supposedly her new partner. Pino Panetta was his name; he was another Italian who'd decided to put down roots in La Eternidad. Slim and blond, he owned the restaurant La Buona Notte and was known in the late nineties—when Margarito and his wife were separating—for being quite the ladies' man. *A real Casanothing*, thought the chief, who couldn't stand the guy and used to encourage his men to park the department's old Jeep in front of his restaurant, blocking the entrance. He smiled at his wife, but she just rolled her eyes. The chief cursed under his breath when his greeting was returned by a nod from her companion.

Seated just behind them was La Eternidad's new generation of politicians, the luxury models. There were the dazzling councilmen, the campaign advisers, and the port's resident moneybags— all of them with fancy moisturizer on their faces and lovely wives on their arms. More than one avoided his eyes. *Ingrates*, thought the chief. All right, so he'd been blackmailing a few of them recently, but he'd also preserved some semblance of order in the port, which meant they weren't bothered by every delinquent with a sense of initiative. Besides, that degree of disdain hardly seemed gentlemanly, to quote his old friend Detective Elijah. *Fucking Elijah, I'd like to hear what he'd have to say about all this.*

"The nerve of that old bastard, showing up here . . ."

The comment came from the middle of the crowd, where the unruliest attendees were sitting. He immediately picked out the ones who'd given him the most trouble over the years: human rights advocates who recently started taking positions in the government, and a few key figures for the opposition—the widow whose husband had been killed at a military checkpoint, the students who'd suffered bullet wounds on their way to class, the woman who led an organization demanding the safe return of missing husbands and relatives, the man who ran an orphanage for children who'd lost their parents to the violence. The only ones who'd shown up to support him were his security detail and the inner circle made up of his secretary, Robusta, plus El Sony, La Gordis, and El Chino.

In the back, flanked by a small detail of soldiers, General Rovirosa greeted him with a wave. *Now there's a professional.* The Three Stooges were also in attendance, standing closer to the mayor's men than to his own; if they'd seen him, they weren't showing much enthusiasm. His seven colleagues from the office, counting Cástulo, the old night watchman, stood in the back with La Caterpillar, who sometimes turned up around there. They were the only ones who shouted "Bravo!" when they saw him; of the group, only La Cat applauded.

"Gentlemen," said the mayor, flashing the journalists a cardboard smile. "The city I've been elected to serve is about to be strengthened by one of the most respected officers who have ever worked for the local police force. His reputation for fulfilling his duties with exemplary zeal precedes him. We have no doubt his presence will help us move past this period of instability that has so negatively affected the image of La Eternidad."

He said a new generation stepped in to replace the old every fifteen years in all human societies, and it was his time to take over. The port was going to become one of the country's foremost tourist destinations.

"There will be palm trees running the length of this street, yachts docked offshore, new restaurants and hotels. We'll lay new cobblestones, build benches for the little old ladies to enjoy, pave the road to the airport. Like all of you, I want to turn La Eternidad into a better place to live."

By that point, Margarito had stopped listening.

"And we are confident that our new chief of police will be a great asset in this decisive war we have declared on crime."

Decisive? thought Margarito. *Only if you mean you've decided to lose. I haven't seen any new weapons, uniforms, or patrol cars.*

Without a single kind word about Margarito's nearly thirty years of service, the mayor talked about the future and the political party that had just risen to power after more than eighty years of corruption in the city. Maybe the chief was being paranoid, but he felt like certain jabs were directed at him. The mayor criticized the many sins of the old system, like hiring untrained, superstitious individuals with proven criminal ties: long-haired, easygoing dead-beats who lived in their swim trunks. His gaze fell on the twenty young men and women fresh out of the academy, standing guard with their backs to the mayor and new police chief, well groomed and purposeful, dressed in white. To Margarito, they looked like they were about to take their First Communion.

"I have one question for you, Ricardo. How far are you willing to take this fight?"

"I'll do whatever it takes."

"You have my full support."

As if they'd rehearsed it, the audience immediately erupted in applause. The politician smiled, his blue eyes and wavy blond hair accenting his warm, earnest expression, and he reached out to shake Ricardo's hand in a flurry of camera flashes. A man to the chief's right commented to the woman beside him that the mayor was on his way to a governorship. When the applause and flashes died down, the young lady from public relations handed Margarito an envelope.

"Your letter of resignation is inside. The mayor asks you to please sign it."

Margarito took the envelope, folded it, and shoved it into his back pocket.

"Tell him I'll send it to him," he said.

The girl seemed horrified by where he'd stowed the letter, but left without another word.

The mayor's communications team had done a good job: most of the questions posed to the group seated at the table seemed to have been set ahead of time. The journalists asked Ricardo if he would give preferential treatment to any of the criminal organizations that were devastating the region. "Absolutely not," he replied, saying he would throw the full weight of the law at anyone who threatened public order. They asked him if he planned to use any of the knowledge he'd acquired abroad, and he answered that he was ready and willing to do so. Finally, they asked if he would be bringing on and training more officers. Ricardo looked discreetly at the mayor, who was still wearing his frozen smile. Catching the gesture, he responded immediately.

"Of course he will. We'll make sure he has all the resources he needs. Otherwise we wouldn't have offered him the job. And that," the mayor asserted, "will be all for the question and answer. The new chief has work to do."

The mayor was already rising from his seat when he saw Juan de Dios, who'd arrived late, raise his hand.

"Juan de Dios Cuevas, for *Proceso*. I was wondering, Chief, if you're going to look the other way on what's been happening around there these past few months or if you plan to do your job. We've had crimes of extraordinary violence here every few weeks for the past two years, and none of those cases have ever been solved. They weren't even investigated by your predecessor. Where do you stand on this?"

Ricardo cleared his throat. "If I may . . ."

The camera lights went on again and the reporters aimed their recording devices at the nearest loudspeaker.

"If you're referring to the mass killings on the outskirts of the city, the law will deal with those crimes as it would with any other. Every crime will be investigated. That's one of my main objectives."

"Even yesterday's massacre of twenty people off Highway 180?"

"That crime is a high priority. In fact, I'm planning to investigate it myself."

There was a moment of enthusiastic applause, but the reporter did not let go of the microphone. Instead, he took the opportunity to address the mayor.

"Your Honor, what are your thoughts on the rumors regarding the hotel industry, specifically those that indicate collusion—"

The mayor pursed his pouty lips. "I'm under no obligation to respond to those slanderous allegations against my administration. I was elected by the people of this city, and I will answer to them if called upon to do so. I will not answer to malicious critics."

To Margarito's surprise, the comment was met by a wave of whistles and applause among the municipal employees. *He's got them all in his pocket,* he thought. He signaled to El Dorado and La Tonina, and they approached his son.

"Whenever you're ready, we'll take you over."

"There's no need. My team is here. I'll see you at the office, to take care of the paperwork."

Margarito shook his head while Ricardo instructed his future assistant on how to prepare the convoy.

"These guys don't look like they have any experience at all. Let me take you."

Ricardo looked him in the eyes and shook his head.

"I'll see you at headquarters. Bring a lawyer."

Margarito gestured to El Dorado and La Tonina, who headed downstairs beside him. They ended up in a shoving match with the new security detail, which wasn't even in the same weight class as them. Without meaning to, they bumped into one of the human rights advocates as they passed.

As he stepped into the hall, Margarito noticed how the nearby gardens were catching the morning sun, flashes of green and yellow illuminating the palm fronds. But he'd have plenty of time to take in the landscape soon enough—that is, if they didn't send him to the clink. For now, he headed down to the parking lot where Ricardo and his secretary had already climbed into the Suburban and closed the doors, indicating they didn't want company. When he saw El Flaco in the pickup La Tonina had been driving back at the airport, he turned and hurried to the truck, which sat there with a door slung open for him.

He watched one of his vehicles, carrying two of the new recruits, pass the Suburban and exit the parking lot. The driver clearly didn't know the port very well, because he stopped when they got to the gate. Eventually, he pulled out to the right and the Suburban followed, with El Dorado at the wheel and Ricardo and his assistant inside.

He caught his son's eye only once. At the very last moment, Ricardo had smiled and waved to his father. The chief tried his best to do the same, though he knew his sadness was written all over his face.

As soon as he sat down in the back seat of the dual-cabin truck where El Flaco and La Tonina were waiting for him, he cursed the fact that the vehicle didn't have air-conditioning in the back. The leather upholstery had gotten as hot as hell itself. He'd have to keep the window open.

"Step on it, goddammit," he said. "Don't lose them."

"All right, boss. I'm on it," La Tonina replied, though at that point he couldn't have cared less about getting anywhere on time.

To the chief's surprise, instead of heading for the waterfront, which would have been the obvious choice, the first vehicle in the convoy took a cobblestone side street that was often jammed with cars parked along the right-hand side. *For fuck's sake, these guys are green*, he thought. But he was in no position to give orders anymore. The first beads of sweat dripped from his forehead; the heat was suffocating. He felt a weight on his chest and opened the top button of his shirt. In the front seat, El Flaco turned the air all the way up.

As was always the case at that time of day, the streets were full of people: women taking their children to school, nine-to-fivers running to work, vendors selling fried food, old ladies on their way to the supermarket, gringos and tourists looking for a nice place to have breakfast.

The chief's mind was on his immediate future. He'd been hoping that one of the politicians he knew would offer him another gig, so he could hang on to some of the benefits of being a government employee. But the hour had come, and none of them were returning his calls, so it looked like the transfer of power would take place as planned in a few minutes. He glanced at El Flaco and La Tonina. Most of his men were probably right behind him on his way out the door.

When the vehicle at the head of the convoy reached the corner of Matamoros and Allende, he saw a gas tanker up ahead of it pull out in reverse, blocking the street. *Nice driving, genius*, he thought. The convoy waited for the tanker truck to park. He saw the typical trio of street kids come running toward them, jockeying among themselves to wipe the vehicles' windshields for some spare change. They smiled like piranhas as they approached. The look of desperation. And what if he stopped messing around and just asked his godson for a job? He knew how to keep an eye out for the law.

"Fuck!"

La Tonina slammed on the brakes. Margarito was about to give him hell when he saw the driver reach for his sidearm.

And then he understood.

He saw the smiles frozen on the faces of the boys—who weren't actually boys, just short and skinny—and he saw that the smiles were just a disguise. If there was one thing he couldn't stand, it was criminals who smiled before they struck.

It felt as if a crowd was throwing stones at the dual-cabin truck; the air around him buzzed as a second wave of hail crashed against the left side of the vehicle. La Tonina and El Flaco began to shake as if someone had dropped scorpions down their shirts, and the spiderwebs covering the front windshield made it impossible to see. The chief felt his shoulder whip back and noticed a hole in his shirt. La Tonina launched forward, a little out of sync with the hailstorm blanketing them. The burning in his shoulder got worse. Before he could grasp what was happening, he saw El Flaco slump over and fall sideways onto La Tonina's lap. The vehicle rolled a few feet and hit something, but that didn't stop another hail of bullets from clattering against its left side like angry protesters banging on its doors. The back window shattered and he understood.

A young man in a green hoodie was killing La Tonina. It looked like he was spraying him with blood. Satisfied that his bullets had found their target, he turned his weapon on Margarito. From where the chief sat, the gun looked like a toy.

The thug in the hoodie stepped onto the curb, looking for a better angle. Margarito lost precious seconds struggling with the door on the right-hand side of the vehicle. When he managed to get it open, he fell rather than jumped out, landing with all his weight on his left shoulder. A jolt of pain brought him to his feet, and not a second too soon, because a spray of bullets had taken the spot where he fell.

He crawled back toward the truck and leaned against the rear tire. He knew he needed to draw his weapon, but the pain in his shoulder wouldn't let him. He heard a sound to his left and managed to catch sight of the Suburban up ahead, where El Dorado had pushed open the passenger door and was trying to get out. He couldn't, entirely, but he did manage to draw his gun and aim it at the man shooting at him from beside the gas tanker. *Fuck*, thought Margarito. *We're fucked.* But El Dorado kept firing until his assailant went down. *That's one asshole less, at least.*

Seeing this, a man dressed in black, who looked to be around forty, stopped shooting at the first vehicle in the convoy and bounded toward the Suburban with the efficient movements of a professional. A young man with a long goatee, wearing track pants, followed close behind him. The man in black took careful aim at El Dorado and *bang*, he ended up like La Tonina.

Then, with the same steady hand, he pointed his gun into the Suburban. As if he were hunting deer. It took Margarito a second to realize he was aiming at his son.

"Hey! Asshole!"

In one motion he struggled to his feet, drew, and fired. The man in black and the kid with the goatee both turned and leveled their guns at him. Margarito took cover behind the open door of the vehicle and exchanged shots with them from there, until the man in black caught a bullet to the leg, momentarily used the kid with the goatee as a human shield, and then limped off, disappearing between two parked cars.

Margarito was trying to get the kid's head in his sights when the thug in the hoodie popped up on the other side of the truck. The chief barely had time to duck before he started shooting at him again.

He launched himself toward the nearest vehicle and slumped down, his back against the car's rear fender. From what he could gather, the guy in the hoodie and the one with the goatee had managed to get on either side of him. If they walked toward him on different sides of the vehicle, it was a matter of seconds before they had him. There was nowhere to run.

The dual waves of bullets hit the car in front of him with a hellish clatter. He tried to figure out the nearest attacker's position, but the only thing he could make out clearly was the sound of tourists running for safety. Just one little boy remained, staring at him through the window of an eyeglass shop.

A chilling silence fell over the street.

The chief tried to catch the boy's eye, but he was looking in horror to the police officer's left. He realized there was someone there, about to ambush him. He reached up and emptied his magazine in that direction. The kid with the goatee fired one last spray of bullets in the direction of the shopwindow before landing faceup on the street.

Before he could turn, the thug in the green hoodie appeared on his right, weapon in hand. Suddenly, the young man's other hand jerked up toward his back in search of the knife he imagined was sticking out of it; spitting blood, the thug collapsed right next to him.

For a few moments, the only sound was the first raindrops of a storm falling on the waterfront.

Then came footsteps on broken glass, more shots, and a woman's voice.

"Chief! Over here!"

He didn't answer, but he recognized La Gordis's voice. The smell of gunpowder hung in the air, and the rain had started falling harder, the drops sharp as knives. At the end of the street, he saw a group of girls running and several people huddled in the doorway of a stationery store. A woman on the ground. A man in a white guayabera, shielding another woman behind a column. He heard a siren approach.

He got to his feet and realized the little boy in the eyeglass shop was actually just an image on a poster. La Gordis and the others had almost reached him. He gestured frantically to them, waving one hand.

"They went that way. Go!"

He ran toward the Suburban, looked inside, and then headed for the corner. With his back to the gas tanker, he scanned the street for the man in black. There were no cars around. Just then, it started to pour so hard it seemed like someone had opened a faucet, and he couldn't see anything anymore.

He counted three bodies and a cholo about to expire on the pavement. Chief Margarito, the highest authority on the police force for thirty years, scourge of the people and friend to evildoers, doubled back, crossing through sheets of rain, toward the giant coffin that used to be the Suburban. He looked at his watch. Two hours and twenty minutes had elapsed between the start of the ceremony and the attack.

Two hours twenty, he thought. *You did better than the guy in La Nopalera.*

5

"Nine-millimeter," said General Rovirosa, tossing him a long cylinder barely thicker than a thermometer. As with many instruments of death, its designers tried to give it an appealing look, in this case by making it golden.

The turret lights on the patrol cars tinted the chief's face red, then blue, then red again as he examined the evidence.

"Shot from a Luger Parabellum," the general added, not needing to mention they were known as cop killers because they could pierce bulletproof vests.

General Rovirosa also chose not to mention that the holes in the sides of the vehicles were exceptionally large. In the crew cab truck where Margarito had been, the only way to tell which was La Tonina was the size of the mass hanging out the front window, as if he'd been trying to open the door from the outside.

With all the cynicism he'd developed over a lifetime dedicated to weapons, the general tried to wrap his mind around how Margarito could still be alive. One look at the constellation of bullet holes in the side of his truck was enough to make him wonder if the chief was in collusion with the attackers. Experience had taught him that the officer in question was capable of anything—except compliance with the law. He looked at the policeman, who, curled up in a ball while a paramedic examined his arm, didn't seem to have heard him, and went off to examine the crime scene, leaning as he always did on his wooden cane and followed by the two soldiers who made up his personal security detail. The news had caught him off guard back at city hall; he hadn't even changed out of his dress uniform. In his blue four-button jacket covered by insignias and badges, his cap emblazoned with three stars, his fair complexion, and his wooden cane, he looked radically different from the taciturn soldiers who hung on his every word.

The first things he examined were the bodies of the gunmen. One of them had fallen across the hood of a car, while the other, a young man with a goatee, lay on the cobblestones not far from the ambulance. The entry wound in his chest looked like Margarito's handiwork. He'd seen others who'd run into that particular thirty-eight in the past. He turned to the nearest crime scene investigator, a man with almond-shaped eyes whose name he could never remember.

"Only three of the assailants were killed?"

"There are two more over there."

The general nodded and stepped onto the sidewalk, where the shooter in the green hoodie was lying near another young man, who couldn't have been more than five feet tall.

There wasn't a single pane of glass left in the truck stopped nearest the gas tanker. It looked as if the front windshield had simply dissolved; not even a shard of glass was left at the edges. Where the new recruits had been sitting there was just a scattered, bloody mass mixed with tatters of clothing and car upholstery, as if a pack of rabid dogs had been let loose on them. The general almost lost his balance on all the shell casings.

In the middle, El Dorado was slumped on the pavement under the driver's side door of the Suburban. There'd be no open-casket funeral for him: his remains were beyond makeup. Two white towels requisitioned from a store on the corner were tossed across the back seat. Under the first one was a young police officer and under the second—*holy shit*—what used to be Chief Margarito's son. *Things are about to get ugly around here*, thought the general, raising his eyebrows. Then he turned and walked back to Margarito.

The first thing he saw was the chief's muddy loafers. The paramedic was almost done treating the flesh wound to Margarito's shoulder, and he must have been wrapping those bandages pretty tight, judging from his expression and the way his body tilted to the left. When he saw the general approaching, the chief growled, "What do you make of it?"

The investigators had gathered the weapons from the four dead men, or was it five, on a black cloth they'd stretched across the hood of a car with its windows blown out. They looked like shiny metal toys.

"Uzis," said the general. "First time I've seen them around here."

The police and the military usually found one of two kinds of weapons on criminals lately: the latest technology from the United States or the oldies but goodies from the former Soviet Union. The first could be purchased from any licensed dealer in California, Arizona, New Mexico, or Texas and brought back easily enough across the border. The second kind found their way into Mexico through guerrilla fighters and Central and South American criminals. But neither of these channels tended to traffic in Uzis.

Margarito looked the small, light submachine guns over: easily concealed under clothing, they were made for secret service agents and ministers' bodyguards, but had come to be used in bank robberies all over the world. The perfect instrument for an ambush. They weren't eye-catching or very heavy compared with similar weapons designed to be intimidating.

The general signaled to the soldier standing nearest to him, who leaned over to pick up one of the guns and handed it to him.

With a fluid movement punctuated by a sharp crack, the general removed the magazine and held it at eye level for a moment. He took out a thick pair of glasses, put them on, examined the object again, and then quickly put the glasses back in his breast pocket. He didn't like to be seen wearing them.

"Son of a bitch."

"What?"

"These are fifty-round magazines. You say they only found one per person?"

"That's right."

The general blinked.

"A strange choice, don't you think? Who sends his men into combat with a single magazine?"

Margarito looked up for the first time and nodded.

"The one who seemed to be their leader carried a thirty-eight," he said.

"Exactly," said the general. "You don't send someone into battle without real firepower."

Margarito was starting to get annoyed. The general had a tendency to let his imagination run wild. At this rate, it was only a matter of time before he declared the attack an international conspiracy.

In the light ricocheting across the stormy sky, the chief's face took on a greenish pallor. He was clearly in terrible pain, but he managed not to touch his sling.

"Why don't you go get checked out at the hospital?" asked the general. "We can handle this."

"No way in hell."

It had stopped raining, but there was still a thick fog hanging over the city, and the streams flowing across the cobblestones from higher elevations made preserving the crime scene impossible.

Margarito looked up and saw General Rovirosa's security detail. He didn't like having those toy soldiers around but couldn't say much about it. Military vehicles were blocking off traffic in both directions, and the rest of the barracks had gone out to patrol the city. He'd even seen a sharpshooter positioned on one of the rooftops nearby. But it was going to take a hell of a lot more than a bunch of soldiers and a tree-hugging politician to take control from him that day.

Forensics Agent Pangtay, a.k.a. El Chino, approached the three men. In public, Margarito always kept some distance from him. Even though he'd been the one who hired Pangtay, and even though the man was part of his inner circle, the chief had always figured that sooner or later he was going to have to arrest him for his side gig as a car thief. But the day of his retirement had arrived, and the scandal still hadn't broken.

"If I may, boss," he said, handing him a newspaper clipping sheathed in a plastic bag. "The one in the green hoodie had this on him."

He took the clipping and examined the two photos that had been published side by side less than forty-eight hours earlier, when they'd announced his replacement. On the right was a picture of his son, taken back when he still worked at headquarters. On the left was a picture of him dirty and disheveled with stains all over his shirt. The chief scowled and Pangtay understood it was time for him to go.

Margarito passed the photo to the general, who took a close look at it—glasses on, glasses off again—and handed it back to the chief.

"I was the target," said Margarito softly. "The primary target, at least."

He thought back on the threat he'd received the night before. *Your days are numbered, Chief. I've got bullets here with your name on them.*

"The order could have come from anyone, even from one of our, ahem, associates. You haven't had any trouble with them lately, have you?"

Margarito shook his head.

"Then look, my friend. While you figure out who did this, stay somewhere else for a few days. Change up your routine. They may not have gotten you today, but they're going to be waiting for you. Maybe not in the next couple of hours, but a few days from now you'll go home and find them there, or else it'll be on your way to work. If you were the target and you walked away from the attack, these guys are going to be in a lot of trouble if they don't complete their mission. But I'm not telling you anything you don't already know. Do what you want. It's your life. Would you like us to admit you to the military hospital?"

General Rovirosa owed Margarito one, and it was time to make good. But the chief of police shook his head.

"Send a detail to protect my wife and another one to keep an eye on my son's funeral in case any of those shits turn up."

"What are you going to do?"

Margarito and the general had been informants and accomplices of the local criminal organizations for years, but he'd have to be crazy to tell him anything, so he just grunted.

"Here," Rovirosa said, offering him the gun one of his guards had been carrying. "Take this. For that time you helped me."

"Did you forget? I have plenty," said the chief, heading back to the scene of the crime.

The general was speechless. When a shipment of weapons fresh from the States had been stolen from one of his men a year earlier, he'd suspected the chief of being behind it and their friendship had cooled as a result. With him, anything was possible. Was Margarito actually admitting he'd had something to do with the guns that disappeared from Captain López's luggage?

La Gordis walked up to the chief and asked if he needed anything.

"Hold on," he said, doubling over. It felt like his arm was going to explode.

"If you don't let someone take a look at that, you're going to pass out," she said, worried.

The chief hadn't stopped moving since the emergency responders covered his son's body: hauling himself around tirelessly, he'd examined different aspects of the crime scene, talked with the investigator in charge, reprimanded him half-heartedly, and had a look at the deceased.

But La Gordis hadn't taken any breaks, either. She was the first on the scene, even though she'd come running from city hall, dragging Pangtay and the other officers behind her. The chief wouldn't be alive if it hadn't been for her: when they arrived firing into the air, they'd scared off the man in black and his thugs. After she'd taken in the horror of the attack, La Gordis located and interviewed the witnesses left inside the surrounding establishments, even though none of them could offer anything substantial. Basically, they saw the police officers start shooting after the attack began, mistook it for a battle between criminal organizations, and ducked for cover wherever they could.

It did not escape the general's attention that the chief hadn't exchanged a word with Bracamontes, who was also on the scene. Or that they were staring at one another like a couple of dogs who'd just been in a fight, the chief at the crime scene and Bracamontes sitting on the hood of an ambulance at the end of the street holding a gauze pad to the side of his face.

If anyone in that city deserved a prize, it was the paramedics. The first ambulance arrived on the scene before the police, and the paramedics proved to be the only compassionate human beings for miles around. When Margarito saw their vehicle approaching moments after the attack, he waved them over with his right arm.

"Over here!"

Two EMTs and a doctor ran toward him. As they approached, their faces reflected their alarm and dismay at the condition of the bodies they passed, but they didn't stop: it was clear that no one could survive injuries like those.

"He's still alive," said Margarito.

Dr. José Luis Rodríguez leaned over the young man in the chief's arms and scanned his chest visually. Then he put on his stethoscope and listened to his heart for what seemed like an eternity while simultaneously checking his wrist for a pulse. Meanwhile, drops of rainwater continued to fall from a few nearby awnings.

"When did this happen?"

"Twenty or thirty minutes ago," La Gordis replied.

The doctor nodded and felt the other arm, then moved his stethoscope.

"There's no sign of life, sir," he finally concluded. "If you're feeling a pulse, it's probably your own. This individual is deceased."

The chief's eyes opened very wide, as if he saw something enormous approaching. It was the feral hound named Sorrow come to visit. She stood almost seven feet tall.

La Gordis furtively wiped away her tears two, three, countless times, until she was eventually forced to turn and move a few paces away. The chief also stepped back from the vehicle, to give the paramedics room to work. A little while later a second, unnecessary ambulance arrived. More people had begun to gather at the corner, asking what was going on. El Sony and

Peralta brought them up to speed as best they could and kept them from getting too close.

After confirming there were no survivors in the Suburban, the doctor apologized to the chief.

"I'm sorry, sir. I didn't realize he was your son. If you'll excuse us, we have to go see to the others," Dr. Rodríguez said and went to check if there were any survivors in the first vehicle.

"Flatliners." The two individuals in the truck were dead.

"Jesus," one of the medics sighed. The victims were in such bad shape there wasn't any point in checking their vitals.

"I've got one alive over here!" called one of the paramedics. The doctor ran over to the crew cab truck. To the chief's surprise, El Flaco was still breathing.

"Entry and exit wounds in the right shoulder, multiple hits to the left arm. Let's get him to the ambulance. He needs immediate medical attention."

El Flaco was alive.

Margarito watched them put him on a gurney and load him into the ambulance.

Bracamontes and the Block had shown up almost thirty minutes after the fact. Thirty minutes in such a small city is inexcusable, especially if you're in a police vehicle and don't have to stop for red lights—even more so if it's your boss who's under fire. They announced their arrival several blocks away with a blaring siren, came to a screeching halt, and got out to examine the scene of the crime in such a hurry they didn't even notice that Margarito was alive and staring at them while Pangtay and La Gordis held him upright.

Bracamontes and the Block made no attempt to avoid the sea of shell casings covering the road as they entered the crime scene. It almost seemed as if they were looking for something. *Or someone,* thought the chief.

"This one's alive!" grunted the Block.

He looked over and saw that the cholo with the goatee was still breathing. He had collapsed between two cars.

The paramedics rushed over immediately.

"Motherfucker!" grunted Bracamontes, trying to keep his balance. "Hold on, hold on," he said, stopping the paramedics with a wave of his hand.

He flipped the cholo over with his foot and aimed his gun at his head.

"Who hired you? Answer me! Who hired you?"

But he wasn't about to get an answer. The man was practically a cadaver. His skin looked like candle wax and his eyes kept rolling back in his head.

"Look," Dr. Rodríguez interjected. "This man is in shock. Step aside."

But Bracamontes didn't move.

"Not talking, kid? Not gonna answer me?"

He lifted his handgun and brought it down hard on the man's face. The cholo passed out on the cobblestones.

"You animal!" shouted Dr. Rodríguez.

Chief Margarito broke free of his assistants, drew his gun, and headed for Bracamontes; the Block alerted him with a movement of his jaw.

Bracamontes paused for a second but pulled himself together and called out to his boss.

"What are you so worked up about, cabrón? You didn't expect him to walk out of here with a smile on his face, did you?"

For a reply, the chief raised his good arm, the one holding his gun, and fired at the ground. Everyone in the vicinity ducked and covered, including Bracamontes. Margarito leveled off at his face.

"Jesus, man!" shouted Bracamontes, but the chief didn't answer, so he took out his piece between two fingers and held it as far away from his body as he could, as if to assure Margarito that he was unarmed and not about to try anything.

"Easy man, easy. You're in shock."

As he said this, though, he signaled the Block, whose hand slowly started to move toward his back. The chief caught this out of the corner of his eye and fired at the ground inches from the Block's feet.

"Fuck!" exclaimed Bracamontes, throwing himself to the ground. If he was hoping to find safety there, he was out of luck: the chief didn't waste a second in pointing his gun at him. Bracamontes went pale. "I'm unarmed, man. I'm unarmed."

Right then, the second ambulance, which had just arrived from the direction of the waterfront, pulled up behind Bracamontes's patrol vehicle. The driver stuck his head out the window and was about to ask a question when he saw the chief pointing his weapon at two police officers, who had their hands in the air.

"Wait a sec, hold on," the doctor cautioned the driver. "We got here a little early this time." Since the violence started, it was a good idea to show up as late as possible to avoid running into trouble.

Bracamontes, trying to reason with Margarito, insisted he was unarmed. "Seriously, cabrón. I swear."

But La Gordis had to intervene, tugging on the chief's good arm to get him to lower his weapon.

"Don't, boss. Don't do anything you'll regret."

She tried to pull him back toward the ambulance, but Margarito kept his gun aimed at his colleague, who eventually got to his feet.

"Get out of here and don't even think about coming back."

"You're fucking nuts, old man," Bracamontes growled.

The chief head-butted the policeman, who fell back down to his knees. Seeing the Block reach for his back again, he aimed his gun at him.

The Block froze. Bracamontes, meanwhile, was writhing on the ground with his face in his hands.

La Gordis wrapped her arms around her boss to keep him from doing anything worse and called the paramedics over, who ran to help Bracamontes.

Miraculously, if one can talk about miracles at the end of a firefight, the military convoy arrived. The soldiers fanned out, securing both ends of the street. For a second, the police officers thought, *They've come back to finish us off.* But no: General Rovirosa stepped from their midst with an escort of half a dozen soldiers and headed straight for the chief.

"We're here to secure the crime scene. What's the situation?"

But the chief was in no condition to explain the situation. His eyes were glued to Bracamontes, who was still holding the piece of gauze to his right cheek while he cursed or spat at the ground behind his squad car, all without taking his eyes off Margarito. Then the chief saw him bring his cell phone to his ear.

At some point, the medics convinced him to let them take a look at him too. He got into the second ambulance so they could clean the wound in his shoulder.

"You're lucky, Chief. It's just a flesh wound."

"I can't move my arm," he said. "It feels dead."

Hearing this, Dr. Rodríguez left El Flaco in the hands of his colleagues for a moment and came back over to examine him.

Margarito flinched when the doctor lifted his arm.

"Oh!" exclaimed Dr. Rodríguez.

The chief, whose pain was getting worse by the minute, noticed one of the paramedics staring at him.

"What are you looking at?"

"Forgive him," the doctor said, apologetically. "He's never seen someone survive a firefight like this one. Good luck is so rare in this line of work."

Dr. Rodríguez lifted the arm again, and the chief writhed in pain.

The young doctor helped him into the ambulance and asked him to lie down on the gurney. He could tell by the look on the chief's face how much he was suffering.

"I'll give you something for the pain," he said. "And in a minute we'll take you to the hospital. I have to cut your shirt in order to examine you."

Before he even finished his sentence, he had already removed the shirt's left sleeve and a good part of the front.

"Hard to believe, coming out of all this with just a flesh wound."

"Should we give him an NSAID?" the paramedic asked.

"It wouldn't do any good," the doctor replied. "Look at him."

The paramedic nodded.

"He's going to need an opioid. The pain will be too much, otherwise."

"Keta?"

"Probably, but first, the diagnosis. Write this down. Lateral and frontal contusions. Superficial lacerations on the elbows and forearms, plus the flesh wound on this shoulder, but that's all. Incredible. Clean that up there. Yes, perfect."

Margarito had groaned when the doctor touched his shoulder, but he almost shot through the roof of the ambulance when he lifted his arm again.

"Ufff! What is that?"

"Your shoulder's been dislocated. I need to . . . Yes, I know it's unpleasant, but I'll get it set in no time."

And, without giving him a moment to object, the doctor put the chief's shoulder back in its socket.

"Mmmphf," groaned Margarito.

"We've treated the luxation, but there's a lot of swelling. If the arm stays that way, you'll need to have it looked at by the hospital staff. We don't want you losing it."

"Why would I lose it?"

"If the swelling keeps up, it could necrotize. They'll need to make a few incisions to relieve the pressure."

"Is it absolutely necessary?"

"You need to keep an eye on this."

"I don't have time to go to the hospital. Give me something to help with the pain. I have to get back to the investigation."

The medics looked at one another.

"We aren't authorized. It would be illegal."

"I'm the chief of police."

"They'd take away our licenses. And anyway, I'm telling you that arm should be kept under observation."

"If you don't give me something," the chief insisted, "the men responsible for this are going to get away. I can't go to the hospital until I catch them."

The physicians exchanged a look.

"I'm sorry, Chief, but I'm not doing anything illegal," said the doctor. "Here's an anti-inflammatory and an analgesic. If you'd like me to take you to the hospital, let me know. That's all I can do for you," he concluded, stepping out of the ambulance.

Once he was out of earshot, the paramedic approached Margarito.

"I've got this friend. I mean, I know this guy who might be able to give you something, if you can't get to the hospital. He's studying to be an anesthesiologist, and he does this. I mean, he'd do this, as like an exception to help you out. But it, you know, would be nice if you'd pass him a little something, a tip. Ask him for buprenorphine. That's what you need."

"Bu . . . pre . . . ? You call him."

"All right. Hold on." The young man walked to the corner with his cell phone in hand and returned almost immediately.

"Okay. He's on his way to buy the stuff now. Where—"

"Tell him to wait for me in the Parque de la Petrolera. By the theater. I'll call him when I get there. What's his number?"

"Whatever you say, Chief." The paramedic leaned forward, wrote the number on a crumpled sheet of paper, and handed it to Margarito.

The general was nearly done surveying the scene when he discovered none other than Flaco Ibarra on a gurney in an ambulance, lying in a pool of his own blood. Rovirosa popped his head in to take a look.

He'd run into El Flaco several times over the years the man had spent as secretary, assistant, partner, and accomplice to Margarito. When their contacts in the trade were feeling appreciative, they would sometimes send a bag of money from the chief's offices to the military base. Sometimes the direction was reversed, but Flaco Ibarra was always the bag man. A loyal, efficient, and discreet individual. *Too bad he never enlisted.*

"How's he doing?" he asked the doctor, noticing that either death or medication had closed El Flaco's eyes.

"Multiple gunshots, not all with exit wounds. We've tried to stop the hemorrhaging, but we've got to get him to a hospital right away," replied Dr. Rodríguez. With the stocky, headstrong EMT who'd earned himself the nickname Speedy González behind the wheel, his was the only ambulance that still made it to every call on time. They threatened his life on a daily basis and blocked his way into certain neighborhoods, but Dr. Rodríguez had become a specialist in firefights over the course of a harrowing three years. Which is why he looked at the general and said, "The chief should go with you. There could be complications if he doesn't get his arm looked at."

When he realized the general wasn't going to do anything to convince the police officer either, the doctor snapped, "Well, then, if you'll excuse me, this man requires immediate attention."

Just as the general was about to step out of the ambulance, El Flaco reached out and grabbed his arm. Terror welled in his eyes. It was fairly common, after a shoot-out, for the gunmen to go after their target in the hospital and finish him off.

"Don't worry," said the general, understanding his fear. "I'll make sure you have a bodyguard. You"—he pointed to one of the men with him—"don't let him out of your sight. Not even in the operating room. And you"—he pointed to the other—"go tell Sergeant Domínguez to set up a security detail at the hospital and to give the ambulance an escort."

To the paramedic's surprise, the first soldier climbed into the ambulance and stood in one corner of the vehicle. The general noticed that El Flaco seemed to have no idea what was going on, so he nodded his good-bye. Dr. Rodríguez banged twice on the vehicle's roof to let the driver know it was time to head out and closed the ambulance door from inside.

Once he was certain the Jeep was clearing a path for the ambulance, General Rovirosa went back to the chief, who was standing next to the Suburban. As he got closer, he noticed that Margarito's cell phone was ringing, but the policeman seemed to have no intention of picking up.

"That one over there," he said quietly, pointing at a soldier who was staring at them intently, "has a package of the usual on him." Meaning coke. "Say the word and we'll slip it in with the gunmen and leave the rest to the attorney general."

In other words, their usual technique for washing their hands of a crime. They'd been doing things that way for years. But the policeman shook his head.

"Don't even think about it."

"Are you sure?"

The chief nodded.

His ears were still ringing, and the pain in his arm had gotten worse.

The general's phone rang. Rovirosa answered, grunted his agreement two or three times, and turned to the chief.

"It's the mayor, for you."

Before he could do anything, the phone was in Margarito's hand.

"Chief, how are you?"

"Alive," he answered, his voice sharp with pain.

"I'm so sorry about what happened. It's a tragedy. They tell me you're badly injured. You have the full support of city hall: If you need to go to a private clinic, we'll cover the expense. I told Bracamontes he should see personally to your safety. Go get some rest."

The chief felt a bitter taste rise in his throat.

"I just gave Bracamontes a different assignment," he retorted. "Thank you for your concern, but until you say otherwise, I'm still the chief of police around here."

"What? No, no, none of that. Get to a hospital. Get yourself checked out. We'll find a replacement for you."

"No, sir. I'm going to handle this myself."

The mayor didn't answer right away. He needed to weigh his options, determine the most politically advantageous move. Would he win more support if he forced Margarito's resignation?

"Let me think," he said. "I'll call you back in five minutes."
And he hung up.

That's when Margarito's arm really started to hurt. He called
over La Gordis, who knew his family, and handed her his cell phone.

"Call Dr. Antonelli and tell her what happened. Tell her we're
going to get him out of here as soon as we can. Then have El
Carcamán ask Robusta for some money from petty cash and start
making arrangements at the funeral home."

And then he went off to yell at the crime scene investigator
who was still busy sketching the victims.

"How much longer, cabrón?"

"I'm almost done."

The general joined them.

"How many do you think there were? How many got away?"

He thought about the guy in black athletic gear and all the
footsteps he heard to his left, toward the stores.

"Three, at least, plus the dead ones. Maybe four."

Rovirosa did the math.

"That makes nine or ten gunmen. You were eight. Ten against
eight? That's no strategy: no one would plan an ambush with
such a narrow advantage unless they were desperate. You might
have better weapons and the element of surprise, but you need
more people for a classic three-on-one."

A little light went on in the policeman's mind.

"They shot at the vehicle up front first, then came for us at
the back of the convoy. They went after the Suburban last."

The general dried his forehead and went on.

"They didn't expect you. If you hadn't been here, it would
have been ten on five: two shooters per target. Now, that would
have been a workable ambush."

The chief looked toward the end of the street where the fog
was still rolling in and said nothing.

"In that case, we can draw one conclusion," the general continued. "The crew might have been improvised. No army would ever enlist these fucking runts. But whoever planned the attack had military training."

To Margarito, this explained the efficiency of the ambush and the stance of the man in black as he approached. He saw it all in front of him, as if the attack were happening again: the man took two steps, paused, and fired; then took another two steps as he readied his weapon, aimed it, and fired; it at the Suburban.

"Anyway," said the general, shaking his head, "what are you going to do?"

"I haven't turned in my resignation yet. I'm still the chief of police."

"What do you mean?"

"I mean I'm going to lay down the law."

The general thought to himself that he was talking to a corpse, but he nodded solemnly and said, "We'll be in touch, then. One squadron will stay here to secure the crime scene." With that, he gave a military salute and left.

Margarito looked out over the scene and thought, *What a fucking farce.*

As soon as the general was gone, the chief opened his left hand and noticed that he'd been holding the nine-millimeter casing the whole time.

Conversation in the dark

"Did you hear?"

"Yeah, I heard. That's why I came. But I didn't have nothing do with it."

"This is the first time something like this happened here in the port."

"It's unbelievable: how could they screw up like that at such close range?"

"His plan was shit. Or his hand shook."

"He choked. Or he's getting old."

"The bastard's going to pay, though. Imagine, screwing up a close-range job like that? This thing just got personal."

"They say there's a reward for anyone who can finish the job."

"Sure, they say that. They also said they were going to retire Margarito, but he's still kicking around."

"The problem was the crew. Why use outside guys? You can't trust them. Our guys, though, you know where their family is, who their parents are, what school their kids go to. You can hold them accountable."

"It doesn't work like that anymore. All of a sudden, we had to start hiring from other states, sometimes even from other countries, to keep the locals in check. It's all because of the competition. That's why he hired guys from outside, and they're all dead now."

"And Margarito's still out there."

"Not for long. They're warming up the pits of hell for him."

"We'll see."

"Yeah, we'll see. One thing's for sure, though: someone's going to pay for his sins."

6

As they were loading his son's body into the second ambulance, one of his cell phones rang—the one only a select few had the number for. He had to take the call. He stepped away to answer and a familiar raspy voice cut right to the chase.

"You alive, Margarito?"

"Still here."

"Your son is dead."

"Seems so. Do you have something to say to me?"

Silence on the other end of the line.

"We need to talk."

"Whenever you like."

"Tonight at eight, at the usual spot. Come alone, no tails."

"I'll be there."

He hung up. As he did, he noticed that his neck hurt. *This is nothing*, he thought. The real stress was just beginning.

Seeing that the street and the rooftops of the nearby buildings had started to fill with onlookers, La Gordis suggested he clear out.

"Give me a minute."

The chief sat on the fender of a patrol vehicle and watched a flock of pelicans flying toward the pier.

"Get El Carcamán and Forensics," he ordered.

La Gordis nodded and noticed that her cell phone was vibrating. It was the mayor again, so she passed him to her boss.

"In light of what happened, you have forty-eight hours to clear this up. But hear this: I need you to go back to headquarters immediately. People are starting to talk about ungovernability. I need them to see you working. My government is not going to run and hide."

The chief said he got it and hung up. Only an idiot would go back to the office at a time like this. He called Roberta, El Carcamán, Villalobos, and Pangtay aside. He hadn't paid most of them their monthly bonuses yet, so they had good reason to want to keep him alive. And a couple of them, like Pangtay and El Carcamán, really owed him. Literally. When they were gathered around, he asked for their attention.

"The mayor wants my resignation, but I haven't signed the letter. He says he'll give me two more days on the job, but my guess is it'll only be twelve hours, until he can name some other son of a bitch to the post. Probably Bracamontes. Whatever happens, this is my case, and you'll report only to me. If you don't like it, that's your prerogative, but get the fuck out."

He looked at each of them in turn. No one moved, so he went on, telling them they weren't going to stop until they caught those bastards, and there was no time to waste. He asked Villalobos to trace the weapons they'd used.

"Check if they forgot to scratch out the serial number. Find out where they got them. Get everything you can."

La Gordis was assigned to locating more witnesses.

"The ones that really matter are the ones who saw them arrive or escape. Ask them what car they got into, who was waiting for them. There was a shitload of tourists around. Go ask at the hotels nearby if anyone suspicious checked in. Don't ask about the shoot-out. Ask what they saw before and after, anywhere around this block. We need to know everything."

He asked Pangtay to seize the security camera footage from all the stores nearby and to talk with private security companies.

"Check out all the movement on this street since yesterday. These assholes must have come through to check out the lay of the land. You don't improvise an ambush. And another thing: El Flaco told me he'd seen a couple of cholos hanging around the airport early this morning. Find all the cameras around there, at the gas station and any ATMs. If anyone refuses to hand over the tapes, get a warrant from Judge Trujillo. And you, Carcamán, tell the morgue to drop everything and examine the bastards we dropped. Every detail matters. While the medical examiner's working, help Robusta collect fingerprints and report back to La Gordis."

He looked at them.

"Got that? Report all leads to Roberta. No sleeping on the job, and I pity the bastard who breathes a word of any of this to Bracamontes or his people. Steer clear of them. Now let's nail those sons of bitches."

He noticed a strange mood among his team. Something like pity. They knew they weren't likely to see him alive again. Pangtay was the first to speak.

"Sir, it's been an honor to work with you."

If anyone had a kind word for him, it was that kiss ass. Pangtay fed a family of seven, not on his salary, but rather on perks the chief had set up for him. So he just gave the man a little nod and didn't take the remark too seriously.

After dismissing the other investigators, he whispered an order to Pangtay. "Go to the parking garage around the corner, on Matamoros and Allende, and subdue the attendant. Pick a nondescript car with tinted windows and a full tank, close the gate, and wait for me there. When I knock like always—three hard, two soft—let me in."

Pangtay nodded and rushed off. He had experience stealing cars; it was his line of work before he joined the force on Margarito's invitation. Thanks to the chief, for the past twenty years he'd been doing it in a legal, orderly way, and Margarito got to keep part of the take. Since he started working with the chief, one luxury car each quarter was enough to feed the family; he made better money and took fewer risks, thanks to the chief's contacts. It's true he was supposed to have given up the gig when Los Nuevos took over, but this was for a good cause: the boss needed something more discreet than a patrol vehicle.

"Carcamán, Roberta, get over here," called the chief. "I'm riding with you."

"Whatever you say, boss." And they headed toward the old man's yellow minivan.

Just then, Margarito's private phone began to ring again. A young voice accustomed to giving orders roared on the other end of the line.

"Padrino. How are you?"

The chief didn't answer.

"What's your position? Are you still at the scene?"

"Yeah."

"I'm on my way."

"There's no need. It's all over, and the army's here."

He heard the clink of ice cubes in a glass and gathered that his interlocutor had poured himself a tall drink.

"Is it true that Ricardo's dead?"

"It is. Have you heard anything?"

"No, I just found out. Do you want me to send some people your way?"

"No need. Better get your folks off the street, they'll be going heavy with the patrols. I'll come to you; will be there soon. What's the car of the day?" Every so often they changed the password that allowed access to his godson's turf.

"Ferrari. What are you going to do?"

"I'm going to make sure justice is served."

"How?"

"Over and out."

Margarito took one last look at the place where his men had fallen, now under the army's guard. He got into the minivan, and they drove off.

Pangtay was waiting for them in the garage in a new SUV. In any flat, low-lying city, a car like that would draw attention, but with all the cobblestones and steep streets in La Eternidad, it was the most popular kind of vehicle.

"Roberta," he said to La Gordis, "you drive. Stay about two car lengths behind Carcamán and yours truly. Pangtay, you can go back to work."

"So that's that, then, sir," he said, shaking the chief's hand. He insisted on saying good-bye as if Margarito were already dead.

Pangtay opened the gate, made sure there wasn't too much activity on the street, and let them out. A few blocks later they hit a red light and a few cars stopped behind them, Roberta's included.

Margarito looked over at the old man behind the wheel: he was skinnier than a piece of spaghetti, more hunched than a question mark, and breathing so heavily it sounded as if he was hyperventilating. He was wound tighter than a spring at the thought that just by being in the same car as his boss—incidentally it was the most eye-catching vehicle in the precinct— he was risking his life. Margarito knew he'd feel terrible if anything happened to the old

man because of him, so he waited until the light turned green
and then jumped out, slamming the passenger door behind him.

"See ya, old man. Thanks for always sticking with me. Go
straight from here until you hit Avenida Águila, then head back
to the office."

"But, boss—" the officer managed to say.

Before El Carcamán could do anything, Margarito was already
walking against traffic toward Roberta's car, amid a sea of honk-
ing horns. He opened the passenger door and sat down next to
her.

"Make a U-turn."

The woman, startled, did as she was told. Margarito noticed
the unpleasant smell of fear coming off her.

"Where to, sir?"

It was nearly four o'clock.

"La Petrolera. Avoid Avenida Pancho Villa, there's sure to be
checkpoints there."

La Gordis hesitated for a second, then stepped on the gas.
The car sped down Avenida Lomas de Rosales, which connected
the two colonias along what used to be an uninhabited ravine.

A few moments later, when they arrived at Parque de la Petrolera, Margarito told her to take a quick spin around, check for
suspicious activity, then park near the small amphitheater, which
looked worse every time he saw it. Roberta brought the car to a
stop between two vehicles and they got out.

The amphitheater was empty. The rain had left its mark: there
were dozens of puddles along the cement risers. A man stepped
out from behind the rusty wall that stood in for a backdrop when
he saw them coming up the main path. The two jumped when
they saw him. He looked exactly like one of the dead hit men. If
the chief had seen him on the street on a normal day, he would
have given the order to bring him in. He was wearing a down

vest over athletic gear and he had the look of an addict: skinny, bulging eyes, hair and nails as unkempt as his beard.

"You're Chief González," the individual announced.

Margarito and Roberta snapped to attention.

"I know you. You arrested my cousin."

"And what was your cousin's line of work?"

"He was a med student. Like me. You arrested him for possession of illegal substances, for doing exactly what we're doing now, and you sent him to federal prison. Who would have thought . . ."

Try as he might, the chief couldn't remember the case.

"You're sure it was me?"

"You're Margarito González?"

The chief grunted.

"Let's get on with it," he said and handed the man a couple of bills.

"Just to be clear, I don't sell these. But your gratuity is appreciated."

"Come on, asshole. My arm is killing me."

"I have to warn you about a few things. First of all, you can't drink a single drop of alcohol while you're on these things. It's a death sentence. You'd stop breathing. Got it?"

The chief nodded and raised his hand to his shoulder.

"One question: how are your bowel movements?"

Roberta had to hold her boss back to keep him from punching the specialist. Once he calmed down, the young man approached again.

"I didn't mean to upset you. It's just that this stuff can cause severe constipation, so I brought a laxative along, just in case." Once it was clear the crisis had passed, he added, "What a temper, jeez."

He showed Margarito the pills, but instead of handing them over, he held them under the chief's nose and sermonized: "One every twelve hours. No more. Don't open them or dissolve them: swallow them whole. They're time-release capsules. If you mess around with them, you could end up in respiratory failure or even die. Don't be alarmed if you experience nausea, vomiting, dry mouth, drowsiness, difficulty concentrating, or if you sweat more than usual. But be very careful if you get a case of vertigo, notice distention in your abdomen, have trouble breathing, or see ghosts."

The two police officers stared at him incredulously. The young man felt obligated to explain.

"I'm not saying that Casper the Friendly Ghost is going to pay you a visit, but you may suffer from auditory or visual hallucinations. Seeing or hearing things that no one else does."

Roberta looked at her boss with concern.

"Last thing: if you stay on these for too long, you'll be addicted for life. Got all that?"

The chief grabbed the pills from him and stuck them into his pocket.

"You don't want the laxative?"

Roberta looked at the young man, who clearly didn't understand the risk he was running.

"Whatever, up to you. Pleasure doing business with you, Chief. I guess I'll be seeing you around."

And he left, singing, "Sorpresas te da la vida, ay Dios . . ."

As soon as he was gone, the chief turned to La Gordis.

"Take me to my apartment. I need to change my clothes."

They were just rounding the corner when Pangtay called.

"Chief, avoid the downtown area. I repeat. Avoid downtown. There are reports of suspicious persons outside your house. Don't go there."

"Shit. What do you mean, suspicious persons?"

"The reports say three white trucks, boss."

"With three letters painted on each side?" The chief was referring to the letters CDP, for Cartel del Puerto. Los Viejos. The members of his godson's criminal organization would spray-paint the initials on the sides of their trucks before heading in a caravan to confront their rivals or carry out an execution. Early the year before, a caravan of thirty vehicles passed through La Eternidad, headed north to wage a take-no-prisoners war on the outskirts of the city. Margarito, who'd been given prior notice, told his people to let them pass. He would never forget El Flaco's face as he counted the immense, identical trucks with tinted windows and looked at the chief without daring to ask. What could Margarito have told him, anyway? Those savages were the law now. No one else had that much authority, that much firepower—no one else in this part of the country, at least.

"No, boss, no letters."

"Got it," he said and hung up immediately. He wasn't about to take any chances.

"To the office?"

"No. Take me to the beach."

La Gordis looked at the pills in the chief's hand.

"Boss, you might not want to risk it."

Margarito looked at her and put the pills back in his pocket. She was right: there were better ways to get to hell.

When they reached the corner, they caught sight of a roadblock of white pickups.

"We can't go that way," said Margarito. "Turn here."

They followed the avenue past the university, turned without stopping at the red light once they got to the brewery, and followed a series of side streets, each named after a thriving oil city. A few minutes later, they crossed the train tracks that served as the border between the city and the coast. After that intersection, they passed fast-food joints, liquor stores with

ample freezers outside, gas stations, pharmacies, shops selling bathing suits, bars where all kinds of business were done,
motels where crimes were committed on a weekly basis, whore-
houses of mixed repute, and warehouses holding contraband
and weapons from the United States and even small shipments
of drugs and people needing a place to rest before continuing
their journey north.

Back when he was starting out, the chief knew where just
about every family in the area lived because he walked those
streets daily. In certain neighborhoods he could choose a block
at random and tell you everyone who lived in each building. But
that was when La Eternidad still had a hundred thousand residents, before the town turned into a city, before the tourism boom
and the fever for building residential complexes for foreigners
and millionaires. For a while already, it had been impossible to
wrap your head around the city. He asked Roberta to stop at a
convenience store and buy him a cola.

"You don't want anything to eat?"

The same thought passed through their heads: no one's
future is certain, much less a police officer's, much less in La
Eternidad. Roberta hesitated a moment before leaving him alone,
but eventually ran into the store as if she were racing to the scene
of an emergency. Margarito released the safety on his gun and
didn't for a second take his eyes off the rearview mirrors. In no
time at all, Roberta was hurrying back to the car. As she got in,
she handed the chief a plastic bag containing, from what he could
tell, ham, cheese, a roll, and a large bottle of cola. Another local
custom: it was easier and cheaper to buy a bottle of soda than a
bottle of water.

They crossed the dump, where the poorest of the poor were
born, lived for a few years, and then died without ever having
left: miles and miles of houses built from cardboard and trash.

Someone had painted a huge, intricately detailed image of La Santa Muerte, Our Lady of the Holy Death, on the wall around the shantytown.

Before they crossed the avenue leading to the beach, they paused to study their surroundings. Margarito was surprised to see such a heavy military presence: two convoys of soldiers were stationed at the refinery's entrance. If they'd been there seven years ago, Los Nuevos probably wouldn't be stealing gas straight from the pipeline today.

"What do we do?" asked Roberta, anxiously.

Margarito pointed to a dirt road that ran alongside the dunes next to the highway. It was the bumpiest drive of Roberta's life. Every few feet the car pitched upward and then fell into a deep trough, tossing its passengers around.

They couldn't afford to pass through a checkpoint: that would just be announcing their whereabouts to their attackers. So they took side roads, passing the charred frame of a vehicle every so often. Their route was so circuitous it would take Roberta hours to find it again if she tried. They passed a white enclosure wall more than two thousand feet long, on the other side of which they could make out an enormous white mansion that belonged to one of the port's union leaders. Then they caught sight of the hill where the oil workers' union had built a recreation center for its members. Eventually, they reached the part of the beach where new luxury homes were being constructed.

"Turn in here," he said.

They passed another unfinished project of the oil workers' union: a hospital the union leader had started just before his political enemies brought him down. Over ten stories tall, it contained a hundred rooms, none of which were ever completed. Rumors circulated about the project for a while; then people gradually forgot about it. When the guards left, no one hesitated

to go in and take whatever there was, break windows, spray graf-
fiti on the walls. Now it was just a huge, rusted-out shell. They
kept driving; when they came to a curve in the road, Margarito
told Roberta to slow down.

They could hear the roar of the sea. The road disappeared
under the weeds. Behind the veil of a row of pine trees stood the
Garza Blanca condominiums.

"Go to the guard station and ask for Panda. Tell him someone from Los Coquitos is here to speak with him. I'll stay here."

He set his two cell phones to vibrate; slid his gun into the
front of his pants, under his shirt; and waited. Roberta came back
two minutes later, reeking of fear, the poor girl. Two steps behind
her, standard procedure in dealing with suspicious characters,
followed the immense Panda Gónzalez, his focus as sharp as an
eagle's and his hand on the butt of his gun, ready to draw. When
he recognized Margarito's profile, he hurried over to the car.

"I thought it might be you! What can I do for you, boss?"

"I have to talk to you in private."

The color drained from the rent-a-cop's face.

"Come on, then. We don't want anyone to see you," he replied,
just the same.

A wave of pain swelled in Margarito's belly and he cursed
his luck.

"Are you alone?"

Panda nodded. "Until tomorrow at three, when the new shift
comes on."

Margarito got out of the car and walked over to La Gordis.

"Sweetheart, I'm staying put. You get back to work and don't
take any risks. When I call," the chief continued, "come pick me
up right here."

She nodded.

"Boss?" she said, before he walked away.

"Yes?"

"Are you going to take them?"

"What?"

"The pills. I was just thinking . . . If I were you . . . I mean, what if they wanted to poison you? That guy didn't seem too trustworthy. I even think I saw him once with the Three Stooges."

"Don't worry about it."

"You're sure you don't want me to stay? I could stand guard."

The chief breathed a grateful sigh before responding.

"No, you're more use to me there. Get back to work and wait for my call. You've got a bright future ahead of you. Just help me close this case."

He grabbed the heavy bag of provisions and headed for the dunes. When he'd climbed to the top of one, he turned and waved to Roberta. She looked as if she might have been crying.

"This way, hurry."

Panda ushered him into the control room. It was much bigger than he'd expected: a six-by-twenty rectangle that served partly for storage and partly as an office for the guards.

"I heard on the radio what happened. I'm so sorry, boss."

Margarito looked him in the eye and thought, *Finally, someone who means what he says.*

"What can I do for you?" the rent-a-cop asked.

"I need a place to hide and if there's one thing you've got here, it's houses."

The big guy's jaw tightened. What Margarito was asking went against every principle of his modest occupation, but he agreed anyway.

"Let me see . . . Yeah, here we are."

Panda opened a little locker and grabbed the key chain hanging from the peg marked with the number 33.

"There aren't many vacancies since it's the high season and all, but I've got something for you. In theory, the owners are gone until next week, so it might work." He checked the surveillance cameras to make sure no one was coming and added, "Follow me."

He led Margarito to a buggy stamped with the logo of the residential complex, told him to lie down in the back, then drove toward a huge roundabout with a fountain and a sculpture of a whale at its center. He swerved onto the broadest avenue leading off it and stayed on that road until he reached a street leading into the dunes.

"It's best if you're not right in the middle of the complex. Wouldn't want any of the neighbors to see you or come knocking on your door."

There were three or four houses set off on their own atop one of the dunes. The rent-a-cop took him to the one nearest the gated community's perimeter wall. He opened the garage with a remote control he'd picked up, parked inside, and closed the garage door behind them.

It was the perfect hideout. To get to him, they'd have to drive up the only street; since he had a clear line of sight on it, he'd have plenty of notice. Or else they'd have to scale the wall between the property and the beach, but first they'd have to get around the row of pine trees, and he'd hear them when they passed on the highway. *But even if I did hear them coming*—the thought struck him like lightning—*I'd need a helicopter to get out of here.* He couldn't go back to the office to restock, so he had only one magazine on him. The rent-a-cop broke his train of thought.

"Here's the master key, which gets you into every room. You want me to bring you something to drink or some dinner, Chief?"

"I'm all set," Margarito replied, showing him the bag.

"If you need me you can reach me on the intercom," he said, pointing at the device. "Try not to turn on the lights."

The chief knew to keep a low profile, or it would mean trouble for the guard.

"Thanks, Panda. You're a lifesaver. Let me know right away if you see any suspicious movement."

As soon as he was alone, Margarito grabbed the bag with his things and went inside to check out the house.

7

Just as Panda had promised, the key slipped easily into the lock, but Margarito still had to throw his weight into the wooden door, which had been warped by the humidity. A fine layer of sand covered the floor.

A large dining room led to the kitchen and laundry room. The wooden furniture was painted white and upholstered in fabrics that were quick to dry, a practical choice for the beaches of La Eternidad. He wanted to lie down right there, but the living room had too many windows and was accessed by two doors: one that opened to the garage and the other to the street. He could easily see the car that just pulled up and parked in front of the house across the way; assuming he could be seen as well, he decided to head upstairs.

His body felt so heavy on the way up it could have been made of cement. It took him a while to reach the second floor, but when he eventually did, he examined the hallway and counted four doors. He chose the fourth and stepped into what was probably the master bedroom.

Whoever owned the place had good taste. There was a king-size bed with cotton sheets and half a dozen pillows under a mosquito net, two nightstands complete with reading lamps and piles of books, a sofa, and a small desk with a record player and a few LPs on it. The finishing touches to this room and its views of the Gulf were a wooden ceiling fan and the requisite industrial-strength air conditioner that could freeze a whole regiment to death.

Because the room was on the second floor, he could see over the wall surrounding the gated community. The dunes and the sea peeked out to the east, and to the north he could see the highway that brought him there, where the only sign of life was a little grocery store brimming with activity. A few children played around a big dog; a group of people, maybe a family or a crew of fishermen, huddled around a small television intermittently broadcasting a soccer match. Little by little, he was able to make out a metal table emblazoned with the Corona logo, innumerable empty bottles resting on its surface, and three men sitting around it, motionless. Inside the compound, two teenagers started up a game of basketball in front of the house across the street.

I'll be damned, he thought. He couldn't turn the light on without attracting their attention.

I wonder how La Muda is doing with her wards, he wondered. *She's been on edge ever since they iced the Bus. I hope she doesn't slip up.* He was dying to listen to the news.

He opened every door along the hallway in search of a television set—*Jesus! This guy doesn't own a TV?*—until he finally found a room dedicated to the purpose. He drew the curtains and turned on the set with the volume all the way down. A banner running along the screen announced that it was ten to six in the evening and that the news was about to come on with updates on what happened earlier that day.

Then he went back to the bedroom and dug around in his bag until he found the opiates. He examined the translucent, amber-colored pill bottle the anesthesiologist had given him: the six white pills inside were either poison or a miracle cure. And if he stopped breathing? It didn't matter; the pain in his arm was unbearable. He opened the bottle and took one of the pills.

He didn't feel anything right away. *This arm could take a long time to heal,* he thought. How the hell was he supposed to defend himself? He pictured the man who'd shot at him with an Uzi coming closer, closer. He managed to focus on the man's features and was surprised by the icy look on his face. *He was going to kill me like a dog.* He remembered his surprised expression when he shot him in the leg and how frustrated he'd seemed when he was forced to drop his weapon and run. He remembered his son's body, and the bitch named Sorrow returned to wrap him in a warm embrace.

Jesus, he thought. *They killed my son, but I was the one who was supposed to die.*

A fresh wave of pain in his arm forced him to lie down on the sofa. In the time it took him to recover, he convinced himself that the kid who'd sold him the pills was bad at math and took another. And then another.

He waited for some indeterminate length of time, then turned off the television because he thought he heard a car coming. There were no cars outside, and night was falling.

Driven by a strange feeling of lucidity, he thought back on his life over the past few years. He asked himself which of the two groups vying for control of the port would benefit more from his death. He couldn't reach any conclusions, but he told himself the answer was there; it was just that sleep was clouding his vision. He sensed the blood moon rising again and heard people talking nearby, so he went to peek out the window.

He saw a fisherman tying up to a float. For a moment, as the medicine began to flow through the policeman's veins, the boat rose and fell, alone in the middle of the bay, and the chief thought how he was like that too: floating in limbo.

His eyes fell on two men walking toward him along the beach. Aware that he was visible where he stood, he hid behind the curtain and observed them cautiously, weapon in hand. When they were even with his hideout, the men looked around and seemed to argue about something, staring at the gated community as if it were an immense pyramid, surprised that someone had built it there. Or maybe they were looking at him, figuring out how to get in.

It was so dark already he couldn't tell if they had weapons. He thought they might just be a distraction, that an armed crew was about to burst through the front door. He struggled to release the safety on his gun: either the pills or the exhaustion had left his fingers clumsy.

He saw one of the men pull some kind of microphone out of his jacket, bring it to his lips, then hold it under the other man's chin. They were obviously communicating with someone. He was about to shoot them both, but then he saw the glow of two red points in the night and realized they were smoking.

A few minutes later, they tossed their cigarettes with an irritated gesture, like they were being forced from their private paradise. Then they took off their shoes and walked toward the water's edge, where a third man was already tossing a small net into the sea. More fishermen.

Toward the other end of the bay, a sizable black rock seemed to be moving across the sand. It was a huge turtle, coming to rest. Then he saw the three men run toward the animal, and he realized their plan was to butcher it.

Before he could scream in horror, a door suddenly opened at the end of the hall. A child, or something that had adopted the appearance of a child, stepped out. When he saw the policeman, he smiled and vanished as quickly as he'd come.

After he managed to close his jaw, Margarito walked haltingly into the corridor, his eyes wide with shock.

With every step, the feeling that what he'd seen hadn't been a child but rather was something else made the hair on the back of his neck stand up.

To his surprise, a door he hadn't noticed earlier stood open at the end of the hall. Its frame was bathed in an intense light, as if it were on fire. He pushed through his inertia and stepped inside.

He found himself in what looked to be a storeroom or a studio, where the master of the house must have dedicated himself to strange pastimes. Aside from a few shelving units as tall as him and full of books and knickknacks that seemed vaguely familiar somehow, the only furniture in the room was a large wooden table. On it was a glass fish tank with a scale model of a boat inside. *Nice*, he thought. *It looks like the* Bella Italia—his first cabin cruiser, purchased back in his jackpot days—and he went over to take a closer look.

What he saw nearly knocked him off his feet.

There, in that fish tank, was an exact replica of the *Bella Italia*, the only boat that had ever meant anything to him. (He'd had two: the first sank in a hurricane and Los Nuevos took the second from him.) He'd bought the twenty-foot *Bella Italia* with somewhat ill-gotten gains early in his marriage: a white boat just like the one in front of him, with a small cabin where he and his wife and son could rest when the sun got too strong. Every weekend for almost six months they'd go out fishing for a few hours and eat their catch for dinner that night. Those days, before their marriage soured, were the happiest of his life. It was his wife who'd painted the name on the side of the boat, at his suggestion, and there it was, right there on the scale model. The boat rested on a wooden board painted to look like the sea, and there was something else: three little pieces of fabric, one with yellow and white stripes, like the Italian bathing trunks his wife had given him long ago, which he always felt so ridiculous in, and the bright yellow bikini she used to wear. *That was it*, he thought. *It was all downhill from there.*

He realized something terrible was happening. He rubbed his eyes, but the little boat was real and it remained right there in front of him: a scale model of reality, sinister in its perfection. *Jesus*, he thought. *Why did Panda send me here? Who owns this place? Who lives here?*

A flash inside the fish tank caught his eye: a hand span away from the boat stood an action figure the size of a tin soldier, holding a shiny pistol. The miniature had white hair and pitch-black eyebrows; was wearing a white shirt, gray pants, and boots; and had his arms and legs fixed in a combative pose. He recognized the figure as Elijah, the man who'd brought him to the force. He felt a chill run up his spine when he noticed that up close there were several vertical slashes in the man's guayabera, right at the chest, and he was holding a coin between his teeth, as if the artists who built the model had gone to great lengths to reproduce the man's horrible death. *It can't be. It can't be*, he thought. *Only a few of us knew those details.*

There was another figure to the man's right, a woman. It took him a long time to realize it was meant to be his mother: a fortune-teller everyone called La Santa. The doll looked like a Barbie, with tan skin and long dark hair, long legs, and a fiery gaze. She was draped in a flowing white dress that ballooned up like a flower in bloom. In her hands, she held a cross and a bundle of herbs. *La Santa*, he thought. *It's been a long time.* She sat in a chair that looked just like the one she'd used in life to read her followers' fortunes. Whoever made the model had gone to the trouble of leaving a miniature bottle of tequila at her feet; it looked just like the ones his mother had emptied day after day when he was a child. There was a suitcase on the floor next to her, and off to the side he saw the old Jeep from the precinct, the one he'd driven when he was just starting out. A black case rested on the passenger seat: he remembered right away where he'd found it, and what he'd done with it. A wave of nausea overtook him.

There were three tiger cubs, too, playing with what looked like a rag but turned out, on closer inspection, to be part of a human torso, rib cage and all, belonging to a fat man with a bushy mustache. The rest of him lay on the ground between the paws of two bigger tigers going to town on the remains.

A buzzing in his ears broke his concentration. The final element in the fish tank was a tanker truck just like the one that had blocked the road in front of his son. And with that, he was sure that some sinister being was observing and distilling his life.

He wanted to defend himself, but he had no ammunition. To be defensible, he needed to have lived a different life.

An intense light shimmering in the fish tank forced him to look away. He had to blink several times before it began to fade and he was able to feel his way to the door.

He made his way down the hall and didn't look back, not wanting to know who lived in that house. He stretched out in the master bedroom, closed his eyes, and breathed deeply until he calmed down.

When he finally awoke, it took him a long time to remember where he was. When he saw the sinuous, fleeting tendrils of light that intermittently played across the room, he thought he'd been thrown to the bottom of a swimming pool. He felt something vibrate in his pocket and realized it was his cell phone: someone had been calling him.

He felt heavy, like he'd been tied to a block of cement. His neck hurt so much he wondered if he'd been run over by a Jeep, and his arm was so unresponsive it didn't seem to be attached to him anymore. From what he could tell, the horse tranquil-izer he'd ingested was having contradictory effects on his body: one minute, he felt like a lead glove tossed into the corner of the room, and the next like a fizzy beverage made of equal parts anger, sadness, and a beast driven by furious longing, though he didn't know for what.

He was still trying to understand what was going on when something hard and pointy walked across his right hand, which was resting on the floor. He pulled it back with a jerk, picturing a scorpion, but the threat proved to be only a small, pink crab that scurried backward, its pincers at the ready, toward the half-open drain grate on the floor of the adjoining bathroom in an attempt to save its little life.

For a moment as long as an Olympic pool, Margarito was a body without a brain stretched out at the bottom of the ocean. As he tried to recall who he was and how he'd gotten there, he felt the sleep leave his body, as if by sitting up in bed he'd spilled a delicious liqueur that could never be recovered. The bitch Sorrow immediately came and sat by his side; moving her huge, dark form, she clasped her jaws around the policeman's head until he hated the whole world. Then, since there was no way around it, he went back to being himself.

I feel like I've been looted, like a car that's been stripped.

The warped wooden doors, the rust clinging to windows and furniture, and above all, the layers of sand scattered across the floor seemed to suggest that the world had ended the night before and no one had thought to inform him.

He didn't know how long he'd slept, but he could tell from the tendrils of light pushing their way through the slats of the blinds that the sun was setting. With a heavy sigh, he decided it was probably best to wait a while longer before contacting La Gordis or the general.

He looked at his cell phone. His battery was down to ten percent, and he had fourteen messages and thirty missed calls, four of which came from the public phone La Muda used for emergencies.

Shit. The girl. His plan had been to let her go that afternoon after turning in his resignation, but the afternoon was almost over. *Jesus,* he thought. *Her father must be beside himself, waiting to hear how he was supposed to pay the ransom.* By that hour, the handoff should have happened already, but he hadn't counted on La Tonina, his assistant in the deal, getting killed in a firefight.

He was fucked. He couldn't call La Muda from his cell phone, much less from the house where he was hiding out, without implicating himself in the kidnapping. He had to get out of there and find a public phone.

He tucked his gun into his waistband, stood, and opened the blinds halfway. The strange light was the result of an intense electrical storm punctuated from time to time by waterspouts. It was an unusual storm, with bursts of light in the clouds looming over the port city answered moments later by lightning on the other side of the bay, not far from the gated community where he found himself. Sometimes lightning would strike two or three times in the same area with varying degrees of intensity before striking once on the other side, so that one lightning bolt in the city would spark frenetic calligraphy across the sky above the open sea; it seemed like an ongoing conversation or the transcription of an urgent message. Or as if two gigantic beings were playing a game of tennis well beyond the grasp of human minds.

Margarito didn't believe in divine beings. Except for that time he was sure he'd met the devil himself.

Margarito would never forget how, during one of the worst crises of poverty he'd experienced as a teenager, when for weeks it had seemed as if things couldn't get any worse but they managed to anyway, he went to police headquarters. He asked for Lieutenant Elijah Cohen, because his mother had told him Elijah was a friend of his father's—back when his father was still alive. They told Margarito he was busy and sent him away, but he tried again every other day or so for a week until he got tired and gave up. When he'd lost all hope, one Monday around midnight a man in a gray suit knocked on the door of the shack where he and his mother lived back then.

His first reaction was confusion: with his goatee and his coyote eyes, the visitor reminded him of the devil, as depicted by the Catholic Church. If the devil was an unusually lively person in constant movement, like a spring.

The newcomer studied him for a moment, then asked if he was La Santa's kid and why he'd been looking for him. Margarito explained that he'd gone looking for him, yes, to ask for work. When the man asked about his mother, he replied that she was on some retreat with her followers, that she'd been gone for ten days already and he didn't know when she'd be back. Then the man with the goatee asked if he could speak to him for a moment out in the street, as if some strange law kept him from setting foot inside without an invitation. Margarito wasn't the type to chicken out, so he went. Out there, on a bench, without so much as shaking his hand first, the visitor began to speak.

"I'm Lieutenant Elijah Cohen. Your father and I worked together a long time ago, down at the shipyard. He was a good man, but gullible. I see he didn't manage his money too well, either, even though he made quite a bit. It's a shame, his son living in poverty like this. Do you want to come work for me?"

Margarito didn't like being around this strange character, who skipped every pleasantry and had the nerve to speak badly or, rather, candidly, about his family's troubles. Then he saw the precinct's famous Jeep parked on the corner.

He was about to make a run for it: he'd stolen a television earlier that day, and he thought they'd come to arrest him. Anyone who worked on the force in La Eternidad during that rough stretch in the eighties would remember Lieutenant Elijah Cohen. It was a tough decade, but headquarters had the right team for the job: Chief Albino was there to lead the force and make nice with mayors, congressmen, and other politicians, while Lieutenant Cohen was there to solve the mysteries of La Eternidad. Cohen was the eldest son and black sheep of a wealthy family of entrepreneurs. He was famous for his intelligence, but even more so for his impatience. Though the people of La Eternidad weren't generally known for their candor, Cohen grew up in a Jewish family that never beat around the bush. While most locals took great pains to surround themselves in a cloud of niceties, Elijah preferred to blow right through them. His life's passion and greatest talent was studying people. He liked to talk with people from all walks of life and hypothesize about their inner workings, their desires, how they pursued them, what resources they had, how they tended to behave.

The years he'd spent needing to work all sorts of jobs to stay alive had given him both an understanding of a wide range of human temperaments and an edge of caustic irony that tended to emerge at the worst possible moment. Unsurprisingly, he'd never had many friends.

"I know you have a criminal record. You steal, either to live or for fun. Aside from that, is there anything I should know?"

"No, sir," Margarito lied.

"I also know you're a man and can handle yourself in a fight. I was standing near you last Carnaval, when you laid those ranchers out. I was going to step in, but then I realized you didn't need the help, that you could manage those three on your own. The one you knocked out was a boxer. Who taught you to fight?"

"Dunno. Picked it up on the street."

Elijah flashed a bitter smile.

"I used to be just like you: a hothead with no one to guide me. It might be that I'm getting old, but I'm tired and need someone around who can jump in when it's time to put on some pressure. If you think you're that person, you just hit the jackpot."

Margarito's life up to that moment had been no picnic. His relationship with his mother had consisted of the following: he would make all sorts of mischief to get her attention, like the time he stole her savings, then she would yell and try to hit him, and he'd run into the street. The more ferocious her insults and her urge to hit him grew, the longer he steered clear of Los Coquitos. No one should have to feel like his own mother hates him. For Margarito, it was the worst feeling imaginable, even worse than knowing his father was dead. That didn't get any easier, either, and it didn't help to hear: *But if you barely even knew your father, why do you care?*

For a while, he made money cleaning windshields along the highway to the airport, until the owner of a grocery store gave him permission to wash cars out front of his place. He'd had to run from the police more often than he would've liked. In those days, it was hard to say who Margarito's friends were; most of the time he'd beat up any kid who went near him. The only one who stuck with him was Flaco Ibarra, who back then was a fat kid with a permanent grin. Margarito would knock him around until he was blue in the face, but El Flaco just kept smiling. Then, because a government inspector—unfazed by her threats to put a hex on him—threatened to report her if she didn't, La Santa agreed to finally send Margarito to school.

"It won't do him any good. Just look at how his brothers ended up: one of them's dead; the other dresses like a woman. I don't know how this one's going to turn out, but he's no angel. None of my children turned out well."

His first days at school were a nightmare. The older kids made fun of his name: *Margarita, Margarita, small and round like a gordita.* They laughed at his threadbare clothes, calling him names like Dumpster and Handouts. They made fun of his mother, calling her La Bruja, the witch. Margarito would shove, scratch, or give them a black eye in response—when he wasn't being pinned down, that is, kicking and biting in self-defense.

The school principal wasn't surprised by the anger little Margarito carried inside him or how often he beat the other boys up. It was pretty much a daily occurrence; you might say it was the only way he knew how to interact with his classmates, as if hitting them were his way of introducing himself. By the end of the first month, he'd already beaten up nearly every one of the boys, even the ones who were bigger than him, and he had started to hassle the girls who made fun of him. He would tug at their dresses, call them names, and shove them as he passed by. *What will become of this child?* the principal would wonder. *It can't be easy to have La Santa for a mother.*

Once, just once, it looked as though his life might go a different way. It was when he met Miss Lupita. Already alerted to the problem child in her classroom by the school principal, instead of punishing him for stealing food from his classmates, Miss Lupita observed him throughout her first day and stayed on the sidelines when he'd get into fights. The next day she asked him to stay behind during recess.

"All right, Margarito. Come share my lunch and let's chat a bit."

Miss Lupita was a very pretty young woman with curly black hair who'd just finished her degree in education. It was the first time anyone had treated him like an adult, and Margarito was so startled by it that he actually acted like one and answered his teacher's questions more clearly than he'd thought he could. When the boy finished telling her about his brothers and how his mother treated him, she seemed to grow very sad.

"You're one of those angry young men," said Elijah, locking him in that blue stare of his that always made Margarito uncomfortable. "I was just like you, at your age. Until Albino handpicked me to work at headquarters. If you want to make a good career for yourself, there are some things you have to learn, and fast. Anyone can learn this stuff by trial and error, but I'm going to show you a shortcut. I only ask one thing: stay loyal. Don't be like those other deadbeats, and you'll make a lot more than they do. More importantly, you'll live a lot longer."

They were regulars at his favorite bar, a little spot with a palm-thatched roof across from the malecón where people would gather to enjoy the seafood, empanadas, and soup. It was one of the only places Margarito always felt at home.

Three months after hiring him, Elijah was already passing him the toughest cases, and everyone said he'd be chief one day. After spending his early years running from the police, he was about to become one of La Eternidad's finest.

Elijah taught him a lot and demanded a lot from him, but what Margarito made working for him was barely enough to live on. His prospects finally started looking up one day when he was out on assignment.

Someone had killed a smuggler known as El Gato just as he was getting home. They were examining the scene of the crime when El Dorado, who'd been assigned as his partner that day, pointed to a briefcase hidden behind a few plants in the entryway.

"Hey, check it out! Look what I found!"

Officer Margarito set the briefcase on his knees and opened it. Inside was an overstuffed manila envelope, and inside that . . .

"Holy shit!"

Stacks of hundred-dollar bills with the bank's currency bands still on them.

"There must be . . . I don't know . . . at least a hundred grand here."

"Son of a bitch, no wonder he tried to run."

Margarito had never seen that much cash in his life.

When they lifted the envelope, out fell a couple of documents and a business card with a message written on it. As soon as he saw the insignia on the card, Margarito knew they couldn't keep the money.

"Are you crazy?" El Dorado asked.

"I might be crazy, but I'm not high. I know who this belongs to. Don't know him well, but I know him."

When he went to return the case to its rightful owner, the men guarding the door of the mansion scoffed at his threadbare pants and worn-out boots. It took him a good forty minutes to convince them he needed to deliver the case to its owner in person, and then another half hour went by before the union leader's right-hand man, a congressman named Camacho, could be bothered to see him. Margarito was sick of counting the palm trees in the garden, but he wouldn't open the briefcase for anyone else. Camacho removed his dark glasses at the sight of the money.

"Did Elijah Cohen send you?" he asked.

"No, sir," said Margarito, swallowing hard. He knew how much of a risk he was taking. "I haven't told anyone about this."

The congressman still didn't trust him.

"You say you're from here, from the port. You're not related to the González family that had that notary's office on Calle Morelos?"

"I don't know them, sir. We're from out on a ranch but we moved here, to Los Coquitos."

"Wait here."

He showed Margarito to a room, from which the young officer could hear him talking loudly on the phone with someone, erupting from time to time in good- and ill-natured laughter. He came out fifteen minutes later, visibly more relaxed.

"So you're La Santa's kid?" he asked. "You should've led with that."

Camacho had put two and two together and couldn't believe what had come out. Under his mustache, his grin nearly reached his sideburns.

"El Gato's dead? Makes no difference to us. The union has nothing to do with smuggling or crime. Nothing, you hear? Our leader is a man of great moral stature."

Based on the stench wafting his way, Margarito guessed that the man had been drinking since the night before. So he answered more shrewdly than he'd thought he could. As if he had no ulterior motive.

"That's exactly why I brought this here, sir. It seemed crucial to remove these papers from the scene of the crime. To protect the union's image," he added, handing him the papers and the business card he'd found at the bottom of the envelope.

The smile faded from the man's face. His eyes moved between the papers and Margarito for a long while. Then he got to his feet.

"Wait here."

Margarito watched uneasily as two bodyguards showed up to secure the room, then patted him down and asked for his weapon, but he didn't put up a fight. *No way is he going to have me killed in his own home. Who'd ever heard of a major public figure hiding a corpse in his living room? He'd have to be stupid.* Five minutes later, he was invited into the union leader's office.

Camacho, holding a Cuba libre, sat next to the man in charge. The briefcase was on a table next to the desk. When he saw Margarito, the great Agustín Fernández Vallarta stood and extended his hand.

"Come in, young man. Come in."

He'd only seen him in photos before, always wearing those iconic dark glasses. As usual, he'd grown his mustache out in a thin horizontal line just above his upper lip, which made his wide mouth look even bigger and gave him a vaguely simian appearance overall. But what surprised Margarito most were the man's stature and the size of his hands. It was easy to imagine him starting out as a longshoreman and working his way up the ladder before jumping over to the administrative side of things and into the leadership of the petroleros, not letting anyone get in his way.

Margarito knew he was face-to-face with one of the most powerful men in the country. All he needed to do was call a strike among his workers, and the price of gas would go up around the world. But this was not a man who often looked beyond his nation's borders, unless it was to survey one of the mansions he'd bought in Las Vegas, Padre Island, or Houston—his favorite cities, where he'd go to get away from it all whenever he got the chance. He traveled whenever he wanted, wherever he wanted. It wasn't unusual to hear of his arrival from Paris, Rome, Spain, or New York—always under the pretext of union business, and always with his mistress and entourage at his side.

He'd read in *Proceso* that the leader of the oil workers had founded the union with the president's support in the 1940s, had traded bullets with Communists bankrolled by foreign interests, and had enjoyed the gratitude and support of the Mexican government until the union grew so strong that the same government suddenly needed to bow down to it.

All the while he was sending his enemies to the funeral home behind the scenes, in public the union leader spent his time taking meetings and weaving a tight web of favors granted in exchange for absolute loyalty and obedience. Nothing more, nothing less. He would treat his most trusted staff to an extravagant meal once a month and meet with the engineers that designed the oil wells, the architects in charge of building the workers' houses, and senators and congressmen from around the country. He would ask each of them what they needed, and they would request personal gifts: money to pay for a daughter's quinceañera, a new car for the wife, a home loan. They almost never asked for the machinery, specialists, or jobs needed in the poorest areas of the state. Inviting his contacts on one of his international trips, paying for their family vacations, giving them cars or even houses—it was all a drop in the bucket for him. Millions of dollars passed through his hands every day. There wasn't a single job in the union that didn't require his approval. No matter how qualified or well-intentioned candidates were, no matter how strong their desire to serve their country, they first had to convince one of the man's inner circle to give them a chance.

He was very impressed with Margarito's sense of ethics, the union leader said, underscoring the word *ethics*.

"I hear you're La Santa's boy. Is your mother still alive?"

Good question.

"The last time I saw her, she was still living in the same neighborhood."

"I see. And your brother was a member of the Caracol collective, no?"

"Yes, sir." Margarito didn't know what to say. How did this man know so much about his family? "That was my brother Antonio, but he's dead now."

"And you have another brother, the son of a Protestant pastor?"

Margarito wasn't sure how to respond without completely humiliating himself.

"That's my brother Enrique."

"Who goes by Raquel these days and works as a dancer out on the docks in Veracruz. Who's your father?"

Margarito shrugged. The union leader and his representative exchanged a glance. It was just a flash, but Margarito caught it. The leader turned, walked behind his desk, and went on from there.

"All right, kid. The union appreciates your support. If this had fallen into the wrong hands, it could have damaged a reputation that was years in the making. What am I saying, *years*? A lifetime. The life of the union. I won't forget this. Here."

The moral leader handed him half the smuggler's money. The policeman refused to take it at first, but the leader insisted. Then the congressman indicated it was time for him to leave and closed the door gently behind him.

To Margarito's surprise, they reached out to him three times over the next few weeks, always through one of the congressman's bodyguards. *Margarito, go find a dancer they call the Russian and bring her to the beach house; Margarito, a few associates in town from Mexico City are looking for boys and a little something to sniff, go pick them up three grams.* And, of course, the king of them all: *Margarito, there's a file sitting on the police chief's desk: a report on those guys that ended up dead on Las Peras bridge. That file's better off here. Go bring us whatever your boss has on the case.* Obviously, he did. When he'd completed this last assignment, the leader surprised him by calling him in at seven o'clock on a Sunday morning. He barely noticed how icy the water was as he showered that morning. He shaved, ironed his best shirt, and splashed himself with the last drops in his bottle of Old Spice. He had a date with destiny.

As had been the case every day since Mr. Agustín Fernández Vallarta took over the leadership of the union, there were vehicles stationed at strategic points along the blocks surrounding his mansion. There were no bodyguards inside, though, because the leader didn't employ any. No sir, not a single one. The people lining the streets were just close friends and associates concerned about his health and well-being, a few of whom *might* have carried a badge or passed through a state prison at some point. They didn't miss a thing behind their dark glasses—courtesy of the leader—as they showed off their shot- and submachine guns, bought by them for their own personal use. The leader never paid for a single gun. You couldn't tie him to the sale of so much as a firecracker. Anyway, there they were, standing on the corners, keeping an eye on everyone who went into and out of that neighborhood, just as they had done every day since Agustín Fernández Vallarta decided there was no reason to go to the union offices when he could work just as well at home. And especially since the union leader became something more like a spiritual leader, always ready with a warm handshake and a word of advice. Every morning, a long line formed in front of his home under the sun's first rays: people begging for an audience, hoping to ask him for a favor, or returning to thank him for a favor bestowed. *This son of a bitch makes more miracles than San Martín de Porres*, Margarito thought. And, lo, a miracle occurred: they did not make him wait.

"The mayor," began the leader, as soon as he saw Margarito, "asked me what it would take to make me happy again. And I said to him: 'You miserable filthy rat, a blind man could see the con you're trying to run a mile away. Don't think for a minute you can buy me. You can't buy me with your little favors. I could end you with a phone call. You can't buy me, but I'll give you a chance. I'll take you at your word, you mangy dog, because I'm smarter and more experienced than you, and I know what this port needs, so listen up: we need a new chief of police in this city.' And the blood drained from his face, because he's a nobody, and he's been a nobody as long as I've known him: he used to shine shoes outside my office, and that's all he deserves. He knows he's on his way out, that he's got his back against the wall, so I say to him: 'The new chief has got to be Margarito González.' What a sigh of relief that bastard gave. You're all right by him, you know that? Actually, it made me wonder about you a little, the sigh of relief that bastard gave. When I said your name, I saw his soul return to his body. He smiled and said, 'Yes, sir, right away.' So there you have it. They fired Albino at two o'clock this morning; he should be down at the office now clearing out his things."

It took Margarito a moment to react. The leader looked at him impatiently.

"What's the matter, kid? Cat got your tongue?"

Margarito leaned forward to shake his hand.

"I won't disappoint you, sir."

"You already are. Look at those clothes. You can't go to work like that. Stop off and see Camacho before you go. He'll help you with whatever you need and give you a little something extra for incidentals. What year is that revolver from? Because that thing's definitely not a pistol."

"It's a Smith and Wesson."

"It looks like it fell out of last century. Buy yourself one of those new ones. No, wait. Fellas!"

Three of his entourage rushed into the room. The leader whispered something to one of them, who ran off and came back carrying a wooden case that he handed to Don Agustín. Without even looking at it, he walked over to where Margarito was standing and handed him the Colt .38 automatic. Margarito had heard of these guns, imagined them—even dreamed of them—but he'd never seen anything like it: solid metal, a real miniature cannon. The alloy on the grip was pleasant to the touch and textured with that famous crosshatch: once you wrapped your fingers around it, you didn't want to let go. Against the pitch-black steel, a silver stud on either side of the manufacturer's imprint gave the piece the elegant look of a cobra. The new chief of police lifted the weapon; it was as heavy as his mother's old-fashioned iron, and he thought to himself, noticing the sharp protrusion on the grip: *I bet this thing would be good for giving someone a knock on the head.* It had a nine-round magazine and a hair trigger: with the safety off, it would take only a sneeze. From the other side of the desk, the union leader seemed pleased by the impression he'd made.

"It's the same one police officers use in the United States. Standard issue."

"Don Agustín," said Margarito, practically on his knees. "I'm at your service."

"I should hope so, my boy. If anyone challenges me, I want you to take care of him. Don't forget who your leader is."

The first thing he did was drive the Jeep back to Los Coquitos, in his civilian clothes. He had an envelope with a thousand pesos in small bills in his shirt pocket and a bottle of good tequila in his right hand. He parked the Jeep in front of the kiosk and took the long way around the block to avoid drawing attention. When he walked up to the wooden house with the sheet metal roof, his old lady was chatting with a neighbor out front, and there was a black cat sitting with them. Both the neighbor and the cat ran off when they saw him coming, but the statuesque old woman dressed in white didn't budge. She simply furrowed her brow as he approached.

"I didn't know I had any children. What? They don't give you my messages?"

"Mother." The chief swallowed hard. "I need to talk to you."

"I don't see why. You've got a roof over your head. I know you're shacked up with that floozy upstairs from Don Cristóbal's bar. That you drink every day and put that powder up your nose."

"Mother," he said. "I'm the new chief of police."

The witch known as La Santa stared at him with eyes as wide as saucers; took another look at the Jeep parked in front of the lottery kiosk, paying special attention to its turret lights; and realized her son wasn't lying—not about this at least. For the first time in as long as he could remember, Margarito saw his mother's face brighten, even if only for a second. She quickly went back to her look of displeasure and her crocheting, which she had set aside when he arrived; just as quickly, her expression softened again and she looked Margarito in the eye.

"You still offering a reward for El Tilapia?"

The new chief of police nodded, stunned.

And that was how Margarito's relationship with his mother was restored, and how her legend continued to grow.

Margarito's working relationship with his mother lasted until shortly before she died. After months on bad terms over something that was said one liquor-soaked night, she asked him through several different channels to pay her a visit. She wouldn't walk again, not on her own, anyway. Margarito remembered how much trouble she'd had moving around those last few months.

"I walk like a parakeet," she would say. All the aches and pains of old age had come crashing down on her at once.

The day he'd gone to see her on her deathbed, La Santa had ordered him to sit down and listen. Convinced she was going to

put a curse on him or criticize him with her last breath, Margarito
was unprepared for what he heard.

"You'll be put to three brutal tests before your time runs out.
And you will understand what you've sown. Why we're put on
this earth."

Margarito looked at the neighbors surrounding his mother,
who shook their heads.

"She's delirious."

"I'm not delirious. There's something else."

She lay back and took Margarito's hand.

"You have another son out there. You have to find him—and
acknowledge him," she said and immediately added: "Strange.
I feel a wave pulling me backward. Am I being carried off by
a wave?" Her house was six miles from the beach, but no one
rushed to correct her.

When it was all over, her faithful neighbor Ubalda and nearly
a dozen girls between twelve and fifteen years old, all of whom
his mother had taken under her wing, stood around her bed
and wept. When Margarito got to his feet, he handed Ubalda
an envelope.

"Here. Make the arrangements how she would have wanted."

He stood there like a zombie while the neighbor and girls
tended to his mother's body. As he was about to leave, he noticed
a flash of red between the dead woman's fingers. He hesitated a
moment before going over to pry them open. Of course he would
have liked for her to reach out all of a sudden, for her death to
have been some kind of mistake (who wouldn't, in his place?).
But La Santa's strange journey through this life had reached
its end, so Margarito opened her hand and turned it over. *How
funny. Now I'm the one reading your palm, mi Santa.* His mother
had one last surprise in store for him: clasped in her palm was
one of the little prayer cards she'd had made up when she was

younger and people still believed in her powers of divination. Scrawled across it in a shaky hand was: *For Margarito*. That, he definitely didn't expect. He took one last look at La Santa, tucked the prayer card away, and hightailed it out of there.

First, they brought in the head of Nuevo León's police force. No one liked that, so he got killed one night as he walked through his front door. Then they made a general from San Luis named Aragón the chief of police, but the little angel only arrested Mr. Obregón's men and didn't hit the new guys with so much as a feather duster, so Obregón's people had him executed on the beach. Next came Chief Albino, then Lieutenant Elijah, sad memories both: the first one forced into retirement, and the second murdered in his own home. And now it was Margarito's turn.

The murder of Elijah Cohen marked Margarito's life as few things had. It's not every day you're called on to identify the mutilated body of your mentor. The crime, which was never solved—yet another of the precinct's many disgraces—was exceptionally vicious, and it gradually became a point of reference. Whenever a cop was about to piss off the oldest criminal organization operating in the port—one that had managed to operate under the radar for decades—whenever anyone was about to act against the best interest of that group, there was always some helpful colleague nearby, ready to repeat the mantra: "Remember what they did to Elijah?"

Of course Margarito remembers. It was 1981, and he'd made a long weekend for himself and gone on a three-day bender. When he got back to the precinct, everyone had seemed nervous around him. No one would talk to him or make eye contact. Cops always know when one of their own is in a bad way. They don't need evidence; their intuition is more than enough.

"What happened?" he asked one of the secretaries.

"Ask the chief," she said. "He wants to talk to you."

And the girl hurried off to deal with some urgent imaginary business at the other end of the office, never taking her eyes off him.

"Where were you last weekend?" asked Chief Albino, who was accompanied that day by the two most trusted members of his security detail. One sat on either side of Margarito.

"I was on a little getaway with a young woman."

"Does this young woman have a name and telephone number? Can she corroborate your story?"

Margarito, surprised, raised an eyebrow.

"I've even got receipts, if you like."

"Let me see them," said the chief, holding out his hand. "And while we're at it, might as well give me your gun."

Margarito obeyed both orders. He was well aware that involving the gorgeous Italian girl he was seeing would be disastrous for the relationship, but the young police officer had no choice but to give up her phone number and address.

"Right now, she's at my place."

The chief sent someone in a patrol car over to check out Margarito's alibi, took the gun, and asked, "So you really don't know what they did to Elijah?"

"What happened?"

The chief explained to Margarito that a bus driver had found his body where it was dumped on the outskirts of the city and had called it in as soon as he got back to the depot. Barefoot, naked from the waist down, blood-soaked shirt, arms and fingers broken, his torso looking like ground meat from all the stab wounds, an expression of intense pain on his face. His arms were outstretched, and a heavy rag had been shoved down his throat to muffle his screams. It almost looked as if his corpse was still fighting against the inevitable. They didn't hack off his tongue or genitals, the way they did with rats and rapists, but they did take his eyes.

Margarito never forgot the image of the man who'd taught him so much. He'd seen something he shouldn't have seen or refused to cooperate with someone, and that was the end of him. To be honest, though, Margarito had seen it coming.

Lieutenant Elijah's lucky star had begun to fade when he started distancing himself from his friends in the criminal under-world. He didn't trust Margarito anymore, so he'd taken to giving him assignments that were total wastes of time: patrolling neighborhoods where nothing happened, serving as a messenger or driver for one politician or another, following up on reports filed by mischievous kids or little old ladies with nothing better to do.

He knew trouble was brewing when Elijah's informants—the skittish, untrusting types he'd meet with in bars—vanished from the piers. They were all on the run. One time, on an errand for a politician in the bar of the port's fanciest hotel, Margarito realized he was somewhere he shouldn't be when he saw Elijah sitting at a table in the back, chatting casually but without a smile on his face with one of the port's better-known dealers: Antonio Gray, who sold marijuana on the malecón. It was him, no question about it: the thick beard, the crisp checked shirt that looked fresh off the rack, the designer pants and fancy shoes. He'd realized that his boss and mentor was into some serious shit when he saw the look on the other man's face. Elijah had pretended not to see him, and a little while later they found his body.

He knew no one was going to step up to investigate Elijah's death. The lieutenant's murder was so shocking that the news-papers treated it with absolute discretion, publishing only an obituary and a notice paid for by the family, indicating where the funeral would be held. That was all. It was the kind of thing the government kept quiet.

He spent the next few weeks searching his soul and wondering which, of all the cases Elijah was working at the time of his death, could have made his mentor as nervous and irritable as he'd been in his final days. Honestly, he'd been unbearable. Margarito questioned the officers who worked with Elijah while he'd been off duty, but all he got was the sense that none of them had anything resembling a lead. He spoke with El Tigre Obregón, who was still alive back then and had gone to the funeral, but the man swore up and down he had nothing to do with it.

"Whoever did this is a monster."

In this general climate of suspicion, Margarito kept a close eye on the officers around him for the next few weeks. Hell if he didn't miss the old man.

He had only one fight with Elijah in more than ten years that he could remember, but it was decisive. Elijah had told him how an organization that had recently arrived from the other side of the country had killed two men in the trade with unprecedented brutality down near the beach. He'd never seen anything like it, he said; it was totally unacceptable. Then he cracked a wry smile.

"You think your buddy El Tigre Obregón was a little angel all those years? He iced his share of enemies and traitors too. We just haven't figured out where he buried them yet. I'm not holding my breath, but I wouldn't be surprised if we got a tip one day and discovered a bunch of missing persons in a secret graveyard out there on one of his ranches in the sierra. The only difference between the guys who were already here and the ones arriving now is that the old guard liked to do things quietly, keep clear of the rest of society, and the new guys are in a hurry. They want to make their presence felt, mark their territory. They want to rule by fear. Like we were all born yesterday."

Elijah leaned toward him.

"Don't forget Mr. Baldomero's ranch—or the one they said belonged to him. Ten years ago, we got a report that there's people buried out there, and we went out to investigate: twelve bodies we found, killed execution-style. Just as we were checking to make sure they weren't people from the port who'd gone missing, an order comes in from the higher-ups: *Leave it alone.* So we did."

"What are you proposing?"

"We've put up with these bastards long enough. Let's get rid of the problem."

"You're nuts, Elijah."

"We've always gone at this thing half-assed. We'll do it right this time. There's an airplane arriving from Bolivia on Tuesday: we take out the pilot, seize the coke, and use what we get for it to buy weapons. Then we run those assholes out."

"Not interested."

"But that's just the beginning. We need to get a group together, people we trust, and go after Los Nuevos and the people close to your godson. Otherwise Los Nuevos are going to gather some serious fucking momentum, and there'll be no stopping them. We need to hit them now."

Margarito hesitated, beer in hand. Long enough that old Elijah saw his window and took it: "So? You in?"

Margarito set the bottle on the table.

"You don't take advice, so I won't bother giving you any."

"I trust you'll keep quiet. Otherwise, you're dead."

"Don't threaten me."

"It's not a threat; it's the truth."

Margarito stood and left without another word. And that was the end of that friendship.

There's a little room deep down inside Margarito, a little room he keeps locked with a dead bolt, where he mourns the way his relationship with his mentor fell apart. He went to see the old man later that night, after several tequilas. La Tonina was with him. When he saw Margarito, Elijah had said, "So it's you they sent."

It went so badly for him because he tried to defend himself. He almost got away a couple of times. Like when he tried to sneak out the kitchen window. If La Tonina hadn't grabbed him by the legs and used those knives, he would have been long gone. It's true: his body ended up in pretty bad shape, so in a gesture of goodwill toward the family, Margarito decided it would be best to dump it somewhere deserted. So it wouldn't be found. His only mistake was leaving the job to La Tonina. It didn't take them more than a half hour to find him, out there on the outskirts of the city.

So, whenever someone asks if he remembers what happened to Elijah, Margarito has to be careful not to give the answer he desperately wants to: "No, not really. I was pretty drunk that night."

8

At ten past seven he picked up his cell phone and, against his better judgment, called the office. He knew that whoever organized the attack could find him if the phones at headquarters were tapped, but even the most skilled technician would need the conversation to last at least sixty seconds to locate the signal. Still, it couldn't hurt to be careful.

La Gordis picked up right away.

"Boss? How are you?"

"Don't say my name, and be discreet with your answers. What's going on over there?"

"Why didn't you pick up? You had us worried."

"You're shitting me, right? I saw you less than an hour and a half ago."

"No, sir. We haven't heard from you in twenty-four hours."

"What?"

La Gordis hesitated.

"You took the pills, didn't you?"

"What are you talking about?"

"Yesterday was the twenty-fourth of August. Today's the twenty-fifth. I dropped you off yesterday at five thirty, and now it's after seven . . . a day later."

The chief couldn't believe his ears. He checked his cell phone, and there it was: a little 25 in the corner of the screen, instead of a 24.

"When you didn't pick up, I called the paramedics and they said if you'd overdone it even a little, you could be out for up to a day. And that's what happened, I guess. I was just on my way to get you. I was worried sick."

Son of a bitch, he thought. *Now I'm really screwed: the girl, the ransom . . . La Muda's nerves must be totally shot, and I'm sure they've run out of provisions and sleeping pills for the girl . . . God-damn it. Gotta get moving.*

"The medicine knocked me out," he apologized. "I hadn't expected that."

"Listen," Roberta interrupted him. "It's not safe for you to be calling the office like this. I'll call you back in two minutes." Then she explained how she'd just bought a cell phone for the sole purpose of communicating with him and that there was no way they'd been able to tap it yet. Two minutes later she called him from a new number.

"What's up?"

"The most urgent thing is that you need to talk to the mayor. He's called three times asking about you. I told him you're fine, that you're recuperating, but he said if you don't call back he's going to have you replaced tonight."

The chief weighed the various risks he faced.

"Get me a line through to him, but first I want a rundown of what's been going on."

"You don't want me to come pick you up? It's kind of a long list."

"No, just give me a quick rundown. There's something I have to do before going to the office."

"Yes, sir. So, you haven't been watching the news? The port's been turned upside down. They're burning vehicles outside Los Coquitos and Colonia Sierra too."

He wasn't surprised. Two of the warring capos lived and worked in those neighborhoods. His godson and the head of Los Nuevos, respectively. As usual, they'd sent someone to burn a few cars as a threat and a way of marking territory.

"The army's checkpoints are still in place, but word has it there were armed men going around to the hospitals last night, looking for you."

"El Flaco's all right?"

"Yes, sir. The army's been with him. They even stationed an armored Jeep in the parking lot."

"And did we get an ID on the dead gunmen? Were they local?"

"I found them. Know where? In the files Interpol left for you. They were from Guatemala. They crossed the border in Chiapas eight days ago."

"Got it. I'll call you back in ten."

He hung up and walked over to the window. The water was calm in the distance, but closer to where the chief was, huge waves were forming on either side of the bay and coming together with a thunderous crash in the middle, as if an enormous child were squatting over it, gleefully slamming the masses of water together with his hands. Was he imagining things, or was there a black pickup parked near the beach?

He took one look at his clothes and realized he needed to change. His shirt and the front of his pants were splattered with blood. *I wouldn't make it to the corner in these rags. I'd draw too much attention.* He went back to the master bedroom and swung open the closet door. *Goddamn! I hit the fucking jackpot.* At least three dozen crisply ironed designer shirts hung above nine drawers full of pretty much anything his heart could desire: pants, pajamas, ties, boxers, T-shirts, socks. When he pulled out the last and biggest drawer, he gave a low whistle of admiration: it contained an impressive collection of sneakers, Top-Siders, loafers, and dress shoes in every color imaginable, even white. He grabbed what he thought was the most attractive pair (crocodile leather with a gold buckle) and noticed with a smile that he and the owner of the place had lots in common: they both wore a size large in clothing and a nine in shoes. Did this asshole wear boots? He opened one of the lower drawers and found half a dozen pairs in different styles, none of them too elaborate. *This closet's unbelievable. It's like something out of Aladdin's lamp. All right*, he thought. *One problem solved.*

He looked out the window. The same two kids were heading out to play basketball again. As he was about to leave, he grabbed an understated guayabera that seemed a little more worn than the rest; he had a hard time finding an old pair of pants, though. *Come on*, he thought. *This guy doesn't own normal clothes?* After finally finding a threadbare pair in white cotton that wouldn't be missed, he gave Roberta a call.

"What else?"

"Another important thing, sir: the gas truck driver was shot point-blank."

"He was killed by his own crew?"

"The man in black was in the passenger seat. Before getting out to join the ambush, he executed him with one shot to the temple."

The chief remembered how the man in black hadn't hesitated for a second as he came at him with his weapon drawn. A real professional.

"I'm guessing the driver was unarmed, right?"

"We didn't find anything on him."

Roberta had confirmed his hunch: they'd hired guys from outside to do the job, guys who'd be disposable, and sent a coordinator along with them to cover their tracks if anything went wrong.

"Here's how it went down: they stole the tanker truck from the refinery that morning. They must've known there'd be hardly anyone there at that hour. They caught them just as they were opening; then one of them cracked the driver with the butt of his gun and they made off with the truck. They blocked the street just as you were passing, and then the rest of the crew pulled up. Oh, and one more thing: the tanker was empty. Our minute's up. Over and out."

As he thought back on the ambush, his head began to ache. It had taken him a while to recognize that whoever planned the ambush was a skilled strategist. There had been at least one moment during the firefight when he'd thought twice about shooting at his attackers, afraid the tanker might blow.

It felt as if someone was trying to rip his head off, and a furious buzzing filled his ears. He rubbed his neck and headed for the television to make sure it was still turned off, but he didn't get that far: the sound was coming from the nearest window. A swarm of bees, probably African, was making a hive out there. Just then, he remembered another possible avenue of investigation and called Roberta.

"At the ready, sir."

"Have you been to the gas company? Did you get composite sketches?"

"We tried, but the crew had their faces covered. They showed up the morning of the attack, held the workers at gunpoint as they were on their way to fill up the tankers, then took one of the trucks that was still empty. Looks like they'd been studying the workers' routines."

That must have taken at least a week, Margarito thought. They must have contacts in the city.

"Find out who the gas company belongs to."

"Yes, sir."

"What are the doctors saying about El Flaco?"

"He's still in intensive care. They tell us the same thing every time we call." Roberta swallowed hard before continuing. "That he's in critical but stable condition."

"And the bastard I hit in the leg?" he asked, referring to the man in black.

"El Chino found the escape vehicle abandoned on a hill nearby. Before he got out he shot the driver, and that was where we lost him. We've visited both hospitals and even checked with local veterinarians, but none of them treated a bullet wound last night, and none of them were missing antibiotics or morphine, not counting the guy from the ambulance."

Son of a bitch, the chief sighed. *The man in black really wanted to vanish into thin air.*

"We're still looking for the attackers, but no one's answered the APBs we put out. There's no trace of the black pickup; it seems like the earth swallowed them whole. No one knows where they are. Your wife called several times, as well. She wants to talk to you, but she says her calls aren't going through."

"Tell her I'll get hold of her. She shouldn't call me. Did you give her my message?"

"Yes, sir. She's been at the funeral home since last night. There are two army Jeeps there with her."

"Over and out."

The chief was silent for as long as it took a few waves to crash on the shore. The bitch named Sorrow, again. He was surprised when La Gordis called a moment later.

"Are you feeling any better, Chief?"

"I feel dizzy and like a fucking idiot. Those pills knocked me on my ass."

"And your arm?"

"It's all right. Getting there."

"That's all?"

"That's all for now. What time . . . Did Dr. Antonelli tell you what time—"

"Yes, sir. The funeral will be today at three, in the Spanish cemetery. Your wife wasn't doing too well after what happened and decided to have it sooner."

Margarito took a deep breath, and the bitch named Sorrow sat down beside him: he wasn't even going to be able to say good-bye to his son.

"And someone's come for La Tonina and El Dorado?"

"Yes, boss. I called their widows. Well, La Tonina's widow. El Dorado lived alone. She was pretty broken up. She came with their kid to claim the body. She cried and cried, spent the whole night going back and forth between headquarters and the morgue until they finally gave her the body. El Carcamán brought him back to their house, where they'll be mourning him."

Poor Tonina, he thought. *You never got those dollars coming to you from the kidnapping.* If everything worked out, he should probably make sure to give the widow a little something.

Before hanging up, he asked, "How's the team?" What he should have said was: *How's what's left of my team?* Roberta sighed.

"Nervous, sir. They don't know where any of this is coming from. What's going to happen. They're scared. And there's something else, sir"—Roberta cleared her throat—"I hate to gossip, but some people around the precinct are saying that you planned the whole thing. That you put Ricardo in the Suburban because you knew it wasn't armored."

"Those motherfuckers. Who's saying that?"

"Bracamontes."

"As far as I know, the only one who has an armored vehicle is him, when he's out running errands for the mayor."

"And what should I tell General Rovirosa? He calls every twenty minutes."

Margarito decided it was too risky to call him from his own phone.

"Find him and patch me through. I'll call you in a bit," he said and hung up.

Man, he thought. *It was too risky to make calls from there, where they could locate him and come after him at any moment.*

Margarito's mind turned to Bracamontes and his accusations. *What is that bastard up to?* The next time he saw him, that asshole was going to eat his words.

Then his thoughts wandered back to the girl, and he suddenly got nervous. He needed to call La Muda. The girl's father would be worried, too, but even though he knew the number by heart, he couldn't call it from his cell phone. That would mean incriminating himself, and he couldn't call from the house where he was staying, because the consul would track him with his little toys. He had to get the hell out of there and go find her, or La Muda was going to drop dead from the stress. His accomplice's only shortcoming was that she had no stomach for being alone: she worried about everything, couldn't handle the pressure. But first he wanted to go back over the attack, starting with the death threat. He was still so dizzy, though. Those pills had really done a number on him.

He had a rash on his forehead. He'd been scratching it unconsciously all night. Of all his different pains—his whole body hurt—the stabbing sensation in his left arm was the worst. Luckily it didn't seem as swollen as the medic had predicted: sure, his muscles were softer, weaker up by his shoulder, but he could still move his elbow, wrist, and fingers. He wouldn't be able to react as quickly as usual if his instincts sent him a telegram, but at least he could shoot or drive with that arm if he needed to. His only worry was that the unbearable pain would come back, now that the drugs were wearing off. Or the bitch named Sorrow, of course.

A drowsy voice inside his head told him to eat something before calling Roberta back, especially if he was thinking about taking more pills, so he grabbed the plastic bag of provisions.

He needed to assemble a team he could trust. *I need an armored vehicle and a team with weapons. Get the general's help. Pressure that asshole until he agrees.*

He knew that every time he picked up the phone he ran the risk of being located by his attackers, so he told himself he'd answer only if it was Roberta calling. And even then he'd think twice about it.

He couldn't stand the rash on his forehead one more minute, so he went into the bathroom to take a look in the mirror: his hair and face were still covered in shards of glass. He ran his hand through his hair and showered the sink with crystalline splinters.

He went back to the closet in the master bedroom and found everything there a gentleman could need to take a shower: not just shampoos and soaps, but also aromatic bath oils—luxuries he'd never allowed himself. In one drawer, he found shaving creams, lotions, a variety of razors, aftershaves, so he placed his weapon on the counter, opened the taps in the sink and the shower, and started to shave before the water even got warm.

While the bathroom filled with steam, he turned on the television he'd found in the next room and changed the channel to his favorite news program. Much to his dismay, he could tune in only to the arts and culture channel. It was still ten minutes before they went through the headlines, so he needed to wait out the talk show currently on the air, which featured a group of local writers discussing the words used most often in La Eternidad. *Well, shit*, he thought.

"I propose we shift the focus of this program a bit," said one of the panelists. "Why don't we talk about the words people use *least* in this city? Like the word *ethics*, or *justice*. It seems to me these terms are fading from sight like boats cut from their moorings, drifting out to sea."

Caught up in the debate, Margarito shaved off a significant chunk of his mustache; if he evened out the other side, he'd look like a 1950s cholo. He figured it probably wasn't a bad idea to change his look a bit, so he got rid of the whole thing and his sideburns, too.

The panelist was right about one thing: when he was a kid, all it would take was one policeman walking into his neighborhood, and people would stand at attention as if they were watching a lion pass. You'd hear the neighborhood parents say, "Look, son. That's Captain Elijah, one of the boys in blue. Let him and his men through. Don't give them any trouble." People could sense that strange aura, the weight, the mystery, and the danger those officers represented. After so many years on the job, Margarito had come to the conclusion that when he and his colleagues were working or when they were on their way home, they didn't move through space the way other people did: there was something different about their walk, their gaze. In those fleeting moments, they transmitted the gravitas of the law, as if people understood what it meant for a guy dressed in blue to be carrying an automatic pistol in his holster. All they had to do was knock on the door of any house and ask for someone by name, and everyone within earshot knew something serious was going down. It only used to take one cop, just one, to make an arrest: the perp would simply accept that the game was up and it was time to submit to a power greater than himself. Of course, as you got older and started hearing more accurate stories about the policemen's motives for visiting the neighborhood, you came to understand that justice and the police force don't always go hand in hand in this country. In a perfect world they'd be joined at the hip, but here—as in many other countries—justice and the police acknowledge one another from afar with a little nod, but they ultimately live separate lives.

"We need to stop there, unfortunately, as we've run out of time. Our program tonight was brought to you by funding from the state. Up next, Agapito Fernández's Ballet Folklórico has prepared a special performance for us."

The three little dipshits, thought Margarito as he turned off the television. He'd listened to enough stupidity for a while, so he went in to take a shower.

When he'd dried himself off, he put on some deodorant and one of the homeowner's aftershave lotions. He reminded himself to ask Panda whose place it was. Before leaving the bathroom, he took a look at his reflection. Clean-shaven with short hair, a white guayabera, and cotton pants, the chief barely recognized himself. *Carajo, it must be twenty years since I saw myself without a mustache.* He tucked his pistol into his belt, outside his shirt, and headed downstairs.

Conversation in the dark

"Did you hear?"

"What? Did they find him?"

"Not yet. But it won't be long. The port's not that big, and there's no way he got past the checkpoints. It's just a matter of time. And then he's gonna pay. Hell yes you will, you son of a bitch."

"The say the devil himself watches over him. That's why the bullets never hit their mark. Did you see the video?"

"How could I miss it? It's been all over the TV. And yeah, he barely made it out of there. The bastard was lucky."

"Sure, but you've got to hand it to him: he's still got nerves of steel. They're turning him into some kind of hero. The survivor."

"I know. He stands up and *pop pop*, there goes the first cholo, then *pop*, he takes the other one out with one shot, then—BANG—he hits a third one, who's coming at him with a fucking machine gun, in the leg. Then he drops the guy coming at him from behind, as fast as I'm telling it now. Not bad for an old man. But his luck is running out."

"Luck had nothing to do with it. Those fuckers were high off their asses. Anyone could have taken them out like that."

"The government's offering a hundred thousand pesos for information on the attackers' whereabouts."

"One fucking hundred thousand pesos? Stingy bastards. They obviously don't want to find them. Who would turn them in for that?"

"There's fifty thousand *dollars* on the table for the other one."

"For Margarito?"

"Uh-huh. At first they offered twenty, then they kept piling it on."

"That's one hell of a death sentence. Bastard doesn't have much time left. I wouldn't want to be in his shoes."

"Who would, man?"

"You know what I do want, though, is to get my hands on him before anyone else does. Who'd turn down fifty grand?"

9

Margarito's phone rang a few minutes later. *Roberta must have patched me through to the general*, he thought. He held up his watch, careful to keep the call under a minute. But it was the mayor.

"Chief! I'd given you up for dead."

"The pills knocked me out, but I'm on my way."

"Listen, I've given it some thought, and I think it would be best if someone else took over from here."

Margarito had seen it coming.

"I'm getting my team together, and we've already made some real progress. If you pull me out now, that's all gone."

"I'd rather—"

"Just give me until tomorrow morning, and you'll have my resignation."

He listened to the buzz of the telephone connection.

"You're that confident? Fine. In that case, you have until nine tomorrow morning. I'll be expecting your letter of resignation by nine fifteen."

"I'll deliver it myself, along with the assailants."

The mayor hung up, and Margarito heard Roberta breathing on the other end of the line.

"You heard the man, Roberta. We have to hurry. Call me back, the minute's almost up."

The call came in a few seconds later. La Gordis cut right to the chase.

"Sir? Bad news. They found one of the two fugitives."

"The man in black?"

"No, the cholo. They'd dumped him in the ravine."

"I'll be damned. Go over everything with a fine-tooth comb, and let me know what you find."

"Yes, sir. And there's something else."

"Tell me."

"They're offering fifty thousand dollars for you."

"What?"

"A few of the officers heard about it while they were taking statements."

"Who put up the money?"

"No one knows who's behind it. Could be guys in the trade, maybe Los Nuevos. But the word is definitely getting around."

Shit, he thought. *I'm going to have to be careful.*

"Another thing. A video from the shoot-out got leaked to the press. One from the security camera in the jewelry store. It's being aired across the country. You totally *drop* those guys."

His head throbbed. That was all the mayor needed to put him away. He needed to hang up.

"Take care of yourself, kid. Stay out of trouble."

"Don't worry, boss."

Fifty thousand dollars . . . If they were offering that for one of his colleagues, he'd be the first to cash in.

He felt like he was going to throw up. He decided he needed to drink something and headed for the kitchen.

His ex-wife would have loved this place; whoever owned it liked to cook. Behind the wooden cupboard doors, shelf after shelf held pans, blenders, and other stainless steel appliances he couldn't identify. As he'd expected, the refrigerator was empty and stank of mildew. It had been unplugged for weeks. He looked through the open cupboard, but found only expired food. He kicked himself for not having Roberta buy him more soda. *Son of a bitch*, he thought. *In a few hours, the whole world will have changed.*

Without his breakfast of champions, he was seized by a headache that was, in fact, a case of withdrawal. *A shame,* he thought. *This fucking house was almost perfect.* He didn't have the strength to keep looking, so he went to the living room to lie down.

Half asleep and with his head still pounding, Margarito spent a long time among the pleasant beach-house couches, watching the light filter through the glass door. Outside, the morning sun cast a calming glow over the sand—but there's no peace for some men without their coffee and cola. He knew he couldn't stay there long, but the light in the palm trees was delightful and, from where he was sitting, his problems seemed so far away. If it weren't for the pain in his arm, he could almost believe it was all happening to someone else. Maybe it was the pills, but for a moment he felt like a guest in his own body and his only company was the bitch named Sorrow.

He got up after five minutes. *I've got to be careful. They're not going to get me like they did the union leader.*

Before the violence started, La Eternidad was one of the best places on earth to live in. It wasn't the most famous port, but it was one of the most peaceful.

Drivers used to stop for pedestrians. You'd get a friendly, sincere greeting from everyone you passed on the street. You could leave your house or your car unlocked, your heart open; you could take your girlfriend for a walk under the stars, let your kids play soccer in the street. But that was then. None of that's possible now, when everyone does whatever they want and your survival instinct screams: *Keep your mouth shut and your eyes down, and get out while you still can. It's every man for himself.*

Margarito knew the men behind the violence, the ones who were fighting over the port. Hell, they'd even worked together. For starters, he'd known the head of the Cartel del Puerto in La Eternidad since before he got into the trade.

One night he and La Tonina were on patrol in the old Jeep when they detected unusual activity at a private home: a guy was taking packages from inside the house and loading them onto a pickup truck. They figured it must be the thief from Colonia Petrolera whose arrest meant a reward, so they drew on him. But the guy said it was his house, showed them the keys, and insisted the vehicle was his too. There was still something strange about that truck full of packages, though, so they put the squeeze on.

"And what do we have here, you little sneak?" The packages were different shapes and sizes, but they were all wrapped in the same brown paper. Margarito tore open one of the bigger ones: it was a fancy new television set from the United States—the latest model, with a remote control and rabbit ears.

"Weeelllll, well, well. You're cooked, papá. Cuff him."

"Son of a bitch," laughed the man. "There must be some mistake."

The officers looked at each other wearily. Which made sense, since they'd been on duty for forty-eight hours straight. When Margarito grabbed his billy club and started walking toward him, though, the man admitted he had contraband.

"Okay, okay." He wasn't begging, so much as he was laughing at the situation. "Just don't hit me. There's no need. I got around gringo customs, Mexican customs, and three federal checkpoints on the highway—and now I'm getting arrested by two cops on my way into my own home to have a cup of coffee. I just got back from the border. Look, this is what I came down here for."

The man pointed to a package and Margarito tore it open. Inside was a small electric coffeepot.

"It's the fucking latest and greatest. You wouldn't believe this thing. It's practically a robot. Listen, it's cold out and I just wanted a cup of coffee. That's it."

"You a smuggler?"

"Come on . . . a smuggler? I deal in building materials and electronics. And the occasional bottle of whiskey."

They loaded him into the patrol vehicle, handcuffed, and made a deal.

"You take him back to the station and lock him up. Tell whoever's at the front desk that we caught him in flagrante for robbery. I'll find a car, load up this stuff, and leave it in your living room."

Margarito, who'd had a talent for strategizing his moves ever since he was young, shook his head.

"Why would you go find a car, kid, when we've got the truck right here? We'll take that too. Waste not, want not."

"And if this numbskull rats us out?"

Margarito sighed.

"Fine. We'll take him to lockup together, then come back for the stuff. Bring the television and the coffeepot as evidence."

"Maybe just the coffeepot," said his partner. "Was thinking I might keep the TV."

"You're making a mistake," said the man in cuffs, still laughing. "Really, though. You guys sure are dense. You don't know a friend when you see one!"

"Shut it, asshole. When we get to the precinct we'll check for priors. Let's see who's laughing then."

The man fell silent.

"Oh, so you've got priors? Uh-oh, papá . . . Looks like someone just stepped in it."

"Doesn't look so tough now, does he?"

"Man, do we get a bonus for bringing this punk in?" asked La Tonina. "'Cause if not, why bother?"

"My dear officers," the smuggler began, leaning forward from the back seat. "What kind of reward are they offering for me? A thousand pesos? Fifteen hundred?"

He was pretty close: it wasn't a lot of money, which is why they had to produce a steady stream of arrests and didn't care whether they handed over the guilty party or some innocent sap they'd dressed up for the occasion. La Tonina looked at him in the rearview mirror.

"Let's say it's two thousand pesos," the smuggler continued. "I can do better than that if you take me to my office. I have a safe there."

The officers barely glanced at one another.

"How much are we talking?" La Tonina replied.

The smuggler looked at them and did a quick calculation.

"Two thousand dollars. Each. In cash."

That's when they realized the man in the back of their car wasn't just any perp. It was the middle of the night, probably three, three thirty. No one was going to be looking for them at that hour.

To the officers' surprise, he directed them to an office building downtown, right across from the Bank of Mexico, one block from headquarters. A night watchman opened the door for them, and they went up to the third floor.

"Congratulations, gentlemen," he said as he walked up the marble staircase. "You're doing the right thing. I'm a peaceable man, I don't want any trouble. I make friends wherever I go."

"Don't get ahead of yourself," said La Tonina. "Try to screw us, and you can kiss your ass good-bye."

Two thousand dollars was the annual salary for cops like them, including bonuses. But at that point they were there out of curiosity as much as anything else. *If this asshole is offering us two thousand dollars,* they thought, *he's got to be worth a hell of a lot more.*

"Don't try anything."

A voice stopped them cold as soon as they walked into the office. He saw the shocked expression on the face of La Tonina, who was looking over his shoulder, and realized they were in a jam. Just as he was about to turn, Margarito felt metal press into his spine and prudently put his hands in the air. Whoever it was behind him withdrew the gun and said, "On your knees, both of you."

"Easy, now. These are my friends," said the smuggler. "Keep an eye on them, of course, but have them sit over there in those chairs. And get their identification."

The man behind them relieved them of their wallets in a flash and tossed them onto the desk. The cops sat down with their hands up while the man they'd arrested just a few minutes earlier walked over to his safe, whistling the mariachi classic "El son de la negra" the whole time. Out of the corner of his eye, Margarito saw that the safe was full of bundled money. Resting on top of the piles was a big serrated knife with a staghorn handle, and off to the side was something that looked horrifyingly like a human limb.

"These two picked me up right after you dropped me off," he said to the man standing behind them. "Good thing I'd sent you here. Now, now," he cautioned one of the officers. "Don't even think about it."

La Tonina, whose right hand had been inching toward a heavy paperweight, put both hands up again. The smuggler exchanged a glance with Margarito, who'd been eyeing the inside of the safe with concern. The smuggler didn't seem like such a nobody any-more. He was around forty, a plump five foot six with blond hair and pale skin. At first glance, he looked like the son of the Span-iards who'd settled in La Eternidad, but it took only a word to give him away: his lack of refinement spelled out a life spent in the sierra. That's when Margarito realized who he was.

For years, his photo—taken when he was much younger, with more hair on top and less flesh around the middle—had hung on the wall of the precinct. He was wanted for the murder of a customs officer, though his name was tied to numerous other crimes. Margarito knew that Elijah had nearly caught him a few times with traps set especially for him. On each of those occa-sions, the suspect had found a way to avoid capture just when Elijah thought he had him.

"He's the slipperiest bastard I've ever seen," his mentor had said. "A tough one, big game."

He was known as the cleverest smuggler there was of alcohol and electronics, able to make the seven-hour trip to the border and back in five. Now, all the coke and marijuana dealers in the state reported to him. El Tigre Obregón. One of the FBI's and DEA's most wanted. A man who butchered anyone who betrayed him. And there he was, right in front of Margarito, getting some-thing from his safe.

The smuggler looked at the two officers, estimating their price, or how much they could cost him. Then he took out two bundles and set them on the desk.

"Two and two make four."

The officers didn't blink.

"Those were the terms, no? Candelario, I'd like to introduce you to two new friends." He glanced at a guy with thick arms and a thick head of hair who was almost as tall as him.

"Is it me, or did it get fucking cold again?"

The smuggler opened a small wardrobe and pulled out a jacket that looked like real leopard hide. Then he grabbed the knife and what turned out to be, to Margarito's and La Tonina's relief, a huge leg of serrano ham. Finally, he sat at his desk, put on a pair of glasses, and went through the two wallets.

"This one here is Epigmenio Torres Merino. The other one . . . Jesus, is your name really Margarito?"

El Tigre Obregón erupted in laughter again.

"Margarito González. You're awfully big for that little name, aren't you?"

La Tonina cleared his throat.

"Well. I'd wanted a cup of coffee, but seeing as how you gentlemen seized my coffee maker, it looks like I'm taking myself off the wagon. Whiskey or tequila? Hmm? Fine. Tequila, it is."

He turned to grab a bottle and three shot glasses from the safe. He filled each until it overflowed and pushed two of them toward the officers. After they'd breathed off the alcohol's fire, the man spoke.

"I'm an entrepreneur, a businessman. I don't want any trouble. I do business with all the federales between here and Matamoros. The chief customs officer is like a brother to me, and those assholes at the checkpoints might as well be my kids. I've never had any problems. Now. Tell me. Just what kind of police are you, to come sniffing around my house? Might I interest you in some serrano ham, gentlemen?"

They talked until six in the morning, when the four of them headed downstairs. They'd finished the bottle, but none of them felt it. They said good-bye with a hug.

"See you around."

When they finally made it back to the Jeep, the man insisted they keep the television and coffee maker. Margarito looked at La Tonina and sighed.

"We were going to seize his inventory, but we ended up being the ones taken in for questioning."

The next time he passed El Tigre's house, he noticed it was being rented out. From then on, the man's legend grew with every new rumor: That he'd moved somewhere safer, to a more affluent neighborhood; that he'd bought this and that warehouse. That business was booming. That he'd joined up with a few of the other young smugglers and the ladies who fenced their black market goods. That he didn't even need to cross the border anymore because he had a whole network to do it for him.

He knew, because Candelario had told La Tonina that the crisis of 1982 was a trial by fire for El Tigre. The middle class, which had always clamored for medicine and merchandise from north of the border, stopped buying because they had no way to pay for any of it. With more than fifty cops on his payroll, El Tigre had to diversify. La Tonina told him that one night when El Tigre really had no idea how he was going to get himself out of the red, they were drinking in one of the restaurants he owned along the highway in Texas and a Colombian showed up. He wanted them to move some of his blow, and that's when it hit him: they knew the roads, the routes; he'd developed relationships—friendships, even—with all the customs agents. Over the years, he'd turned them from a vicious pack of dogs used to extorting and robbing travelers, into docile house pets trained to collect a commission on every truckload of contraband that crossed the border. He knew every gas station, every motel, every warehouse: the stretch of map between La Eternidad and the north held no mysteries for his organization. The problem was the merchandise, which just wasn't profitable anymore. So he joined a new league: he stopped transporting alcohol and electronics (tequila for the Texans, televisions for the Mexicans) and dedicated himself to moving weed and blow. He traded his fleet of cars for pickups, trucks, and trailers. He founded phantom businesses, pretended to become a farmer, a rancher, a fisherman. It went so well that he stopped working for the Colombians and they started working for him. Back then, in the seventies and eighties, the best weapon for keeping people in line was a fat wallet.

Margarito's friendship with El Tigre only got stronger when he was promoted. Under the protection of La Eternidad's new chief of police, El Tigre bought mansions, hotels, travel agencies, art galleries, movie theaters, even entire shopping malls—businesses he could use to justify his income—and no one blinked an eye. The same thing that happens anywhere in the civilized world these days. El Tigre had set up his network so well that his money and drugs could move between the Texas border and the marijuana fields in Oaxaca and Guerrero or the labs in Cali without ever being disturbed. Who was going to mess with the state police? Margarito occasionally escorted El Tigre's trucks to Gringoland himself, looking for a change of scene and a little pocket money. In five years, he was stopped only once by a Mexican border agent, who was surprised to see him in those parts.

"What's a patrol vehicle from La Eternidad doing in Matamoros? You're seven hours out of your jurisdiction, kid. And why is your trunk full of tomatoes?"

Margarito wasn't intimidated.

"Man, you have no idea how good these fucking tomatoes are."

The agent scowled at him. Before things escalated, Margarito shifted tactics.

"You know Pepino Calles, the chief customs officer?"

"Fuck yes I do."

"Give him a call and tell him Margarito's here. I'll wait for you."

The agent returned five minutes later.

"Okay, I get it. You're just passing through on a little joyride. Wasn't there some kind of tip?"

Margarito handed over two hundred dollars, they shook hands, and he was let through.

In the late eighties, El Tigre had such a tight grip on the highways in Tamaulipas that he started renting them out. Knowing how safe it was to use those routes, and how they wouldn't have any trouble with the police as long as they sent El Tigre Obregón's regards, distributors from across the country would come to La Eternidad to strike a deal: they'd pay the fee to pass through, and it was settled.

So you could say Margarito knew El Tigre from the beginning. Or, in his own words, since before they became compadres.

They got together often to cut loose. The chief would show up at one of El Tigre's many restaurants with a few girls and get the party started. Then, when they were good and hammered, the bad jokes would begin.

"Tigre . . . you're going to the slammer."

"Oh? For what?"

"Illegal transportation of military weapons, money laundering, drug trafficking."

"No shit! Tell me something I don't know."

Anytime they had a problem, El Tigre would say, "No, no, no. We're going to talk this out, like men. What do you want? A friend or an enemy?"

When El Tigre's first son, Joel, was born, Margarito agreed to be his godfather.

For years, Margarito was under the impression that Don Agustín's people and El Tigre's left one another alone. He knew all too well that the union leader didn't think much of El Tigre and didn't expect him to be around too long, though El Tigre ultimately outlasted him by a bit. Margarito would never forget the call he got from El Tigre late one night toward the end of the nineties.

"Compadre, I need to talk to you right away. Drop whatever you're doing and come see me. Please."

Margarito, who had been wrapping a few things up at the office, headed for Los Olivos, El Tigre's favorite meeting spot. Of all his restaurants, it was the fanciest and most pleasing to the eye. There was a huge party going on, with mariachis and girls in miniskirts. *Strange,* thought Margarito. *His birthday is still a way off.* When El Tigre saw him, he waved him over to his table and sent everyone except his chief of security away. El Tigre's eyes were teary, but the smile never left his face. He asked Margarito to join him in a tequila before they got to talking.

"Are you on my side, cabrón? Are you with me? Time's run out on someone close to you. If I can count on you, I'd suggest you stay here with me tonight. Let's see if we make it to morning. Big things are coming."

"What are you talking about?" asked Margarito. "Do you want me to send for my men?"

"No, no. Nothing like that. You just do as I do. What's coming is so big there's no running from it."

And he turned his focus to serving himself a tequila every five minutes. As soon as Margarito finished his, and, hell, that didn't take long, El Tigre poured him another right away.

"Have another. Now, cabrón."

If Margarito didn't obey, El Tigre would quietly insist: "We're not just drinking, here. I'm saving your life. You'll thank me for this one day. I know how to repay a favor."

"But what's this all about?"

"Just wait, cabrón. Or are we not friends, anymore?"

Every hour or two, El Tigre would look at one of his men and ask: "Now?"

"Not yet, boss."

And two hours later: "Now?"

"No, sir."

This went on until exactly seven in the morning, when even the mariachis had started to fade. El Tigre's bodyguard approached him.

"Now, sir."

His compadre jumped.

"It's time?"

They brought him a telephone so he could take a call. El Tigre called for silence, listened to what was being said on the other end of the line, said good-bye, and hung up. Then he waved the mariachis over.

"Play us 'La Golondrina,' if you would. That's it for the great leader." He looked at Margarito. "There are some soldiers over at your friend's office. They're taking him away."

The shock cut through the haze of tequila.

"What do you mean, soldiers?"

"Soldiers. Those guys who run around in green with a nasty look on their face, sometimes, and an ax to grind. Not too many. No more than fifty."

And that was how Margarito learned of the events that turned the port upside down. He learned that a military convoy arrived that night in a plane that landed on a government airfield, and within twenty minutes they were busting down Don Agustín's front door with heavy artillery for betraying the new president and supporting the opposition party. That they arrested him and transported him in the same military airplane to a maximum security prison outside Mexico City. That they'd arrested the leader of the oil workers' union, who'd been in charge for some fifty years. Some of Don Agustín's closest associates followed in his footsteps through the prison gates, while the others, like Camacho, looked like they'd been through the wringer. No saint could protect them: all the saints were busy watching over El Tigre.

He never paid much attention to the other ones, the more violent ones. Los Nuevos. It's not as if they appeared overnight. They started out in the military, but they defected when El Tigre invited them to lock down the tougher routes and keep things running smoothly whenever a big shipment came in. Sometimes he'd even call Margarito in the middle of the night to ask if he could receive a package for him or give some friends an escort from the black bridge to the US border. That was how Margarito first met those guys out of their military uniforms. That was also how he ended up going with them on runs, to make sure the crew cab pickups and trailers supposedly full of produce, eggs, cutlets, clothes, or designer shoes made it safely to their destinations. When the customs agents saw them coming, they'd wave them into a special lane and they'd pass through without so much as showing their papers.

It went on like that until they decided they could branch out on their own, without El Tigre, and founded their organization. That's when things started getting really ugly. *How could I not have seen this shit coming?* Margarito often reproached himself. *Elijah was right.*

These days, the residents of La Eternidad lock themselves in at sundown. They're suspicious of their neighbors, their in-laws, their teachers; they don't even trust the nuns at the Sagrado Refugio de los Pescadores.

10

The buzzing of his phone woke him up again. *Goddamn fucking pills.* He had three messages waiting for him from La Muda. Margarito opened them one by one, praying the battery would last.

THE GIRL WONT DRINK WATER HOW DO I GIVE HER THE MEDISIN?

And then:

THE GIRLS AWAKE THE OTHER TRIED TO RUN. WHEN R U COMING BACK? SEND HELP

His phone was almost dead. Margarito answered:

GIVE THE GIRL A SCARE AND SHOOT HIM IF YOU HAVE TO

She answered immediately. She must have been glued to her phone.

TO LATE THE BASTERD GOT OUT OF HIS CHAINS

To which he responded:

ON MY WAY

No, thought the chief. *Hell no. That money is my retirement fund. It's mine, even if we have to take Treviño out of the picture sooner than planned.*

He looked out the window and saw the neighbors still playing basketball. He couldn't leave with them out there, so his mind wandered back to the attack. *What the fuck did I do to some fucking Guatemalan to make him come up here and ambush me? Someone definitely hired them to do the job and helped them plan it, but it wasn't La Cuarenta. They had nothing to gain from it, and it'd put their whole organization at risk.*

He considered Los Nuevos, then thought about his godson and wondered if he might have it out for him. The kid was capable of anything. *We were all screwed when he developed a taste for the product.*

Then there was the matter of the fifty thousand dollars. Margarito knew all too well what to expect. On the force, he'd had a front-row seat to observe what happened when that kind of price was put on someone's head. It was just a matter of time before even the people closest to you started trying to cash in. Hell, he'd even done it himself. Like they didn't slip him a little bonus for Elijah?

In the distance, three fishermen tossed fish carcasses to the pelicans from their boat. The sea crashed against the rocks. *Fuck.* He still felt shaky, but he had to jog his memory: he needed to remember every word, every inflection of that phone call. Like a song. He had zero clues, no team he could trust. They'd killed his son and two of the three guys who'd always been at his side. They took out La Tonina and El Dorado, and they would have done the same to him and El Flaco if Roberta hadn't shown up.

He'd hoped his contact with the federales would help him trace the call. Now he knew it was impossible. With technology out of the picture, he'd have to rely on plain old intuition, the way he did thirty years ago, before the Internet and cell phones.

All right, he thought. *Who's the cabrón that called me?*

It was ten at night.

Let's see . . .

The machine of his intuition rumbled back into operation.

It was a man's voice. Not a teenager or some old geezer, either. A powerful bastard in his prime. Self-assured, the kind who thinks the world is his for the taking. All that, for sure, but there was something else. He had pronounced each word with exceptional care, as if he'd been planning his speech for a long time. As if he didn't so much want to communicate information as cast a spell. *That's it: the bastard wanted to scare me, and he's been planning it for a while.*

The windows of the house across the street reflected the sun's light straight into his eyes and he needed to look down. *All right. What did that asshole say? Your days are numbered; I've got bullets here with your name on them.* He finally understood: the key to the whole thing was in that call.

In his first moments of lucidity, Margarito asked himself what had bothered him so much about that phrase. He struggled with the question like a straitjacket before it hit him: *The fucking punk said it like a prayer, or a spell, or a slogan.*

That's it. That's how I'm gonna get you, you son of a bitch.

Things were about to start moving very quickly.

According to his dying phone, it was seven thirty. If he hurried, he could still catch the perp and claim the ransom for the girl.

Just as he was about to leave, he heard someone walk up to the door. He breathed a sigh of relief when he saw Panda González.

"You awake? I went home and came back and you were still out. You didn't answer when I talked to you, just gave me this blank stare."

Now that he mentioned it, he thought he'd seen his former report pass through his field of vision a couple of times. *Fucking pills. Goddamn, was I wasted.*

"Take your time. I brought you something."

The guard handed him a small metal thermos.

"Drink this."

"What is it?"

"Chamomile. Cut fresh by my wife."

The chief took a sip from the container. It was the best thing he'd had to drink in a long time.

"This is delicious. Best thing I've ever had."

"It's fresh. That's why it tastes so good."

He'd had only two sips, and he already felt something like calm settling into him. *Amazing.*

"I need to pop out of here like a cork, Panda. Lend me your car."

The guard looked worried.

"You're not going to do anything illegal, are you?"

"What do you think? I'm an officer of the law."

Panda handed over the keys.

"I hope you know what you're doing."

Margarito climbed into the black compact car parked outside. It smelled of chiles and onions. He started the motor and cursed his luck when he noticed it was a stick shift: he'd have to figure something out if he was going to drive with that injured left arm.

La Muda didn't need words to insult him. She was so angry her frenetic stream of gesticulations lasted a good three minutes. The sweeping movements of her hands berated the chief in every tone imaginable. *What happened to you, you piece of shit? Can't you tell time? I've been waiting here for you for two days!* She informed him they'd run out of water, the bathroom stank—she kicked in the door to prove her point—the fridge was empty, there was nothing to eat or drink. She had no dope left for the girl—who, by the way, would scream for help now and then—the guy kept trying to escape, she hadn't slept in two days, the chief was the worst good-for-nothing son of a bitch the port had ever seen, and how dare he leave her hanging like that.

"All right, all right! Goddamn it! What's the matter, haven't you seen the news?"

With that, La Muda pointed to the television's broken screen and kicked the wall. You had to hand it to her, the woman was expressive.

"I'll come for her first thing in the morning, okay? I'll come for the girl tomorrow. Relax," he said, passing her the bag of food and the bump of coke he always kept in his wallet. "And here's the girl's medicine. We'll give it to her in a second. Now quit bitching at me and let's get to work."

They put on their ski masks and got into character. He grabbed the voice distorter, grateful it was still working, and called the girl's father. He picked up after three rings.

"Get the money ready and place it in three trash bags. I'll call you tonight to tell you where and how to make the drop. If there's so much as a penny missing, your daughter dies."

"Hey, wait! Prove to me that she's still alive."

Margarito kicked the metal door and slid open the peephole.

"Say hello to Daddy."

"Dad! Dad!" wailed the girl.

"Wait," said De León. "Your ransom note mentioned my daughter's birthmark. What does it look like?"

"A triangle, with the three corners stretched out. And don't you start second-guessing me or the girl gets it."

He closed the peephole and went back to the dining area.

After he hung up, Margarito removed his ski mask and called for La Muda.

"Come here, give me a hand with this."

They went to open the three locks on the closet in the back where Margarito kept his personal arsenal. The chief pulled out a menacing-looking shotgun, a Remington machine gun, and two assault rifles, then bent over to grab a very thick rope and a few magazines for his sidearm. Then he smiled with something that resembled serenity. On his way out, he turned and grabbed a duffel bag with the words FOR THE EXCLUSIVE USE OF THE ARMY OF THE UNITED STATES OF MEXICO printed on it. It looked heavy. He locked the door behind him and gave the rope to La Muda.

"Come with me."

They opened the door to the room where they were keeping Treviño. Margarito released the safety on his gun with a loud click.

"Come out from there or I'll skin you alive, cabrón."

Treviño stepped out from behind the door and put his hands up.

"Tie him up again," he directed La Muda.

As they headed for the front door, he told his assistant he'd see her at six.

"Got it? See you here at six a.m. I have a few things to take care of first."

Half the city was looking for him, but he still had time to go to the cemetery. As usual, there was only one guard, who made the rounds with his flashlight a couple of times every night. The man had a deep respect for the law and led Margarito to the corner where his son had been laid to rest. He even lit the area for him.

"Give me a minute."

Margarito had just noticed that someone, probably his wife, had placed one of their son's old stuffed animals on his final resting place. A little stuffed turtle. That was the only time he broke down. The night watchman recited the words he had ready for moments like this: "There, now. You'll be together soon."

"You have no idea," said Margarito. "But not just yet."

After a heavy, uncomfortable moment, the chief leaned forward and slid the turtle to the middle of the boy's tomb. The night watchman was silent as Margarito got to his feet and said aloud: "To be continued, Ricardo." Then he turned to the guard. "How do I get out of here?"

11

LOS NUEVOS

Two black pickups parked in front of the cathedral at quarter to eight in the evening. At the sight of them, a line of little old ladies wrapped in shawls and overcoats on their way to evening Mass did their best to hurry along. Once five armed men had checked the area for unusual activity, a man in a black hat stepped out of the second truck and into the cathedral, escorted by three of his associates. *He practically came alone,* thought an old man sitting on a bench, feeding the pigeons. He tossed the rest of the corn at the birds, picked up the trash bag at his feet, and headed toward the cathedral.

The two guys guarding the door scoped out everyone who walked down that street. They thought they'd been doing their job well, but like many who thrive in La Eternidad, they'd been dense and too conservative, and their day was about to get a lot worse.

They didn't see him until it was too late. He placed the bag on the ground and put his hands in the air. The two watchmen were slow to react.

"What the hell was that? Quit sleeping on the job. I'm here to see the bald man, and I'm packing, at the waist."

The one with the bigger mustache and a serpent's smile lifted the man's checked shirt and removed his weapon. Before letting him pass, the guard rummaged around the plastic bag with it.

"The piece stays here. Go on in."

Just as the man was about to enter the church, the guy with the mustache hit him in the back with the butt of the gun. The chief fell to his knees, and before he could defend himself, the same guy gave him a kick in the gut. A few moments later, while he was still getting his breath back, the two watchmen lifted him up by the arms.

"That was so you don't get any ideas in there."

Margarito picked up the bag and made his way inside as best he could. The one with the serpent's smile followed him into the church and made sure he limped over to one of the middle rows, where the man in the black hat was conferring with his escorts in a low voice. The chief knew the tallest of them, a former Kaibil with two cauliflower ears, who was in charge of teaching new recruits all there is to know about terror. The Colonel sneered, revealing his canine teeth.

"Get a load of this punk."

The three hit men stood and didn't take their eyes off the chief the whole time he sat beside the fifty-year-old Colonel. Margarito scanned the cathedral and counted a total of twenty people scattered around: a few young couples, but mostly old or sickly women. When they saw the chief approaching, the three women nearest them stood and headed for the exit. The chief knew that when they got to the men standing guard at the door, they'd be told to go back where they came from. *The church is closed, no one goes in or out.* The priest, who was performing the introductory rites of the Mass with his back to the congregation, was unaware of the situation. El Coronel de los Muertos stared into Margarito as if he was giving him an X-ray.

"You kept me waiting a whole day," he accused the chief in his raspy voice. "Our meeting was yesterday."

The chief noticed that the bodyguard with the swollen ears was staring him down and had angled his torso toward him. There was another guy to the left of the Colonel, and two more standing behind Margarito, including the one with the smile.

"Your son stuck his nose where it didn't belong," the Colonel continued, then waited to see Margarito's reaction. "But it wasn't us. And you've got a lot of balls coming here to ask."

The policeman gave the man a look that made it clear he couldn't care less about what he said or did.

"I knew that already. I didn't come here to ask questions."

For the first time in a long while, the Colonel felt his authority being challenged. His men felt it, too, and even the giant with the cauliflower ears shifted his weight. The Colonel leaned in until he was face-to-face with the policeman and said, not caring whether the little old ladies sitting nearby could hear him: "I'm the one who raises the dead. I'm the one who chooses. One snap of my fingers and you'd end up worse off than your little friend Elijah. If I had wanted it, you'd have been taken apart already with machetes in the middle of the street. I don't need to waste time with a man who's already been sentenced to death."

"I didn't come here to waste time."

The priest, who had caught part of the conversation, swallowed hard. The little old ladies prayed with particular fervor.

"You already know the Guatemalan's specialty," said the Colonel, referring to the former Kaibil with two cauliflower ears, who was looking at Margarito as if he was trying to figure out which part of his body to start with when the time came to break him.

The chief rested a hand on the pew in front of him.

"I'm here to offer you a deal."

He opened the plastic bag and pulled out twenty-five thousand dollars from amid the trash.

The Colonel looked at the money, unfazed.

"I can get you more," Margarito said, carefully setting the bag between them. "They're offering fifty. It's yours if I'm left alone long enough to catch a guy."

The Colonel stared at him for an eternity.

"The people who killed your son aren't with us. Someone outside our organization decided his fate, but we would have done the same thing if push came to shove. That's all I'm going to say."

"I appreciate your candor," Margarito said, tossing him the bag. "But I already knew that. If you want the other half, tell your people not to follow me or give me any trouble while I close this case."

"Impossible. There's too many of us, and not everyone's in the barracks. We've got some gate-crashers, too, who do business on their own and give us a cut of every deal. Them, I can't control."

"I'm sure you can manage. I don't want any hunting parties getting in my way—or my team's—until this case is closed."

"I can't hold them off forever."

"I just need time for two more meetings. Let's say I'm asking for your help until dawn."

The Colonel looked at him.

"Now, you tell me: do you know how to find a guy named Carlos Treviño? Used to be a cop . . ."

"Wish I did," said Margarito, rolling his eyes toward heaven. "Swear to God."

"I need him alive. This guy sneaked in somewhere he shouldn't have and found some sensitive information. I think he's working for the DEA or the marines. We want him alive and conscious. No one's ever made it that far and gotten out alive."

"All right."

"And if someone's helping him lie low, I'll kill him myself."
Margarito flashed him a big smile.

"You think the Cartel del Puerto sent him?"

"Why? What have you heard?"

"Let's call it a hunch."

"We took out twenty of their men this week. These stunts of theirs are getting to be a real pain in my ass. Anyway. What are you going to do?"

Keeping his eyes on the front of the church, where the priest was holding up a Communion wafer, Margarito answered: "I'm going to enforce the law. Even if that law is the Ley de Fugas."

The Colonel didn't move or say a word for a moment. Then he asked, "How did you know it wasn't me who gave the order?"

"Because you'd be killing the goose that lays golden eggs—or one of a few. When you arrived, I'd saved up enough to grow old peacefully. Now I have nothing. First you asked me to stop selling stolen cars, which I did, as a gesture of goodwill. Then you asked me to help with the bars. Then you wanted me to pay you more and more, until you'd emptied my bank accounts. I never complained. All I've ever done is go along with you. You know I still have money coming in from my friends in the cartel and from other deals, and that interests you. You need the scratch to finance your little war."

The Colonel stared Margarito down with a look intense enough to melt a candle.

"How do you plan to catch these guys, when you can't even move? Not to mention that as far as I know you don't have anyone around you that you can trust."

"I'm not crippled. I just need to be able to move around without running into problems until nine in the morning, and there's more in it for you if I can. Twenty-five thousand more."

The bald man stroked his mustache.

"The last time I checked, your accounts were empty, which either means you've got it well hidden or it's in an international back account. If it's far away, I'm not interested."

"It's close, and you'll have it in cash."

"All right. But I want it in my hand, and this stays between me and you. Tomorrow at nine. Where?"

"In the bar where I saw you last time."

"Don't even think about standing me up, you hear me? And I'm not going to lift a finger for you after that. Stay sharp, because at nine o'clock you're worth fifty grand again."

"I'd better get going. My godson sends his regards."

The Colonel hit him with a radioactive glare.

"That kid's only alive because we want it that way."

Margarito smiled.

"Well, he's been going around saying you haven't been able to get anywhere near him, and I get the impression that his neighborhood is a goddamn fortress. You haven't seen the banners inviting you to take a tour of the place? They're pretty funny."

"All he's managed has been to shoot a couple of fairies who thought they were tough. They weren't trained by me."

"I went by there yesterday and they've got an impressive army going. The place is impermeable."

The bald man pointed a finger at his face.

"There's only one army in this country, and it's made of real men."

"If you say so," said Margarito, looking at his watch. "I'd better get going, I'm running out of time."

He stood to go, but he must have gotten dizzy, because he careened sideways, toward where the bodyguards stood. The one with the thick mustache smirked as Margarito nearly collapsed, then barely moved when he tried to steady himself on him. That was his mistake. By the time the bodyguard realized what was going on, the chief had locked his good hand onto the man's shoulder, straightened up a bit, and brought his knee up hard. The man with the thick mustache dropped to the ground. Seeing his other bodyguard reach for his weapon, the Colonel shouted, "Stand down!"

The man with the mustache got to his feet with difficulty, coming first to one knee, then the other. "Stand down, I said," the Colonel repeated as the man with the mustache gasped for breath, his face so red it was almost purple.

"Don't go looking for trouble, Margarito."

"The cash I just handed you covers a little payback," said Margarito before putting his hands in the air and smoothing his clothes. "My weapon, please."

The man with the mustache reached into his waistband and handed Margarito the thirty-eight. From the pulpit, the priest yelled to them.

"Settle down back there. This is a church, not a boxing ring."

Margarito said his good-byes with a gesture of his good hand.

He looked up as he left the church: the clouds had parted and a full red moon looked down over La Eternidad.

THE FEMME FATALE

Completely worn out and dressed from head to toe in black, Dr. Antonelli turned her key in the lock. After closing the front door of her house, she flicked on all the lights in the living and dining rooms so each of her movements could be seen from outside, then went to the kitchen to make herself a cup of tea. She lit the stove and put water on to boil. Then she retraced her steps, turned off all the lights, and left the front door ajar. Deep in the shadows, Margarito took a moment to react.

He'd been out there a while sniffing the breeze for danger, but the only suspicious movement was coming from the fig tree, so he dashed from his hiding place to the house in just a few strides. She didn't even turn around.

"What do you want?"

The first time he saw her, he'd felt the kind of rush that comes only in the presence of a new love. When you realize something good is about to start between you and the other person.

She had been wearing a colorful skirt, slit to the middle of her thigh. He figured she had to be a foreigner, because no one wore skirts like that in La Eternidad. He couldn't take his eyes off her: her full, athletic thighs had a sun-kissed glow that would have made a peach jealous. He watched her climb a flight of stairs as if she were stepping onto a stage, her hair in a ponytail that fanned out to completely cover her back. She never could tame that thick head of hair. Her shoulders, made to be rubbed; a long, swan-like neck that instantly sparked his desire; the triangular shape of her back and wide hips that swayed so gracefully; those long, long legs. But three things, above all: feminine hands that never stopped moving—it was an incredible sight, the way they accompanied every shift, every comment, as if they were a shortcut to the essence of her thoughts—those round breasts that would fit so well in his hands, and that unique face of hers: sharp chin, high cheekbones, ample forehead, almond eyes. The first time he saw her, he thought, *You'd need two artists to paint those lips, three sculptors to get the face right, a team of painters to reproduce the color of her skin, the light glinting off each strand of hair.* Margarito didn't know how to act around respectable women, and he felt a butterfly make its way from his knees to his throat. Just then, she stopped, straightened up as if an electric current had run through her, and turned to see who was staring at her so intently. Margarito swallowed hard and opened his mouth. She smiled and kept going, perhaps a little slower than before. He couldn't follow her, though. He had to work. That evening he left early and went into tourist territory—the malecón, the beach, the bars, even La Eternidad's most expensive restaurants—hoping to find her again, without any luck. He hated the false levity of the binge drinkers, the fake laughter of their friends, all the women who weren't her that he saw in the street. He went to sleep upset.

He thought about her every day for eight days. He compared her with every actress he saw on the screen and concluded, *That woman was more beautiful.* Based on her clothing and the color of her hair, he'd guessed she was foreign. Maybe he'd seen her on her last day in the port and she was already back in her country. He changed his routine and started eating, drinking, and dancing at different hours. After two weeks, he gave up and went on an epic bender. It took two bottles of tequila and several ladies in heavy makeup to blur the memory of that mysterious woman. Of course, when he went out the next day in search of something to ease his hangover, he ran into her at a seafood stand in the market. She was with a group of friends. He was alone and in bad shape, looking disheveled and operating at half his typical lucidity. But the fog seemed to lift when he saw her. He smiled and went over to say hello as if they were old friends.

"May I join you, miss?" He'd never called anyone *miss* before. She blushed and, to his surprise, nodded.

"I'm Italian," she explained. "I came here to see your country."

Margarito, a police officer who worked for the worst types of folk in the port, was a full-time roughneck. As he sat across from her, though, it seemed like it had all been arranged ahead of time. Everything went smoothly: she responded well to his questions and observations. She kept smiling at him, gazing at him softly from behind her glasses. *Where did this girl come*

*from? Why did it take her so long to find me? I know there's going
to be something big between us.*

"What do you do?" asked the Italian.

"I'm a cop," Margarito confessed.

She blew a perfectly vertical column of smoke into the air,
as perfectly vertical as she was, and blurted out, "I thought you
were a criminal."

He shrugged.

"It happens. People get us mixed up all the time."

She said good-bye to her friends and they went for a walk
along the malecón. The sea rose and fell like a pounding heart.

A huge smile spread across her face when he took her hand
and kissed her. Then she pulled him toward her and kissed him
again. They leaned against a palm tree and before Margarito
could ask, she said, "I just finished school and want to move to
Mexico. I'm still deciding which city."

Margarito was so happy he thought his chest might explode.
Until she asked him what he thought of Monterrey. He was
about to curse the capital of Nuevo León, but managed to con-
tain himself.

"They say the people are nice and you can live well there.
That there are plenty of universities and job opportunities for
foreigners like me."

"That's what they say," Margarito had replied, kicking a can.

"What's it like to live near the sea?" The woman stretched
out her arms to feel the breeze on her fingertips.

"Do you want me to tell you?"

"Yes."

But Margarito's hand was already running along her hot neck,
the little beads of sweat forming under her thick blond hair, and
she smiled. Margarito had thought to himself that a woman like

this was what had been missing from his life. Just then, out of
nowhere, she'd confessed: "I adore making love."

Over the next six months, she'd convinced him to take the
exams to graduate from middle and high school: Margarito
bought the answers from one of the faculty beforehand. One
day she seemed withdrawn. They'd recently had a fight. She
locked herself in the bathroom for a long time and when she
came out, she said, "I'm pregnant."

Those who know say that Margarito never pulled a more
perfectly idiotic face than he did that day. Unfortunately, it didn't
take the two of them long to go from *I love you* to *If you were
honest, you wouldn't be a cop.* From the fifth year on, they stayed
together only for their son, but when even the kid doesn't keep
you from fighting, it's time for the relationship to end. At first,
the major differences between them had seemed unimportant,
because love conquered all: She was a voracious reader; he only
wanted to watch television. She was thinking of pursuing a doc-
toral degree; he barely had a handle on Spanish grammar. She
would indulge in the occasional glass of red wine; he drank
beer like water and could polish off a bottle of tequila on his
own if the occasion called for it. She hated Mexican cigarettes;
he loved his Raleighs. She watched what she ate and exercised
every day; he claimed to have cut a deal with his arteries. She was
incapable of touching someone else's property; he, well, he was
Margarito. That's where the attacks began. *Corrupt son of a bitch,
thief, conceited animal,* and his favorite: *stronzo.* His car became
the stronzomobile. People would say, "There goes the chief's
wife. Only a naive foreigner could marry a guy like Margarito.
But one day she'll realize what a mistake she made and it'll be:
'Ciao, Margarito, hit the road.'" And so it was. One day he came
home to find her in the front hall with divorce papers in hand.

"What do you want?" his ex-wife repeated, snapping Margarito back into the present. "What do you want and why are you here? Have you no heart?"

Dr. Antonelli's question was unfair. Of course he was upset about Ricardo's death. Had she forgotten who taught him how to walk, drive a car, clean and load a gun? *Give me a fucking break. This job isn't like other jobs: you walk out on a tightrope the minute you put on that badge, and you don't come down until you die of natural causes or they pick you off with a bullet, because being a cop is forever.* That's what he wanted to say, but he didn't. If anyone in the world was suffering right then, it was that woman.

"Shut the door, please. There's a draft."

The chief carefully closed the door and settled into the shadows next to the refrigerator. The first thing he noticed was the sweet scent of plantain empanadas. The memories came flooding back.

"I came to tell you it wasn't me. I'm going to get whoever did this."

"You're an asshole."

"I had to tell you."

"Who was it?"

When Margarito didn't answer, she lifted her face from her hands and howled like a cornered animal: "Who was it?"

Margarito took a deep breath.

"I'll get him. For our son."

"Ricardo is dead. And they're going to kill you too." The kettle started to whistle on the stove, but the Italian didn't seem to hear it. "You poor thing," she went on, sarcastically. "The world has been so hard on you! You didn't go to the funeral. You didn't say good-bye to your son because you were out there doing your job."

"I couldn't go," he explained. "I sent those soldiers. If I'd shown my face, I would have been shot. You have no idea how many people are after me. There's a fifty-thousand-dollar price on my head."

She looked up.

"I need to know what the two of you talked about these last few times. Right now everything matters in solving this crime. I haven't asked you for anything in twenty years, but I'm begging you now. Please. Try to remember."

His wife turned off the stove and poured herself a huge cup of hot water. She dropped in two bags of linden flower tea, collapsed onto the living room sofa, and took off her shoes. She took a long sip of the tea and fixed her eyes on the ceiling.

"Until around two months ago, he'd tell me how things were going with him and eventually ask me about you. It was always the same. Then we didn't talk for a while. As you can imagine, I was surprised when he took this job. I had a hard time understanding that this was how we raised him: to be great at what he did and work for the good of others. The last time we spoke, I asked him if he wanted a special meal when he came back, and he said he wanted plantain empanadas. He was going to come over for dinner . . . I asked if he and his wife had reconciled. Did you know he and Laura weren't living together? They separated when he took the job. She didn't want to come back here, didn't want him to risk his life. Poor Laura . . . She was always so wrong about Ricardo, but she was right about this. She's coming tomorrow to say good-bye. I don't know what I'm going to say to her."

His wife rubbed her eyes: apparently the mildly soporific tea was taking effect. Margarito blinked and asked, "What else did he say?"

She didn't answer.

"Sandra?"

"Hold on. I'm trying to remember." The doctor closed her eyes and rested her head on the cushion behind her.

Just when the chief thought she'd fallen asleep and was about to leave, she spoke.

"He told me he was thinking of moving into one of the three luxury buildings they're putting up along the beach, the ones with that flamingo sculpture. Someone offered him a good deal and he was thinking of buying the place when he got here."

Deep in the shadows, Margarito opened his eyes wide. A moment later, his ex started snoring and he decided it was time to go. As soon as he started to move, she added, "Close the door behind you," and kept snoring.

She'd said it peacefully, almost pleasantly. He hadn't heard that tone of voice in nearly twenty years. Not since they were married and still lived together, back when she still thought her husband was a good person.

Maybe there was a better place in some corner of the dream she was having, one where the three of them still lived together, where Ricardo was happy and still alive. He left on tiptoe, not wanting to disturb that dream.

THE THREE LETTERS

Margarito parked Panda's car a few yards from his godson's office, safe from prying eyes in the shadows of the red-light district. The only business there, aside from the three little bars for down-and-out types looking for a good time (La Lucha, Angel's, Motel Flair), was a twenty-four-hour convenience store. In better days, there had been a dozen of these shops, and they could hardly keep up with the demand for condoms and alcohol from the patrons of the dives nearby; judging from the only customers visible from outside, they now made their money selling instant soup, heated up behind the counter, to a few rent boys, panhandlers, and hookers. The neighborhood had turned into a self-sustaining ecosystem: from the look of things, the kids hanging around the bars—the only other people who hung around there—were the offspring of the prostitutes who worked them.

Ten years ago, the hill facing the malecón teemed with activity. Ever since the red-light district became part of the turf war between heavily armed crews, though, people stopped spending time there. Especially the clueless tourists with a knack for losing their wallets. He turned the corner and saw an old prostitute flirting with a few drunken soldiers; one of them was carrying a gigantic bottle of Bacardi. Margarito found it all very depressing. *What a hand she's been dealt,* he thought and immediately corrected himself. *Who are you kidding, buddy—you're not that much better off.*

The place changed names every four years or so. It had been called Blue Skies, Arriba Juárez, the Wild Rose, the Captain, Mystic, Magic, Ramses, and, most recently, Manhattan—the unifying concept behind the gaudy decorative failure that was its current facade.

He's nothing like his father, who hated drawing attention to himself. The infamous Tigre Obregón was far from the sociopathic monster the press made him out to be. On the contrary: he counted a district attorney, three representatives from the governing party, a senator, the leader of the national union of electricians, a secretary of the economy, and two governors among his closest friends. He also had strong family values, of course, and respected the noble institution of marriage: after all, he'd fathered nine children with five different women. At the turn of the millennium he suffered a stroke and handed control of the business, as he called it, to the most competent of his sons, the reckless Joel Obregón, godson to the chief. But there was a world of difference between Joel and his father.

Unlike his progenitor, the son started dipping into the organization's product at a young age. Margarito couldn't understand
how he slept or kept his head enough to keep himself on the
throne. Between the ages of twelve and fifteen, before he became a
regular at luxury rehab centers (and long before he founded one of
his own to ensure a pleasant stay), the only things he cared about
were Ferraris. His horizon broadened when he turned twenty and
discovered Lamborghinis. Then came the Porsches, and now it
seemed he was on to Jaguars. When he finally developed a taste
for girls and partying, both his father and the chief breathed a sigh
of relief. Lately he'd been spending his days conceiving (and bank-
rolling) nightclubs known for their design in cities across Mexico.

Under the Statue of Liberty sketched in neon lights above
Manhattan's door, three guys watched Margarito approach. Their
movements indicated they'd been partaking enthusiastically of
the house special. They weren't particularly tall or built, but,
with their guns barely concealed under their shirts, they were
the only ones smiling in that depressing place. As he got closer
to the first bouncer, the chief flashed his badge.

"I'm with the guy who drives that Ferrari," he said, pulling
the velvet rope back for himself.

"Hey . . . hey!"

Margarito turned, and the bouncer flashed him a wide, wide
smile.

"Aren't you Chief Margarito?"

He didn't stop to answer. He was already halfway inside when
he heard: "How long you think it'll be before the bullets start
flying?"

He made an effort to keep himself from going back and laying
the guy out. He didn't have the time. Given what he was paying
the Colonel, every hour cost him two grand. So he ignored the
comment and headed straight into the club.

There weren't twenty girls on the dance floor, but they were all euphoric. As always, the VIP table was set up right under the DJ booth, and there was his deadbeat godson, enjoying the company of four gorgeous teenagers, his entourage, and the sycophants du jour in their respective Panama hats. Margarito's godson signaled to his bodyguards to let the chief pass, and Margarito walked over and sat in the space that had been cleared next to him.

"You have no idea how sorry I am, Padrino," he said, giving the chief a hug and thumping him loudly on the back. Margarito nodded and examined the boy's face. The boy rubbed his nose.

"Would you like something to drink?" Before the chief could respond, he'd already called over the waiter. "Bring him a tequila, from my personal stock."

He looked at the grayish hue of Margarito's face and his bandaged arm and patted him on the back again.

"I see you shaved. Looks good. How have you been holding up?"

"Hanging in."

The four long-legged babes with him wore tight miniskirts, plunging necklines, and towering heels. Their manicures alone would be enough to keep a salon in business. When Joel finally figured out that the chief wasn't going to talk in front of them, he gave them a nudge.

"Don't you ladies wanna go dance a little?"

The tallest of them, a beautiful girl with sad blue eyes, stood and the others followed suit. The chief's godson signaled the DJ and a wave of electronic music flooded the space. Clouds of dry ice swirled around the girls as they stepped onto the dance floor. The only ones who stayed were two guys with the look of hungry jackals sitting to the left of his godson. *They're just waiting for the right moment to strike. One of these guys is going to end up in charge.*

The chief's godson patted him on the back.

"C'mere, c'mere. I can't hear you over there," he said and turned to the first jackal. "You, Sticks, give my godfather here something to take the edge off."

His subordinate opened a briefcase, pulled out a bag of cocaine, and placed it on the table. Margarito declined. His godson looked him over again.

"Your shoes are all worn out, Padrino. They're ratty as fuck. Have you been walking everywhere?"

"I borrowed a car."

"I saw on the news what they did to the one Papá gave you. Those fucking bastards. But don't worry. They're gonna pay for this. Pepe!" he shouted to the second jackal, "Give my godfather your truck."

His assistant pulled a Ford key ring from his pocket and held it out to the chief, who declined the offer with another movement of his head. His godson was getting uncomfortable. More to feel the chief out than anything else, he asked, "What happened to your arm? And your face?"

"My shoulder got dislocated during the attack, and this"—he touched his face—"this was Los Nuevos."

"You saw them?" asked his godson, a glimmer of lucidity finally flashing across his face. Margarito nodded.

"Let's just say they called a meeting, and I couldn't say no."

"Son of a bitch." Margarito's godson sprang forward in his chair. "Why'd you go see that pack of mangy dogs, huh? You don't trust me? You could've come here. We'd have taken care of you." Then he added, under his breath, "The next time they call you, give me a heads-up. Whenever, wherever. You know I value that kind of information."

The chief looked at his godson. He was running out of patience. This time it was Margarito who rested a hand on the young man's shoulder.

"And you, who runs such a large organization and who's become so powerful, what have you heard about what happened?"

His godson, visibly uncomfortable, tried to wriggle out from under the paw resting on his back.

"Did you come here to interrogate me?"

The jackal sitting closest to them shifted forward in his chair, and Margarito saw his hands drift toward the mother-of-pearl grips of the two guns sticking out of his waistband.

"What do you take me for, son?"

"It's just that you seem pretty tightly wound, Padrino. Here, drink your tequila," suggested his godson, taking the opportunity to put some distance between them. Margarito didn't move or take his eyes off him, so his godson had a sip of his own drink.

"I haven't seen much of you lately, Padrino. You wouldn't happen to be cozying up to Los Nuevos, would you?"

Margarito shook his head.

"I risked my life to save your father, I got him out of jail. I was the only one there at his side when Los Nuevos rose up and the bullets started flying. I lost my reputation and my son to keep his business afloat. And now you can't even answer a simple question for me."

"Those fucking dogs," the heir to the Cartel del Puerto said, shaking his head, as if the men who'd planned the attack that killed Ricardo were evil incarnate. "Who the hell would've thought things would get so bad here?"

"You haven't exactly been standing on the sidelines."

"Los Nuevos want to destroy us. We have to defend ourselves. Those fucking dogs. They started out working for us, licking my father's boots. Then they decide to branch out on their own. You know my father always said we had to be invisible—only make our moves in the dark, like owls. That's not an option anymore.

There are too many people from other organizations out there, and they're gaining ground. They're out there during the day, threatening our dealers and our turf; they spread out and do whatever they have to do to get a foothold here. If they take La Eternidad from us, they control the route going north. The border. We have to defend ourselves."

Margarito looked at him impatiently. "You still haven't answered my question."

"I'll answer you. But give me your pistol first, Padrino."

The chief noticed one of the jackals move a hand toward his gun, so he took out his piece with two fingers and placed it on the table.

"All right. Thanks, Sticks. Better safe than sorry. Look, Padrino. Two days ago, a man dressed in black with a thick mustache came by and had a talk with our head of security. He wanted us to recommend some guys for a job. They had to be Maras, from Guatemala. Now, hold on . . . He didn't mention you at all, he just said he needed to straighten out an associate who wouldn't listen to reason. That's what he said. My head of security, I trust him completely, he asked me about it and I recommended a couple of Maras I'd worked with before. I had no idea you were the mark. We brought them in, made the introductions, and took our cut. That's it. For us, it was just another transaction."

Margarito struggled not to hit his godson. "Who hired them?"

His godson looked at him cheekily. "So you're not angry?"

"I'm not angry. How could you have known?"

"Thanks, Padrino. I knew you'd understand, man-to-man."

He motioned to the waiter, who immediately came over with another drink.

"Guy's got money. We thought he was going after one of his associates; he's done it before. Enterprise, Padrino. Papá always used to say it's the root of all evil: if the guys running this country hadn't just been looking to get rich we'd all be singing a different tune right now. Businessmen used to be wolves among men, but now they're just jackals, fighting over the scraps. That's enterprise for you. Bottoms up."

As he finished his drink and looked out through the base of his glass, the godson noticed that everyone had joined in the toast except the old man, who hadn't taken his eyes off him. Margarito didn't speak, so he went on.

"Man, Padrino, I admire your restraint. Why don't you stop messing around with the law? You see where that's gotten you. Come work for us. We'll take good care of you. This is a business, you know. We need all kinds."

Margarito shook his head. "No, thanks."

"No? And why not?"

Margarito stared him down. "What would the mother of my son think when she heard I agreed to go work for the men who hired his killers?"

His godson had no response. "So what are you going to do?"

"Go after them with the full force of the law."

The boy's jaw dropped. "Ricardo's dead. You do get that, right? You know I'm really sorry about it, Padrino, and I never meant for it to happen . . . But listen, I'm worried about you. You know there's a fifty-thousand-dollar price on your head, right? What are you going to do?"

Margarito finally lit the cigarette he'd been holding, inhaled deeply, as though he wanted to blow out another flame inside him. He released a thick white cloud between them. "I just told you. I'm going to lay down the law."

The color drained from Joel's face. "If you leave here, I'm afraid I can't protect you," he hissed. "Just so you know."

"We're all riding this wave, kid, and no one knows where it's taking us."

He noticed that the song was ending and the girls were on their way back from the dance floor.

"Who was it?" Margarito insisted as they got closer.

"I can't tell you that. I've got my own principles to uphold, and that includes respecting private enterprise. Give him his gun back at the door," he said, turning to the jackals, "and don't let him back in."

Margarito's godson turned back toward the chief and looked at him as if he were watching a suicide walk straight into the ocean.

"Take care of yourself, Padrino. You already dodged a bullet once. Don't let them get you."

"You take care," Margarito said, returning the embrace. "I saw the Colonel a while ago and he let something slip. I shouldn't be telling you this, since you're not helping me, but he's getting ready to come at you with everything he's got."

"Are you sure?"

The kid and his cronies leaned in.

"He'll start in Colonia Morales: he's going to throw everything in his arsenal at La Cuarenta, and then he's coming for you."

"Son of a fucking bitch." His godson stood and started pacing the floor. "Why didn't anyone tell me?"

"Are you sure?" asked the most lucid-looking of Joel's companions.

"That's what he said. Something about a 'final showdown.'"

"I told you!"

"Cabrón, you're fucked for real."

"Let's go to the bunker!"

The next song came on, accompanied by a cloud of smoke, and Margarito slipped away.

As he stepped through the door he saw two of the bouncers headed toward him, guns drawn. He shot the closest one in the gut and leveled off at the other's head. The man dropped his piece and burst out laughing.

"Sorry, sorry," he said, kneeling. "Sorry."

Margarito cocked his gun.

"Why'd you try it?"

"No, please."

"Why did you try it?"

"He talked me into it," the man pointed at the first bouncer. "For the reward."

Margarito pressed the barrel of his gun into the man's forehead.

"Who put up the reward?"

"I have no idea! He was the one who knew about it."

But the gut-shot dude's eyes had already rolled back in his head. Margarito nodded, pulled his arm in slightly, and slammed the butt of his gun into the bouncer's forehead. He crumpled to the ground.

"What's going on out here?" his godson asked as he stepped outside, flanked by three men.

Margarito slid his piece into his waistband and looked over at the guy who'd taken a shot to the gut.

"Free enterprise."

He scanned the street for unusual activity and, seeing none, climbed into Panda's car.

"General? Do you have a minute?"

"Of course, Mr. Joel. At your service. What can I do for you?"

"How's the family?"

"My family? Good, fine."

"Your daughters?"

"Macorina is still studying in Berlin. You know what she's like. Aureliana's at Harvard, getting straight A's."

"That's wonderful, General. Congratulations. You're an excellent role model."

"What can I do for you?"

"What are your thoughts on our friend?"

"A terrible thing, what can I say. What a waste. He was so young and had just gotten his first big break."

"No, man. I'm talking about Margarito. All the rage he's carrying around. I just spoke with him, and he's just not thinking straight. There's something about the way he's acting. I don't know if I can trust him. What do you think?"

The general let the wind die down before he answered.

"I don't know . . . He's going through a difficult time."

"Exactly. He's going through a hard time, and it's making me nervous. Do you think someone as desperate, exhausted, and as far out of his mind as my godfather might do damage to my organization?"

The general swallowed hard. "I do."

"All right. Let's do something about it, then. No way are we gonna close the shop because of some screwup. Am I right?"

"Understood, Mr. Joel. I'll handle it."

"I fucking love the way you military types talk, you know that? Zero bullshit. Let me know when it's done."

"I will."

"That's what I wanted to hear. Talk to you soon."

The general had barely hung up before his phone rang again.

"What's going on, you little bitch? Why haven't you been picking up?" It was the Colonel. "Where's Margarito?"

"I have no idea."

"Don't lie to me or I'll come over there and cut your balls off. What do you know?"

"I haven't seen him since yesterday."

"You're taking too long to lay him out. Don't play dumb with me," he said and hung up.

The general let out a stream of profanities and punched the glove compartment. His phone rang again. The last thing he wanted to do was take another call, but he recognized the number and picked up.

"Hi, sweetheart. How are you? How's everything over there?" He looked at his watch. "Isn't it a little late for you to be awake? . . . Oh, I see . . ." And, a moment later: "But don't you spend a lot of time with her? Why don't you come home by yourself this time to see me and your mother? . . . Okay, okay. Forget I said anything. I'll transfer the money for the tickets soon. See you at Christmas. Bye, sweetheart."

The general slipped the phone into the pocket of his pants and shot a glance at his driver.

"What are you looking at?"

"Nothing, General, sir."

"Damn straight."

Panda's ride, still smelling of onion and chile, glided along a side street downtown. Bonfires had started all over La Eternidad: La Cuarenta, Los Viejos, and Los Nuevos were burning cars again. Some asshole had lit the fuse, and now they were going after each other with everything they had. *Maybe now the good guys can move around this town freely, for a change.*

12

Illuminated by powerful spotlights, the marble facade of the modern twenty-story building sparkled like a diamond in a display case. The structure was probably green certified, built for sustainability and engineered to take advantage of the area's abundant solar energy. But everyone in La Eternidad knew it had gone up on protected land, right on top of a mangrove swamp whose rightful inhabitants had been driven out. They also knew that the financing for the project had come almost exclusively—always through roundabout and highly irregular channels—from the government, and that the apartments were going for several million dollars each. The stakeholders made a tidy profit, while—contrary to what had been promised—few to none of the proceeds were reinvested in the community or the creation of new jobs. What's more, the bulldozing of the mangroves had affected several species on the brink of extinction, like the long-clawed spiny lizard; the black howler monkey, with its flowing mane and its habit of hurling avocados at anyone who invades its territory; the majestic white-tailed flamingo, which dances en pointe once a year to draw the attention of the female of the species; and the Frigga spider, which can jump up to five feet to deliver a bite. What made the whole thing even more scandalous was the fact that the developer, from one of the best families in the city, went around making a point of his respect for nature and wildlife. *Yeah, right.* Since the building went up, the only flamingos left in La Eternidad were the two metal sculptures standing in front of it.

Margarito chose a dark corner under the outstretched arms of an imposing walnut tree and parked the car. He took a deep breath before getting out: what mattered now was catching his quarry and squeezing him under the full weight of the law. He'd handle the girl afterward. It was hard to stay on top of both things, but not impossible, and he still had time left. It was only three, and the Colonel wouldn't be looking for him until nine. He was sure if he got the ransom money by eight, he'd be able to make a deal for his life. *But first,* he thought, *the law's going to come crashing down on this bastard.*

His sidearm was ready, and he was carrying handcuffs and a second magazine in his waistband, plus two grenades hidden up his pants leg. He took another deep breath. *Justice will be served tonight.*

He opened the car door and shut it behind him as quietly as possible. He hadn't taken more than one step toward the building when he heard the familiar hum of a walkie-talkie a few feet up ahead. He hung close to the wall around a nearby home and studied the darkness. Before he could locate the source of the sound, a guy in a security guard's uniform came out of nowhere. He drew on Margarito, who did his thing and shot first, emptying almost an entire magazine at him. The problem was that there were two more guards right behind the first one. Margarito ducked behind the flamingos to reload and figure out how to drop the newcomers when something slammed into the base of his skull. Before checking out, his brain managed to comment that someone must have been playing baseball nearby. He felt the ground slide out from under his feet, and a moment later the world was upside down.

They took him to a room as small and dark as a coffin. He felt two ocean currents pulling him into the depths. *Fuck 'em*, he thought. *No one's gonna drag me around.* He kicked his imaginary legs with all his strength and was overcome by relief when his toes finally touched the ground. All he could make out was the surf crashing against the coast. But he understood what was really going on as soon as he opened his eyes.

What he'd thought was the surf crashing against the coast was actually a pair of bodyguards giving his rib cage a brutal working over, undeterred by the fact that he was lying semiconscious on the floor. He tried to get up to dodge the blows, but his attackers were always a step ahead, kicking his legs or stepping on his fingers before he could stand.

He told himself that if he could just grab one of the aggressors' legs in midkick, he'd be able to knock him over. *I could get him with a head fake.* But when the opportunity to launch himself at them arose, he realized his body wasn't responding the way it did before, or it responded with things he hadn't asked for, crumpling into a heap when he'd wanted to stand or move gracefully aside. So he rolled over as best he could and focused on curling up in a ball when he sensed a kick coming.

Eventually he watched one of his attackers take a few steps back and, with a running start, aim a kick at his temple.

He was happy, way down there in the depths, until an icy liquid soaked his face and neck and there was light.

He was in the living room of a fancy apartment. One he already knew. The first face he recognized belonged to a beast in a leather jacket: Bracamontes, his second in command, who was standing next to the bar with his arms crossed. Next to him, seated on a black leather sofa, was another man; he gradually made out the features of the former congressman, senator, and founder of the environmentalist party, and current mayor of

La Eternidad: Mr. Tomás Cárdenas Vidaurri. The one with the lovely locks and pouty lips. The politician observed him from where he sat.

"He's coming to."

"I didn't tell you to kill him."

"It'll take more than that to kill him," the Block assured him from behind Margarito. "Old dogs have thick skin."

"Hello, Your Honor," said Margarito. "I knew I could count on you."

A man in black limped up behind the mayor. He wasn't carrying an Uzi or riddling Suburbans with bullet holes, but Margarito recognized him right away.

"Nice limp you've got."

The man in black picked up a baseball bat and hit Margarito in the bad arm. The chief writhed in pain.

"Enough, enough," the mayor said, crossing his legs. "So, what's up, Chief? Why are you trying to break into my home?"

Margarito glared at him.

"Have you already forgotten what you said to me yesterday? 'I've got bullets here with your name on them.'"

The mayor scowled. Then he stood, walked over to the bar, and pulled out a bottle full of a honey-colored liquid.

"I met your son when I started on the campaign trail. I threw a dinner party to introduce him to my advisers, and he promised to restore order around here. I really thought he could do it. I'd heard his situation in Canada wasn't ideal, so I told him I'd be happy to facilitate his transition back to the port. You know what he said? That he was going to help you. He knew that Los Nuevos were giving you trouble, that you'd distanced yourself from Los Viejos, and that La Cuarenta weren't too fond of you, either. I eventually convinced him to arrest you: he thought you'd be safest behind bars, given how many people are after your hide.

He was sure it would be the best thing for you, sending you to a maximum security prison. Of course, he asked me to find work for your drivers so they wouldn't be fired so abruptly. I told him I would. The deal was only going to last a few minutes, after all."

Margarito managed to sit up a bit. He searched for something to defend himself with, but came up empty.

"The city's worse than it's ever been, but it's a passing phase. We're just waiting for the right moment. We needed a martyr, someone who would give his life to bring peace to the port, someone to be the last innocent authority in the region. I picked Bracamontes to be your successor and thought your son would do nicely as the martyr. I've always believed change should be absolute: otherwise, it's not change. Your son is dead, but you survived, and the situation demands another sacrifice. Someone has to pay for the crime, and it's best if that person is you. Just do as Bracamontes and his colleagues tell you. Don't try to fight it."

The mayor held the bottle up to the light and opened it.

"Three years ago, I had a shot at the presidency. I was seen as a dedicated, educated young man who spoke English well. I showed the dinosaurs I could follow orders and keep their bank accounts fat. By the time of that ill-fated get-together in my building, my name was one of two being tossed around as likely candidates for the presidency. And it was the ruling party that was going to nominate me, not my own. Can you imagine? I was going to be the first president from this part of the country. But you put an end to all that when you insisted on investigating that girl who fell to her death during that party my friends organized for me. You didn't think twice about calling the press, airing the details of the case, making me look like a conceited ass who orders European prostitutes from local thugs. I still regret trying to reason with you. 'If you help me out,' I said, 'I'll make it worth your while. Hide her,' I said.

'Send her back to her country, take her for a swim in the Gulf, toss her to the crocodiles.' But you wouldn't listen. I offered you money, power, but here we are: if I'm lucky, I'll hold on to the mayorship of this town, because they're never going to let me run for any real office again. I accepted the mayorship like a consolation prize, thinking that at least I could do a little business. I promised myself that if I was going down, you were going first. Yesterday was just a preview. Today I'll make sure you die the way you lived and that you're remembered as the scum who killed his own kid. Get him out of here, Bracamontes. Finish him off in the sierra. And see to it that someone cleans the floors. Look at this mess."

As if Margarito were already gone, the mayor fumbled with the bottle until he got it open.

"This whiskey is thirty years old," he said, serving himself a generous pour. "Same age as your son, no? Let's see how it tastes."

Margarito watched him breathe in its fragrance.

"Take him."

As Bracamontes and the Block lifted the chief roughly to his feet, El Braca whispered into his ear: "Just wait till we get out to the sierra."

They were dragging him out of the building when he heard shouts: "Drop your weapons!" The Block and Bracamontes let go of their quarry and tried to draw their guns. Margarito saw them fly through the air as he fell to the ground. His hands were still over his ears when someone leaned over him.

"Goddammit, Margarito. You're a real pain in the ass, you know that?"

It was General Rovirosa.

"I recorded the whole thing. We've had an eye on him for months. Some very powerful people want to bury this guy alive.

You were lucky my team saw you arrive, but you rushed our operation a bit. Care to join me? I'm going up to have a civilized chat with him. He's got a choice: he can either walk himself to prison on his own two hooves, or take a swan dive off the building, like that girl. You coming?"

Margarito shook his head. "What time is it?"

"Six thirty."

His letter of safe passage was about to expire. "Take me over to that car."

"That heap? Are you sure? Now I *really* think you need a doctor. The city's in chaos, they're burning cars in every neighborhood. It's all we can do to keep things from escalating. It's not a good idea for you to be going around like that."

"I have an important appointment to keep. Just get me my phone and keys."

"You don't want us to drop you off? Wait just a minute and I'll take you myself."

"No. I'm running late, and I have to go alone."

"All right. Someone lend him a jacket. Here are your keys. Now where the hell, may I ask, are you going? There are armed men all over the city looking for you."

"This is where we part ways, General. Don't try to follow me."

"All right. You know what you're doing. But we're even now. Got that? If you were smart, you'd get out of the city."

"I've got some things to take care of first." Margarito could barely speak. Just as he was about to get into the car, the general added: "I deserve a cut, don't you think?"

The police officer turned to see Rovirosa put his glasses on, look at him, then put them back in his pocket.

"Go on, it's getting late."

He struggled to get into Panda's car and called Roberta with the last juice in his cell phone.

"I'm just calling to thank you. For everything. The way things are going, I don't expect to see you again. So, thanks, kid."

Roberta started to cry.

"Where are you, Chief? We've been trying to reach you for hours. Get somewhere safe and we'll come find you!"

"There's no need for that, kid. Thanks for everything you've done. You're a better cop than I am."

"Boss, there's something I need to tell you."

Right then, his battery died.

He finally made it to Shark Bar, his favorite spot in La Eternidad. It had been months since the last time he'd settled in under the establishment's giant awning. As soon as he got out of the car, he noticed the few people still in the streets at that hour—drug dealers and underslept thrill seekers—backing away from his unsteady walk and bloodstained clothes. He was grateful the place was open as usual. He pushed open the bar's wooden doors and headed inside.

Only two of the bar's tables were occupied. At the first, a group of tourists had made their way through three bottles of vodka. At the second, he saw Fearless Juan, the reporter so fond of criticizing him, with a few of his colleagues. Everyone turned toward Margarito when he walked in.

"Welcome, boss," said the owner, Don Omar, as he stepped out from behind the bar to greet him. He was unfazed by Margarito's swollen face. It wasn't the first time he'd shown up looking like that.

"I'm so sorry about your son, Chief. Can I get you a drink?"

Margarito almost smiled at the sight of the tiled walls and the giant stuffed and mounted shark that had been hanging from the ceiling for more than thirty years.

"How have you been, Don Omar?"

"Just fine. At your service. Have a seat. Are you feeling all right?"

Just as he was about to answer, Fearless Juan wobbled over to talk to him. Margarito could barely understand what the man was saying.

"Chief . . . Cn I ask you uh quessstion?" The reporter was blind drunk.

"Go ahead."

The bar went absolutely quiet. Not even a fly buzzed at the table where the reporters were sitting. Far from getting angry, Margarito just looked wearily at the reporter.

"Pinche Juanito. I thought you had a question for me. There's not much to say. You'll find out all about the thing in a bit. They're going to hold a press conference."

The chief sat down at the next table over. The reporter stumbled and looked like he might fall over, but he caught himself on the table.

"If you donn mind, theressomething I have to tell you."

"Juanito, leave the chief alone. You're drunk," one of his companions shouted.

"Go on."

"I met one of your es-girlfriens. Miss Azucena."

Margarito scowled, but let him continue.

"She got married, n took the guy's lasname. You look for her under her old name, you'll never find her. And there's something you dunno."

"Get to the point." Margarito was on edge. Los Nuevos might show up at any minute.

"Misssazucena had your baby. But she never told you. I dunno wha she named him, but I know he worked with you, and wanned to get to know you, but you didn't want. Miss Azucena told me tha . . . that he was a really smart . . . But you two diddn get along. And so he left. Quit."

The reporter fell silent and rubbed his eyes. His friends took advantage of the moment to stand and grab his arms.

"Let's go, Juan."

"See you, Boss Margarito," the reporter added before the group left the bar.

The chief was trying to remember which of his men had suddenly quit on him when Don Omar interrupted him.

"What can I get you, sir?"

Margarito looked at his watch. It was seven thirty.

"Tell me something, Don Omar. Have I been a good customer all these years?"

"Of course! What kind of question is that?"

"So you'd rent me the bar for a private party?"

"Of course! When?"

"Right now."

"Caray! I wasn't expecting that. What would you need? Food? Snacks? Waiters? I'm not sure if I can get everything ready right away."

"I just need you to clear out the place and leave it open for me. Send everyone home. Right now."

The owner looked at his bloodstained clothes with concern.

"How many are you expecting?"

"Just a few, but they can get rowdy. I'd like to pay in advance for any inconvenience they might cause."

Margarito passed him the roll of US currency he'd been hiding.

"This is too much," the owner replied. "What kind of party do you plan on having?"

"Nothing fancy."

The old man paled when he saw the police officer set his gun on the bar.

"Well, around here the customer is always right. When should I plan to come back?"

"In an hour. Before you go, would you make me a Conga? I had one the first time I came here, and it was delicious."

"With pleasure, boss."

"You have five minutes."

Three and a half minutes later, Don Omar served him what looked like a crystal ball with different colors swirling inside.

"Is this how you remember it?"

"Just like that, boss."

The old man headed for the door. Before he left, he grabbed a photo of himself with a famous actress who visited his bar that one time.

"Adiós, Chief."

"Adiós, Captain."

The waiters and the tourists followed him out.

Margarito was alone, and the light coming in from the beach refracted through his glass to form a rainbow on his white shirt. *Incredible*. For a moment, all the meaning and mystery of the universe seemed to be focused right there in front of him.

At five minutes to nine he nearly shot two guys who walked through the front door looking fairly lucid and gave the bar a once-over. They stopped short when they saw Margarito's gun.

"Is the bar open?"

"Go fuck yourselves. Get the hell out of here."

They backed out without taking their eyes off him.

Margarito thought about how much the beach had changed. *Fifteen years ago, it was almost all families who came here.*

He remembered the time he'd brought his son to that same beach, long before the buildings and restaurants went up on that part of the malecón. When the bar with the thatch roof and its little stretch of sand was a favorite local hangout. *That was another life,* he thought. *Another incarnation.* Before he fell into infamy.

Back then, on one of those afternoons, they'd seen a man eagerly taking pictures of something in the sand. A crowd of gringos huddled around the photographer, emitting squeals of delight. Margarito and five-year-old Ricardo, who had been play-ing in the sand, went over to see what was going on.

In front of the photographer there was a small pit, and inside that, a red pail filled with water and sand. The gringos leaned over it, rapt and beaming. Margarito's wife ran up to get a look at what was in the pail.

A large black splotch formed by smaller splotches swirled at the bottom. Margarito thought they must be crabs.

"They're turtles," said his wife.

At first Margarito thought the güero was fixing to rob them, so he was surprised when he identified himself as a marine biologist from the University of California. *Oh, I get it,* he thought. *He's one of those crazy gringos who camp out at the end of the beach and say they're here to help.* They'd been there for a week.

"They were born this morning," he told the onlookers. "Now we have to help them reach the sea."

He pointed to the pit.

"Eighty of them didn't make it out. Only these little guys are left."

Ricardo peered into the magnificent red pail, teeming with life.

The güero—a skinny man with a big nose and long, fine hair—pointed to the sky.

"There are too many birds right now. We have to wait until it gets dark, so they have a better chance of surviving. It won't be long. The sun's already starting to set."

So it was. Shadows were falling over the hills of La Eternidad.

When he saw how fascinated Margarito's son was by the contents of the pail, the man leaned over and asked, "Would you help me with one of the turtles?"

Ricardo, who was very shy at the time, nodded.

The güero knelt in front of the pail, picked up a turtle between two fingers, and handed it to the child.

"Hold it like that, right around the belly, with just your fingers."

His son, transfixed, watched the tiny creature wriggle its four obsidian limbs.

"Don't be scared. They don't bite or scratch."

Ricardo looked up at the güero and then at his mother, whose neon green bathing suit accented her cinnamon skin in the last rays of afternoon sunlight. Margarito had been so happy then.

"Go on, son," his wife said, smiling.

Ricardo held the turtle with both hands. The güero pointed toward the frothy sea.

"Take him to the water and let him go, so he can swim home."

But Ricardo seemed shaken. He looked up and out at the horizon, the darkness that was settling over the bay.

"What about his mom?"

"His mom is far away. He has to go find her."

The boy studied the waves crashing against the rocks closest to the shore.

"Let him go," the güero repeated.

Ricardo shook his head.

"Go on, son, let him go," urged his mother. But the boy shook his head again and held the turtle close to his chest, so she leaned over him and asked quietly, "Why don't you want to let the turtle go? Are you afraid something will happen to him?"

The boy pursed his lips, nodded, and burst into tears.

"He's all alone . . . He's going to die."

His mother tried to calm him, but Ricardo went on hiccup-
ping as though someone had just told him he was going to be
left alone on the beach too. *What the fuck*, thought Margarito.
The man who was about to be La Eternidad's chief of police for
nearly thirty years felt the need to assert his authority, so he
leaned over and grabbed the boy's arm.

"Listen to the man or you'll catch a beating."

"No."

Ricardo tried to back away, hoping that everything—his parents, the güero, the whole universe conspiring against them—
would disappear and that someone, something would come to
the rescue of him and that turtle.

"Don't scare him."

His wife grabbed his arm, making him let go of the boy.

"Oh, God," said the güero, trying not to cry. "This always
happens. May I?"

The man walked calmly over to the boy, leaned over, and said
something to him that his parents couldn't make out. First, the
boy shook his head furiously. Then his expression turned serious
and he looked up at the güero and the water behind him. He
walked toward the shore and slowly put the turtle down on the
sand. The animal scurried away as if it had just been released
from prison. Ricardo watched the little black dot drag itself across
the sand and then let itself be carried away by a sliver of wave.
The dot floated there for a while before reaching the part of the
sea where everything gets dark, and they couldn't see it anymore.
The boy stood there looking out over the water, and the güero
went back to his pail.

"What did you say to Ricardo?" Margarito's wife asked. "How
did you convince him?"

"Oh, it's something you pick up with experience. I told him
if he let the turtle go, he'd be his friend for life and would come

back to say thank you. It's true. Did you know they always come back to the beach where they were born? They travel the whole world, but they always come back. If they survive, of course. Only one in a hundred does."

Margarito watched his son for a long time. His wife was upset too. If she had any idea about what he'd lived through as a kid. He came from a world where you didn't hang out on the beach playing with turtles like some sissy. The opposite, actually: you had to be faster than a hare.

At five past nine the sun flooded into the bar, filling it with flashes of light and unexpected colors. *Who would have thought? All these years coming to this dive, and I'm just now figuring out how much nicer it is in the morning.*

That's when he noticed the silence.

Something was up. *They're outside. It won't be long now.* He wondered if he should receive them seated or standing. He decided to remain seated with his back to the concrete column, not because it offered protection, but because that was his table and he wanted to wait for them there.

He was still holding his weapon, still aiming it at the street. His arm was getting tired.

Someone knocked on the door. He pricked up his ears and confirmed it wasn't his imagination. *Oldest fucking trick in the book. If they're trying to distract me, they may as well just come in. I'll be waiting right here.*

But the knocking went on for a few minutes more. Annoyed, Margarito got to his feet.

It was nine forty.

With his weapon in hand, he tiptoed to the door. He wasn't expecting what he saw: a young woman was putting the finishing touches on her three-year-old's turtle costume. A little parade of schoolchildren dressed up as different types of animals was already half a block ahead of them. The boy was out there knocking on the door for fun. When he saw Chief Margarito's terrifying figure behind the door, his eyes opened very wide and he stopped knocking right away. His mother, whose back was to the chief, never saw Margarito at the door. She was focused on getting her little one ready.

"Hurry, or you'll be late," she chided.

And then she left, dragging her turtle by the hand. Margarito sat back down and rested his elbows on his favorite table.

The gun was so heavy he laid it down on the metallic surface of the table for a moment. *Goddamn it, I can't take another minute of this. I'm Chief Margarito,* he thought. *And I'm going to die. Here come the turtles.*

Last conversation in the dark

"Did you hear what happened?"

"I'm afraid to ask. What now?"

"Nothing. The girl's home with her parents, and guess who collected the ransom?"

"I don't want to know. Margarito?"

"Yes and no."

"Cut the crap. Did he collect or not?"

"Collect, collect. If you mean *Did he collect the money,* then, no. Listen. Ten thirty came and went, and no one had gone looking for Margarito. The only person who showed up at the bar was Don Omar, the guy that runs the place. He went by to see if the party had ended yet. When he saw Margarito fast asleep with the widow-maker next to him on the table, he gave him a shake and asked if he wanted to call a taxi, told him he should go get some rest. Margarito woke up, totally out of it, looked at his watch and realized that the Colonel, who decides who'll be taken and who'll be forgiven, wasn't coming for him. That he'd fallen asleep and was dreaming."

"The Colonel's never late, though."

"Exactly. Margarito knew that too. So he headed straight to the secret lockup he had over behind the church, you remember? He lit out of that bar like the devil was after him, cutting between the burned-out cars the two warring organizations had left behind the night before, probably kicking himself for not going there first. As soon as he got out of the car, the nuns ran up to him, terrified and shouting. They'd heard shots out back, behind the chapel. He didn't like the sound of that at all, so he hobbled as fast as he could toward the dilapidated safe house. When he got there, his worst fears were confirmed: the front door was open and the place was empty, except for La Muda, who was chained up. Treviño and the girl were gone, and the place still smelled of gunpowder."

"La Muda really is a hostage by nature. The whole world ties her up and pushes her around."

"Margarito untied her and when he looked around, he saw that Treviño had taken the assault rifle."

"Then what?"

"Margarito searched the place with his thirty-eight drawn and figured out that Treviño had set a fire. Who knows how he did it, but he found a way to light the mattress with the few things he had on hand. With all the smoke, La Muda had to open the door to see what was going on. She's not new to this. She followed procedure, but Treviño was still able to hit her with the door and subdue her. Not that it was easy work: it looked as though she fired the rifle and they fell to the floor. Judging by the state of her hands, Margarito figured that Treviño had probably needed to break a few of her fingers to disarm her. Then he chained her up and went for Cristina. *I'll be damned,*

Margarito thought. *All that work, for nothing.* The mattress was still smoldering, so he figured the detective couldn't have gotten far. He untied La Muda and went looking for a telephone: he was going to call La Gordis for help. He was just turning the corner, angrier than he'd ever been, when he saw the side door of the convent, where the nuns keep their old Volkswagen, being swung open by Treviño himself. He'd covered the girl in a habit and put her in the passenger seat, and they were about to make their escape. Margarito drew on him, but Treviño was faster. 'Don't move,' he said, aiming the rifle at him. Then he cracked half a smile and added, 'Toss me the thirty-eight.' Margarito was so furious he thought it might kill him, but he handed over his weapon. Still smiling and without taking his eyes off Margarito, Treviño got into the car and closed the driver's side door. Aware that his money was driving away with them, Margarito said, 'You won't make it across town on your own, Treviño. You need my help.' But the detective shook his head and started the motor. Only when the car was in motion did he lower the rifle. 'See you never, Chief.' And then he and the girl were gone. Treviño was in pretty bad shape. He'd been hit, kicked, and tortured. But he managed to cross the city. They say he was paid, that the family handed over the money they'd promised, and that Treviño barely gave it a second glance, like he didn't care about it anymore. Eventually, he took the dough, got into the nuns' car, and no one's seen him since."

"That dude's got some serious luck."

"Not really. Did you hear they burned down the Hotel de las Ballenas that same day? The place he ran with his wife? No one knows what happened to her."

"Shit, tough break. That's what he gets for coming back, I guess."

"But that's not all."

"I know. They promoted La Gordis: she'll be the first female police chief in this part of the country. You've gotta have a real set of brass ones to take that job, the way the city is these days, right?"

"She can handle it. And get this: they're pinning a medal of honor on La Muda for her service on the force. They're saying that without her, the kidnapping never would have gotten solved."

"Seriously? She's police?"

"For ten years, already. Every now and then she'd help the chief out with a side operation, as Margarito put it. Who do you think found the spot where they were keeping the girl?"

"What I didn't like was what happened to El Coronel de los Muertos."

"Tell me about it. Who'd have thought he'd end up caught in the cross fire between his people and the other organization?"

"I mean, he's not bulletproof. That's why he never made it to his meeting with Margarito. Did you know his truck wasn't even armored? I saw his body myself."

"And what about the godson?"

"It seems a light went on upstairs for the first time. Instead of standing by his people, the kid hopped on a private jet to Mexico City. Looks like he hooked up with a pretty big player in exchange for agreeing to bankroll his presidential campaign. It doesn't look like the feud between the old and the new guard will be ending anytime soon."

"So nice to know there's justice in this land."

"They're turning Margarito into a national hero. Seven million people have already seen the video of him protecting his son. If only they knew the skeletons their angel has in his closet."

"Yeah, well. The bad thing about this country is that we have a terrible memory."

"Get this, though. The best part? He's been named the director of a regional anti-kidnapping institute."

"That's it. This city's about to get intolerable. I'm sending myself into exile."

"Don't go anywhere. This is about to get good. Anyway, we have to pay our respects to Margarito, like everyone else. There's a religious service later today in memory of his son, since he couldn't make the other one. At the Sagrado Refugio de los Pescadores. He'll probably send some work our way sooner or later, now that he ended up without any muscle. Who knows, maybe we'll even be able to come out of the shadows. What do you think, should we send a wreath or a bouquet?"

Epilogue

Panda wanted to keep talking, but Margarito was busy with a phone call to La Eternidad's new chief of police—his former report, Roberta. Every so often, he'd tell him which road to take. As they drove across the black bridge, the rent-a-cop was struck, as he always was, by the sight of the city's main avenue at that hour of the morning: the huge palm trees growing on either side of it had been there since long before the road came through. They passed the new hospital and kept going. When the vegetation changed and they came up on some pine trees planted alongside a gated community, the former police chief told him to turn.

They took an unpaved road, its potholes bouncing the fancy compact car into the air. At the top of one hill, two kids with a shovel asked for a donation "for maintaining the roads" and climbed up on the car's fenders. It didn't escape Margarito's attention that the older one had a cell phone clipped to his waistband and stared insolently at the passenger and driver as he walked up to the window. *He's checking to see how many we are and whether we're armed. These little bastards aren't here for spare change. They're lookouts.* As he suspected, they hadn't gone ten feet before the two kids started fighting, not about the tip he'd given them, but about which one would use the phone. *Who are you calling, boys?* the rent-a-cop wondered. *Who's paying you to keep watch?*

"From here on out," Margarito ordered, "don't you fucking stop, Panda. If we see anyone coming our way, flash your brights twice and keep moving."

They continued along the dirt road surrounded by the thick rows of pine trees until it opened to a huge, completely deserted soccer field. That was the end of the road.

Panda never thought he'd run into this kind of thing next to a residential area on the outskirts of La Eternidad and thought he'd taken a wrong turn. He was just getting ready to turn around when Margarito told him to drive over to the nearest goal.

"What?"

"Drive onto the field and park near the goal." The order didn't make any sense, but Panda obeyed.

What's the point of having a soccer field out here in the middle of nowhere? the guard wondered.

As they passed between the pines, the rent-a-cop noticed that the soccer field was much longer and narrower than usual and that there were no bleachers or chairs for the spectators, but the ground was marked with thick layers of quicklime and there was a regulation goal set up on either end.

As soon as they cleared the pines, a loud whistle to their left turned their heads.

"Hey, assholes!"

At least twelve people, standing in front of three pickups and one stake-body truck were waving at them frantically from the other side of the goal. When he saw the guard draw his piece, Margarito stopped him cold.

"Fucking Panda. Put that thing away."

He hurried to park alongside the other vehicles. He noticed that only three or four of the people standing around them carried weapons in holsters clipped to their belts. The rest of them were dressed in the simple clothing of manual laborers: boots, denim, wide belts, some embellished with charro embroidery; durable plaid shirts, leather jackets or Windbreakers. When he realized that they looked more like cargo loaders than mercenaries, Panda breathed easy again. Of course, he'd feel a lot better if someone would tell him what the hell was going on.

Margarito told him to cut the motor.

"Wait for me here."

"I'd rather go with you."

"All right. But whatever you do, don't take out your gun or your badge."

"What the fuck?" yelled one of the armed men, staring at them reproachfully. They could hear a high-pitched buzzing in the distance, as if someone were using a chainsaw on the pines. "You could have caused an accident."

"Sorry. My driver doesn't know the place," Margarito replied. "Who's in charge here?"

The man shouted over to his associates.

"Eleazar! Someone here to see you."

A man with a thick mustache and a ten-gallon hat got out of one of the pickups and walked over to the newcomers. He had a huge sidearm holstered at his waist.

"What can I do for you?"

"My name is Margarito González. I'm a friend of La Colombiana's."

Margarito reached out his right hand, but the rancher didn't move. When he realized a formal greeting wasn't going to happen, Margarito added, "We were at a cookout La Colombiana hosted a long time ago. Remember? She made us bandejas paisa."

"Oh, yeah. That's right. Well, what do you want?"

"I'm trying to find her. And a guy named Carlos Treviño."

The rancher looked at him for an instant, then at Panda, and said he didn't expect anyone would be seeing Carlos Treviño for a long time to come.

"Payback's a bitch," he said, and spat angrily.

Margarito asked him what he meant.

"I hear they've sent the troops out after him."

"The army?" asked Margarito. He found it hard to believe he wouldn't have heard about that.

"No," Eleazar answered. "Not those pricks, or the marines. I hear it was Los Nuevos, that he ran into them the day they were burning all those cars and there was an argument. Seems he ran into one he didn't like so much, some colonel. They say shots were fired, and your guess is as good as mine what happened to him."

"Heads up!" shouted one of the men.

The buzzing they'd heard in the distance became a roar, and a sizable light aircraft appeared on the other end of the pine forest as if it had been skimming the treetops the whole time, landed, and finally came to a stop just before crashing into the second goal. The plane made an elegant circle and settled right outside the penalty area, as if it were getting ready to take a free kick. The name of the aircraft, *El Mexicano*, was painted on it in ornate calligraphy. Everyone there, except Eleazar and the newcomers, ran toward the plane.

"You shouldn't be here," Eleazar said, releasing the safety on his gun.

Shit, thought Panda, as he noticed the armed man standing behind Eleazar staring at them.

The door of the plane opened and a young woman with an immense smile dressed like a pilot in an action movie—big sunglasses, long white scarf, leather cap and jacket—ran her eyes over the crowd and raised an arm in greeting when she saw Margarito.

"What a surprise! Wait right there, Margarito."

"Everything all right, Parce?" asked Eleazar.

"Stellar," the pilot answered. "This fellow here's a friend of mine."

"I was about to run them off. They looked lost."

As soon as the pilot exited the plane, six of the ranch hands hurried in and rushed out carrying packages of all sizes wrapped in brown paper, which they handed carefully to the men waiting by the trucks.

"Don't touch the Blu-rays," the woman shouted. "Those are for my personal collection." She walked over to Margarito.

"Good to see you, sir," she said, giving him a hug. She looked Panda over but didn't say hello. "What can we do for you?"

Margarito cleared his throat. Eleazar wasn't going to miss a word of the conversation.

"I'm looking for our mutual friend, Carlos Treviño."

"Treviño?"

"Some people think he died last week. Others say he fled to the United States. That he took off from a secret airstrip. That he paid handsomely for the flight and got some help with his escape. That he was seen getting into a plane like this one."

The woman took a deep breath.

"Why not? There are lots of airstrips like this one around here. And Treviño knows the area well." A spark flashed in her eyes. "May I ask why you're so interested in Treviño?"

"We have some personal business."

"Hey!" shouted Eleazar. "Dick around on your own time!"

Three guys passed them carrying what appeared to be a refrigerator and loaded it onto one of the trucks.

"It's too late in the day for them to be fucking around," said Eleazar, checking his watch. He stepped between the pilot and the newcomers. "You, too. Don't waste time. We need to stick to the schedule."

"Look, friend—" Margarito tried to intervene, but the rancher wouldn't be swayed.

"Time for you to be going."

"Yes, of course, Eleazar. They were just leaving. See you around, gentlemen. It would be best if you didn't come back here."

Margarito sighed. "See you around, my friend. In the meantime, let me know if you see him."

The pilot smiled mischievously.

"The only passenger I've had recently was a young lady going to meet her boyfriend at the border."

The woman turned and walked toward the plane. Before boarding, she examined the bottom of the aircraft.

"I thought I scraped the bottom of the plane on those trees," she said to the ranchers. "But, no, we're fine. It's not easy flying that low."

Margarito González, former chief of police to La Eternidad and current director of the Tamaulipas Anti-Kidnapping Initiative, watched in frustration as the pilot pulled the door of *El Mexicano* closed. By the time he got back in the car, the other drivers already had their motors running.

"Who were those assholes?" Panda asked.

"You don't want to know, partner. But I'll tell you this: that goddamn plane is the key to the only mystery I give two shits about."

"Back to La Eternidad, then?" the driver asked as they passed the young lookouts.

"Take me to my beach house. I deserve a break."

As they got back on the highway, the plane appeared over the tree line. Panda watched its ascent in the rearview mirror, taking one last look at its twin engines and unusual form as it set off along its course.

The Last Word

This novel is dedicated to those who told me several of the stories that appear in its pages, and to those who declined to share theirs, offering instead an even more eloquent silence.

In literature: to Danilo Moreno, Francisco Goldman, Mario Muñoz, Christilla Vasserot, Luis Carlos Fuentes, Fernanda Melchor, Jorge Harmodio, Augusto Cruz, Antonio Ortuño, Claudio López Lamadrid, Andrés Ramírez, and Fernanda Álvarez, for their insightful comments on the first draft of this book. To César Aira, Bernardo Atxaga, Almudena Grandes, and Héctor Abad Faciolince, for the kindness they showed this Tampiqueño. To Dominique Bourgois, Amy Hundley, Tomasz Pindel, and Morgan Entrekin, for their collusion and their loyalty to my writing.

In memory: this book is for my father, Martín Solares Téllez; and for Daniel Sada and Federico Campbell: thank you for the games, the books, the words, the haiku, and the cappuccinos. But not in that order.

In life: this novel is for Florence Olivier, José Manuel Prieto, Quino and Alicia, Pietro and Maddalena Torrigiani; for my friends in La Paz: Paloma, Edmundo, Jorge, Mariana, and Sandino; for Alejandro Espinoza, Cristina Fuentes, Izara García,

ⅼⅼⅼ⊏ ∟∩∽⊥ ∨∨∪ⅼ ∪

and Cecilia Medina Basave; for Diana Carolina Rey and Guido Tamayo, Diana Agamez, Mar Meléndez and Emiro Santos; Alina Interián, Forrest Gander, Rubén Gallo, Magali Velasco and César Silva, Gabriela León, Ricardo Yáñez, Guita Schyfter, and Hugo Hiriart; Luis Albores, Gerardo Lammers, Patricia Pérez, Ulises Corona, Rogelio Flores Manríquez, Gabriel Orozco, María Álvarez and Jaime Ashida, Lorenza Barragán and Jaime Martínez, Trino Camacho, Yael Weiss, Marcelo Uribe. For the Herrerías and the Cuevas in the streets of Veracruz, and for the Barragáns and Heredias around the world. For Taty and Armando, and for Gely, Luis, and Rosario in Monterrey.

For Vesta, Mateo, Mariana, and Joaquín. With all my love.